Three delicious,
impossible bet
surrounded b
days without sex!

DESIRING
THE REILLY
BROTHERS

Three favourite authors bring you
three sizzling romances

We're proud to present

MILLS & BOON SPOTLIGHT™

A chance to buy collections of bestselling novels by favourite authors every month – they're back by popular demand!

January 2010

Desiring the Reilly Brothers
by Maureen Child

Featuring

The Tempting Mrs Reilly
Whatever Reilly Wants...
The Last Reilly Standing

Triplets Found

Featuring

The Virgin's Makeover by Judy Duarte
Take a Chance on Me by Karen Rose Smith
And Then There Were Three
by Lynda Sandoval

DESIRING THE REILLY BROTHERS

MAUREEN CHILD

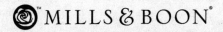

DESIRING THE REILLY BROTHERS © Harlequin Books S.A. 2010.

First published in Great Britain 2010
Harlequin Mills & Boon Limited,
Eton House, 18-24 Paradise Road, Richmond, Surrey TW9 1SR

The publisher acknowledges the copyright holders of the individual works, which have already been published in the UK in single, separate volumes, as follows:

The Tempting Mrs Reilly © Maureen Child 2005
Whatever Reilly Wants... © Maureen Child 2005
The Last Reilly Standing © Maureen Child 2005

ISBN: 978 0 263 88028 1

64-0110

Printed and bound in Spain
by Litografia Rosés S.A., Barcelona

THE TEMPTING
MRS REILLY

Maureen Child is a California native who loves to travel. Every chance they get, she and her husband are taking off on another research trip. The author of more than sixty books, Maureen loves a happy ending and still swears that she has the best job in the world. She lives in Southern California with her husband, two children and a golden retriever with delusions of grandeur.

Visit her website at www.maureenchild.com.

To Desire readers –
You guys are the best. The reason we do what
we do. Thank you for your continued support!
Happy reading!
Maureen

One

"Ten thousand bucks is a lot of money," Brian Reilly said and, grabbing his beer, leaned back against the scarred, red Naugahyde bench seat.

"Don't make plans," his brother Aidan added quickly as he snatched a tortilla chip from the wooden bowl set in the middle of the table. "You don't get it all, remember."

"Yeah," Connor added. "You have *us* to share it with."

"And *me*," Liam said with a smile, "to guide you."

"Don't I know it." Brian grinned at his brothers. Liam, the oldest by three years, looked completely at home, sitting in the dimly lit barroom. Not so unusual, unless you took into account the fact that Liam was a priest. But first and foremost, he was a Reilly. And the Reilly brothers were a unit. Now and always.

As the word *unit* shot through his brain, Brian turned his gaze on the other two men at the table with him. It was like looking into a mirror—twice. The Reilly triplets. Aidan, Brian and Connor. Named alphabetically in order of their appearances, the three of them had been standing together since the moment they took their first steps.

They'd even joined the Marine Corps together, doing their time in boot camp in stoic solidarity. They'd always been there for each other—to give moral support or a kick in the ass—whichever was required at the time.

Now, they were meeting to celebrate a windfall.

Their great-uncle Patrick, himself the last surviving brother of a set of triplets, had died, and having no other relations, he'd left ten thousand dollars to the Reilly triplets. Now all they had to do was figure out how to split the money.

"I say we split it *four* ways," Connor said, shooting Liam a glance. "Reilly's—all for one and one for all."

Liam grinned. "I'd like to say no thanks," he admitted. "But, since the church really needs a new roof, I'll just say, I like how Connor thinks."

"Twenty-five hundred won't buy you a new roof,"

Aidan said. "Won't buy much of anything for any of us, really."

"I've been thinking about that, too," Liam said and looked at each of his brothers. "Why not have a contest? Winner take all?"

Brian felt the zing of competition and knew his brothers felt it, too. Nothing they liked better than competing. Especially against each other. But the quiet smile on Liam's face warned him that he wasn't going to like what was coming next. Sure, Liam was a priest, but being a Reilly first, made him tricky. "What kind of contest?" Brian asked.

Liam smiled. "Worried?"

"Hell no," Aidan put in. "The day a Reilly backs off a challenge is the day when—"

"—when he's six feet under," Connor finished for him. "What've you got in mind, Liam?"

Their older brother smiled again. "You guys are always talking about commitment and sacrifice, right?"

Brian glanced at his brothers before nodding. "Hell yes. We're Marines. We're all about sacrifice. Commitment."

"Ooh-rah!" Connor and Aidan hooted and high-fived each other.

"Yeah?" Liam leaned back and shifted his gaze between the three other men at the table. "But the fact is, you guys know zip about either."

Aidan and Connor blustered, but it was Brian who shut them up with a wave of his hand. *"Excuse me?"*

"Oh, I'm willing to acknowledge your military commitment. God knows I spend enough time praying for the three of you." His gaze drifted from one to the other of the triplets. "But this is something different. Harder."

"Harder than going into battle?" Connor took a sip of his beer and leaned back. "Please."

"Anything you can come up with, we can take," Aidan said.

"Damn straight," Brian added.

"Glad to hear it." Liam leaned his elbows on the tabletop and gazed from one triplet to the next as he lowered his voice. "Because this'll separate the Marines from the boys." He paused for effect, then said, "No sex for ninety days."

Silence dropped down on the table like a rock tossed from heaven.

"Come on," Connor said, shooting his siblings a look of wild panic.

"No way. Ninety *days*?" Aidan looked horrified.

Brian listened to the others, but kept his mouth shut, watching his older brother while he waited for the other shoe to drop. He didn't have long.

"I'm only talking about three months," Liam said, that wily smile on his face again. "Too hard for you guys? I've made that commitment for *life*."

Aidan shuddered.

"That's nuts." Connor shook his head.

"What's the matter?" Liam challenged. "Too scared to try?"

"Who the hell *wants* to try?" Aidan added.

"Three months with no sex? Impossible." Brian glared at Liam.

"You're probably right," the oldest brother said and smiled as he took another long drink of beer. Setting the bottle down onto the tabletop, he cradled it between his palms and said with a shrug, "You'd never make it anyway. None of you. Women have been after you guys since junior high. No way could you last three months."

"Didn't say we couldn't," Connor muttered.

"Didn't say we *would,* either," Aidan pointed out, just so no one would misunderstand.

"Sure, I understand," Liam said, shooting each of them a look. "What you're saying is, that clearly, a priest is way tougher than *any* Marine."

There was no way they were going to be able to live with *that* statement. In a matter of a few seconds, Liam had his deal and the triplets had signed on to the biggest challenge of their lives.

How they'd been sucked into the rest of it, Brian wasn't able to figure out, even days later. But he was pretty sure that Liam had missed his calling. He should have been a car salesman, not a priest.

"No sex for ninety days," Brian said, his gaze shifting to each of his brothers in turn. The other two Reilly triplets didn't look any happier about this than he did. But damned if he could see a way out of it without the three of them coming off looking like wusses. "Loser forfeits his share to the whole."

"And if you *all* lose," Liam added cheerfully, "my church gets the money for a new roof."

"We won't lose," Brian assured him. Not that he was looking forward to a short spate of celibacy, but now that he was in the competition, he was in it to win. Reillys didn't lose well.

"Glad to hear it," Liam said. "Then you won't mind the penalty phase."

"What penalty?" Brian eyed his older brother warily.

Liam grinned.

"You've been planning this, haven't you?" Connor demanded, leaning his forearms on the table.

"Let's say I've given it some thought."

"Quite a bit, obviously," Aidan mused.

Liam nodded. "The church *does* need a new roof, remember."

"Uh-huh." Brian glared at him. "But this isn't just about a roof, is it? This is about torturing *us*."

"Hey," Liam said with a crooked grin. "I'm the oldest. That's my job."

"Always were damn good at it," Connor murmured.

"Thank you. Now," Liam said, enjoying himself far too much, "onto the penalty phase. And I'm especially proud of this, by the way. Remember last year, when Captain Gallagher lost that round of golf to Aidan?"

Aidan grinned in fond memory, but Brian's brain jumped ahead, and realized just where Liam was going with this. "No way."

"Oh yeah. Gallagher looked so good in his costume, I figure it's perfect for you guys, too. Losers have to wear coconut bras and hula skirts while riding around the base in a convertible," Liam said, then added, "on Battle Color day."

The one day of the year when every dignitary, high-ranking officer and all of their families was on base for ceremonies. Oh yeah. The humiliation would be complete.

Aidan and Connor started arguing instantly, but Brian just watched Liam. When the other two wound down, he said, "Okay, big brother, what's *your* stake in this? I don't see you risking anything, here."

"Ah, I'm risking that new roof." Liam picked up his beer again, took another long swallow, then looked at each of his brothers. "My twenty-five hundred is riding on this, too. If one of you guys lasts the *whole* three months, then he gets all the money. If you *all* fold, which I suspect is going to happen, then the church gets it all, and the new roof is mine. Ours." He frowned. "The church's."

"And how do you know if we last the three months or not?"

"I'll take your word for it." Liam grinned. "You're a Reilly. We never lie. At least not to each other."

Brian looked at the mirror images of himself. He got brief, reluctant nods from each of them. Then he turned back to Liam. "You've got a deal. When does the challenge start?"

"Tonight."

"Hey, I've got a date with Deb Hannigan tonight," Connor complained.

"I'm sure she'll appreciate you being a gentleman," Liam said, smiling.

"This is gonna suck," Aidan said tightly.

Brian admitted silently, that Aidan had never been more right. Then he shifted his gaze to each of his brothers and wondered just which of them would be the last Reilly standing.

He fully intended that it would be *him*.

Tina Coretti Reilly parked her rental car in her grandmother's driveway, then opened the door and stepped out into the swampy heat of a South Carolina early-summer day.

She instantly felt as though she'd been smacked with a wet, electric blanket. Even in June, the air was thick and heavy, and she knew that by the end of August everyone in town would be praying for cooler weather.

Tiny Baywater, South Carolina, was barely more than a spot on the road outside Beaufort. Ancient, gnarled trees, magnolia, pine and oak, lined the residential streets, and Main Street, where dozens of small businesses hugged the curbs, was the hub of social activity. In Baywater, time seemed to move slower than anywhere else in the South, and that was saying something.

And Tina had missed it all desperately.

She stared up at the wide front porch of the old bungalow and memories rose up inside her so quickly, she nearly choked on them. She'd grown up in this house, raised by her grandmother, after her parents' death in a car accident.

From the time she was ten years old until five years ago, Baywater had been home. And in her heart, it still was, despite the fact that she now lived on the other side of the country. But California was far away at the moment.

Not far enough away though to block the memory of the conversation she'd had only yesterday.

"Are you insane?"

Tina laughed at her friend Janet's astonished expression. She couldn't really blame her. Janet had, after all, been the one to listen whenever Tina complained about her ex-husband.

"Not legally," Tina quipped.

"You are nuts. You're volunteering to go back to South Carolina, for God's sake, in the middle of summer, when the heat'll probably kill you, not to mention the fact that your ex is there."

"That's the main reason I'm going, remember?"

"Yeah," Janet said, easing her six-months pregnant bulk down until she could sit on the edge of her friend's desk. "I just don't think you've thought this all through."

"Sure I have." Tina sounded confident. She only wished she were. But if she stopped to think about this anymore, she just might change her mind and she didn't want to.

At twenty-nine years of age, she could hear her biological clock ticking with every breath she took. And it wasn't getting quieter.

"Look," she said, staring up into Janet's worried brown gaze, "I know what I'm doing. Honest."

Janet shook her head. "I'm just worried," she admitted, running the flat of her hand across her swollen belly with a loving caress.

Tina's gaze dropped to follow the motion and she swallowed back a sigh that was becoming all too familiar lately. She wanted kids. She'd always wanted kids. And if she was going to do something about it, then it was time to get serious. "I know you're worried, but you don't have to be."

"Tina, I didn't meet you until six months after your divorce," Janet reminded her. *"And you were still torn up about it. Now, five years later, you still carry his picture in your wallet."*

Tina winced. *"Okay, but it is a great picture."*

"Granted," Janet agreed. *"But what makes you think you can let him back into your life and not suffer again?"*

A nugget of hesitation settled in the pit of Tina's stomach, but she ignored it. *"I'm not letting him into my life again. I'm dropping into his life. Then I'm going to drop out again."*

Janet sighed and stood up. *"Fine. I can't talk you out of this. But you'd better call me. A lot."*

"I will. Don't worry."

Of course, Janet would worry, Tina told herself as she came back from the memory. If she wasn't so determined on her own course, maybe she would be worrying, too. Her gaze slid from the front porch to the driveway and the garage and the apartment over that garage.

Maybe, she told herself, Janet was right. Maybe this was a mistake.

But at least she was doing *something*. For the past five years, she'd felt as though she'd been standing still. Sure, her career was terrific and she had good friends and a nice house. But she didn't have someone to love. And she needed that. Now, whether she was making the wrong move or not, at least she was *moving*.

That had to count for something.

"Of course," she muttered, tearing her gaze from the apartment, "you're not moving at the moment. And you've only got three weeks, Coretti—so don't waste time."

Grabbing her luggage from the trunk, she pulled up the handle and rolled the heavy case along the bumpy brick walk leading to the front door. The suitcase thumped against the four wooden steps and the wheels growled against the wide planked front porch.

When she unlocked the front door and stepped inside, Tina stopped in the foyer. The big front room was bright with sunshine streaming through the picture window. The air was cool, thanks to the air-conditioning her grandmother insisted on running even when she wasn't home and a vase full of lemon-yellow roses scented the room. It was just as she remembered and for a moment or two, Tina just stood there, enjoying the sensation of being home again.

Until the frantic barks and yips cut into her thoughts and reminded her that she wasn't entirely alone.

Closing the front door, she abandoned her suitcase and walked through the living room, into the kitchen and straight back through the mudroom to the back door.

Here, the noise was deafening. Tina chuckled as

she fumbled with the deadbolt. Thumps and scrapes against the outside of the door blended with more high-pitched barking that had the same effect as fingernails scraping across a blackboard.

In self-defense, she whipped open the back door and the noisemakers tumbled in, as though they'd been balanced against the door. Which they probably had been. Instantly, the two little white puffballs leaped at Tina. What felt like dozens of tiny feet with needlelike claws clambered over her legs and feet.

Muddy paw prints decorated the legs of her pale green linen slacks, looking like smudged black lace. The two little dogs tumbled over each other in their quest to be the first one petted. The sniffing and licking continued until Tina gave up trying to calm them down and fell to the floor laughing.

"Okay, you guys, I'm glad to see you, too." She tried to pet them but they wouldn't stand still long enough. And, as if sitting on her lap wasn't nearly good enough, both teacup poodles tried to dig their way inside her, squirming and pushing each other off Tina's lap.

Muffin and Peaches, one a pale cream color and the other, well, the color of ripe peaches. Nana's unimaginatively named, unclipped poodles were nuts about women and hated men. Which, Tina thought, put them pretty much in the same boat with a lot of Tina's friends.

Tina on the other hand, didn't hate men.

She didn't even hate the one man she should have.

In fact, that one man was the real reason she'd come back to Baywater.

Oh, Nana had asked her to stay at the house and take care of "her girls" while the older woman and two of her friends were taking a tour of Northern Italy. But the timing of Nana's trip and Tina's private epiphany seemed destined by fate. It was as if the universe had grabbed Tina, given her a shake and said *Here you go, girl. Go get what you want.*

Because as happy as Tina was to do Nana a favor, there'd been another, more important reason for agreeing to come home for two weeks.

She wanted to get pregnant.

And the man she needed to get the job done was living here, over the garage.

Her ex-husband.

Brian Reilly.

Two

The two spoiled mutts sent up a racket the minute Brian pulled into the driveway. Scowling, he shut the engine off and shot a grim look toward the back-yard where the little bastards were probably trying to scratch through the gate to get at him.

Shaking his head, he climbed out of the car and wondered again why the little dogs hated him. Maybe in a past life he'd been a dogcatcher or something and they could still smell it on him.

"Knock it off, you guys," he bellowed, not expect-ing his shout to do a thing about shutting them up. And he wasn't disappointed. If anything, the noise level climbed and the frantic urgency in their yips and high-pitched barks escalated.

One downside to living in the garage apartment at Angelina Coretti's house was putting up with those dogs. But, it was the *only* downside as far as Brian was concerned.

Renting that small, one-bedroom apartment worked out well for both him and Angelina. The older woman liked having him around—knowing he was handy if she needed help. And he had privacy, no worries about losing his apartment when he was deployed for months at a time, and a sweet old lady who enjoyed cooking, to make him the occasional home-cooked dinner.

On the whole, a situation worth putting up with Muffin and Peaches.

And there was another good point to his living arrangements. Since Angelina was his ex-wife's grandmother, Brian could keep a tenuous connection to Tina Coretti Reilly. It wasn't much, and probably wasn't real healthy, but Tina, even though they'd been divorced for five years now, was never too far out of his thoughts.

The barking got sharper, louder, as he stalked up the driveway toward the stairs at the side of the garage. Brian tossed another scowl at the whitewashed wooden gate and the hell hounds beyond. Then the back door opened and that scowl froze on his face.

It was as if all the air had been sucked from his lungs. His guts twisted and a hard ball of something hot and needy and just a little pissed landed in the pit of his stomach.

"Judging by that expression," Tina said, over the din of the dogs, "you're not real happy to see me."

Afternoon sunlight lit her up as brightly as if she'd been an actress standing at center stage. Her wide brown eyes danced with amusement. Her long, thick black hair hung down around her shoulders. She wore a pale green tank top that bared her tanned arms and chest, and he was only grateful that the gate was there, minimizing his view of her. He wasn't at all sure he'd be able to take seeing miles of long, tanned leg.

"Tina." He swallowed hard and cleared his throat. Damn it, if he was shaken to find her standing practically on top of him, he wouldn't let her see it. "What're you doing here?"

"I'm here to take care of the girls while Nana's in Italy."

The girls being Muffin and Peaches.

"Angelina didn't tell me you were coming."

"Any reason why she should?"

His eyes narrowed as he watched her. "Any reason why she shouldn't?"

"Ah," Tina said smiling, as she let the back door swing closed behind her. "Same ol' Brian. Answer a question with a question. Stall for time."

The dogs kept barking and he and Tina were shouting at each other just to be heard. His head was buzzing, brain racing. And he didn't want to think about the jolt his heart had just gotten. Damn it.

Angelina should have warned him.

Should have given him the chance to get the hell outta Dodge.

And, he admitted silently, since Angelina knew him well enough to know that he *would* have left, that's probably exactly why she hadn't told him about Tina's visit. The older woman had never made it a secret that she thought the two of them still belonged together. It would be just like Angelina to try for a little long distance matchmaking.

Too late to do anything about it now, anyway, Brian thought and told himself to get a grip. It wasn't easy.

Tina took the steps down from the back porch, opened the gate and the minute she did, the two little fleabags were on him. Stalking and pouncing as though they were the size of wolves instead of especially hairy rats, they attacked the laces of his tennis shoes and grabbed at the hem of his jeans. He glanced down at them, almost grateful for the distraction. "Cut it out."

"They really *don't* like you, do they?" Tina mused. "I mean, Nana told me they weren't very fond of you, but I figured she was exaggerating."

Brian heard her, but he wasn't listening. Instead, he

was watching her and wishing to hell she'd stayed behind the safety of that gate. It was just as he'd thought. She was wearing denim shorts that hugged her hips and displayed way too much smooth, tanned leg.

Blood pumped and rushed to the one spot in his body that had always responded to Tina. From their first date, the attraction between them had been electrical. And time hadn't changed a damn thing.

Which just made his black mood even blacker.

It had been two solid weeks since he'd made that stupid bet with his brothers. Two full weeks of no sex and he was already a man on the edge. By the end of three months, he'd be a gibbering idiot. And Tina's presence wasn't going to help anything.

"Damn it, Angelina should have warned me you were coming."

She stiffened slightly and lifted her chin in a defiant, *I'm ready to rumble* pose he remembered all too well. Damn. Their fights had been almost as good as the sex. And the sex had always been incredible.

"I asked her not to tell you."

"Why in the hell would you do that?" he demanded, and kicked his foot, trying to dislodge Peaches from his ankle. It didn't work. She managed to hang on.

"Because I knew if she told you that you'd find a way to disappear."

That rankled a little, but only because she was right. He would have signed on for extra duty, pleaded for a top-secret mission, asked to be deployed to a base several thousand miles away.

When, Brian suddenly wondered, had he become a coward about Tina?

Then he dismissed the question, because it wasn't relevant at the moment.

"Why would I do that?"

"I don't know, Brian," she said and cocked one hip as she folded both arms across her chest.

Well, *under* her breasts, pushing them higher, giving him a closer look at the smooth, tanned curve of flesh peeking up from the top of her low-cut shirt. He forced himself to lift his gaze to meet hers.

"But," she continued, keeping her gaze locked with his, "you always do. Every time I've visited Nana in the past couple of years, you've 'coincidentally' been called away."

Nothing coincidental about it. Ever since the divorce, he'd purposely avoided running into Tina. He reached up and shoved one hand across the side of his head. "I just wanted to make it easier on you. Visiting family without having to—"

"—see the man who divorced me without an explanation?" she finished for him.

She was still mad. Easy enough to see in the sparks shooting out of her dark brown eyes. He couldn't really blame her, either. "Look, Tina…"

"Forget it." She waved whatever he'd been about

to say away and shook her head until her hair whipped back behind her shoulders. "I didn't mean to start anything. I just wanted to see you. That's all."

Brian studied her and wished to hell he could read her mind. Dealing with Tina had never been easy, but it had always been an adventure. And if he knew her, then there was something else going on besides just wanting to say hi to her ex.

Still, he told himself, *did* he know her anymore? They'd been married for one year and divorced for five. So maybe he didn't. Maybe she'd changed. Become a stranger. The thought of which left him a lot colder than it should have.

"Why'd you want to see me?" His eyes narrowed suspiciously.

Her eyes went wide and innocent. "Jeez, Brian, lighten up. Can't an ex-wife say hello without getting the third degree?"

"An ex-wife who flies in all the way from California to say hello?"

"And to take care of two sweet little—"

"—furry monsters," he finished for her and snarled at Peaches who was trying desperately to crawl up his leg. Probably wanted to bite through his jugular.

Tina laughed and everything inside him went still.

He looked at her from the corner of his eye and watched her like a hungry man eyes a steak. *Di-*

vorced, he reminded himself, but still just the sound of her laughter could reach down inside him and warm all the cold, empty spots.

Five years since the last time he'd touched her and his fingertips could *still* feel the softness of her skin. Her perfume, a soft blend of flowers and citrus, seemed always to be with him, especially in his dreams. And the memories of their lovemaking could make him groan with need.

Hell.

Especially now.

Man, he so didn't need Tina in town with this stupid bet going on.

"I don't know why they don't like you," Tina said as she bent down to scoop Muffin into the crook of her arm. The little dog quivered in excitement and affection and gave Tina's neck a couple of long swipes of its tongue.

Brian wouldn't mind doing the same.

He spoke up fast, to keep that image from coalescing. "Because they know it's mutual."

Tina scratched Muffin behind her ear, giving the dog a taste of heaven and giving herself something to do with her hands. If she hadn't picked up the dog, she might have given in to the urge to grab Brian. Her mouth watered just looking at him.

His black hair was still militarily short, showing

off the sharp angles and planes of his face to model perfection. His dark blue eyes were still as deep and mysterious as the ocean at night. His black USMC T-shirt strained over broad shoulders and a muscular chest and his narrow hips and long legs looked unbelievably good encased in worn denim.

She'd forgotten, God help her.

She'd forgotten just how much he could affect her.

Maybe Janet had been right. Maybe this wasn't such a good idea after all.

She wanted a baby, sure.

And she wanted Brian to be its father.

But if simply standing beside the man could make her weak in the knees, what chance did she have to keep herself from falling back into the *stupid-with-love* category?

As soon as that thought flitted through her mind though, she firmly pushed it aside. She could do this. It had been five years. She wasn't in love anymore. She wasn't a kid, trusting in one special man to make her dreams come true.

She'd worked long and hard at her career. She was respected. She was mature enough to handle Brian Reilly without getting her fingers burned again. And if she was still breathlessly attracted to him, that was a good thing.

It would make seducing him that much easier.

"Look, Brian," she said, keeping a tight grip on

Muffin while Peaches scrabbled at the hem of Brian's jeans again, "there's no reason we can't be civil to each other, is there?"

"I guess not."

"Good." It was a start, anyway. "So, I'm going to barbecue a steak tonight. Want me to add one for you?"

For one small second, she thought he was going to say yes. She could see it in his eyes. The hesitation. Then he apparently got over it.

"No, thanks. Gotta go see Connor tonight. He's uh…having some problems with his uh—"

Tina smiled and shook her head. "You never were much of a liar, Brian."

He stiffened. "Who's lying?"

"You are," she said, smiling. Then she turned for the gate leading to the backyard and the house. "But that's okay, I'm not taking it personally. Yet. Come on, Peaches. Dinner."

Instantly, the little dog released her hold on Brian and scuttled for the backyard and her food dish.

"Tina," Brian said.

She stopped at the gate and flashed him a smile. It was good to know she could still get to him so easily. If he hadn't been worried about being alone with her, he never would have lied about having to meet Connor.

And now, he looked…confused. Also good. If she could just keep him off his guard for a week or two, things would work out fine.

"It's okay, Brian," she said, giving him a shrug and a brighter smile. "I'm going to be here for almost three weeks. I'm sure we'll be seeing plenty of each other."

"Yeah." He shoved his hands into his jeans pockets and hunched his broad shoulders as if trying to find a way to balance a burden that had been dropped onto him without warning.

She wasn't sure she liked the analogy much, but it seemed to fit.

"Have a good night," she called out as she closed the gate behind her, "and say hi to Connor."

"Right."

Tina went into the house with the dogs, and once the back door was closed, she fingered the edge of the white Priscilla curtains until she could see the stairway leading to the garage apartment. Brian climbed those stairs like a man headed for the gallows.

And when he reached the landing, he paused and looked back at the house.

Tina flinched. It was almost as if his gaze had locked with hers instinctively. She felt the heat and power of that steady stare and it rocked her right to her bones.

Long after he'd gone inside his apartment, Tina was still standing in the kitchen, looking out the window. And she couldn't help wondering which of them was really off their guard.

* * *

Two hours later, Brian was finishing dinner and listening to Connor laugh at the latest development. It was his own fault. Not that he'd been expecting sympathy, but outright hilarity was a little uncalled for.

"So, Tina's back in town," Connor said, grinning. "Man, I can almost feel that money sliding into my wallet as we speak."

"Forget it," Brian snapped, still feeling the effects of Tina's smile hours later. "She's not going to help you win this bet. *I* divorced *her*, remember?"

"Yeah," Connor said and signaled to the waiter for another beer. "Never did understand why, though."

None of his family had understood, Brian thought, momentarily allowing himself to drift down memory lane. Hell, even *he'd* had a hard time coming to grips with the fact that divorcing Tina had been the only right thing to do.

It hadn't been easy. But it had been right.

He still believed that.

If he didn't, he wouldn't be able to live with the regrets.

Tina Coretti still haunted him. At the oddest times, his brain would suddenly erupt into images of her. Cooking, laughing, singing off-key with the radio while on one of their notorious road trips. He remembered arguing with her, both of them shouting until one of them started laughing and then how they'd tumble into bed and rediscover each other.

The sex had always been amazing between them.

Not just bodies coming together, but in his more poetic moments, Brian had convinced himself that even their souls had mated.

And once she was gone from his life, he'd had to believe it, because he'd been left hollow. Empty. His heart broken and his soul crushed, despite knowing that what he'd done, he'd done for *her*.

That hadn't changed.

He shoved what was left of his burger and fries to the edge of the table for the waiter to pick up, then leaned back in his seat.

The Lighthouse Restaurant was packed, as it generally was. Families crowded around big tables and couples snuggled close together in darkened booths. Overhead, light fell from iron chandeliers bristling with hanging ferns and copper pots.

Studying his brother across the table from him, Brian shifted the talk from himself by asking suddenly, "So how're *you* doing on the bet front?"

Connor choked on a swallow of beer and when he was finished coughing, he shook his head. "Man, it's way uglier than I thought it was going to be."

Brian laughed.

"Seriously," Connor protested. "Getting to the point where I'm hiding from women completely."

"I know what you mean," Brian said, though for him, hiding had just gotten a lot harder. Staying away from women at work was easy. There weren't that many female pilots or female personnel assigned to the F-18 squadrons. And those that were there made a point of avoiding the *guys*. Couldn't blame them. They had to work twice as hard as the men just to be accepted and they weren't going to blow a career by flirting with their fellow officers.

So work was safe and Brian had planned to hide out at home, staying away from the usual spots, bars, clubs and whatever, to avoid women in his off-duty hours. But now, home wasn't a refuge. Instead, with Tina in town, home was the most dangerous territory of all.

"It's only been two weeks," Connor admitted, "and already, I've got way more respect for Liam."

"I'm with you there," Brian said.

"Talked to Aidan last night and he says he's think-ing about joining a monastery for three months."

The thought of that was worth a chuckle. "At least he's suffering, too."

"Yeah." Connor narrowed his eyes, nodded at the waiter, who stopped by to deliver their check, then said, "At least I get to take out my frustrations by screaming at the 'boots' every day."

Brian smiled but couldn't help feeling sorry for the new recruits under Connor's charge in boot camp.

Then his brother spoke up again.

"Have you noticed the only one who's *not* suffering is our brother the priest?" Clearly disgusted, Connor shook his head. "He's just sitting back laughing at the three of us. How'd he talk us into this, anyway?"

"He let us talk ourselves into it. None of us could ever resist a challenge. Or a dare."

"We're that predictable?"

"To him anyway. Remember, priest or not," Brian said, "he's still the sneakiest of us."

"Got that right." Connor reached for his wallet and pulled out a couple of bills, tossing them onto the tabletop. "So, what're you gonna do about Tina?"

"I'm gonna stay as far away from her as I can, that's what."

"That was never easy for you."

Brian tossed his money down, too, then grumbled, "Didn't say it was gonna be easy."

Connor stood up, looked at his brother and gave him a smile. "We could try the old switcheroo trick. Since you have a hard time being around her, I could talk to her. Ask her to leave."

Brian looked at him and slowly slid out of the booth. They hadn't used the switcheroo since they were kids. The triplets were so identical, even their mother had sometimes had a hard time keeping them straight. So, the three of them had often used that confusion to their advantage, with one of them pre-

tending to be the other in order to get out of something they didn't want to do. They'd fooled teachers,
coaches and even, on occasion, their own mother
and father.

But, Brian reminded himself, as the idea began to
appeal to him, Tina had always been able to tell them
apart. They'd never once fooled her as they had so
many others. Still, he thought, watching Connor
smile and nod encouragingly, it had been *years* since
she'd seen the three Reilly brothers together. *Years*
since Tina and Brian were close enough that she'd
been able to pick him out of a crowd of three with
pure instinct.

"I'm willing if you want to give it a shot," Connor prodded.

What did he have to lose? Brian asked himself. If
Tina didn't catch on to the trick, maybe she would
leave, making Brian's life a little easier. And if she
did catch on…well, it had been a long time since he'd
seen Tina Coretti's temper.

And as he remembered it, she looked damn good
when she was fighting mad.

Three

Tina heard Brian's car when he returned to the house late that night and she breathed a quiet sigh of relief. Moving to the curtains of the upstairs bedroom that had been hers since she was a child, she peeked out to watch him walk up the driveway. When he paused long enough to snarl insults at the barking dogs, she smiled.

She'd been half worried that he might bolt. It would have been easy for him to up and move to the base for a few weeks just to avoid her. But he hadn't. And she was pretty sure she knew why.

Brian would never admit that he wasn't up to the challenge of seeing her every day. He'd never allow himself to acknowledge that there was anything to worry *about*.

He took the flight of steps to the garage apartment two at a time and her heartbeat quickened just watching him move. By the time he opened his door and went inside, without a glance at the house, her mouth was dry and her breath came in short fits and starts.

"Okay," she muttered, "maybe *I'm* the one who should be worried."

When the phone rang, she lunged for it gratefully. Sprawled across the hand-sewn quilt covering her double bed, Tina snatched at the "princess" style telephone and said, "Hello?"

"So, you're there."

"Janet." Tina rolled over onto her back and stared up at the beamed ceiling. Smiling, she said, "Right back where I started, yep."

"Have you seen him?"

"Oh yeah."

"*And…?*"

Tina grabbed the twisted cord in one hand and wrapped the coils around her index finger as she talked. "And, he's just like I remembered." Actually, he was *more* than she remembered. More handsome. More irresistible. More aggravating.

"So you're still set on this."

Tina sighed. "Janet, we've been all through this. I don't want to go to a sperm bank. Can you imagine *that* conversation with my child? 'Yes, honey, of course you have a daddy. He's number 3075. It's a very *nice* number.'"

Janet laughed. "Fine. I'm just saying, it seems like you're asking for trouble here. I'm worried."

"And I appreciate it." Tina smiled and let her gaze drift around her old bedroom. Nana hadn't changed much over the years. There were still posters of Tahiti and London tacked to the walls, bookcases stuffed with books and treasures from her teenage years and furniture that had been in the Coretti family since the beginning of time.

There was comfort here.

And Tina was surprised to admit just how much she needed that comfort.

Though she'd been born and raised in this house, this town, she'd been gone a long time. And stepping into the past, however briefly, was just a little unnerving.

"But you want me to back off," Janet said.

Tina heard the smile in her friend's voice. "Yeah, I do."

"Tony told me you'd say that," Janet admitted, then shouted to her husband, "okay, okay. I owe you five dollars."

Tina laughed and felt the knots in her stomach slowly unwinding. "I'm glad you called."

"Yeah?"

"Yeah. I needed to hear a friendly voice," Tina admitted. With Nana in Italy and Brian holed up in his cave, Tina had been feeling more alone than she had in a long time. "Even I didn't know how much I needed it."

"Happy to help," Janet said. "Call me if you need to talk or cry or shout or…anything."

"I will. And I'll see you in three weeks."

After her friend hung up, Tina sat up and folded her legs beneath her. She looked around her room and felt the past rise up all around her. She'd still been living in this room when she and Brian had started dating.

It felt like a lifetime ago.

Back then, she was still working part-time at Diego's, an upscale bar on the waterfront, and studying for her MBA during the day. Brian was a lieutenant, the pilot's wings pinned to his uniform still shiny and new. He'd walked into the bar one night, and just like the corniest of clichés, their eyes met, flames erupted and that was that.

In a rush of lust and love, they'd spent every minute together for the next month, then infuriated both of their families with a hurried elopement. But they'd been too crazy about each other to wait for the big, planned, fancy wedding their families would have wanted.

Instead, it was just the two of them, standing in front of a justice of the peace. Tina had carried a single rose that Brian had picked for her from the garden out in front of the courthouse. And she'd known, deep in her bones, that this man was her soul mate. The one man in the world that she'd been destined to love.

They'd had one year together. Then Brian dropped the divorce bomb on her and left the next morning for a six-month deployment to an aircraft carrier.

"So much for soul mates," Tina whispered to the empty room as she left the memories in her dusty past where they belonged. Then she flopped back onto the bed, threw one arm across her eyes and tried to tell herself that the ache in her heart was just an echo of old pain.

The next day, Tina dived into work on her grandmother's garden. Nana loved having flowers, but she wasn't keen on weeding. She always claimed that it was because she had no trouble getting down onto the grass, but getting back up was tougher. But Tina knew the truth. Her grandmother just hated weeding. Always had.

The roses were droopy, the Gerbera daisies were being choked out by the dandelions and the pansies had given up the ghost. Tina knelt in the sun-warmed grass and let the summer heat bake into her skin as she leaned into the task.

Classic rock played on the stereo in the living

room and drifted through the open windows to give her a solid beat to work to. The sounds of kids playing basketball and a dog's frantic bark came from down the street. Muffin and Peaches watched Tina's every move from behind the screen door and yipped excitedly whenever something interesting, like a butterfly, passed in their line of vision.

She'd already been at it for an hour when she straightened up, put her hands at the small of her back and stretched, easing the kinks out of muscles unused to gardening. In California, Tina lived in an apartment and made do with a few potted plants on the balcony overlooking Manhattan Beach. At home, she was always too busy working, or thinking about working, or planning to be working, to do anything else. And when had that happened? she asked herself. When had she lost her sense of balance? When had work become more important than living?

But she knew the answer.

It seemed as though everything in her life boiled back down to Brian. She'd buried herself in her ambition when he'd divorced her. As if by immersing herself in work she could forget about the loneliness haunting her. It hadn't worked.

It felt good to be out in a yard again, she thought. Good to not be watching a clock or worrying about a lunch meeting. It was good just to *be*, even if the

South Carolina humidity was thick enough to slice with a knife.

A thunderous, window rattling roar rose up out of nowhere suddenly and Tina tipped her head back in time to see an F-18 streak across the sky, leaving a long white trail behind it. Her heart swelled as it always did when she spotted a military jet. Every time, she imagined that Brian was the pilot. She'd always been proud of him and the job he did. There'd been fear, too, of course, but when you married a Marine, that was just part of the package.

She lifted one hand to shield her eyes as she followed the jet's progress across the sky.

"Pretty sight," a voice from behind her said, loud enough to be heard over the music still pouring from the house into the hot, summer air.

Tina sucked in a breath and slowly turned around to look up at him. She hadn't heard him drive up. Hadn't expected him to come back home in the middle of the day. In fact, she'd figured him for spending as much time away from the house as possible.

Yet, here he was.

Taller than most pilots, Brian used to complain about the cockpit of an F-18 being a tight fit. But she'd always liked the fact that he was so much taller than her. Unless she was on the ground having to tip her head all the way back just to meet his eyes. She stood up, brushing grass off her knees and then peeling the worn, stained, gardening gloves from her hands.

The sun shone directly into her eyes, silhouetting Brian, throwing his face into shadow. But she felt him watching her and knew that his gaze was locked on her. "What'd you say?" she finally asked, then remembered and said, "Oh. The jet. Yes, it is pretty."

"Didn't mean the jet, but, yeah," he said, "it looked good, too."

Tina felt a rush of warmth spin through her and told herself that a compliment from Brian meant nothing. Only that he was alive and breathing. He'd always been smooth. Always known just what to say. Known how to talk her down from a mad and how to talk her *out* of her panties.

Instantly, memories dazzled her body and the resulting warmth turned to heat and Tina had to fight to keep her knees from wobbling.

"Brian—"

"Tina—"

They started talking together, then each of them stopped and laughed shortly, uncomfortably. A twist of regret tightened in her chest as she acknowledged that discomfort. How had they come to this? she wondered. How had the passion, the love they'd once felt for each other dissolved into this awkward courtesy between strangers?

"You go first," he said tightly.

Shaking her head, she said, "No, it's okay. You go ahead."

Nodding, he jammed his hands into the front pockets of his jeans, rocked on his heels and shifted his gaze to one side briefly before slamming back into hers. "Tina, this isn't easy for me, but…"

While he talked, Tina watched him. And as she watched, her brain, dazzled at first by his unexpected arrival, began to kick in. She noticed the way he held his head. The shrug of his shoulders. The way he stood and the way one corner of his mouth tilted up when he spoke. But it wasn't just how he looked that was different. It was how he *felt*. Or rather, how he *wasn't* making *her* feel. There was no buzz of electricity jumping up and down her spine. There was no hum of energy bristling between them. And no matter what else had passed between them, they'd always shared a combustible chemistry.

Whenever she was near Brian, the very air changed, and she felt that tingle right down to her toes.

Except, at the moment, she felt absolutely *nothing*.

As her brain calculated all of this information and more, Tina's temper flared.

"…I know I don't have the right to ask you to do anything," he was saying.

She should call him on it now. He deserved it. Had to be Connor, she told herself. Aidan wouldn't have tried it. In seconds, dozens of thoughts raced through her mind as she tried to decide how to handle the last of the Reilly triplets. When the solution finally dawned on her, she smiled.

So did he. "See? I knew you'd be reasonable. No sense in you staying here when it would just make it awkward for both of us."

"Awkward?" she said on a deep, throaty purr. "Brian, honey, we know each other way too well to be awkward together."

"Huh?" He looked confused.

Good. Tina chuckled gleefully inside, but on the outside, she gave him a sultry smile and stepped close enough to walk her fingers up his chest and then stroke his cheek. "I missed you, Brian," she breathed and took a deep breath before letting it out slowly. "I'm...*lonely*."

She let that one word hover in the air between them and watched with some small sense of satisfaction as panic lit up Connor's eyes just before he backed up a step. "Now, Tina, I don't think you really mean that and—"

"Brian, baby," she cooed, closing in on him with unerring instinct, "haven't you missed me, too?"

"Uh, sure." He looked around wildly for help that wasn't coming.

Tina moved in even closer and reaching up, wrapped her arms around his neck and leaned into him, pressing her breasts to his chest. He pulled his hands free of his pockets and tried to hold her away from him. But she'd felt the frantic beat of his heart and knew she'd gotten payback. "So, kiss me, Connor."

"Kiss you—" he broke off and looked down into her eyes. *"Connor?"*

"You idiot." She released him and took a step back while having the pleasure of watching him mentally trying to backtrack.

"Look, Tina…"

"Did you really think you could fool me?" she demanded hotly, all kidding aside.

"Whoa," he said, swallowing hard and shaking his head. "Tina, I don't know what you're talking about—"

The temper she'd felt building a moment before leaped into pure rage, and she wouldn't have been surprised to feel steam coming out of her ears. "Sure you do. But it looks like both you *and* Brian have forgotten a few things. See, I can tell you guys apart. Always could. Remember?"

He scraped one hand across his jaw, then shoved both hands into his pockets again. "Okay, it was a bad idea."

"Bad idea?" She stared up at him in openmouthed fascination. "I don't believe you guys. What? Are we in junior high? What were you supposed to do, Connor? Talk me into leaving so Brian wouldn't have to face me again?"

A short bark of laughter shot from his throat as he pulled his hands free of his pockets and held them up in surrender. "Come on, Tina. It was just—"

"What?" she demanded, moving in on him, keeping pace as he backed up toward his—*Brian's*—car parked in the driveway. "A joke?"

"No!" He scraped one hand across his jaw and stumbled over the hose that had been stretched out across the lawn. He recovered quickly, did a fast two-step and kept moving toward the safety of the car. "Brian just thought—I mean *I* just thought—"

Muffin and Peaches sent up a din of barks and frantic yelps that had Connor throwing an uneasy glance at the screen door.

"This was his idea, wasn't it?" she challenged, so disgusted with Brian *and* Connor, she could barely squeeze the words out of her tight throat.

"No—yeah—I mean…" He looked at her again and threw both hands high in an *I'm innocent* pose that didn't convince her. "It was just an idea."

"A bad one."

"I see that now." He nodded and swallowed hard. "Believe me. But hey, you gave me a couple bad minutes there, too, you know."

"Where's Brian?" she demanded, still moving closer.

"Now, Tina…"

She glared at him as she saw his mind working

fast, trying to come up with a stall. Then she realized that the triplets solidarity would work against her here. Connor wouldn't squeal on his brother. But then, he didn't have to.

"Never mind," she said tightly. "He has to come back here sometime, doesn't he?"

"Uh, you bet." At last, he backed into the car and reaching behind him, grabbed the door latch. Unwilling to take his gaze off her, he opened the door and slid inside as fast as he was able.

But before he could slam the car door shut, Tina grabbed the edge of it and leaned in toward him. It did her heart good to watch those blue eyes so much like Brian's suddenly sparkle with trepidation.

Served him right.

"Now you listen to me, Connor Reilly…"

"Oh, I'm listening, Tina."

"You tell your brother that I want to talk to him."

"Right." He reached for the keys dangling from the ignition and fired up the engine. "I'll tell him."

"And don't you even think of trying this on me again, Connor."

He looked at her for a long moment, then slowly gave her a wide smile. "Not a chance, ma'am. You're just too scary."

Now that the first, furious blast of anger had dissipated a little, she could appreciate the humor in the situation. At least as far as Connor was concerned.

Tina's mouth twitched, but she refused to smile back at him.

"You know something, Tina?" he said softly, "even though you just took about five years off my life, it's good to have you home."

Now she did smile. It would have been impossible not to. No woman could stand against a Reilly man for very long. "Go away, Connor."

"Yes, ma'am."

She stepped back, slammed the car door, then stood and watched as he pulled out and drove away. The minute he'd turned the corner though, Tina headed for the house. If she and Brian were going to have a confrontation, then she'd be damned if she'd do it sweaty and dirty from the garden.

Four

Connor's laughter still ringing in his ears, Brian winced as he pulled into the driveway. What his brother had found so damned funny, Tina was sure to be pissed about.

He'd known going in that the trick would never work. Just the fact that he'd let Connor try to put one over on Tina proved the level of Brian's desperation. And in a weird sort of way, he was glad it hadn't. At least he knew that Tina could still tell him apart from his brothers. It had always been like that. Even though everyone else considered the Reilly triplets interchangeable, Tina was different. So different from every other woman on the face of the damn planet, that if Brian couldn't get her to leave town soon, he was a dead man. He'd never survive the bet with his brothers.

Hell, any other time, Tina's visit would have been bad enough. She was a distraction no matter how you looked at it. But now, when he was already a man on the edge, Tina was enough to push him over.

He'd never wanted another woman as badly as Tina. And that still held true. They'd been apart for five years, but just knowing she was in town had his body tightening and his blood pumping. Knowing that she was alone, in the house next door, made sleep impossible and every waking moment a torture.

Oh, yeah. He was in bad shape.

Still grumbling about the coming confrontation with Tina, he stepped out of the car into the cool of twilight. The sun was down, the first stars were just starting to wink into life and jasmine scented the air.

The front door to the main house was open, lamplight spilling into the darkening yard, laying out a path of welcome that he was willing to bet Tina hadn't meant for him. Brian scowled at the house and told himself he didn't give a damn what she thought about his plan. He'd had to try, and it didn't really matter if she was mad about it or not. He didn't owe her anything anymore. They were exes.

So why then, did he feel so blasted guilty?

And so damned hesitant about facing her?

Hell, he was a Marine.

Trained for combat.

Which, he told himself as he started for the door, might just come in handy when talking to Tina Coretti Reilly.

He took the steps in a couple of long strides and stood in the slice of lamplight, staring through the screen door. From the living room, came the muted, plaintive wail of good jazz playing on the stereo. The dogs had to be outside, or they'd have had their nasty little faces pressed to the screen in an attempt to chew right through the mesh and get to him. So, there was one good point. No dogs to deal with.

He knocked. No response.

He knocked again, louder this time.

"Brian?" she called, "Is that you?"

"Yeah, it's me."

"Come in."

Well, so far, she sounded reasonable. Good. That was good. He stepped into the house, walked through the living room and tossed his USMC cap at the closest table. He rounded the corner into the kitchen and found her sitting at the table, a glass of white wine in her hand.

She was mad. He could see it. Her eyes danced

with it. And damned if she didn't look great. That extra sparkle in her eyes appealed to him, which let Brian know he was in deep trouble.

"Sit down."

"No, thanks," he said, letting his gaze slide over her smooth, tanned legs, her pale green cotton shorts and one of the skimpiest tank tops he'd ever seen. No, he wouldn't sit down. He wouldn't be staying that long. Couldn't afford to be around a woman who could torment him this easily. So, best to just say what he had to say and get out of there. "Look, Tina, I'm sorry about—"

"—sending Connor to get rid of me?" she finished for him, then paused for a sip of wine.

He lifted one shoulder in a shrug. "Well, yeah."

"That's it?" She swiveled on her chair, crossed her legs and swung her foot lazily.

Her toes were painted a soft pink and she wore a silver toe ring. *Oh, man.*

"That's all you've got to say?" One finely arched dark eyebrow lifted.

Brian scraped one hand across his jaw. "What do you want from me? I gave it a shot." Oh, he had to get out of the room. Fast.

She stood up, set her wine on the table and took a step toward him. Her tank top had those tiny little spaghetti straps and they were the *only* straps across her smooth shoulders. No bra. His gaze dipped to her pebbled nipples, outlined to perfection beneath the clingy, white fabric. *Oh, man.*

"Why are you so anxious to get me out of town, Brian?"

"Not anxious," he said, then corrected silently, *desperate.* But he couldn't say that to her. Couldn't let her know what she could still do to him with a single look.

"Connor didn't fool me," she said, hitching one hip a little higher than the other and tapping her bare toes against the cream-colored linoleum.

"Yeah, I know," Brian said, doing his best to keep his gaze locked with hers. It wasn't safe, God knew, since her big brown eyes had a way of sucking him in and holding him close. But it was safer than admiring her skin or the way her tank top rode up on her flat belly or the way her shorts molded so nicely to the curve of her behind. Oh, yeah. Safer.

"Why'd you do it, Brian?" she asked, and her amazing eyes locked on to him again.

She was like a damn polygraph. Looking into Tina's eyes *forced* a man to tell the truth. At least, that's how her deep brown eyes had always affected him.

"Because," he muttered thickly, "I just don't want you around."

Her head snapped back as if he'd slapped her, and he cursed himself silently. Then she took a step closer and Brian caught of a whiff of her cologne. She still wore the stuff she'd worn five years ago. A magical blend of flowers and citrus, it smelled like summer and warm nights in her arms and, damn it, he told himself, *stop breathing*.

A heartbeat later, she'd recovered. "That's honest, at least. Why?"

He tore his gaze from her eyes, stepped past her and picked up her wine. Chugging a long drink of the cold, white liquid, he swallowed hard and glanced over his shoulder at her. "What's the point, Tina?"

Tina watched him avoid looking directly at her and a ping of something sad and empty resounded inside her. She'd been so furious all afternoon, waiting to face him, and now that the time was here, all she could think was how different they were together now. The attraction was still there, no doubt about that.

She'd seen his eyes glaze over when he first walked into the room and she'd felt that instant rush of something powerful sweep through her. But then he'd distanced himself without moving a step and she'd felt as though she could reach for him for years and never really touch him.

But she wouldn't let herself be hurt. Wouldn't allow him to chase her off. Not until she'd done what she came here to do. And if that meant that she had to fight past his defenses, then she was just the woman to do it.

"Geez, Brian," she said, just a little hotly, "does

there have to be a point? Can't we just be friends again?"

He laughed shortly and set her wineglass carefully back down. "We were never friends, Tina."

True. She hated to admit that even to herself, but it was true. From the moment they'd first met, they'd been lovers. There'd been no "friendship" period between them. It was all flash fires and fireworks. It was need and hunger and passion.

If they'd been friends, too, maybe they would have lasted. Maybe Brian wouldn't have been able to walk away as easily as he had.

"We could be now," she said.

"Why?"

"Because you meant something to me once," she said and hoped to heaven he couldn't see that he *still* meant something. What, she wasn't sure, but it was there. "Because what we had was good."

"What we had is over."

His quiet voice jabbed at her with the strength of a punch to the stomach, but she didn't waver. Didn't let him see how much it hurt to know that all he wanted from her was for her to be gone.

Instead, she asked the question that had been haunting her for five years. After all, if he wanted to be distant, he could give her the reason. He could tell her why he'd suddenly announced he wanted a divorce—without ever saying why.

"It's over because *you* decided it would be."

He sighed. "Tina—"

"Tell me why, Brian," she said and took a step closer. She saw his blue eyes darken, his expression tighten. "Tell me why you threw us away and maybe I'll think about leaving."

She wouldn't but he didn't have to know that.

"It was five years ago, Tina. Let it go."

"You still won't tell me?" she asked. "Not even for the chance of getting rid of me?"

One corner of his mouth quirked, and Tina felt a tug of reaction down low in her belly. Brian Reilly had one great mouth. Instantly, her brain filled with images of just what that mouth was capable of. Memories crowded into her brain, stealing her breath and making her blood hum with a sense of expectation.

"You wouldn't leave," he said, shaking his head. "Not until you're good and ready."

Still feeling the rush of attraction, she smiled and admitted, "True."

"You always were a hard head."

"Coming from the Rock of Gibraltar, not much of an insult."

"Didn't mean it as an insult," he admitted. "I always sort of enjoyed our arguments—at least, I enjoyed the making up part."

A rush of heat swamped her, and Tina had to

breathe deeply a few times, just to keep her brain on track. "If you enjoyed our marriage so damn much, why'd you—"

"So, why're *you* here?" He interrupted her neatly, clearly refusing to talk about the past. Again. Shifting position slightly, he leaned one hip against the chipped, blue tile counter. "Why now?"

He looked dangerous.

Always had, which she had to admit, if only silently, had been part of his appeal. Black hair, blue eyes, a broad chest, narrow hips and the ability to wear blue jeans like no one else she'd ever known. Of course he could get to her in a heartbeat. There probably wasn't a woman on the planet between the ages of sixteen and sixty he wouldn't affect.

Swallowing hard against a sudden knot of need that had lodged in her throat, Tina said, "Nana went to Italy. She needed help with Muffin and Peaches."

"And that's it?" he asked, eyeing her suspiciously. "The only reason? You didn't talk to my brothers or anything?"

"What are you talking about?" she asked, trying and failing to read his expression. "The only one of your brothers I've talked to is Connor."

He didn't look as though he completely believed her, and she wondered what he was thinking. Wondered just what else was going on. And even as she wondered, Tina knew she'd never find out from Brian, so she'd just have to snoop around a little.

Brian had the decency to wince when she said Connor's name. "Yeah. Sorry about that. I knew it wouldn't work and still let him try." Clearing his throat, he added wryly, "If it's any consolation, you scared the hell out of him."

Tina smiled. "Actually, yes, it is some consolation. But it doesn't tell me what I want to know. Which is, why'd you do it in the first place? Why is it so important to get me out of town?"

His features closed up and a shutter dropped over his eyes. It was the only way to describe the sudden distance in him. One moment he'd been less than a foot away from her and the next, he might as well have been on Venus.

"Doesn't matter anymore."

"It does to me," she admitted.

"Just forget it all right?" He pushed away from the counter and half turned toward the back door.

"The dogs are out there."

"Damn it." He did a quick about-face and stalked across the kitchen and into the living room.

Tina was right behind him.

He snatched up his cap off the table and marched across the dimly lit living room to the front door. As he stepped out, Tina reached for him and grabbed his upper arm.

He stopped dead, as if he'd been shot. He looked down at her hand on his arm, then slowly lifted his gaze to hers.

She knew what he wanted, but she didn't let go of him. It wasn't only stubbornness that had her hanging on, it was also the direct heat that had zipped through her body at the first touch of him. Electric. It felt as though live wires were dancing and skittering inside her veins and she didn't want to lose that sensation so quickly. It had been way too long since she'd felt it.

"I'm not leaving," she said firmly, meeting his gaze so tightly, she saw the shift of emotions in his eyes, but they came and went too fast to identify them. "I'm going to be here for three weeks, Brian. So you'd better find a way to deal with that."

His jaw clenched and she was pretty sure he was grinding his teeth. Which, actually, made her feel a lot better about the whole situation. Sure he wanted her out of town. Sure, he didn't want her to touch him.

Because whether he wanted to admit it or not, he experienced the same short-circuiting sense of excitement from her that she did from him.

Which meant, all in all, that Tina was going to have an easier time seducing him than she'd thought she would.

After all, that's why she was here, right?

To get Brian into bed.

To get pregnant.

And then to leave.

She let him go on that thought because the idea of leaving was less pleasant than the other thoughts had been and she didn't want him to see any hesitation on her face.

"Fine." He nodded and stepped out onto the porch. Settling his cap on his head, he looked at her from eyes shadowed by the black brim of the cap. "Three weeks. I can handle it if you can."

Then he stomped down the steps, circled the house and headed for the stairs to his apartment. The dogs erupted into howls, yips and barks and Tina chuckled when she heard Brian mutter, "Shut up, you little beasts."

Handle it?

He might think he'd be able to handle it, but Tina knew that she was getting to him. Knew that before the next week was up, she'd have him just where she wanted him.

The only question was, would *she* be able to handle leaving him again when the three weeks were over?

Bright and early the next morning, Tina dressed carefully in cream-colored linen slacks and a pale russet blouse. Then she snapped Peaches and Muffin onto their leashes and headed down the street.

It felt strange to go for a walk. Too long in California, she thought. Out there, people drove a half a block to a store rather than walking. Traffic was awful because carpooling had never taken off. Californians liked their cars and their sense of independence too much to share rides. They wanted to be able to go, when and where they wanted to.

Here in Baywater though, the quiet streets were made for walking. The sidewalks rose and fell like waves on the ocean as they climbed over tree roots. But when the sidewalks split, the city came out and patched the cement. A much better solution to Tina's way of thinking, than the California answer to growing trees—which was to rip them out at the roots and plant newer, smaller trees. And then when they grew, rip *them* out and start over again.

The trees in Baywater, left alone to do what trees did best, stretched out leafy arms toward each other, making thick green arches over the wide streets. Kids rolled by on skateboards, neighbors worked in the garden and everyone had a swing on the front porch, just made for sitting and watching the world roll by.

God, she'd missed it.

"Hi, Mrs. Donovan," she called and grinned when the old woman pruning her roses lifted a hand and smiled.

"That's another thing," Tina said, talking to the dogs as they pulled her forward, "neighbors actually talk to you here. They smile. Nobody ever smiles on the freeway."

The dogs didn't care.

Tina'd never really thought about the differences between South Carolina and California much before. Mainly, she guessed now, because if she had, the homesickness would have crippled her. Always before, her visits to her grandmother were quick and so full of activity or just plain sitting at the kitchen table talking, that she didn't get the chance to wander around her hometown. To appreciate the quiet beauty and the peaceful atmosphere. To give herself a chance to wind down from all the hurry up and wait in California.

Now that she had, it was addictive.

Muffin and Peaches strained at their leashes, wandering back and forth until the twin, red leather straps were hopelessly tangled and they were just short of strangling each other in their enthusiasm. Tina laughed and skipped over Peaches as she darted backward to smell something she'd missed.

Quickly, Tina bent down and did a hand over hand thing with the leashes until they were straight again. "Now, how about single file?" she muttered and laughed as Muffin's tongue did a quick swipe across her chin.

Straightening up, she started walking again and as the dogs' tiny nails clicked against the sidewalk, she thought about her latest plan.

Tina had spent a long, sleepless night thinking about Brian and what he'd said. Or more importantly, what he hadn't said. And just before the first streaks of light crossed the dawn sky, she'd realized what she had to do.

Talk to the one Reilly brother who wouldn't lie to her. The one man she knew who was obliged, by virtue of his career, to tell her the absolute truth.

Father Liam.

Five

The rectory at St. Sebastian's Catholic church was old and elegant. Built in the same style as the small church, the rectory, or priest's house, looked like a tiny castle, squatting alongside the church itself. Ancient magnolia trees filled the yard and their wide, silky leaves rustled in a barely felt breeze as Tina approached.

The rectory's weathered gray brick seemed to absorb the summer sunlight, holding it close and giving the building a sense of warmth, welcome. Sunshine glinted off the leaded windows and the petunias crowding huge terra cotta pots on the porch were splotches of bright purple, red and white in the shadows.

Muffin and Peaches raced up the sidewalk, dragging Tina in their wake and she was laughing as she rang the doorbell. An older woman, tall, with graying red hair and sharp green eyes, opened the door and asked, "May I help you?"

"Hello. I'd like to see Father Liam, if he's here."

The woman gave Tina a quick but thorough up and down look, then nodded and stepped back, issuing a silent invitation. Tina stepped into the room and gathered up the leashes tightly, keeping the dogs close at hand. She looked around and smiled at the dark wood paneling, the faded colors in the braided rugs and the sunlight spilling through windows to form tiny, diamond shapes on the gleaming wood floor.

"He's right in there," the woman said, reaching for the leashes. She spared a sniff as she added, "I'll take your dogs to the backyard while you talk to Father."

Before Tina could agree or not, the woman had Muffin and Peaches in hand and headed down a long, narrow hallway toward the back of the house. Shrugging, Tina crossed the hall to the door indicated, knocked and pushed it open.

Liam was sitting in an overstuffed chair, his feet up on a magazine-littered coffee table. He dropped the book he was reading, grinned and jumped to his feet when he saw her. "Tina!"

He crossed the room in a few long strides and enveloped her in a fierce, tight hug. Tina held on for a long minute, grateful for the warm welcome. Brian had certainly made it a point to let her know she wasn't wanted. Getting this kind of reaction from Liam soothed her bruised feelings.

When he grabbed her shoulders and held her back for a long look, he grinned. "You look terrific. And it's so good to see you."

"Thanks, Liam. Good to see you, too."

"Come in, sit down."

"Sure you're not busy?" She glanced around, but all she saw were the magazines and the open book, now lying on the carpet.

"Nope. Just reading a murder mystery, but it can wait." He took a seat beside her on the couch. "When did you get in? How long are you here for?"

"A few days ago and three weeks," she said, smiling. Priest or not, Liam Reilly was the kind of man women noticed. His black hair, longer than his brothers' military cuts, was thick and wavy and his deep blue eyes were framed by long, black lashes. Tall and lean, he walked with an easy grace and his mouth was usually curved in a grin designed to win female hearts. There'd been a lot of disappointed women in Baywater when Liam entered the priesthood.

He looked at her carefully, tipped his head to one side and asked, "What's wrong?"

She laughed shortly. "You must be psychic as well as a priest."

"Nope," he assured her with a grin. "Just incredibly handsome and charming." Then he added, "But I know my people and my instincts are telling me there's something bothering you."

"Score one for Father Liam."

"Good. Now why don't you tell me what it is."

Where to start? It had seemed like a good idea at the time, coming here, to talk to Liam. But priest or not, he was also Brian's brother. Would he really side with Tina against his family? Or would he just clam up and keep whatever secrets Brian was hiding?

"You're thinking," Liam said softly. "I can practically see the wheels turning behind your eyes."

"I'm just wondering if maybe I shouldn't have come."

"Of course you should come to see me." He reached out and took one of her hands with both of his. "Especially if there's something bothering you."

A knock at the door sounded and the older woman poked her head into the room. "Would your guest like some tea, Father?"

Covertly, Liam shook his head at Tina, but she ignored him. It had been a long walk. "That would be great, thank you."

When the woman was gone again, Liam sighed. "Mrs. Hannigan makes the world's worst tea, poor woman."

"Sorry."

"Doesn't matter," he said on a sigh. "I'm almost used to it now anyway. But it may kill you."

"I'm tough," Tina assured him.

"Not tough enough to hide whatever's bothering you. So spill it."

She did. Right or wrong, she'd made the choice to come to Liam, so she would see it through. She started at the beginning and hit only the high points. How she'd decided to become a mother and how the only man she wanted to father her child was Brian and how she was now starting to worry about it all because Brian was so determined to stay away from her and "...so," she said, winding the story up, "Brian had Connor try to get rid of me, and then refused to tell me why he wants me out of town so badly. I know something's up, I just don't know *what*."

Liam laughed.

Throughout her story, he'd watched her eyes and she'd noticed first, understanding, and then the amused sparkle in his concerned blue gaze. But outright laughter seemed a little harsh.

"Hello?" she said, reaching out to slug his upper arm. "I came here for comfort, you know. And some answers."

"I know, I know," Liam said, still laughing as he rubbed his arm and then stood up to greet Mrs. Hannigan as she reentered the study. He took the tray from her and set it down on the coffee table. Once the woman was gone again, Liam poured a murky brown liquid into one of the tall glasses filled with ice. Giving it a wary look, he passed it to Tina. "Drink that, if you're feeling brave, and I'll explain."

She did and at the first sip, she shuddered and felt a caffeine reaction punch through her like a bunched fist. The woman must have brewed the tea for days. It was almost thick enough to chew.

"I did warn you," Liam said, obviously watching her reaction.

"Right." She set the glass onto the tray, then turned to face her ex-brother-in-law again. "Start talking, Liam."

He did. And when he was finished, she just stared at him for a long minute.

"You bet your brothers that they couldn't abstain from sex for three months."

"Yep." He grinned again and leaned back into the faded floral couch.

"You're a *priest*."

He held up one finger. "I'm also a Reilly. And I know my brothers. They'll never make it."

"And you're enjoying this."

"Oh, yeah," he said with relish and rubbed his palms together. *"And,"* he said, "with you back in town, the odds just went even higher in my favor."

"How do you figure?"

Liam smirked at her. "Please. You and Brian are *meant* to be together."

"We're divorced, remember?" Tina cringed inwardly at the word. She still didn't like it. Still hadn't accepted it, even five years after the event.

She'd dated over the past five years, but Brian had always been there. In her heart. In her mind. He was the shadow she couldn't quite lose. The memory she couldn't quite forget. He was the love of her life. Or, at least, he had been.

Liam waved one hand at her, waving away her objections. "I blessed your marriage," he said. "And the marriages I bless don't dissolve."

"Nice in theory," she said.

He shook his head, sat up and leaned in toward her. "Tina, you guys are both Catholic. You know as well as I do that Catholic marriages are forever."

"Until the state of South Carolina says they're not," she reminded him.

"*My* boss has a lot more clout than the governor," he said, with a smile.

"I guess so," she admitted, but shook her head again.

"Look," Liam told her, giving one of her hands a squeeze. "Brian's a man on the edge already. It wouldn't take much for you to push him over."

"So my priest is suggesting I seduce a man who isn't my husband?"

He winked at her. "According to the church,

you're still married. Besides, this is a poor parish. We need that new roof."

In spite of everything, Tina laughed. "You Reillys are really something."

"We thank you."

"I don't think Brian will," she mused, reaching for her iced tea, before remembering and drawing her hand back empty.

Liam scooted around on the couch, dropped one arm across Tina's shoulders and gave her a brief hug. "That's where you're wrong, Tina. Brian made a big mistake letting you go. Maybe it's time you showed him how big a mistake it was."

She leaned into the solid comfort of Liam's embrace and thought about everything he'd said. As she did, she smiled. The only reason Brian would be trying so hard to get rid of her, is if he didn't trust himself around her. Which told Tina that seducing Brian Reilly just got a lot easier.

Now all she had to do, was convince herself that she really was doing the right thing.

No problem.

By the time Brian got home from the base, he was worn out. He'd done everything he could to run himself ragged so that he'd sleep tonight, without the taunting dreams he'd been experiencing the past few nights.

Ever since Tina came back to town, he'd hardly dared close his eyes. The minute he did, she was there. Surrounding him in living breathing color. He could feel her, hear her, smell her. She filled his mind and tortured him in his sleep.

For three nights running, he'd awakened in the middle of the night, with his only recourse an ice-cold shower.

Not the way he wanted to spend the next two and a half weeks.

So until she left, he'd just work himself into the ground so exhaustion would take care of shutting down his too-busy mind. Today, after taking his jet up for some qualifying runs, he'd hit the weight room, then talked three of the guys into doing a five-mile run. The summer heat had pounded at them and the humidity was enough to make a grown man weep.

But as he pulled into the driveway that night, even exhaustion couldn't completely stamp out the instantaneous reaction his body went into at Tina's nearness.

The house was lit up like a fistful of birthday candles. Every light in the living room was on and a wide slice of lamplight spilled from the kitchen windows onto the flower-lined driveway. Music, something soft and entreating, drifted through the partially opened window overlooking the drive. It all looked warm and friendly, but he knew that inside that house was the biggest danger of all.

Brian walked along the driveway and stopped just short of stepping into the patch of light. Instead, he stayed in the shadows and looked through the kitchen window. Tina was there, alone, dancing slowly to the beat of the music playing on the stereo. His breath caught as he watched her move around the room in time to the music. Her body, long and lean and tanned, looked great in the shorts and skimpy tank top she wore. Her hips swayed, her eyes closed and when she lifted her arms like a gypsy dancer, it was all he could do to keep from storming into the room and grabbing her.

He rubbed both hands across his face and told himself to get a grip. But it was impossible. When he was thirty thousand feet above the ground, in the cockpit of his F-18, blasting across the sky, he felt in control. Sure of himself. But with his feet firmly on the ground and Tina in Baywater, Brian was a drowning man going down for the third time.

God, why was this so hard?

He'd let her go five years ago because he'd believed, deep in his heart, he was doing the right thing for her. For both of them. And it was fairly easy to keep himself convinced of that when she was on the opposite end of the country.

But now that she was home again.

Here.

Within arm's reach—he wasn't so sure anymore.

As that thought skittered uneasily through his mind, he headed toward the stairs, determined to ignore Tina and sneak—correction—*go* home without seeing her. And take another cold shower.

Of course, he'd forgotten about the damn dogs.

Muffin and Peaches erupted into a cacophony of sound that damn near deafened him and Brian shot the closed, backyard gate a furious glare. The little mutts had it in for him.

Suddenly the back door flew open, he turned to look and there was Tina, silhouetted in the doorway. His heart did a quick spin, jump and lurch and it was a second or two before he could draw an easy breath.

"Quiet, girls," she said and instantly, silence dropped over them.

It was almost eerie.

"Thanks," Brian said with another glare for the two little meatheads hidden from sight behind the gate. "I'm still not sure why they hate me."

Tina cocked a hip and leaned one shoulder against the doorjamb. "Maybe they love you and they're just too shy to show it."

He snorted. "Yeah, that's it." He lifted a hand and started for the stairs.

"Brian?"

He stopped and looked back, wishing he could just keep walking. "Yeah?"

"Would you mind taking a look at Nana's TV?"

"What?"

"The TV. It's all fuzzed out and I can't get a picture."

Go into the house? With her? Alone? Feeling like he did right now?

Not a good idea.

She saw him hesitate and spoke up before he could say no. "You're not afraid of me, are you?"

Brian snapped her a glance. He knew exactly what she was doing. She was challenging him. Throwing down a gauntlet. Making a dare. Because she knew he'd respond to it, damn it.

"Don't be ridiculous," he said tightly.

"Good. Then come around the front and you won't have to fight your way past the dogs."

She let him in the front door and the music from the stereo reached out for him. Tina stood back for him to come inside, but he took a whiff of her perfume as he passed, just to make sure the torture continued. Seriously, he should try to find a way not to breathe when she was around. Because the only way he'd be safe from Tina was when he was buried six feet under and even then, he had a feeling she'd still be able to get a reaction out of him.

"What's wrong with the TV?" he asked, moving directly for it, hoping to make the repair and get out of there as fast as possible.

"Now, if I knew that, I'd have fixed it, right?"

She stood right beside him and from the corner of

his eye, he got way too good a picture of her smooth, silky-looking legs. He shifted his gaze to the TV, telling himself to do the job and move on.

Moving closer, Tina squatted down beside him until they were practically nose to nose. Her brown eyes glittered in the lamplight and her perfume reached for him, invading him. "You're in my light," he muttered.

"Sorry," she said, but didn't move.

Muttering beneath his breath, Brian punched the power button on the TV and was rewarded instantly with a screen full of flickering gray snow. No picture. No sound. Great.

"What do you think?" she asked.

"I don't know," he said, turning to look at her and finding her mouth was just a breath away from his. Why the hell was she leaning into him like that? How did she expect him to fix a damn television when she was practically sitting on his lap?

His body tightened, his breath shortened and his heartbeat took off at a wild gallop. Gritting his teeth, Brian said, "You need to move so I can look behind the set."

"Okay." She shrugged and the skinny little strap of her pale blue tank top slid down her right shoulder.

Brian swallowed hard.

"What's the matter?" she asked, brown eyes wide with innocence.

"Nothing," he said, and inched past her to see the back of the television. He pried off the black plastic casing and stared blindly at the wires and chips he'd exposed. If his brain was working, he could probably figure this out, but at the moment, the only thing working was his groin.

"Wow," she murmured, leaning in to get a look at the television's inner workings, "I wouldn't even know where to start."

Her hair was in his face now and the soft, silkiness of it brushed against his skin and filled his mind with the scent of flowers. Brian closed his eyes tightly, grabbed her by the shoulders and pushed her out of the way as quickly as he could. And even then, it didn't diminish the flash of heat rippling from his fingers, straight up his arms to rattle around in his chest. Touching Tina was like touching a live electrical wire.

"If you'll stay the hell outta the way," he muttered, not daring a look at her again, "I'll try to fix it."

"Pardon me," she said, but she smiled and didn't move away. Instead, she settled down and crossed her legs. Leaning her elbows on her knees, she rested her chin on her hands and watched him. "You always could fix just about anything," she said.

He tried to shrug that away. He wasn't going to be led down memory lane. Not when he was already on pretty shaky ground. "I was always good with my hands."

"Yeah," Tina said on a soft sigh, "I remember."

Oh man, he was in deep trouble here and sinking fast.

"Look," he said as he backed out from behind the TV while still trying to keep a safe distance from her, "maybe you'd better call a TV guy tomorrow and—"

"What?"

He looked back over his shoulder at her and narrowed his eyes suspiciously. Then he held up a thick black cable with a silver connection head on it. "I think I found the problem," he said.

"Really?" Her lips twitched and the dark brown of her eyes shone with amusement and…something else.

Tearing his gaze from hers, Brian turned around, screwed the silver head back into the wall plate and instantly the picture and sound on the television set blasted into life.

Tina reached out and shut it off.

"Why'd you unplug the cable, Tina?"

She shrugged again and this time, the strap on her other shoulder slid down. The only thing holding her tank top up now, was the swell of her breasts.

"Why've you been avoiding me, Brian?"

"Doing things my way now?" he asked, "Answering questions with a question?"

"Oh," she said and shifted around until she was kneeling on the floor right in front of him. "I have an answer, I just don't think you'll like it."

"Try me."

"Okay," she said smiling, "but remember, you asked for it.

Then she leaned forward, took his face between her palms and kissed him until Brian was sure his eyeballs were going to pop right out of his head.

And he wouldn't have missed them.

Six

Instantly, Tina realized her mistake.

She'd thought it a simple thing, getting Brian to kiss her. After all, years ago, she'd had plenty of practice in turning Brian on.

But what she hadn't counted on, was her *own* reaction to the kiss.

She'd planned on being the logical one.

The cool-headed one.

The one in charge.

But there was no one in charge now.

They were on a runaway train and with every passing second, that train picked up speed.

Brian pulled her close and with one hand at the

back of her head, held her in a bruising grip. Her heart raced, her blood pumped and her brain clicked off.

All that was left was sensation.

The feel of Brian's mouth on hers. The warm slide of his tongue as he tasted her, explored her. The strength of his hands on her body and the hot brush of his breath on her cheek.

He groaned tightly and Tina felt an identical response shuddering within her. It had been too long since she'd felt anything like this. Too long since her blood sparkled like freshly opened champagne. Too long since her brain fuzzed over and her body tingled.

She kissed him back, putting everything she had into it, claiming his mouth with the same ferocity he took hers. Their tongues tangled together in a wild dance of need and she held on to him as the earth beneath her seemed to tilt dangerously.

His hands moved over her, roughly, demanding, and she loved it. His calloused palms scraped her flesh and sent chills racing along her spine. He tore his mouth from hers and hungrily trailed his mouth along her neck, following the line of her throat and down, lower and lower until Tina held her breath, let her head fall back and silently prayed for more.

And then he gave her more and she sighed his name like a blessing.

He slid the edge of her tank top down, pushing it

over her breasts until he'd freed them from the fabric and Tina held her breath again, waiting.

"Tina…" he murmured and dipped his head, to take first one, then the other of her nipples into his mouth.

Her breath sighed from her lips as she felt the dazzling sensations rocketing around inside her.

His lips and tongue defined the rigid points and as he suckled at one of her breasts, his fingers teased the other until Tina couldn't think. Couldn't breathe.

He seemed insatiable. As if he couldn't taste enough of her. As if the taste of her were more important than his next breath. And his hands continued to move over her, stroking, sliding, up her back, over her breasts, and down over her hips to her thighs and then inward, to the warmth of her center. He cupped her and even through the linen fabric of the shorts she wore, Tina felt his heat. Felt the incredible pressure of his touch on her and knew she needed more. Needed to feel flesh on flesh.

"Brian," she murmured, kissing his neck, his jaw, nibbling at his bottom lip as he lifted his head to look at her through dazed eyes. "I want you. I want you so much."

Brian struggled for air. It felt as though an iron band was around his chest, squeezing. Every inch of his body was alive and screaming. Need radiated from him, and his instincts were all telling him to stretch her out on the floor and take her, hard and fast.

She rocked her hips against his hand and he groaned, gritting his teeth and fighting the hot flash of desire nearly choking him. He touched her center and even through the soft fabric covering her body, he felt her heat, pulling at him.

"Brian, please—"

He looked at her, meeting her gaze and momentarily, he lost himself in the shadowy depths of her eyes. She wanted him. He wanted her. Why did this have to be any more complicated than that?

But it was.

On too many levels.

Sure, the bet, he thought and knew that one more minute in her arms and he'd throw away the stupid bet and any amount of money for the chance to be with her. But there was more at stake here, too. They'd been apart five years. It hadn't been easy, but it had been the right thing to do. Did he dare risk screwing it all up now, making it harder on both of them, just for the sake of losing himself in her one more time?

Her hips rocked again and she pulled herself closer, tighter, to him. One arm went around her and he allowed himself a moment to revel in the feel of holding her again. To feel her hair soft against his neck, the press of her breasts against his chest and the soft brush of her breath. He knew her sighs, her moans, her every mood.

And he'd missed her more than he'd ever thought possible.

"Brian…"

"Tina," he said her name on a sigh that ripped from his chest and tore free of his soul.

"Don't—" she warned, shaking her head and holding on to him even more tightly. "Don't walk away. Don't deny us—"

He touched her.

Because he wanted to.

Because he *needed* to.

His thumb scraped across the fabric strained tight over her center and Tina reacted instantly. She clutched at his shoulders and opened her legs further, giving him access.

"Touch me, Brian," she whispered and her voice echoed inside his head, his heart.

She turned over onto her back and lay across his lap and Brian shifted his hand far enough to dip beneath the waistband of her shorts, slide across her abdomen and then slide down farther. She rocked in his grasp and her every movement created torture for him as she moved against his hard body, pushing him closer to the ragged edge.

And still he couldn't stop. He could at least have this. Give her this.

His fingers deftly moved beneath her panties to touch her warm, damp flesh.

At his first touch, she arched her back, moving into him, sighing his name. Again and again, he stroked her, at first slowly, teasingly and as she crested closer and closer to her climax, he quickened his rhythm and watched her expressive face as the first tremors of delight shook through her.

Her eyes widened, she bit down hard on her bottom lip and lifted her hips into his hand, his touch, claiming him as much as he claimed her. When she cried out his name, he groaned again and held her while she reached her peak and then fell to earth.

"Brian?" she asked a moment later, lifting both arms to encircle his neck.

She looked more beautiful than he remembered. Her brown eyes were warm and rich and filled now with a lazy satisfaction that was already giving way to new needs. Needs he wouldn't—couldn't—fulfill. Brian grabbed her wrists and shook his head.

"What?" she asked, wariness creeping into her expression.

"I've gotta go," he said and gently lifted her off his lap and pushed himself to his feet. Pain radiated through him and Brian realized he hadn't been that frustrated since he was a kid. A cold shower probably wasn't going to do it this time. With an ache this big, this deep, he'd need an oceanful of cold water.

"Are you kidding?" she demanded, slipping her arms through the straps of her shirt and rearranging her clothing as she stood up to face him. "You're leaving? *Now?*"

"Especially now," he said tightly.

His hands itched to hold her again and other parts of his body were even more interested in getting close again. Deliberately, Brian turned his back on her and stalked to the front door.

"Was that just me, Brian?" she demanded and the tone of her voice prodded him to turn around to meet her gaze just as he hit the front door.

He saw hurt and confusion along with the anger in her eyes and told himself it was his own damn fault. He never should have trusted himself inside this house alone with her.

"Was I alone in there?" she asked, waving one hand behind her toward the living room.

He wanted to say *Yeah, I felt nothing,* because that would surely be the easier way. But the whole Coretti polygraph thing had him in its clutches again and Brian discovered he couldn't lie to her. Not about this.

"No," he said, his voice just a ragged hush of sound, "you weren't alone."

"Then how can you leave?" she asked. "If you feel *anything* of what I'm feeling, how can you leave?"

"Don't you get it, Tina?" he asked, hitting the screen door with the flat of his hand and stepping out onto the porch, "It's *because* I'm feeling what I am that I'm leaving."

She threw her arms across her chest and held on tight. Glaring at him, she snapped, "That makes no sense at all."

His body aching, his mind hurting, his soul emptying, Brian just said, "Yeah, I know."

Then he left.

While he still could.

For the next three days, Brian stayed as far away from Tina as humanly possible. He even considered moving onto the air base for the duration of her visit. But he just couldn't seem to make himself do it. Oh, he didn't trust himself anywhere near her, but at the same time, he didn't want to cheat himself out of at least seeing her from a distance.

Stupid.

Losing control of the situation had been stupid and Brian couldn't even remember *how* he'd lost it. All he could remember was the feel of Tina in his arms again. The soft sigh of her breath. The amazingly responsive woman he'd missed so desperately.

"When are you going to admit it?"

Brian snapped out of his thoughts, which had once again been centered on Tina, and looked at Aidan, across the table from him. "What?"

Aidan sneered at him and jutted his elbow into

Liam's side for emphasis. "D'ya hear that?" he demanded. "He's not even willing to admit to *us* that Tina's getting to him."

"She's not," Brian lied and didn't even feel guilty for it. What was between he and Tina wasn't anyone's business. Not even his brothers.

"Right," Connor said from beside him and reached for a tortilla chip out of the basket in the center of the table. "You're just avoiding going home because you hate the dogs."

"I do," Brian reminded him.

"Uh-huh," Liam put in, "but they've never kept you away from home."

"Fine." He threw both hands up in mock surrender, then reached for his beer. Taking a long swig, he swallowed, then said, "You guys win. Tina's making me nuts. Happy now?"

While his brothers grinned and nodded knowingly, Brian shifted his gaze to the crowd dotting the tables at the Lighthouse. Always, there were families. Kids, of all ages, parents, grandparents. He'd never really paid attention to them before, and maybe that was because it hurt too much to see happy families when his own marriage had ended.

But for some reason, the last few days, all Brian had been noticing were families. His friends and their kids. Military wives driving into Parris Island to hit the Commissary for groceries. And he couldn't help wondering if he and Tina would have had kids by now if he hadn't insisted on a divorce. But following that thought, he wondered if he hadn't saved them both a lot of heartache by ending things when he had.

What if they had had kids, and then divorced? How much harder would everything be? And how unfair to children, torn between two parents.

His gaze fastened on a little girl, no more than two or three. She had dark, curly hair and big brown eyes and looked just as he imagined a daughter of his and Tina's would have looked. She was beautiful, he thought, just a little wistfully. And if a ping of regret sounded in his heart, then he was the only one who would know it.

"I don't know about the rest of you," Aidan said, snagging a chip for himself, "but I'm *real* happy to hear it."

"Oh, me, too," Connor put in. "Good to know I'm not the only one suffering here."

"You guys are lightweights," Liam said with a sly smile.

"Hey," Connor argued, "you've had a few years to deal with this whole, 'no women' thing. We're new to it, thank God."

"And not long for it," Aidan remarked, pointing his beer at Brian. "At least, one of us isn't."

Brian bristled. Sure, things were tougher than he'd

thought and damn, he'd come close to losing the bet—and himself—in Tina the other night. But he'd stayed strong. Stayed dedicated.

Stayed frustrated.

"Don't worry about me, boys," he said tightly. "I'm doing fine."

"Right. That's why you're here with us instead of at home."

Brian ignored Connor and looked at his older brother. "You enjoying this, Liam?"

"I am," he said and cradled his bottle of beer between his palms. Slanting a look at Brian, he said, "You know, maybe there's a *reason* Tina's in town right now."

"Sure. It's fate, huh?" Brian said with a snort.

"Would it be so surprising?"

"Yeah, it would. I don't believe in fate," Brian said flatly. "We make our own decisions."

Aidan and Connor exchanged a glance and a shrug, then kept quiet and listened.

"And if you make the wrong decisions?" Liam asked.

"Then you pay for them."

"Like you're paying now?" Liam mused.

"Who says I'm paying?" Brian argued and when his voice got a little loud, he winced and hunched his shoulders as a woman at the table next to them gave him a quick look. "Damn it, Liam, Tina has nothing to do with this bet."

"I'm not talking about the stupid bet, Brian," his brother said softly, as if only the two of them were at the table. "I'm talking about you letting Tina walk out of your life."

"That's over and done," he murmured, refusing to look at any of his brothers. Instead, he stared at the label on his beer bottle and picked at the edges of it with a thumbnail.

"Is it really?" Liam said on a sigh. "I wonder. If it were really over, wouldn't you feel safe going home?"

Brian snapped him a look then swept his gaze over Connor and Aidan who were both doing their damnedest to look invisible.

Scowling at his sudden discomfort, Brian reached for his wallet, pulled out a bill and tossed it onto the table. Then standing up, he looked down at his brothers, but focused solely on Liam. "I'm trying to stay away from Tina for *her* sake, if you've just really gotta know what I'm doing."

"Okay," Liam said nodding. "I'll buy that, if you can."

"What's that supposed to mean?"

"I think you know, Brian. You just don't want to admit it."

"I don't remember asking for advice, *Father*," Brian pointed out, feeling his temper spike.

"You're right," Liam said and he smiled again, even wider this time, as if to prove to both of them that Brian's temper didn't worry him. "But consider this a freebie." He leaned forward, forearms on the table and stared steadily into Brian's eyes. "You're not avoiding Tina for her sake, Brian. You're doing it for your own. You're hiding from her because you don't want to admit that you never should have let her go."

"Bullsh—"

"Ah," Liam said grinning, "fascinating, well-thought-out argument."

Brian huffed out a breath, dug in his pockets for his car keys, then glared at the booth full of Reillys. "You guys are making me even more nuts than Tina!"

He stomped off, and after a second or two, Aidan held up one hand toward the waitress and silently ordered another round of beers for the table. Then he glanced first at Connor, then at Liam. "Brian's a dead man," he said, smiling.

"Oh, yeah," Connor said, "a goner."

"I'll drink to that," Liam said and lifted his beer. "A toast. To Brian. May Tina make him suffer before taking him back."

"Amen."

"Ooh-rah."

Tina sat on the edge of the bathtub in the tiny bathroom, dressed only in a towel and reminded herself that this was what she'd come home for. Since she'd first hit town, Tina had started off every day the very same way—taking her temperature. And every day, she'd waited, wondering if this was the optimum day for conception or not. Then every day, she'd faced a mixture of disappointment mingled with relief.

Until today.

She pulled in a deep breath and let it slide from her lungs in a slow rush. Nerves twisted in the pit of her stomach, but she resolutely squashed them. Her temperature was right. Her eggs were ready. The time was now. If she was going to do this, she'd never have a better day than today.

And if she was a little nervous about the romantic ambush she'd been forced to plan, well, that was Brian's fault. He'd been sneaking into his apartment and sneaking out again in the mornings, avoiding her at all costs. "So what other choice did I have?" she asked, more to hear the sound of her own voice in the stillness of the apartment than anything else.

She crossed her legs, uncrossed them, then crossed them again in the other direction. Her stomach twisted and pitched and every nerve ending in her body seemed poised for panic.

"Silly." She muttered the word aloud, as if to convince herself. "This is Brian. We were *married* for Pete's sake. It's not like we've never—" her voice droned off into silence as memories, old and new, flooded her brain.

Of course, there were the memories of she and Brian, first married, and loving each other so desperately, so frantically, they could barely stand to be separated from each other. Then there were the long, empty years and then—images of the other night crowded her brain and Tina's stomach twisted again. This time from need. From want.

Brian had pushed her higher and faster than anyone else ever had and the crashing climax she'd found in his arms had only fed her hunger for more. She wanted his hands on her. She wanted to feel the rush and roar of her own blood racing through her veins.

And she wanted a baby.

Her head snapped up as a slight sound reached her. The front door of the apartment had opened.

Standing up, Tina smoothed her palms over the pale blue towel knotted between her breasts and falling to the tops of her thighs. She soothed her stomach with a deep gulping breath of air, then pulled open the bathroom door and stepped out.

Brian's gaze locked with hers.

His mouth fell open.

Tina smiled. "Surprise."

Seven

Brian just stared at her.

He tried to talk, but his throat closed up tight.

He'd been thinking about her all the way home from the restaurant. Liam's words had rattled around inside his brain until Brian was forced to wonder if maybe his big brother was right. But if Liam *was* right, then that meant that Brian had wasted five years of his and Tina's lives. So, his brother wasn't right, Brian told himself. Liam didn't realize that Brian had only divorced Tina to protect her. To save her years of misery.

Sure he regretted letting her go.

Never more than right now.

The old-fashioned wooden clock on the wall ticked loudly, sounding like a much steadier heart-beat than Brian's at the moment. Moonlight filled the shadowy room, streaming in the front windows like a silvery fog. Lamplight from the bathroom behind her, backlit Tina, defining her outline with a glow that was almost otherworldly.

But she was all too real.

And Brian was a doomed man.

Every inch of him went on red alert. He felt like he was strapped into a jet, parked on a carrier, ready-ing himself for the roar of engines and the heart-stopping jolt of takeoff. Adrenaline pumped and his blood raced.

A second later, Tina started talking, and he fought the hunger to pay attention.

"...I locked myself out of Nana's house after my shower—"

He held up one hand for quiet. "You went outside dressed like that?" he managed to croak, and won-dered if the fact that he found that idea incredibly sexy was a sign that he was truly twisted.

She smiled, slowly, wickedly. "I'm perfectly de-cent," she said. "Not like I went for a walk down Main Street. Besides, it's a big towel."

Not big enough, Brian thought frantically. She looked...beautiful. And edible. And irresistible. And so many other things, he could hardly name them all.

Her dark, curly hair brushed her shoulders, and her darker eyes glittered with expectation and a hunger he remembered only too well. His fingers itched to explore the length of her tanned, smooth legs and when she smiled, her lips looked full and luscious.

Then his gaze locked on the towel, knotted between her breasts. His breath hitched. Was the knot slipping?

Please.

Slip.

"Anyway," Tina said and strolled—there was no other word for it—*strolled* to the double bed on one side of the room and sat down on the edge. He swallowed hard as that towel edged apart slightly and rode high—too high—on her thighs. "I know you have a spare key for Nana's place and I didn't think you'd mind if I waited for you up here."

He watched her and wondered if she'd sat just there on purpose. Moonlight played over her, gilding her in a soft silver glow that made her even more beautiful than usual.

"No. Don't mind," he ground out and swallowed hard. His brain was clouding over. Not good. His body was pumped and eager. Also not a good thing.

Tina scooted around until she was stretched out on the bed, long legs crossed at the ankle, her back against the headboard. The moonlight loved her. As he watched, she lifted both arms and stretched lazily, as if she didn't have a care in the world. As if she wasn't nearly buck naked in *his* bed.

As if she wasn't driving him crazy with a wild desire that had a stranglehold on him.

"It's a nice apartment," she said, letting her gaze slide around the small room.

Now she's making small talk? he thought furiously. He was a man on a knife's edge and she wanted to talk about home furnishings? Bullshit. She was playing this out, deliberately torturing him. She knew what she was doing and knew what it was doing to him. No way was she actually admiring his place. He knew exactly what she was seeing. The studio apartment was small, efficient and anything but homey. But it had always suited him fine.

Until now.

Now, he didn't think the place would be big enough if it were a castle.

He'd still be able to smell her perfume.

Okay, key to his survival here, was to get Tina the hell out of his place as fast as possible. Preferably, without touching her or smelling her hair or…hell. *Anything.*

"C'mon," he said, grabbing up his keys and shifting his gaze away from her. There'd be no help for him at all if he kept looking at her. "I'll take you downstairs and let you in."

"What's your hurry?"

He looked.

She turned slowly onto her side.

Brian stifled a groan, but it almost killed him.

Head propped up in one hand, Tina kept her gaze locked on him as with her free hand, she inched the hem of the towel up a little higher on her thigh.

His heart pounded in his chest. He forgot how to breathe. His eyes glazed over.

And then the towel parted. One half of the pale blue terry cloth fell away, displaying a tantalizing slice of Tina's naked, curvy body to perfection.

Brian groaned. "You're killing me."

"*So* not what I had in mind," Tina said softly, making no move at all to cover herself.

He scraped one hand across his face, frantically trying to get a grip. And losing. "Your towel fell."

"I know."

"I know you know." Damn it. Why was she doing this? Was this a game? Payback maybe, for him getting the divorce? But if that's all it was, why wait five years to claim it?

And if it was more, what did that mean?

And if he asked himself any more questions, that didn't have answers, he really would slip over the edge into insanity.

"This is nuts," he blurted.

"Maybe."

His gaze locked with hers, studiously avoiding noticing her bare, beautiful skin. "You'll be sorry."

Tina smiled and shook her head. "Not if you're as good as I remember."

Like a punch to his gut, her words hit him hard and left him shaky. He was only human, right? Mere mortal? And faced with Tina Coretti, Brian was willing to guess there wasn't a man alive who could have walked out that door.

Still, he had one last hope. "I, uh…don't have any condoms here." Actually, he'd gotten rid of his stash purposely, since he figured with the bet on, keeping a supply handy would only submarine his chances of winning.

She smiled again. "Doesn't matter."

"Uh, yeah," he said tightly. "It does."

"Brian," she said, her voice dropping to a husky note that damn near killed him, "as long as you don't have some socially icky disease, you don't have to worry."

Don't have to worry. So she was on the pill. Okay, there went the last wall standing between him and glory.

It didn't matter anymore why she was here or what she wanted. Maybe it never had. Maybe since the day she arrived in Baywater, they'd been heading right here. To this place. Maybe it was something they both needed.

She trailed her fingertips up, over her hip, pushing the other half of the towel aside.

His mouth went dry.

His heart hammered in his chest.

"So?" she asked, her voice a whisper in the moonlight as she repeated her earlier question. "*Are* you as good as I remember?"

Even a Marine knew when to surrender.

Brian grinned and pulled off his shirt. "Babe. I'm *way* better."

She held one hand out to him. "Prove it."

He tore off his clothes, and in seconds, he was there, beside her on the bed. He peeled the towel off her body, then cupped one of her breasts.

"Brian…" she whispered, arching into him, pushing herself into his touch, "I want you so badly."

"I want you too, baby," he murmured, dipping his head to taste her nipple. A lick, a nip of his teeth and his words muffled against her flesh. "I've always wanted you."

She put her hands at the sides of his face and tipped his head up until she could look into his eyes. Brian read the hunger in those dark chocolate eyes of hers and something more. Something he didn't want to think about. Or acknowledge.

She pulled him close and kissed him, nibbling at his bottom lip for a long moment before saying, "Then take me, Brian. Take me and let me take you."

He was lost.

Groaning, he covered her mouth with his and swept his tongue into her warmth. Grabbing her tightly, he held her close, and took everything she had to give. His tongue mated with hers and his breath filled her as she filled him. He felt the heat of her, pressed along his body and thought wildly that he'd been so cold for five years. So damn cold and he'd never realized that it was because he didn't have her.

She was the heat.

The light.

Tina Coretti was the missing piece in his life and even if it was for this one night, it was good to have her back. To feel the connection blistering between them. To realize that here, at least, there was nothing else in the world that mattered. Here there was only the two of them and the magic they created together.

She moved against him, and slid her hands up and down his back, scoring his flesh with long swipes of her short, neat nails. And he wanted more. He wanted her to somehow mark him permanently, so that he would always carry a reminder of this night. This moment.

His brain raced, blood pumped and an ache he hadn't known in five long years built within. Sweeping one hand down the length of her body, he defined every curve, every line of her. He touched, caressed, explored. He tasted, as he shifted over her, trailing his lips and tongue along the line already drawn by his hands. She moved in his grasp, wriggling and sighing softly into the night.

And no music had ever sounded sweeter.

He ached for her.

Sliding down her length, he kissed every inch of her as he moved along her body. She lifted her hips, arching into him, digging her head deeper into the pillow beneath her. Her fingertips scraped across his shoulders as she reached for him, but he evaded her touch, determined now to explore all of her. To rediscover every hidden delight. To touch her as he had before—and as he'd dreamed of doing since.

"Brian," she whispered throatily, "I need you inside me."

"Not yet, babe," he answered, then nibbled at her abdomen, making her hiss in a breath. "Not yet."

Tina didn't think she could stand much more. Oh, she'd thought herself prepared. Thought that she remembered what it was like, being with Brian. Being the sole focus of his attentions.

But she hadn't.

It was so much more than mere memory could provide. The sensations coursing through her ebbed and flowed and rose up again, nearly swamping her with their strength. Her mind fogged over and her heartbeat tripped and staggered. Breathing was almost impossible. She couldn't think clearly enough to draw a breath—only remembering when she was on the verge of passing out from lack of air. Her vision swam and silvered in the moonlight and she lifted her head from the pillow to look down at the man moving over her.

She reached for him again, but he shifted, sliding around and down the front of her as though he were determined to taste every square inch of her body. She felt the fluttering nips and licks of his tongue and teeth and she shivered in his grasp.

Oh, she hadn't counted on this, Tina thought wildly, frantically as his hands moved over her hips, her thighs, exploring, defining. Then he was kneeling between her legs and Tina sucked in a gulp of air like a dying woman hoping for five last seconds of life.

"Brian—" she reached for him.

"Shut up, Coretti," he said, smiling, then scooped his hands beneath her bottom and lifted her hips off the mattress.

Tina grabbed fistfuls of the quilt beneath her and held on. He held her suspended, then deliberately hooked her legs over his shoulders and Tina watched him as he lowered his head and took her.

His mouth covered her, his lips and tongue did incredible things to flesh suddenly extremely sensitive. She held on tightly, fingers cramping in the fragile quilt fabric. The world tilted and only Brian's grip on her behind held her steady.

She couldn't look away. Her gaze locked on him.

He swiped her center with a long stroke of his tongue then nibbled at her core, and Tina groaned, rocking her hips into him, following the rhythm of his touch. She staggered toward a release that hung just out of reach and with every intimate caress, Brian pushed her higher, further.

Her breathing quickened and she reached for him again, and threaded her fingers through his hair as she held him to her. Kept his talented mouth in place as her body quickened and raced toward completion.

And when she screamed his name, she let herself fall, knowing that he held her safely.

Seconds trembled past and she shivered again, then opened her eyes to find him watching her, hunger dazzling his eyes. Slowly, he eased her back down onto the mattress, then moved to cover her body with his.

"I've really missed you, Tina," he said, dropping a soft kiss at the corner of her mouth.

"Oh, Brian, it's been too long." Her hands swept up and down his back, sliding over the familiar as though it were new.

"Don't think about that now," he said, frowning as he bent to kiss her once, twice. "Don't think at all."

"Don't give me time to think," she said and lifted her arms to encircle his neck, holding him tight, welcoming him with her body as well as her words. Welcoming him with everything she had. Everything she was.

He entered her body on a sigh and she felt—for the first time in far too long—*complete*.

Instantly, they were caught up in the rhythm. The slap of flesh to flesh, the thunder of hearts beating in time and the desire that pulsed around them, drawing them closer and uniting them into a single unit— as it always had.

Tina held on to him, lifting her legs, locking them around his hips and holding him tight, pulling him in deeper. Rocking her hips in time with his, she followed the frantic pace he set and gave herself up to the wonder of being in his arms again.

Her body quickened, sparkling with a renewed need that Brian hurried to meet. He thrust in and out of her heat, claiming and reclaiming all that had once been his. And she felt the strength of what they'd had and lost shimmering in the moonlight around them.

Her heart ached as her body sang and all Tina could do was hold him, cradle his body within hers and make these moments with him a memory that would sustain her long after she went home.

As the first tremors rocked her, Tina held him even tighter and raced with him to a climax that shook the foundations of everything they most believed. And as his body emptied into hers, she heard him whisper her name like a prayer.

"Damn it."

Tina tipped her head back on the pillow of his

chest and looked up at him. Smiling, she ran the tips of her fingers across his broad chest and said, "Not exactly the reaction most women look for after incredible sex."

"Incredible, huh?" His mouth twitched, then a heartbeat later, he was scowling. "That's not what I meant."

"Well," she said, turning into him and sliding up the front of his body in a deliberately slow, sinuous move, she brushed her hardened nipples against his chest. "Then I don't want to talk about whatever you *do* mean. Not now, anyway."

"No, we have to talk about this…." His voice trailed off as she slid slowly back down his body, trailing kisses and long swipes of her tongue over his flesh as she went. "Tina, cut it out."

She smiled against his abdomen. "You don't really want me to stop, do you?" she teased and shifted even lower.

"Yes—no—"

"Well, that's clear." Tina couldn't let him talk. Not now. She didn't want him regretting what they'd done because she wanted to do it again. And again. And again.

And not just because she wanted his baby growing inside her.

She did.

But more than that, she wanted Brian's *body* growing inside her, filling her, pushing her to heights she'd never reached with anyone else. She wanted him to want her as much as she did him.

She wanted him to *love* her as she did him.

That thought crashed through her mind and she at last admitted the plain, pitiful truth.

She'd never stopped loving her husband.

She'd never gotten over Brian Reilly.

And she didn't want to try.

That's why she wanted his child. If she couldn't have him in her life, she at least wanted a *part* of him to love.

"You're distracting me," he muttered.

"Good," she said and lifted her head long enough to smile at him. Then she bent and kissed his hard flesh, stroking the sensitive tip of him with her tongue. He gasped, dragging air into his lungs.

"Still distracted?" she asked.

"Come here," he demanded and sitting up, reached for her, dragging her along his body until he could flip her onto her back on the mattress. He kissed her, taking her mouth, stealing her breath, giving her his. His tongue met hers in a tangled dance of promise.

"No more talking."

"Who wants to talk?" she countered, grabbing at his shoulders, pulling him close. This is what she'd missed, she thought wildly. Being a part of Brian's life. Being able to turn to him in the night and find this warmth, this need, this hunger for her.

How she'd missed Brian.

She parted her legs for him and he moved quickly, eagerly, to enter her again. As if he couldn't bear another moment apart from her. Tina took him inside and felt the first staggering blasts of reaction dazzling within. He moved, his hips rocking, and sent waves of dizzying pleasure surging through her.

Tina planted her feet on the mattress and rocked hard against him, taking him deeper, higher inside. She moved, and he tormented. His mouth continued its tender assault on hers and as their bodies mated, they clung together, each taking something of the other.

He groaned and Tina swallowed the sound, burying it deep within. The first tiny tremors shook her as they built to an all encompassing finale and as Brian's body tightened, she held him to her, and this time, they took the fall together.

Eight

The rest of the night passed in a glorious haze of passion. Minutes crawled past and bled into hours that swept them both along on memories and a rush of desire that had been dammed up too long.

Dawn was just tracking colorful fingers across the horizon when Tina stretched, yawned and turned her head to glance out the window.

Every square inch of her body felt thoroughly used. Brian hadn't missed a trick and had, in fact, picked up a few new ones since the last time they'd been together. If her heart ached a little at the knowledge that he'd undoubtedly been with other women since they'd separated, she wouldn't let him know it.

She would bury that ache and keep it to herself. After all, she hadn't exactly lived like a nun for the past five years either.

But she was honest enough to admit, at least to herself, that no one had ever touched her the way Brian did. With another man, it was simply sex. With Brian, it was lovemaking that bordered on the spiritual.

She shifted her gaze back to him and smiled. Even sleeping, Brian didn't look innocent. He looked—*dangerous*. And he was. At least to her sense of well-being.

But with his dark blue eyes closed, she could indulge herself by studying him as she would any other gorgeous work of art. His chest rippled with muscles tanned to a deep, rich brown, despite his Irish heritage. A scattering of black hair swept down the center of his chest and disappeared beneath the pale green sheet they'd at last crawled under sometime during the night. One arm cocked behind his head, he slept with a smile on his face and damned if it wasn't an arrogant, self-satisfied smirk.

But, since she knew a like smile was currently curving her own mouth, she couldn't really blame him for it. One night with Brian was better than a hundred nights with anyone else. And how sad for Tina to discover that truth only to have to leave him again.

Hopefully though, this time when they parted, she would take a small piece of him with her. She dropped one hand to her abdomen and spread her fingers wide across it, as if already cradling the minute child that might be within.

"When a woman smiles like that," Brian said softly, "makes a man wonder what she's thinking about."

Tina started, then guiltily moved her hand from her belly to reach for the sheet, pulling it up to cover her breasts. "Um…"

He grinned. "Good answer." Then he turned onto his side, swept the sheet aside and cupped one of her breasts in his palm.

Tina sucked in a breath as his thumb and forefinger teased and tweaked her nipple.

"You're not feeling shy all of a sudden, are you?" Brian asked.

"No," she said, "just a little tired."

"Not surprising," he admitted. "Even I usually require more than an hour's sleep at night."

But that's all they'd had, she realized. Because neither of them had wanted to stop touching the other long enough to snooze, however briefly. Finally, exhaustion had slapped them both into sleep just before dawn.

When she didn't answer, his hand on her breast stilled and his gaze narrowed on her. "Are you all right?"

"Sure," she said, biting back her second thoughts, tamping down on the first stirring of guilt that was already beginning to nibble at the edges of her conscience.

"Yeah," he said, sitting up to look down at her. "I'm convinced."

The back of his neck itched.

Just like it did whenever he was in the field. Even at thirty thousand feet above the earth, a pilot could sense when there were missiles targeting his ship. And it was that very sixth sense that was jangling inside him now like a mission bell blowing in a hurricane wind.

"It's nothing, Brian. Really."

"It's something," he countered and told himself that he was pretty sure he wasn't going to like it. All night, he and Tina had connected just like the old days. Despite the lack of sleep tugging at him, he'd never felt more alive than he had at this moment. And he knew without a doubt that once Tina started talking, that well-being was going to fly out a window. And still, he had to *know*. "Why don't you just spill it?"

"I don't think that's a good idea," she said.

"Now I know we've gotta talk," Brian told her and felt his stomach clench into fists of anxiety. Something was definitely up.

"Let's not do this, okay?" she said and abruptly scooted to the edge of his bed and scrambled around on the floor, looking for the towel she'd discarded the night before.

"Okay, when Tina Coretti doesn't want to talk,"

Brian muttered darkly, "there's trouble. And I want to know what it is."

She shot him a look over her shoulder, blew her hair out of her eyes and gave him what she no doubt hoped would look like an innocent shrug.

"No trouble. Really. Just looking for a shower and some clothes now." She didn't want to have this talk now. Not when she knew it would lead to an argument of apocalyptic proportions. And Tina wasn't sure she was ready for that. Not when her body was still humming from his touch and her heart was still aching with the knowledge that she loved a man who didn't want her.

Where did the stupid towel go? she wondered. Not like it could walk off on its own.

"Why don't I believe you?"

She glanced at him again, tugged the sheet with her, draping it around her body before dropping to the floor. "Beats me," she said. "Maybe you have a suspicious nature?"

"Talk to me, Tina," he complained and she heard the impatience in his voice and winced at it.

So much for the happy afterglow thing, she thought as she continued to grope her way across the floor, looking under tables and the edge of the bed for her wayward towel. "You know what?" She staggered to her feet, caught her toe on the hem of the sheet and stumbled forward a step or two. "Screw the towel. I'll just borrow this sheet to go back to Nana's house in. I'll bring it back to you tonight."

Then she made the mistake of turning around to look at him. Naked and comfortable with it, he was sprawled across the rumpled sheets, braced on his elbows as he watched her. Every square inch of him was gorgeous. He looked like a statue carved by a master craftsman. Well, except for the suspicion gleaming in his eyes.

"Not a chance," he muttered.

"You don't trust me with your *sheet*?"

"I don't give a good damn about the stupid sheet, Tina," he said, sliding off the bed and stalking toward her. "I want to know what's going on inside that head of yours and you're not leaving until you tell me."

Tina took an instinctive step backward, then stiffened her spine and stood her ground. After all, she wasn't ashamed of what she'd done. Well, not totally, anyway. It wasn't as if she'd had to hold a gun to his head to get him to have sex with her, right? He'd enjoyed himself. *Many* times.

Although, said a little voice in the back of her mind, *if he'd known what you were doing, he never would have slept with you.*

But then, she reasoned, however faulty, that's precisely why she hadn't told him.

Until now.

She forced herself to look into his eyes, because

looking anywhere else would only send her blood into a frothing rush—and she knew darn well that once he knew what was going on…there wouldn't be any more rolling around on those rumpled sheets.

Their gazes locked and Brian studied her features for what felt like forever. Then slowly, her gaze shifted to one side as if she couldn't quite look him in the eyes. Not a good sign.

"Last night," he said, his voice low and dangerous, "when you said I didn't have to worry about not having condoms…"

Tina reached up and pushed her hair back from her face. With her free hand, she clutched the sheet to her chest like some ancient battle shield. "Yes?"

"You *did* mean that you were on the pill, right?"

"Not exactly."

His features froze over. Some unidentifiable emotion—panic maybe, or fear—clawed at his chest. She still wouldn't look directly at him. Oh yeah, his sixth sense was never wrong.

"Not *exactly*?" he repeated, remembering just how many times he'd made love to Tina during the night. How many times his little warriors had stormed her undefended beaches. The air in the room got a little thin and he had to gulp in oxygen like a drowning man. "Just what the hell does 'not exactly' mean?"

"It means that I'm not on the pill, but you don't have to worry."

Not on the pill.

Four words guaranteed to strike fear into the hearts of men everywhere. The world shifted just a bit and he felt as though he were perched on the edge of a cliff and already sliding swiftly toward a crevasse that was going to swallow him whole. And there wasn't a damn thing he could do about it.

Don't have to worry? he thought. What the hell kind of man did she think he was? Did she really believe he could make a child and walk away? Didn't she know him at all?

Oh, God.

A baby?

His blood pumped and the furious roaring in his ears sounded a backdrop for the bass drum beating of his heart.

"And I shouldn't worry because…"

Here it comes. Tina had known all along that she'd have to tell him. That she wouldn't be able to *not* tell him. But it was different, now.

Back home in California, when she was talking to Janet, planning all of this, thinking it through, she'd done it objectively. She'd reasoned it all out and the plan had seemed fair to her. She would have the child she'd always wanted and Brian would have the opportunity to either be a part of the child's life or not, as he chose.

Now though, guilt was a living thing inside her.

Now, she regretted the lie to him—though she didn't regret her actions, not one bit. She wouldn't trade the past several hours with Brian for anything. And hopefully, they'd created a child—and she would love it with all her heart.

The problem was, she loved Brian, too. And loving him, she could feel badly for tricking him into this. For taking advantage of the nearly magical chemistry they'd always shared. But if she had to live with guilt to have his child, then that's just the way it would have to be.

She looked up at him and etched this image of him into her brain. Stern, his face set in hard planes and sharp angles, his eyes glittering with impatience and the first stirring of temper. Outside, the sun was creeping into the sky, sending the first pale rays of light reaching into the shadows of the room. Birds chirped, the wind blew softly and the day moved forward even while time seemed to click to a standstill here in Brian's apartment.

He reached for her, his hands coming down on her shoulders, his fingers digging into her flesh, branding her skin with heat. "Tell me what the hell you think you're doing, Tina. I've got a right to know."

She steadied herself, taking a deep breath and blowing it out again before trying to answer him. Then tossing her hair behind her shoulders, she looked him dead in the eye and started talking. "Yes, you do. And I was going to tell you anyway, I want you to know that."

"Tell me *what*?"

"That I want to be pregnant."

He blinked, opened his mouth, then slammed it shut again, clearly waiting for more.

She gave it to him.

"And I'm really hoping that we made a baby last night."

He let her go so suddenly, she staggered backward a step or two before regaining her balance. His eyes went wide and he looked at her as if she were a stranger who'd wandered into his room accidentally.

"A *baby*?"

Tina winced slightly at the horrified tone in his voice, but she stood her ground defiantly. A Coretti didn't hide from responsibility. "That's right. I wanted a baby and I wanted you to be the father."

He reached up and shoved both hands along his skull, as if he were trying to keep his brain from exploding. "*You* wanted," he said after a long, painful moment of silence. "You didn't think I should get a vote in that?"

Tina's lips quirked and her gaze slid past him to the bed and back again. "You voted yes, Brian. Many times as I recall."

"I voted for *sex*," he pointed out harshly. "Don't remember voting for *fatherhood*."

That stung and because it was true, she only nodded. "I know. But when I said you didn't have to worry, I meant it."

"Right. Don't worry. Make babies, move on."

"Brian, I *want* this baby."

"Don't say that," he snapped. "We don't know that there *is* a baby."

She slapped one hand to her abdomen, as if she could block the ears of the microscopic life that might already be forming inside her. "I hope to heaven there is."

"Tina, what in the hell were you thinking?"

"I just told you."

"Uh-huh," he muttered thickly and moved past her, grabbing up his jeans and tugging them on. "Your biological clock ticks and the alarm goes off on *me*?"

"For God's sake, Brian," she said, gathering up her sheet and holding it even tighter around her body, "you don't have to act like I pulled a gun on you and *forced* you to have sex with me."

His head snapped up and he pinned her with a look that would have terrified a lesser woman. But Tina was used to the Reilly temper. And had one of her own to match.

"You tricked me," he said.

"I tempted you," she corrected, clinging to that distinction.

"You knew damn well what you were up to and didn't tell *me*."

"Oh, please," she said, pushing her stupid hair back out of her eyes again. He was dressed now. So unfair. He had the advantage here. Hard to fight for your rights with dignity when you're wearing a pale green toga. "Don't act like some poor little virgin who was taken advantage of. You were more than willing, thanks to that idiotic bet you and your brothers made."

He stopped. "You know about the bet?"

"Yep."

He scowled. "Liam."

"Yep."

He lifted one finger and pointed it at her like a physical accusation. "So you set this up deliberately. You caught me at a weak moment."

One dark eyebrow lifted. "And your point is?"

Furious now, Brian buttoned up his jeans, planted both hands at his hips and glared at her. "You should have told me."

All of the air left her lungs in a rush and she almost felt like a balloon deflating in the hands of a greedy child. Hindsight was always twenty-twenty, she reassured herself. And he might have a tiny, tiny, point. "Maybe."

"No maybe about it, babe."

Tina winced. Funny. He'd called her "babe" all

night and it had sounded sexy, titillating. Now it sounded cold and dismissive. "If I'd told you, you wouldn't have cooperated."

"Hah!" He grinned victoriously. "Exactly my point."

Sighing now, Tina felt regret pool in her stomach and spread cold tentacles throughout her body. How sad it was, she thought, that the two of them had come to this. How sad that so much fire was now only an empty chill in a shadowy room. "Brian, I don't want anything from you."

"No, why should you?" He threw both hands high and let them slap down against his thighs again. "You've already gotten what you needed from me."

From outside, the roar of a jet streaking by overhead thundered through the room and Tina felt a hard jolt. Soon enough, she'd be home again in California, alone, and praying for the existence of the child Brian didn't want. And Brian would be here, flying those jets, preparing to step back into danger at a moment's notice.

She'd thought she could come into town, sleep with Brian and make a baby, then slip right back into her world. But the truth was, she would never really be free of Brian. It was the plain and simple truth.

No wonder none of the men she'd dated over the years had been able to touch her heart. Her heart had always been here, in Baywater with her ex-husband.

She couldn't fall in love with anyone else when she still loved Brian Reilly.

As if he, too, felt the sense of misery creeping into her heart, he said, with regret rather than temper, "Don't you get it, Tina? I don't want to be a part-time father."

"You don't have to be, Brian," she said and wondered if he knew what it cost her to say this. "I'm not asking you to be an active parent. You can be as involved or as distant as you choose to be."

"Oh," he said quietly, "*now* I get a vote?"

"Yes," she said, just as quietly, "when I told you not to worry, I meant it. If you want to, you can never speak to me again."

"Just like that."

Okay, she was willing to admit that maybe, *maybe,* what she'd done had been a mistake. Unfair to him. But she wasn't going to stand here and let him pretend that he'd rather things were different between them. "Yes, Brian. Just like that. It's been five years, remember? And we've talked maybe three times in all that time."

"This is different," he snarled. "What's between you and I is one thing. What's between me and a child I created, is something else altogether. You think I could let my child not be a part of my life?"

"That'll be up to you."

"Gee, thanks."

Despite the already growing heat, Tina felt a chill snake along her spine and she wished fervently that they'd never had this conversation. She should have waited to see if there was a baby before confronting him with the possibilities.

"There's no point in talking about this anymore," she said suddenly, turning as she spoke to head for the door. "I'm going back to the house."

"What about locking yourself out?" he said, sarcasm dripping from every word.

She stopped, one hand on the doorknob, and shot him a look over her shoulder. "I lied."

"Big surprise."

Her shoulders hunched as his words slapped at her. "I'm sorry you're mad, Brian," she said, never taking her gaze from his, despite inwardly flinching from the fury she saw written in his eyes. "But I'm not sorry about last night. And I'm not sorry that we might have made a baby." She opened the door and paused again. "I am sorry that you are, though."

Then she stepped through the door and closed it softly behind her.

Brian stood alone in the growing patch of sunlit warmth and had never felt so bone-deep cold in his life.

Nine

Later that morning, Brian really lived up to his call sign, Cowboy. Every pilot had his own nickname used during flights. Some of his best friends were known as Bozo, or Too Cool, or Goliath. Brian though, had come by his call sign because of his aggressive approach to flying.

Nothing he liked better than doing loops and spins miles above the ground. Ordinarily, too, he emptied his mind of everything but the task at hand—much safer to be thinking *only* about flying when you went faster than the speed of sound.

But today, Tina was flying with him.

She was there beside him in the close confines of

the cockpit. She was in his blood, in his brain, and to get her out again, was going to be far tougher than anything he'd ever faced before.

"She *tricked* me," he muttered, still unable to grasp the fact that his ex-wife had deliberately set him up to father her child.

"What?" The voice came from the seat behind him. His radar officer, Sam "Hollywood" Holden.

"Nothin'."

"Okay, Cap'n," Hollywood said, "that's the way you want it. So if you're finished trying to make me upchuck my breakfast, why don't we turn this puppy around and head home?"

Brian grinned. "What's wrong, Hollywood? Late night last night?"

"Hey," his friend pointed out with a chuckle. "Not all of us signed up for that stupid bet."

Groaning, Brian shook his head and stared into the clouds whizzing past the plane. Impossible to keep a secret on a military base. At least *this* kind of secret. Spies, battle plans, sure. You were safe. A humiliating, personal problem—fair game.

He never should have agreed to the bet. If he had told Liam to get lost, he never would have been in such a vulnerable condition when Tina hit town. And he never would have spent a long, endless night exploring her body.

Hard to regret that, even considering the way it had ended.

However, he'd be damned if he'd just sit back and let the guys get a good laugh at his expense.

"Just for that," Brian said with an evil chuckle, already maneuvering his jet into an upside-down position, "I think we'll just fly home inverted."

"Oh, *man....*"

"I really made a mess of this, didn't I?" Tina looked down at Muffin and Peaches, sprawled across her bed. "Not that I'm really regretting it. I mean, that *is* why I came here, right?"

Peaches yawned and rolled over.

Tina paced, marking off the same steps in her old room that she had as a teenager when she was angsting over the serious problems that had faced her back then. Things like, would she ever get her hair straightened? Would she ever get a date? Would she ever get out of AP Chem?

Well, times had changed and the problems had gotten bigger. But her solutions were still the same. Pace and talk to herself.

"It's not like I *forced* him, you know," she said aloud, shooting a look at Muffin, since Peaches, the little traitor, was snoring. "He was more than willing."

Muffin yapped.

"So why do I feel so blasted guilty?" she demanded and knew the answer, though she didn't really want to look at it too closely. Using Brian had been wrong. "Fine. I'm a rotten human being. Stand me up against a wall and shoot me." She stopped at the foot of the bed and plopped down onto the edge of the mattress. "I just wanted—"

What? A baby? Sure. But that wasn't all, was it? No. She'd wanted Brian back. She hadn't been able to admit it even to herself before she'd arrived back in Baywater. But it was impossible to deny now.

It wasn't just his child she wanted.

It was his heart.

And that was the one thing she couldn't have.

Pushing herself to her feet, Tina stalked around the edge of the bed, grabbed the phone and punched in a familiar number. It rang twice.

"Hello?"

"Janet." Tina sighed, reached down to scoot a limp Peaches over and then sat down. "Thank God."

"Tina! How's it going girl?"

"Not so good."

"Oh." Janet was silent for a long minute. "So you couldn't get him to—"

"No," Tina said, toying with the pale blue, coiled cord of the ancient Princess phone. "Mission accomplished."

A long pause. "Really? You mean you really went to bed with your ex?"

"No," Tina said, scooting back farther on the bed. "I asked him for a donation, then I took it to the clinic and had them douse me with a turkey baster."

Janet laughed. "Well, for someone who just had sex, you seem a little cranky."

Frowning, Tina said, "I'm sorry. I'm just mad at myself and you're easier to yell at."

"Happy to help."

"Janet, it didn't go like I thought it would."

"It wasn't as great as you remembered?"

"It was better."

"So what's the problem?"

"I told him." Tina closed her eyes and saw Brian's face again. The betrayal in his eyes and the fury stamped on his features. She couldn't really blame him. *He'd* divorced *her,* after all. And if he hadn't wanted her as his wife, why would he want her as the mother of his child? A child, by the way, he hadn't realized he'd been conceiving. Maybe.

"Ahh…" Janet's sigh was long and eloquent. "You knew going in he wouldn't be happy about it."

"I know," she said and shook her head even as she dropped one hand to Peaches's back and stroked the little dog gently. "But I didn't know I'd—"

"—still love him?" Janet finished for her.

"Well, yeah."

"Tina, honey, this way lies pain."

"You're right, but—" Tina's brain went back to the

night before. The passion, the desire, the hunger that had risen up and engulfed them both. It had been stronger somehow, *bigger* than what she and Brian had shared five years before. Was it because they'd been apart so long?

Or was it because they were meant to be together?

"So what are you going to do about it?"

Tina scowled. "What can I do?"

"Honestly, Tina," Janet said, clucking her tongue loud enough that it sounded as though she were right beside Tina instead of at home, more than three thousand miles from South Carolina. "You love him and you're just going to walk away again?"

Tina stiffened slightly. "I didn't walk the last time, remember? Brian did."

"And you let him decide for both of you what was going to happen."

"Yes, but—"

Janet didn't let her finish. "How about this time, the two of you actually *talk* about what happened?"

Good idea, in theory, Tina thought grimly. But as she remembered the look on Brian's face when she'd left his apartment only that morning, she had a feeling that he would be a little less than receptive.

"And say what?"

"I don't know," Janet said, sarcasm dripping from every word, "how about, *I love you?*"

Those three words echoed over and over again in

Tina's mind as she stared blankly out the window. Outside, sunset pulsed in the sky, gilding the cloud-streaked horizon in brilliant shades of crimson and lavender.

"I said that five years ago," Tina whispered, remembering the pain. "It didn't help."

"Couldn't hurt, either."

"Maybe," she said, then changed the subject abruptly. There were no easy answers here. Nothing had really changed between her and Brian. And though she loved him and probably always would, she wasn't going to tell Brian. What would be the point? Another chance at humiliation when he told her *again* that he didn't want to be married to her? No, she thought. Passion was one thing—love was another. And all during the long night with Brian, he'd never once mentioned love.

While Janet talked about her pregnancy and the plans she had for her baby, Tina kept one hand firmly atop her flat abdomen. Silently, she prayed that inside, a child was already beginning to grow.

And if she was lucky, a small part of Brian would always be a part of her life—and no one would be able to take that away from her.

"I'm out."

Connor, Aidan and Liam stared at Brian for a long minute. He shifted under that steady regard, then bounced the basketball a few times before turning, jumping and shooting for the basket. The ball ricocheted off the backboard and crashed through the pretty stretch of flowers lining the rectory's driveway.

"Perfect," he muttered. Couldn't even make a basket. When he snatched up the ball again, he turned to see his brothers still watching him, wide grins on their faces.

"You didn't even last a month," Connor pointed out.

"Pitiful," Aidan said and came toward him, grabbing the basketball and shooting, making a perfect *swish* through the net.

"What happened?" Liam asked.

Brian wiped sweat out of his eyes with his forearm, then squinted at his brother the priest. The backyard lights spilled onto the wide driveway, lighting up the makeshift basketball court where he and his brothers fought vicious games of two-on-two ball a couple of nights a week.

Brian snapped his fingers a couple of times. "Keep up, Liam. I said I'm out of the contest. Measure me now for the hula skirt and coconut bra."

"I love this," Aidan said, taking another shot. "I can already feel that money bulging in my wallet."

"Yeah?" Connor countered, making a jump for the ball as it rebounded, "don't start spending it yet, pal."

The two of them argued and fought for the ball as Liam strolled across the driveway toward Brian.

Scowling, Brian watched his brothers shooting hoops and listened to the metallic *twang* as the ball slapped against the rim with every shot. A full moon shone down from a clear night sky and the scent of jasmine floated on the thick, summer air.

"You don't look so good," Liam said.

"Told you," Brian snapped, giving his older brother a quick, heated glance, "I lost the bet."

"This isn't about the bet."

"Yeah? Then tell me, *Father,* what's it about?"

Liam smiled and shook his head as if he were watching a particularly stubborn five-year-old. "It's about Tina. And *you.*"

Thoughts, questions, doubts, nibbled at the edges of his mind, as they had all day. He'd gotten through work, but he'd avoided going home. He wasn't ready yet to face Tina. To look at her and remember the night before. To remember that she'd tricked him. That even now, his *child* might be nestled inside her body.

Brian's stomach twisted and a knot lodged in his throat. Wasn't sure what that meant, but he had an idea and he didn't want to acknowledge it. Even to himself.

"There is no me and Tina," he said softly.

"Maybe there should be," Liam told him, and turning, steered Brian farther down the driveway, away from Connor and Aidan's shouting. "Maybe you've been given a second chance, Brian."

"A chance to make a jackass of myself in a hula skirt?"

Liam shook his head. "This isn't about the bet, Brian. You're not paying attention." He stopped at the end of the driveway and took a long moment, to look up and down the street. From a distance, came the sounds of kids playing, a car engine firing up and a stereo system blasting out some classic rock and roll.

Smiling, Liam lifted one arm and pointed at the houses crouched behind ancient trees. "What do you see?"

Brian snorted. "Maple Street."

"And…?"

Blowing out a breath, Brian turned and looked. "Houses. Trees. Dogs."

"Families," Liam said. "Homes."

Brian scraped one hand across his jaw and narrowed his gaze. "What's your point, Liam?"

"How many of those families are military, do you think?"

"What difference does that make?"

"All the difference to some, none at all to others," Liam said.

"Are you a priest or Confucius? For God's sake, make your point."

"You're an idiot, Brian." Liam shoved his younger brother and watched him stagger before regaining his balance.

Brian instantly lifted both hands, curled into fists. "Hey, you wanna go a round or two, fine by me."

The streetlight nearby spotlighted them in a circle of white and cast deep shadows on Liam's face. But despite the shadows, Brian saw a look of utter disgust on his brother's features.

"I don't want to fight you," Liam snapped. "I'm trying to tell you that instead of being here, with us—" he waved one hand at the driveway behind him, indicating Aidan and Connor, still throwing hoops. "You should be back at Angelina's house, talking to Tina."

The urge to fight dissolved and Brian shifted his gaze to the street and the houses beyond. "We're done talking."

"Just like five years ago then, huh? Your way or nothing?"

"You don't know what you're talking about," Brian warned.

"I know you, Brian." Liam shook his head, clearly disgusted. "I know Tina was the best thing that ever happened to you. And I know you *loved* her and you were *happy* until you decided to chuck it all."

"My business."

"Undoubtedly. All I'm saying is that maybe fate just handed you a second chance and you'd be an idiot to turn your back on it."

"I didn't ask for a second chance."

"That's what makes you *lucky,* you moron."

Brian snorted. "Nice priestly manner."

"You want a priest?" Liam asked, already turning to head back to the game, "show up at Mass once in awhile. Here, all you'll get is a brother."

Brian stared after him for several long minutes. Absently, he listened to the sounds of his brothers laughing and talking trash. Then he turned his gaze on Maple Street. And for the first time, he really thought about something Liam had said.

Probably half of those tidy little houses with neat lawns and carefully tended flower beds were lived in by military families. Husband or wife—and sometimes both—lived their lives according to the Corps, going where they were told, when they were told, never sure if they were going to be coming back.

And yet…Brian listened to the sound of a dog's excited bark and a kid's delighted laughter, drifting to him on the summer breeze. Somehow, most of those families made it work for them.

Five years ago, he'd decided that he couldn't put Tina through the misery of a life dictated by military needs. He'd told himself at the time that it wasn't fair to her. Wasn't fair to expect her to pick up, pack up and move across the country, sometimes around the world, whenever his orders changed. It was too much to ask her to live alone for months at a time when he was deployed. He'd thought it wasn't right to keep her in a marriage where her husband had a damn good chance of never coming home at all.

And he'd let her go.

For her sake.

It had cost him everything to cut Tina out of his life. And he'd felt the hollow emptiness ever since.

Now that Tina was back, he felt that emptiness even more sharply. It was a razor, slicing his soul, tearing at his heart. She'd wanted a baby.

His baby.

And he wondered if he'd made a big mistake five years ago.

Was he really the moron Liam claimed?

Ten

Two days later, and Brian was still thinking. Not that it was doing him much good.

He'd been able to avoid Tina so far, but that couldn't last. His ex-wife was *not* a woman to be ignored. He smiled as he remembered just the night before, her footsteps pounding up the stairs to his apartment and her voice demanding that he open the door and talk to her.

Naturally, he hadn't. He'd only shouted at her to go away and she'd left. Eventually.

But he knew damn well this armed truce couldn't last.

He pulled into the driveway, casting a quick

glance around to make sure the coast was clear. Man, what was the world coming to when a *Marine,* for God's sake, was skulking in and out of his house to avoid a woman?

Twilight was just beginning to fall and the air was a bit cooler as a soft sigh of wind drifted in off the ocean. From down the street came the unmistakable scent of a barbecue being fired up and a couple of kids were tossing a baseball in the street. Situation normal.

So why did he feel as knotted up and wired as he did when about to fly a combat mission?

The answer to that question opened up the screen door and stepped onto the porch. The two dogs hot on her heels followed after, yapping and snarling as they pelted off the porch and across the yard toward him. Presumably, they were ready to chew on what was left of his sorry butt once Tina was through with him.

She had blood in her eye and an expression of fierce determination on her face as she marched toward him. Looked like his stalling time was up. Briefly, Brian considered firing up the engine, throwing the car into gear and roaring back out of the driveway. But that smacked just a little too much of retreat, so he ignored the urge and stepped out of the car.

On the street, the kids hooted and jeered at each other as the ball flew wildly. In the yard, Muffin and Peaches were headed directly toward Brian and he imagined they were looking at him like a giant chew toy.

Then one of the kids missed a catch and the base-ball shot past him, landing in the yard and rolling fast toward the flower bed. Peaches shifted direction and took off after it as though it were a gazelle and she a mighty lion. Her little feet flew and her ears flapped. She was almost on the ball when one of the kids threw a rock, hit her on a hind leg and the dog dropped with a yelp.

"Hey!" Furious, Tina shifted direction, heading for the downed dog.

Scared, the kid started backing off, but Brian was already moving to intercept. Anger pulsed through him as he heard loud whimpers from the injured dog. God knew he and the little ankle biters weren't close friends, but he wouldn't stand for one of the little dogs being hurt.

He reached the kid in a few long strides and dropped both hands on the boy's shoulders. Couldn't have been more than ten, Brian thought and right now, he was looking scared enough to cry. Good.

"What the hell are you doing?" Brian demanded.

"It's my ball, is all," the boy said, shooting a glance at the dog now being petted and stroked by Tina, kneeling on the ground beside it.

"And you thought that little dog was going to eat it?" Brian demanded.

"No," he said, his voice hitching close to the same note as the dog's whimper.

"You threw a *rock* at a three-pound dog," Brian growled, using his best, put-the-fear-of-God-into-your-enemy voice.

"I didn't mean to hurt her…"

The kid's friend, Brian noted, had already deserted the field, scampering out of range of punishment or retribution. The boy still in his grasp was trembling and Brian, keeping a firm grip on one shoulder, steered him toward the yard. "What do you think your mom would have to say about you throwing rocks at animals?"

"Oh, *man*," the kid whined pitifully. "Don't tell her, okay? I'm really sorry. Honest I am. C'mon, mister, don't tell my mom."

Brian heard the desperation and could appreciate it. When he and his brothers were ten, there wasn't anything they wouldn't have done to get out of letting their parents know they'd screwed up. "All right, I won't. But, you're going to go check on that dog. Make sure she's all right. *Then* you're going to apologize to the lady. Then you can have your ball back."

The boy blew out a relieved breath, then ran the back of his hand under his nose and sniffed dramatically. Every step dragged through the grass as if it were thick mud, sucking him down. He kept his head lowered and shot a wary glance up at Brian before shifting his gaze to Tina.

"I didn't mean to hurt her," he said and his voice shook a little.

"Then you shouldn't have thrown a rock," she said tightly.

"I'm really sorry." He went down on one knee next to the little dog and petted her head gently. Looking at Tina he promised, "I won't ever do it again, I swear."

Tina glanced at Brian and he smiled, nodding. He figured the kid was scared enough to make good on his word. And after all, what kid *didn't* throw a rock at the wrong time at one point in his life?

"All right then," Tina said, as she watched Peaches lick the boy's hand. "If Peaches can forgive you, so can I."

"Thanks, lady," the boy said, reaching for his ball and standing up again. He lifted his chin and met Brian's steely stare with more courage than he'd shown before. "I *am* sorry, y'know."

"Yeah," Brian said, jerking his head toward the street. "Go on."

The kid ran—as if he might not get a second chance at escape. Brian watched him, baggy jeans, torn sneakers and faded T-shirt, as he sprinted for his own house and safety. And just for a minute, Brian wondered what it would be like to have a child of his own.

Which of course, brought him full circle, right back to where he'd started.

He thought about the night with Tina and the chances of their having made a baby. And for the first time, that possibility felt real. He could almost see the kid's face. A fascinating combination of his and Tina's features. Unexpectedly, a curl of something warm unwound inside him.

A baby.

Brian Reilly, *father*.

And the notion of that didn't seem as weird, or terrifying as it had a couple of days ago.

"Ooh," Tina said, "I wanted to shake him so badly."

"He's pretty shook already," Brian said, going down on one knee in the grass. "How's the dog?"

"She's all right," Tina said. "It wasn't a very big rock, thank heaven."

Muffin sidled up close to Brian and leaned into him. Without even thinking about it, he stroked her cream-colored curls. Peaches slipped out from under Tina's gentle hand and trotted to Brian, too. Planting both front feet on his knee, she sat down and stared up at him in adoration.

He looked down at the dogs who'd been the bane of his existence for years and couldn't believe it. Neither one of them was trying to go for his jugular.

"Looks like they're in love," Tina quipped.

Brian's gaze snapped to hers. "What?"

"You're their hero, apparently."

He frowned at the two tiny dogs.

They sighed.

"Oh, this is weird."

"You'd rather they were snarling at you?"

"At least I know what to expect then."

"And that's important?" Tina asked.

He looked at her again. "I don't like surprises."

"Brian—"

He cut her off. "Tina, I don't want to talk about it again."

"Again?" she countered. "We haven't talked about it *yet*."

Peaches tried to crawl up his body, so Brian gently picked her up and set her back down again. Muffin leaned harder against him.

Brian tried to ignore the dogs and focus on the woman watching him. He could already see the fires of indignation beginning to kindle in her eyes and he braced himself. "Fine. Can we at least take this inside?"

"You bet." She jumped to her feet, snapped her fingers and said, "C'mon, girls."

Neither dog moved.

"Muffin? Peaches?"

Brian scowled at the little animals.

They sighed.

He sighed, too, as he stood up and the dogs fell into step behind him. He headed for the front porch, ignoring the stupefied expression on Tina's face as he and his entourage walked to the house.

"I'm sorry I tricked you," Tina blurted the minute they were in the door.

"Old news," Brian said, walking past her to the

couch where he sat down and winced as both dogs jumped into his lap at once.

Tina frowned at the three of them. The dogs, the little traitors, had shifted their affections to him and she felt like a complete outsider, now. She buried the irritation and took a seat on the sofa opposite him.

"Old or not, I wanted you to know that I've thought about it and I realize that it was wrong of me to do it."

"Thanks," he said, shoving both dogs off his lap and leaning forward, his forearms on his knees. "But that doesn't change the fact that we have to deal with the consequences."

"So businesslike," she murmured, shaking her head. "Very admirable."

"Would you rather I shout and stomp around the room?"

"Actually?" she mused, "Yes."

"Already did that," he pointed out. "Didn't change anything."

"Look, Brian," she said, hating the calm, indifferent tone of his voice. She'd much rather have one of their legendary arguments. An Irish temper and an Italian temper could get pretty loud when they clashed. But the making up had always been worth the storm. "I meant what I said the other night. If I am pregnant—"

He winced and she tried not to notice.

"—then I'll deal with it myself. You don't have to—"

"Just stop right there," he demanded and shifted when Peaches made a try for his lap again. "If you're pregnant, then it's *our* baby and *we* deal with it."

"How do you mean *deal*?"

"Take care of it, of course. What the hell do you think I mean?" His temper spiked a little and Tina immediately felt better.

"I can raise a child, Brian," she said.

"Not my child. Not alone."

For one brief second, Tina entertained the notion that just maybe he'd missed her as much as she'd missed him. That maybe he was going to suggest that they might still work this out. That there was a future for the two of them after all.

And when that heartbeat of time passed, reality struck.

"I've been thinking about this," he said. "For two days now. And if you're pregnant, I can make arrangements."

Wary now, she asked, "What kind of arrangements?"

"Well," he said, in an abstracted tone, almost as if he were thinking aloud and didn't really like his thoughts very much. "I could leave the Corps. Take a civilian job. For one of the airlines."

"What?" Tina stood up and looked down at him. "You can't leave the Marines."

"I admit it's not my first choice, but—"

"Brian, don't be stupid. Being a Marine isn't your job. It's who you *are*."

Slowly, he pushed himself to his feet. "Tina—"

"No," she said, cutting him off before he could get started. "I would never ask you to leave the Corps. I know what it means to you. And I would never want you to be less than you are."

He pushed one hand along the side of his head. "Families are hard enough under the best of circumstances," he muttered. "But military families have a tougher road than most."

She stared at him as if she'd never seen him before. Where was this coming from?

"I've seen families splintered," he said tightly. "My friends, leaving their wives for months at a time. The spouse of a Marine gets all the crap jobs. Handling cross-country or around-the-world moves alone. Raising kids, paying bills, worrying about every damn thing all on their own." He started pacing and as he walked, the words bubbled up and out of him as if they'd been dammed up for way too long and just had to escape. "There's no one there to help, you know? It's hard. And that's not even counting all the worrying. Money's tight and housing stinks. You get deployed to danger zones all over the world and sometimes can't even tell your wife where the hell you are."

"Brian—" She stood stock still and followed him with her gaze.

He held up one hand and kept talking. "There's long hours and a lot of alone time. It's a hard life, and I wanted you to have better. I wanted you to be happy, and didn't want to think about you doing without or being alone or spending your whole damn life worrying about me and where I was and—"

Tina trembled. She felt twin waves of regret and fury rock through her as she listened to the man she loved tell her exactly why he'd ended their marriage five years before. He may have started out talking about their current situation, but she knew damn well, he'd somehow drifted back and was finally giving her the answers she'd wanted so badly five years ago.

Now that she had those answers though, she was furious.

"Are you telling me," she said, loudly enough to interrupt him at last, "that you divorced me because you wanted me to be *happy*?"

He stopped pacing and shot her a look. "Yes," he said. "I did it for you."

"You moron."

"You know," he said, every word ground out from between clenched jaws, "that's the second time this week somebody's called me a moron. Don't much like it."

"Don't much care," Tina snapped, stalking around the edge of the sofa to walk straight up to him. She stopped only inches from him and jabbed him in the chest with an index finger. "You divorced me for my own sake? *You* decided that I wouldn't be a good Marine wife?"

"That's not what I said—"

"It's exactly what you said," she cut him off again, and let herself go, riding the crest of the fury that was threatening to blow the top of her head clean off. "You thought I couldn't hack it. You thought I was too soft, or too weak or too stupid to be able to take care of myself while my big, strong husband was off protecting my country?"

"No…" Wariness tinged his voice.

"You thought I couldn't be trusted to raise our children, to pay some bills, to pack for a move, for heaven's sake?"

"I didn't—"

"You figured that without my husband standing close by, I'd curl up into a ball and cry?"

"Tina—"

"Did you really think so little of me?"

"I loved you."

"But obviously, you didn't *respect* me at all."

"Of course I did."

"If you did, you wouldn't have done this. Wouldn't have treated me like a child sent off to my room," she snapped. Really, Tina thought, your blood pressure could get so high that the edges of your vision actually shook and wobbled. "You cheated us both, Brian."

"What?" He backed up a step as she stepped forward.

"*You* decided for both of us that I should be protected. You decided that I wasn't woman enough to stand beside my husband."

"No, I—"

"You decided that I was unworthy to be a Marine wife."

"You're twisting all of this around, Tina."

"No, I'm not," she said, and wondered if the hurt and the anger would ever completely drain away. Five years of their lives lost. Five years when they could have been happy, been building a family, been together, living and loving. All gone because Brian Reilly had willed it so. "I've got it straight," she said. "At last. And you were wrong. So wrong. I was *proud* of you. Proud to be the wife of a Marine. Do you think I don't know how important your job is? Well, I do. Sure, it would have been hard, being separated. But I'm strong, Brian. And as long as we loved each other, I could have handled it."

"I know that," he managed to say, "I just didn't want you to have to."

Pain rippled through Tina and she wanted to weep for everything they'd lost. "So to save us from being separated for months at a time," she said, shaking her head sadly, "you separated us permanently. Nice logic. Good choice."

"I did what I thought was best."

"You were wrong."

Brian reached for her, but Tina stepped back quickly. She didn't want him to touch her, to hold her. She didn't want comfort from him. She wanted what he'd never be willing to give her.

She wanted his respect.

And she wanted his love.

"Go away, Brian," she said softly, turning for the kitchen at the back of the house.

"We haven't talked about the baby."

"We'll do that *if* there's a baby," she said, her words drifting back to him as she moved farther away. "For now, I'm through talking to you."

Another week flew past and Brian could still hear Tina's words echoing over and over in his brain. Had he really been so damn wrong? Was it a bad thing to want to protect someone you loved?

He couldn't talk about this with anyone. Not even Liam, because he sure as hell wasn't in the mood to be called a moron again. And he had the distinct feeling that he wouldn't get any sympathy from his family on this one.

Maybe he didn't deserve any sympathy though. Over the past several days, he'd paid closer attention to his friends and their families. Five years ago, he'd been worried about the hardships. But he hadn't really noticed the partnerships.

His friends had good, strong marriages. There was laughter and trust and respect on both sides. If life got hard, they leaned on each other.

Why hadn't he noticed the good along with the bad?

As he waited to find out if Tina really was carrying his child, Brian was forced to rethink decisions made so long ago. And to consider what life might be like if she was pregnant.

If she was, he wanted to be a part of the child's life. That was fact. He couldn't live knowing he had a child out there somewhere who didn't even know him.

But could he be a part of his kid's life and *not* a part of Tina's?

Eleven

A few days later, Tina had deals to manage, even if they were closing three thousand miles away.

Sitting at her grandmother's kitchen table, she cradled the phone on her shoulder and took notes while her assistant talked.

"The Mannerly house is in the final days of escrow," Donna said, her perky voice just a shade too cheerful for Tina. "Are you going to be back in time to walk them through the closing?"

A week, Tina thought. "Yes, I'll be back by then." She'd be home. Back in her neat little condo, with her tidy little world and the occasional date for dinner and a movie and maybe, just maybe, she'd be pregnant.

"That'd be great," Donna cooed. "Suzanna Mannerly called this morning and wanted to thank you for finding her dream house. Turns out she's pregnant. Isn't that great? She's all excited."

"I'm sure," Tina said, and made all the right noises while Donna went on.

"Suzanna said she's going to do up the nursery just the way you suggested when you first showed them the house and—"

Zoning out, Tina only half listened as she remembered, walking through the big old Victorian in Manhattan Beach. Suzanna Mannerly had loved it the minute she'd walked through the front door. And Tina, having been the number one saleswoman in her real estate office for three years running, had known that she had a sale.

But, when she'd taken Suzanna on a tour of the big old house, and proudly showed the woman the nursery that had sheltered generations of children, Tina'd had an epiphany. The very epiphany that had dragged her all the way back to South Carolina to trick her ex-husband into getting her pregnant.

It had suddenly dawned on her that while she'd spent years helping families find homes, build dreams and invest in their futures…she'd neglected her own.

As Suzanna had oohed and aahed over the nursery and its bay window and window seat and conical ceiling, Tina had felt her biological clock erupt into a series of thunderlike tick-tocks. She'd known, just that quickly, just that absolutely, that what she needed wasn't to be found in the hustle and bustle of L.A.—in the thrill of a sale and the quiet cha-ching of money adding up in her savings account.

What she needed, what she *craved,* was a family of her own. Children. A husband.

Now, she had the chance for one and she'd lost the other, one more time.

"Thanks, Donna," Tina interrupted her assistant neatly. As her stomach twisted and her head ached, she realized she just didn't want to talk about other people's dreams coming true anymore. Maybe that made her a small person, but she'd just have to live with it. "Tell Suzanna I'll be back in time to personally hand her the keys to her dream house."

She only wished she could do the same for herself.

As soon as she hung up, the doorbell rang and she grumbled as she pushed up from the chair and stalked to the front door. She was in no mood for company.

Especially if it was Brian. He'd been coming by the house every day, asking if her period had arrived. If she was feeling sick. Telling her that they had to make a decision. Well, her period hadn't arrived yet. And though hope was still lifting inside her, a part of her wanted to tear her own hair out in frustration.

How much harder was it going to be, she wondered, having Brian's child and yet not having Brian?

Oh, she'd been an idiot, no way around it. Thinking she could get pregnant and waltz away again with no twinges of guilt, no regrets. Janet had been so right to advise her against this.

Too bad she hadn't listened.

Because knowing that she still loved Brian was going to make living without him unbearable.

Grabbing the doorknob, she turned it and gave it a vicious tug. She nearly snarled at the woman on the porch, but cut it off when she was greeted by her former mother-in-law's smiling face.

"Maggie."

"Tina, honey," the older woman said, stepping into the house and grinning like a kid at Christmas. "I'm so glad to see you."

Maggie Reilly was short and a little on the plump side. She had Celtic blue eyes as dark as her sons and black hair she kept short and wispy around her pixie-ish face. Her understanding heart and warm nature had made her the perfect mother-in-law and Tina had missed her desperately.

Muffin and Peaches scrambled around her ankles and Maggie spared each of them a quick greeting before straightening up and looking Tina dead in the eye. "I've been on a bus tour of New England with my travel group or I'd have been to see you before this." She cocked her head, folded her arms over her chest and said, "So, have you come back to knock some sense into Brian's head at last?"

Tina laughed and the laugh choked off at the knot in her throat and before she knew it, the tears she'd been holding in for days burst free. Maggie took a step forward, enfolded her in a tight embrace and murmured to her while she cried.

"It's all right now, love. I'll hit him *for* you." Patting her back, Maggie whispered sympathetically. The soft whisper of her native Ireland sang in her voice, giving her speech a rhythm as soothing as a lullaby. "You come with me." Leading Tina back to the kitchen, she sat her down in the closest chair. Turning for the stove, Maggie snatched up the teakettle, filled it at the sink and set it on a burner to heat. "We'll have a little tea, and you can tell me all about my idiot son and what he's done now."

Tina smiled through her tears and blinked her watery vision clear. "Maggie, I've missed you."

"And I've missed you, too." Bustling around a kitchen as familiar to her as her own, Maggie got down cups, teapot and a plate of cookies. "Hasn't Angelina been keeping me up to date on you and what you've been doing out in Hollywood?"

"Not Hollywood," Tina corrected. "Just L.A."

Maggie waved a hand dismissively. "Same difference, if you ask me. All those pretty people and fast parties. I read the papers."

Tina laughed again and this time felt better. It was good. So good, just to sit and be understood.

"And Brian's kept up with you as well," she said, nodding from her position by the stove, as if just by standing there, she could arrange for the water to boil faster.

"He has?"

"'Course he has. Silly man." Maggie shook her head. "Liam's the only one of the four of them that makes a lick of sense to me most times."

"I should have married *him*."

"Well, now," Maggie said with an impish grin, "the church might have been a little cranky about that idea."

Tina tried for a smile, but failed. "Oh, Maggie, I should never have come back here."

"That's where you're wrong, darlin'," the older woman said. "You should never have *left*."

"He didn't want me."

"Nonsense."

"He *divorced* me."

"He *loves* you."

Tina snorted. "He has a strange way of showing it."

"Well, he's a man, isn't he, poor thing." Maggie shook her head, picked up the teakettle and filled the pot on the table. After the kettle was back on the stove, Maggie took a seat opposite Tina and stretched out one hand to her. "Mind you, I love my sons. Every hardheaded, stubborn, prideful one of them. But I'm not the kind of mother who overlooks their faults. I see them as they are, not as I'd wish them to be."

"Meaning?"

"Meaning," Maggie said, "Brian Reilly has been miserable since you two split up."

"Really?"

"Really." Sighing, Maggie gave Tina's hand a pat, then reached for the teapot and poured each of them a steaming cupful. "He's as thick-headed as his father was before him, God rest him." She made a quick sign of the cross, then went on as if she hadn't paused at all. "But the heart of him was gone when you left, Tina. He's never told me why he divorced you. Couldn't pry that out of him, and Liam couldn't either, though he tried, and reported back to me," she added with a smile. "But I can tell you this. He hasn't rested easy since he lost you."

Small comfort, Tina thought sadly. Although, it some weird way, it might have been easier to take if she thought he had moved on. If he'd found someone else to love. If she thought he'd divorced her because *she* wasn't what he'd needed. But how was she supposed to feel knowing that the man she loved had let her go—and still loved her? What kind of peace could she find in that knowledge?

None.

"I don't know how I'm supposed to feel about that, Maggie," she admitted, cupping her hands around the fragile, rose-patterned teacup.

"Do you love him?"

Tina stared at Brian's mother. "That has nothing to do with anything."

"Not an answer at all," Maggie muttered, shaking her head until her silver hoop earrings clashed against her jaw line. "If you two aren't peas in a pod with your concrete skulls."

Tina smiled.

"I'll ask again. Do you still love Brian?"

"I do."

"Well then, that's settled."

Tina snorted. "Maggie, it settles nothing. Love isn't enough. Not for Brian, anyway."

"Faddle." She waved one manicured hand and blew out a dismissive breath. "Love is *everything*, Tina. The only thing that matters."

If she could believe that, maybe it would be enough to make her stay and fight, Tina thought. But if love had been enough, then surely Brian wouldn't have walked away five years ago.

As if she could read her mind—and Tina wouldn't have been the least surprised to find that she could—Maggie leaned in and said, "The question here is, what're you willing to do about it?"

"About what?"

"Brian."

"What can I do?"

Maggie sighed, took a sip of tea, then shook her head. "Tina, an Irishman's head can be as thick as a brick. Sometimes, you need a two by four just to make a dent."

Tina laughed, and though it sounded a little shaky, it was better than crying. "You're telling me to hit him?"

"No, I could do that myself—and will, if you ask me, make no mistake."

She looked so hopeful and eager, Tina had a hard time saying no. But she did.

"Ah, well then, it'll be up to you, dear. You've only to decide if you want him badly enough to fight through that hard knob of a skull of his." She picked up her teacup and leaned back in her chair. "Then you've only to dig in your heels."

"And if I don't?"

"Then, Tina, love, you and my Brian both will have sad, lonely lives when you could have had so much more."

Brian stalked up the shadow-filled driveway and stopped at the gate leading into the backyard. Just beyond that gate, he heard the excited whimpers and scrabbling of tiny nails as his two tiny fans tried to get through the gate to him.

Scowling, he told himself he didn't know which was worse. The way those two dogs had hated him before, or their abject devotion now. Shaking his head, he opened the gate and stepped through, moving cautiously, so as not to stomp on tiny paws. "Okay, okay, I'm here." He bent down and Muffin and Peaches were all over him.

As he petted and stroked quivering little bodies, the back door opened and a slice of lamplight speared into the shadows, spotlighting him.

Tina stood in the doorway, but she didn't look welcoming. No surprise there, of course. Things had been pretty damn cool between them for days now. And damned if he didn't miss talking to her, watching her, hearing her voice.

Every night, his mind tortured him, by replaying images of the hours he'd spent in her arms. With crystal clarity, Brian recalled every touch, every sigh, every whispered word and caress. And he wondered, in those long, sleepless hours, if he'd ever be able to forget. If there would ever come a night when he'd be able to sleep without dreaming of her. Without remembering what he'd lost—not once, but *twice*.

"I've been waiting for you," Tina said and her voice sounded thick, as though she'd been crying.

Brian's heart twisted and he stood up, barely feeling the two little dogs as they jumped at his legs. His hands felt empty, useless, so he stuffed them into his jeans pockets.

She stepped out onto the porch and he studied her. Hair soft and loose around her shoulders, she wore a skinny strapped tank top and a pair of worn denim shorts with frayed hems. Her long, lean legs were bare and the silver toe ring winked at him in the light. He imprinted her image on his brain without even trying.

She would haunt him.

Always.

He swallowed hard. She was right in front of him and yet, she seemed farther away from him than she ever had before. A single thought raced through his mind before he could stop it and he wondered what they would be like now if he hadn't ended their marriage five years ago. He wondered what it would be like to be coming home to her at night. To hear the sounds of kids playing in the house. To know that the lights left burning were for him, to guide him home to warmth.

And he wondered how in the hell he would ever be able to stand returning to a dark, empty apartment night after night for the rest of his life. Suddenly, the years stretched out in front of him and all he saw of the future was a black void, yawning in front of him like a black hole opening up in space. He was a doomed man.

If he'd stayed married to her, he would have sentenced her to a life of hardship. By setting her free, he'd sentenced himself to a lifetime of emptiness.

But that was a decision he'd made long ago and now he just had to live with it. Blowing out a breath, he squared his shoulders, lifted his chin and asked the question he'd put to her every day for the last week or so.

"Everything all right? You feeling okay?"

"I'm fine."

He nodded, and knowing she didn't want him around, turned for the gate. He had one hand on the worn, weather-beaten wood when her voice stopped him again.

"I'm fine. But there's no baby."

His hand clenched on the top of the gate and his grip was so tight, he wouldn't have been surprised to feel the wood snap clean off. His insides twisted and a laser shot of pain sliced him in two. Somehow though, he managed to stay upright. Swiveling his head, he looked at her. "You're sure?"

"My period started this afternoon," she said and her voice sounded...*hollow*. "So you don't have to worry anymore. You're in the clear."

Was he? He would always wonder about that.

No baby.

There'd never been a baby.

So why then, did he suddenly feel like he was in

mourning? Why did the pain tighten like a vise around his heart and twist in his guts? Why the sorrow? The regret?

Wasn't this what he'd been hoping for?

Wasn't this for the best?

And if it *was* for the best, shouldn't he be feeling happy? Instead, he was feeling as though the earth had opened up beneath him and he was tottering on the lip of a rocky chasm.

Deliberately, he forced himself to loosen his grip on the old gate. "I don't know what I should say," he admitted quietly.

"There's nothing *to* say, Brian," Tina said softly. "Not anymore."

Then she snapped her fingers and the dogs reluctantly left him, scampering up the steps and through the open doorway into the lamplit house. Tina stared at him for a long minute and looked as though she was going to speak again. But she changed her mind and quietly closed the door.

That spear of light was gone.

The promise of warmth was shut off.

And Brian was alone.

In the dark.

Twelve

By noon the next day, Angelina Coretti was home, greeting her nearly hysterically-glad-to-see-her dogs, and Tina was packing.

"You should stay," the older woman said to her granddaughter, trying to look stern as she cradled first one tiny dog and then the other, giving each of them equal attention.

"I can't, Nana," Tina said as she tossed shorts and T-shirts into the oversized, navy blue suitcase. "I just can't stay."

Angelina clucked her tongue, set Muffin down on the floor, then walked to her granddaughter. Laying one hand on her arm, she waited until Tina was looking at her to speak again. "Is it Brian?"

It was *always* Brian, Tina thought, diving into the pool of misery that lay deep in the bottom of her heart. All night, she'd been torn by the knowledge that she had to leave.

Talking to Maggie hadn't helped. If anything, it had only made Tina feel worse. Knowing that Brian had been miserable without her was small consolation. If Tina'd been able to convince herself that he'd divorced her because he wanted someone else, it would have been hard to swallow, but she'd eventually have succeeded. But knowing that the damn man hadn't wanted anyone but her and had *still* divorced her only made the whole situation more heartbreaking.

How could she possibly argue with a man so willing to walk away from love? From what they'd had? From what they might have had?

Angelina sighed and sat down on the edge of the bed. Reaching into the suitcase, she pulled out one of Tina's shirts and absently folded it as she spoke. "I'd hoped that the two of you would find a way back to each other during these weeks."

"Nana." Tina stopped what she was doing and stared at her grandmother. Angelina Coretti was tall and slim. Her silver hair was still long and thick and she wore it in a braided knot at the back of her head. Her features were lined in patterns created by years of smiling and her dark brown eyes were filled with the warm understanding that Tina had grown up with.

The older woman shrugged and reached for another shirt to fold. "Do you think I don't know why you never visit except when you know Brian will be gone?" she asked with a shake of her head. "Did you think I couldn't tell that you still love him?"

Sighing, Tina dropped her makeup bag into the suitcase, then took a seat beside her grandmother. "Never could put one over on you, could I?"

"Surprising that you still try." Angelina patted her hand, then gave it a squeeze. "Brian was the one for you," she said softly. "Right from the first. And it was the same for him."

"Doesn't matter," Tina said and fought the rising pain within. No point in worrying her grandmother. There'd be plenty of time for tears, for regrets, once she got home.

"Of course it matters," Angelina snapped. "It's the only thing that *does* matter. I thought you knew better than that."

Tina smiled grimly. "Even if I do know better, Brian doesn't. And I can't make a marriage all on my own, Nana."

"You're both too stubborn, you know." Angelina huffed out a disgusted breath.

"That's what Maggie said yesterday."

"Smart woman."

"I'll miss you," Tina said, turning her hand over so she could link fingers with her grandmother.

"Oh, honey, I'll miss you, too." Angelina turned slightly on the bed. "Why don't you stay?" she urged. "Don't give up so easily. Stay here where you belong. This is your *home,* Tina."

Home.

She was right. Baywater was home. Here, there was Nana and Maggie and Liam and the slower lifestyle Tina'd forgotten how much she loved. Here there were warm breezes and magnolia trees and the scent of jasmine flavoring every breath. Here, there were neighbors and the streets she'd grown up on. There were people who knew her, loved her.

Here, there was Brian.

And that's why she couldn't stay.

Everything she'd come home for was gone. The hope for a baby, the yearning for Brian. It had all dissolved like a piece of sugar in the rain. Her wishes, her dreams, were puddled around her.

She needed to get away—she wouldn't think of it as *running*—from the death of those hopes. She needed to see everything that had happened recently more clearly. And for that she needed distance.

Three thousand miles might be enough.

"I can't," Tina said and heard the regret in her own voice. "I hope you understand, Nana. But even if you don't, I have to go."

Her grandmother sighed, gave Tina's hand an-other pat, then stood up and laid a pair of pale green shorts on top of the clothes in the suitcase. "I under-stand, honey. Wish I didn't, but I do."

"Thanks for that."

Nodding, Angelina shot her a look from the cor-ner of her eye. "Are you going to at least say good-bye to Brian?"

"No." Tina stood up, too, and reached for another shirt to throw into the bag.

"Too scared?"

She sighed. "Too tired."

Brian left the base early, but he didn't go home.

He still wasn't ready yet to face Tina.

If that was cowardly, then he'd have to suck it up.

Instead, he went to the Lighthouse to meet his brothers. Now, he was trying to remember why it had seemed like a good idea at the time.

"You're letting her go, *again?*" Connor snorted, leaned back in the booth and took a long swig of his beer.

"I'm not *letting* her do anything," Brian pointed out in his own defense. "Tina goes where she wants, does what she wants."

"Uh-huh," Aidan said with a smirk at Connor. "And she's leaving because…?"

"How the hell do I know?" Brian countered, but

he *did* know. He knew all too well why Tina was leaving. Because there was no baby. No future. With him. And that was a good thing. She was better off without him. And God knew, they were better off without having made a child they'd have to figure out a long-distance way to share.

He rubbed the center of his chest when the ache came again. He was almost used to the nagging pain now. It came whenever he remembered that there was no baby. That Tina was leaving. That he'd never see her again once Angelina came home.

Scowling, he told himself that he'd gotten used to Tina's absence five years ago, he'd get used to it again. With that thought in mind, he signaled the waitress for another beer.

"You do know though, don't you, Brian?" Liam asked, jabbing him in the ribs with an elbow.

Turning that fierce frown on his brother, he snapped, "If you're looking for a confession here, I suggest you head back to your flock."

"Ooh," Connor said, grinning. "Touchy."

"Pitiful," Aidan said. "Just pitiful. Man can't even admit it to himself."

"Admit what?" Brian thanked the waitress for the fresh, icy cold beer she'd brought him and took a long pull at it. Life would have been much simpler, he thought briefly, if he'd been an only child.

"That you love her, you moron," Liam said softly.

Brian's breath hitched in his chest and it felt as though a cold hand were fisting around his heart. *Love.* What was it about that one little word that could bring a man to his knees? What was it that made a man so reluctant to look at that word honestly? Objectively?

His gaze shifted around the restaurant. He took it all in. The same, familiar faces that he usually saw there at this time of day. The same families. The same children, turning to their parents. The same couples, huddled together in booths, sharing whispered conversations and unspoken promises.

And it suddenly hit him that there wasn't a damn thing objective about love.

You either felt it or you didn't.

Wanted it or ran from it.

Appreciated it or threw it away.

Damn it.

Brian slid a glance at his older brother. "You know, I'm getting really tired of you calling me names."

"Then stop being stupid."

"Do they teach you those comforting little sayings in the seminary?" Brian wondered aloud.

"Shut up," Connor said and snickered when Brian sent him a you-are-dead-meat glare. "If you think you worry me, you're wrong."

"Why am I here?" Brian asked no one in particular.

"Because you're too dumb to admit you'd rather be with Tina," Connor said.

"You already lost the bet, Bri." Aidan picked a tortilla chip out of the basket in the middle of the table and crunched down on it. "What's holding you back?"

"This is not about the bet."

"Then what?" Liam prodded.

"It's about being fair," Brian argued.

"To who?" Connor demanded.

"To Tina." Brian leaned in over the table, and swept his gaze across his brothers' faces, one after the other. "Being a Marine wife is hard. Harder than any other job out there and you guys know it."

"What's your point?" Aidan asked.

"I want Tina to have better," Brian snapped. "She deserves better."

"Better than loving and being loved?" Liam asked.

Brian slumped back against the booth seat and cradled his beer between his palms. Shaking his head, he muttered stubbornly, "She deserves better."

Connor snorted.

Aidan opened his mouth to speak.

Liam held up one hand to silence him and then looked at Brian. "She deserves the chance to decide for herself," he said quietly. "She deserves to have the man she loves respect her enough to give her a *choice*."

"You don't underst—"

Liam cut him off. "She knew when she married you that you were a Marine. She grew up in a military town. She knows what being a military wife means. And she *chose* to love you. To marry you."

Brian heard the words and let them sink in. As he did, he felt a flicker of light shimmer in the darkness within and hope bubbled up inside him. Images of Tina raced through his mind, one after the other. Her eyes flashing, her mouth curving, her arms encircling him. He heard her laugh again, felt the soft sigh of her breath on his cheek and relived the sensation of her turning to him in her sleep.

And he knew.

Damn it, he'd always known.

Hard or not, life wasn't worth living without her.

"I gotta go," he muttered, reaching for his wallet and tearing a couple of bills out. He tossed them onto the table and slid out of the booth. Staring down at his brothers, he gave them a quick grin and said, "Gotta talk to Tina."

"Better hurry," Connor said, lifting his beer in a half-assed salute.

"Yeah," Aidan added, "before she remembers what a jerk you are."

As Brian darted between the crowded tables, the three remaining Reilly brothers clinked their beer bottles together and smiled.

* * *

Three days back in California and Tina knew what she had to do. Actually, to be honest, she'd known before she flew back to the land of perpetual sun and smog.

But she'd had to come here to be positive.

Now she was.

Smiling to herself, she shuffled the papers on her desk, straightened them up and set them in the file marked "urgent." Janet would take care of it all. She knew Tina's cases as well as or better than she did herself.

Everything would be fine.

And now, so would she.

"Are you sure about this?" Janet rubbed her swollen belly as if rubbing a good luck charm. "I mean, you just got back, maybe you should take more time and—"

Tina shot her a quick grin and shook her head. She would miss Janet, but they'd keep in touch. Telephone calls, e-mail, visits, somehow, someway, they'd do it.

"Trust me on this," Tina said. "I've already had five years. I've thought this through and it's what I have to do."

Janet sighed. "Okay, but it's not going to be the same around here without you."

"Thanks." Tina came around her cluttered desk and hugged her friend tightly. "I'll miss you, too."

* * *

Brian hated L.A.

Always had.

He'd been stationed at Pendleton for a couple of years once and the crowds had chewed at him. Just too damn many people. And they all seemed to be on the freeway at the same time.

While he sat in traffic, his brain kicked into high gear, as if trying to make up for the standstill by revving at top speed.

He'd left the restaurant, determined to talk to Tina. To apologize. To do whatever he had to do to make her listen. To make her know that he loved her. Always had. Always would. He'd finally gotten it through his thick head that love wasn't something fragile to be protected. It was something strong, something to lean on when things got rough. And there was nobody stronger than Tina.

He'd just been so determined to take care of her, that he hadn't realized that a marriage was about taking care of each other.

But when he got home, he'd found Angelina, back from Italy and just mad enough at him to tell him that Tina had left for L.A.

Gone.

Just like that.

With no word.

No warning.

But then, he hadn't really deserved one, had he? he thought now. Remembering the blind panic that had shot through him, he nearly strangled on it. He'd tried to catch her at the airport but her flight had already left by the time he got there.

He could have called her, but he knew that what he had to say couldn't be said on a phone. He had to be standing in front of her, so she could see his eyes, so he could reach out for her and hold on if she decided to make this harder than it had to be.

So, he'd spent the next two days wangling a brief leave and then talking his way onto a transport plane headed to Camp Pendleton. Now, his rental car was overheating and he was stuck in traffic next to a teenager in a black truck with a stereo system loud enough to reach Mars.

And all he could think was, he hoped he hadn't waited too long. Hoped he wasn't too late.

Tina looked around her office, exhaled deeply and smiled to herself. Finished. It was done and she was ready.

More than ready, she told herself, she was anxious to get started.

"Tina!"

She jolted and spun around, one hand reaching for the base of her throat. "Brian?"

"Damn it," he shouted again, his voice carrying

from the main office with no trouble at all, "I'm here to see Tina Coretti, and I'm not leaving until I do."

Heart pounding, brain reeling, Tina hurried through the open doorway leading from her office to the real estate business's main room. She spotted him easily. A tall, gorgeous, totally built Marine, surrounded by men who suddenly looked much smaller in comparison, was hard to miss.

He saw her instantly and his features shifted from angry frustration to desperation. "Tina, tell these yahoos who I am."

"It's okay," she called out and ignored the questioning looks being tossed her way. "He's my ex-husband."

Brian pushed through the rest of the people standing between him and Tina and headed for her.

"Oh, wow," Janet said from directly beside her and Tina was forced to agree.

Brian in uniform was something to see. His chest was broad and the medals pinned to his left breast glittered in the sunlight streaming through the bank of floor to ceiling windows. His blue eyes were focused on Tina and his jaw was locked tight.

He stopped just a foot from her and took a long deep breath before blurting, "You left without telling me."

"What?" she asked and nearly shook her head as if to clear it.

"You heard me," he said and his voice boomed out

around them. "I went to Angelina's to talk to you and you were gone."

"You knew I wasn't staying," she said and shot a quick look at the interested faces turned toward them.

"Yeah." He shoved one hand along the side of his head then let his hand drop. "But I want you to stay."

"Brian—"

"I came to take you home," he said, not letting her get more than that one word out.

Tina felt the earth shift beneath her and decided she liked it. "You did?"

"I can't live without you, Tina. Not anymore. Not one more day." He reached for her, dropping both hands onto her shoulders and squeezing, as if holding her in place should she decide to make a run for it.

But Tina wasn't going anywhere.

"You can't?" she asked, wanting to hear it all. Hear everything she'd waited five long years for.

"I thought I was doing the right thing before," he said and at last his voice dropped until it was as if just the two of them were in the room. "When I let you go. Being a Marine wife is hard. A tough job not everyone can do."

"I could have," she said, needing him to know that he'd made a mistake.

"I know that now," he agreed. "You're plenty tough enough," he added, then lifted one hand to stroke her cheek. "Tougher than me, because you were able to leave and I couldn't let you."

Tears rushed up from her heart, filled her throat and blurred her eyes. "Not so tough," she said, catching his hand with hers and holding on. "It killed me to leave."

"Then come home," he said, softer now, more intimately. "Come home with me, Tina. Love me. Let me love you. I've always loved you, Tina. Always will love you."

"Brian…"

He pulled her close, wrapping his arms around her until all Tina could feel was him. His heart pounded and she felt the thud of it echo inside her.

"Make babies with me, Tina," he whispered, his breath a hush on her ear. "Make lots of babies with me."

Joy rippled through her, one wave after another, like circles on the surface of a lake after a pebble had been tossed in. She held on to him, holding him as tightly as she could and whispered for him alone. "I love you, Brian Reilly. Always have. Always will. I was always proud to be a Marine wife. And even prouder to be *your* wife."

Relief crashed through him like storm surf and left his legs shaky. Brian had never felt better in his life. Pulling her back so that he could look into her beautiful, teary eyes, he said, "So then. How fast do you think we can move you back to South Carolina?"

"Does tomorrow work for you?"

Stunned, Brian just stared at her. "Huh?"

Laughing, Tina grabbed his hand and ignoring everyone else, dragged him down the short hall to her office and closed the door behind them. Then she flung herself at him, wrapping her arms around his neck and grinning up into his face.

"I sold my half of the business to my partner," she said. "Movers are coming tomorrow to pack up my stuff."

"You—but—how—" He sounded like an idiot and he was so damn happy, he didn't care.

Shaking her head, Tina leaned in and planted a long, deep kiss on him before pulling back again. "I decided two days ago that I couldn't stay here—that I couldn't live without you."

His arms tightened around her and his heart gave a lurch that jolted him.

"I was going home to you, you big dummy," Tina said, smiling. "To make you love me. To make you see that we belong together."

"Baby," he said, pausing for another soul-searing kiss, "I'm convinced."

And when they finally came up for air again, Brian gave her a tight squeeze and warned, "You realize you're marrying a man who's going to have to be seen in a hula skirt and a coconut bra."

"I'll bring a camera," she said on a teary laugh.

"And I'll even pose for you," Brian told her, "because I've never been happier about losing a bet."

* * * * *

WHATEVER REILLY WANTS...

For Kathleen Beaver.
Thanks for being an emergency reader,
for always being a friend
and for never getting tired of meeting me
for a latte to talk about writing!

One

"**O**ne down, two to go." Father Liam Reilly grinned at his brother, sitting alongside him, then lifted a beer in salute to the two identical men sitting opposite him in the restaurant booth.

"Don't get your hopes up." Connor Reilly took a sip of his own beer and nodded toward his brother Brian, the third of the Reilly triplets, sitting beside Liam. "Just because Brian couldn't go the distance, doesn't mean we can't."

"Amen," Aidan said from beside him.

"Who said I *couldn't* go the distance?" Brian demanded, reaching for a handful of tortilla chips from the basket in the middle of the table. He grinned and sat back in the booth. "I just didn't *want* to go the distance. Not anymore." He held up his left hand, and the gold wedding band caught the light and winked at all of them.

"And I'm glad for you," Liam said, his black eyebrows lifting. "Plus, with you happily married, the odds of *my* winning this bet are better than ever."

"Not a chance, Liam." Aidan grabbed a handful of chips, too. "It's not that I begrudge you a roof for the church…but *I'm* the Reilly to watch in this bet, brother."

As his brothers talked, Connor just smiled and half listened. Once a week the Reilly brothers met for dinner at the Lighthouse Restaurant, a family place, dead center of the town of Baywater. They laughed, talked and, in general, enjoyed the camaraderie of being brothers.

But for the last month their conversations had pretty much centered around *The Bet*.

A great uncle, the last surviving member of a set of triplets, had left ten thousand dollars to Aidan, Brian and Connor. At first, the three of them had thought to divide the money, giving their older brother, Liam, an equal share. Then someone, and Connor was pretty sure it had been Liam, had come up with the idea of a bet—winner take all.

Since the Reilly triplets were, above all things, competitive, there'd never been any real doubt that they would accept the challenge. But Liam hadn't made it easy. He'd insisted that as a Catholic priest, his decision to give up sex for a lifetime was something not one of his brothers could match. He dared them to be celibate for ninety days—last man standing winning the ten thousand dollars. And if all three of the triplets failed, then Liam got the money for a new roof for his church.

Connor shot his older brother a suspicious look. He had a feeling that Liam was already getting estimates from local roofers. Scowling, he took another sip of his beer and let his gaze shift to Brian. A month ago the triplets had stood together in this bet, but now one had already fallen. Brian had reconciled with his ex-wife, Tina, and, now there was just Connor and Aidan to survive the bet.

"Don't know about you," Aidan said, jamming his elbow into Connor's rib cage, "but I'm avoiding all females for the duration."

"No self-control, huh?" Liam grinned and lifted his beer for another long drink.

"You're really enjoying this, aren't you?" Connor glared at him.

"Damn right I am," Liam said laughing. "Watching the three of you has always been entertaining. Just more so lately."

"Ah," Brian said, "the *two* of them. I'm out, remember?"

"Didn't even last a month," Aidan said with a slow, sad shake of his head.

Brian's self-satisfied smile spoke volumes. "Never been so glad about losing a bet in my life."

"Tina's a peach, no doubt about it," Connor said,

just a little irritated by Brian's "happy man" attitude. "But there's still the matter of you in that ridiculous outfit to consider."

Not only did the losers lose the money in this bet, but they'd agreed to ride around in the back of a convertible, wearing coconut bras and hula skirts while being driven around the base on Battle Color day...the one day of the year when every dignitary imaginable would be on the Marine base.

Brian shuddered, then manfully sucked it up and squared his shoulders. "It'll still be worth it."

"He's got it bad," Aidan muttered, and held up both index fingers in an impromptu cross, as if trying to keep Brian at a distance.

"Laugh all you want," Brian said, leaning over the table to stare first at one brother, then the other. "But I'm the only one here having regular—and can I just add—*great*, sex."

"That was cold, man." Aidan groaned and scraped one hand over his face.

"Heartless," Connor agreed.

Liam laughed, clapped his hands together, then rubbed his palms briskly. Black eyebrows lifting, he looked at his brothers and asked, "Either of you care to back out now? Save time?"

"Not likely," Aidan muttered.

"That's for damn sure." Connor held out one hand to Aidan. "In this to the end?"

Aidan's grip was fierce. "Or until you cave. Whichever comes first."

"In your dreams." Connor'd never lost a bet yet and he wasn't about to start with this one. Of course, the stakes were higher and the bet more challenging than anything else he'd ever done, but that didn't matter. This was about *pride*. And he'd be damned if he'd let Aidan beat him. Besides, "No way am I gonna be riding in that convertible with Brian."

"I'll save you a seat," Brian said, grinning.

"Oh, man, I need another beer." Aidan lifted one hand to get the waitress's attention.

Another beer would be good. All he had to do was *not* look at the waitress. Connor's gaze snapped from Aidan to Brian and finally to Liam. "This game's far from over, you know."

"There's two, count 'em, *two* long, tempting months left," Liam reminded him.

"Yeah, well, don't be picking out roof shingles just yet, *Father*."

Liam just smiled. "The samples are coming tomorrow."

The next morning Connor sat in the sunlight outside Jake's Garage and sighed heavily. South Carolina in July. Even the mornings were hot and steamy. The heat flattened a man until all he wanted to do was either escape to a beach and ocean breezes or find a nice shady tree and park himself beneath it.

Neither of which Connor was doing. He was on leave. Two weeks off and nothing to do. Hell, he didn't even want to go anywhere. What would be the point? He couldn't date. Couldn't spend any time at all with a woman the way he was feeling. He was a man on the edge.

Two more months of this bet and he wasn't sure how he was going to survive. Connor *liked* women. He liked the way they smelled and the way they laughed and the way they moved. He liked dancing with 'em, walking with 'em and most especially, he liked making love to 'em.

So he'd never found the *one*.

Who said he was looking for her?

His mother, Maggie, had been telling her sons the story of her own whirlwind courtship and marriage to their father since they were kids. They'd all heard about the lightning bolt that had hit Maggie and Sean Reilly. About how they'd shared a dance at a town picnic, fallen desperately in love and within two weeks had been married. Nine months later, Liam had arrived and just two years later, the triplets.

Maggie had long been a big believer in love at first sight and had always insisted that when the time was right, each of her sons...well, except for Liam, would be hit by a thunderbolt.

Connor had made it a point to steer clear of storms.

"Boy, you look like you could chew glass." Emma Jacobsen, owner and manager of Jake's Garage, took a seat on the bench beside him.

Connor smiled. Here was the one woman he could trust himself with. The one woman he'd never thought of as, well...a *woman*.

She wore dark-blue coveralls and a white T-shirt beneath. Her long, blond hair was pulled back into a ponytail and braided, falling to the middle of her back. She had a smudge of grease across her nose, and the cap she wore shaded her blue eyes. She'd been his friend for two years, and he could honestly say he'd never once wondered what she looked like under those coveralls.

Emma was safety.

"It's this damn bet," Connor muttered, and leaned his elbows on the bench back behind him, stretching out his legs and crossing them at the ankles.

"So why'd you agree to it in the first place?"

He grinned. "Turn down a challenge?"

She laughed. "What was I thinking?"

"Exactly." He shook his head and sighed. "But it's harder than I thought it'd be. I'm telling you, Em, I spend most of my time avoiding women like the plague. Hell, I even crossed the street yesterday when I saw a gorgeous redhead coming my way."

"Poor baby."

"Sarcasm isn't pretty."

"Yeah, but so appropriate." She smiled and punched his shoulder. "So if you're avoiding women, what're you doing hanging around *my* place?"

Straightening up, Connor dropped one arm around her shoulder and gave her a quick, comradely squeeze. "That's the beauty of it, Em. I'm *safe* here."

"Huh?"

He looked at the confusion on her face and explained. "I can hang out with you and not worry. I've never *wanted* you. Not that way. So being here is like finding a demilitarized zone in the middle of a war."

"You've never wanted me."

"We're pals, Em." Connor gave her another squeeze just to prove how much he thought of her. "We can talk cars. You don't expect me to bring you flowers or open doors for you. You're not a *woman,* you're a *mechanic.*"

Emma Virginia Jacobsen stared at the man sitting next to her and wondered why she wasn't shrieking. He'd never *wanted* her? She wasn't a *woman?*

For two years Connor Reilly had been coming to the shop she'd inherited from her father when he passed away five years ago. For two years she'd known Connor and listened to him talk about whatever female he might be chasing at the moment. She'd laughed with him, joked with him and had always thought he was different. She'd believed that he'd looked *beyond* her being female—that he'd seen her as a woman *and* as a friend.

Now she finds out he didn't even think of her as female *at all?*

Fury erupted inside her while she futilely tried to reign it in. Not once in the past two years had she even considered going after Connor Reilly herself. Not that he wasn't attractive or anything. While he continued to talk, she glanced at his profile.

His black hair was cut militarily short. His features were clean and sharp. High cheekbones, square jaw, clear, dark-blue eyes that sparkled when he laughed. He wore a dark-green USMC T-shirt that strained across his muscular chest and a pair of dark-green running shorts that showed off long, tanned, very hairy legs.

Okay, sure, he was gorgeous, but Emma had never thought of him as dating material because of their friendship. Now, she was glad she *hadn't* gone after him. He would have laughed in her face.

And that thought only tossed gasoline on the fires of anger burning inside her.

"So you can see," he was saying, "why it's so nice to have this place to hang out. If I want to win this bet—and I do—I've gotta be careful."

"Oh, yeah," she murmured, still watching him and wondering why he didn't notice the steam coming out of her ears. Of course, he hadn't noticed *her* in two years. Why should he start now? "Careful."

"Seriously, Em," he said, and stood up, turning to look down at her. "Without you to talk to about this, I'd probably lose my mind."

"What's left of it," she muttered darkly.

"What?"

"Nothing."

"Right." He grinned and hooked a thumb toward her office, located at the front of the garage. "I'm going for a soda. You want one?"

"No, but you go ahead."

He nodded, then loped off toward the shop. She

watched him and, for the first time, *really* looked at him. Nice buns, she thought, startling herself. She'd never noticed Connor's behind before. Why now?

Because, she told herself, he'd just changed the rules between them. And the big dummy didn't even know it.

While the sun sizzled all around her and the damp, hot air choked in her lungs, Emma's mind raced. Oh, boy, she hadn't been this angry in years. But more than the righteous fury boiling in her blood, she was insulted…and hurt.

Just three years ago she'd allowed another man to slip beneath her radar and break her heart. Connor had, unknowingly, just joined the long list of men who had underestimated her in her life. And this time Emma wasn't going to let a guy get away with it. She was going to make him pay for this, she thought. For all the times she'd been overlooked or underappreciated. For all the men who'd considered her *less* than a woman. For all the times she'd doubted her own femininity…

Connor Reilly was going to pay.

Big-time.

A few hours later Emma was still furious, though much cooler. In her own house, she had the air conditioner set just a little above frigid, so a cup of hot tea was enjoyable at night. Usually she found a cup of tea soothing. Tonight she was afraid she'd need a lot more than tea.

Even after Connor left the garage that afternoon, she hadn't been able to stop thinking about him and about what he'd said. Anger had faded into insult and insult into bruised feelings, then circled back around to anger again.

There was only one person in the world who would understand what she was feeling. Alone at home, she set one of the last remaining two of her late mother's floral-patterned china cups on the table beside her, picked up the phone and hit the speed dial.

The phone only rang once when it was picked up and a familiar voice said "Hello."

"Mary Alice," Emma said quickly, her words tumbling over each other in her haste to be heard, "you're not going to believe this. Connor Reilly told me today that he doesn't think of me as a *woman*. I'm a 'pal,' A 'mechanic.' Remember I told you about that stupid bet he and his brothers concocted?" She didn't wait for confirmation. "Well, today he tells me that the reason he's hanging out at the garage is because he feels *safe* around me. He doesn't *want* me, so I'm neutral territory. Can you believe it? Can you actually believe he looked me dead in the eye and practically *told* me that I'm less than female?"

"Who is this?" An amused female voice interrupted her.

"Very funny." Emma smiled, in spite of her anger, then jumped up off the old, worn sofa in her family's living room and stalked to the mirror above the now-cold fireplace. "Weren't you listening to me?"

"You bet," Mary Alice said. "Heard every word. Want Tommy to call out the Recon guys, take this jerk out for you?"

Emma grinned at her own reflection. "No, but thanks." Mary Alice Flanagan, Emma's best friend since fifth grade, had married Tom Malone, a Marine, four years ago and was now currently stationed in California. It was only thanks to Mary Alice that Emma had ever discovered the mysteries of being female.

Emma's mother had died when she was an infant, and after that she'd been raised by her father. A terrific man, he'd loved his daughter to distraction, but had had no idea how to teach her to be a woman. Mary Alice's mother had filled the gap, and when they were grown, Mary Alice herself had given Emma the makeover that had helped her attract and then win the very man who'd left her heart battered and bleeding three years ago.

The two women stayed in constant touch by phone and e-mail, but this was one night Emma wished her oldest and best friend was right here in town. She needed to sit and vent.

"Okay then, if you don't want him dead, what *do* you want?" Mary Alice asked.

Emma faced the mirror and watched her own features harden. "I want him to be sorry he said that. Sorry he ever took me for granted. Heck, sorry he ever *met* me."

"You sure you want to do this?" her friend asked, and the worry was clear in her voice. "I mean, look how the thing with Tony worked out."

Emma flinched at the memory. Tony DeMarco had done more than break her heart. He'd shattered her newfound confidence and cost her the ability to trust. But that was different and she said so now. "Not the same situation," she said firmly, not sure if she was trying to convince herself or her friend. "I *loved* Tony. I don't love Connor."

"You just want to make him miserable?"

"Damn skippy."

"And your plan is…?"

"I'm gonna drive him crazy," Emma said, and she smiled at the thought of Connor Reilly groveling at her feet, begging for just a *crumb* of her attentions.

"Uh-huh."

"I'm going to make him lose that bet."

"By sleeping with him?"

"Sleep's got nothing to do with my plan," Emma said softly, and ignored the flutter of something warm and liquid rustling to life inside her.

TWO

Saint Sebastian's Catholic Church looked like a tiny castle plunked down in the middle of rural South Carolina. Made from weathered gray brick, the building's leaded windows sparkled in the morning sunlight. Huge terra-cotta pots on the front porch of the rectory, or priests' house, were filled with red, purple and blue petunias that splashed color in the dimness of the overhang. Ancient Magnolia trees stood in the yard of the church, draping the neatly clipped lawn with welcome patches of cool shade.

The church's double front doors stood open, welcoming anyone who might need to stop in and pray, but Emma drove past the church and pulled into the driveway behind the rectory.

She turned off the engine, then stepped out of the car and into the blanketing humidity of summer. The heat slapped at her, but Emma hardly noticed. She'd grown up in the South and she was used to the heat that regularly made short work of tourists.

Besides, if she was looking to avoid the heat, she could have stayed at the shop, in the air-conditioned splendor of her office, and had one of her mechanics drive Father Liam's aging sedan back to him. But she'd wanted the opportunity to talk to Connor's older brother.

Ever since her enlightening conversation with Connor the day before, Emma'd been fuming. And thinking. A combustible combination. She'd lain awake half the night, torn between insult and anger and even now, she wasn't sure which was the stronger emotion churning inside her.

She'd thought that maybe talking to Liam might help sort things out. Now that she was here, though, she didn't have a clue what to say to the man.

Muttering darkly, she headed past the small basketball court in front of the garage, down the rose-bush-lined driveway and around to the front door.

She knocked, and almost instantly the door was opened by a tall, older woman with graying red hair and sharp green eyes. Her mouth was pinched into its perpetual frown. "Miss Jacobsen."

"Hi, Mrs. Hannigan," Emma said, ignoring the woman's usual lack of welcome. Practically a stereotypical housekeeper, she was straight out of an old Gothic novel. So, Emma never took her grim sense of disapproval personally. Mrs. Hannigan didn't like anybody.

Stepping into the house, she glanced around and smiled at the polished dark wood paneling, the faded but still colorful braided rugs and the tiny, diamond-shaped slices of sunlight on the gleaming wood floor. "I brought Father Liam's car back. Just want to give him the keys and the bill."

"He's in the library," the housekeeper said, already turning for the hall leading back down the house toward the kitchen. "You go in, I'll bring tea."

"That's okay—" Horrified, Emma spoke up quickly, trying to head the woman off. Everyone in Baywater knew enough to say no to Mrs. Hannigan's tea. But it was too late. The housekeeper ignored Emma's protest and strode down the hallway, filled with purpose, and Emma knew there would be no getting out of having to drink the world's worst tea just to be polite.

Grumbling to herself, she crossed the hall, opened the door into the library and paused, waiting for the young priest to notice her. It didn't take long.

Father Liam Reilly set aside the book he was reading, stood up and smiled at her, and Emma had to remind herself that he was a dedicated priest. As she was sure *every* female was forced to do when face to face with Liam.

As tall as his brothers, he was every bit as gorgeous, too. His black hair, longer than the triplets' military cuts, was thick and wavy and his deep-blue eyes were fringed by long black lashes any woman would envy. His generous mouth was usually curved in a smile that set people immediately at ease, and today was no exception.

"Emma! I'm guessing your arrival means you were able to save my car again?" He crossed to her and dropped one arm around her shoulder, leading her to a pair of overstuffed chairs near a fireplace that held, instead of flaming logs, a copper bucket filled with summer roses.

"I brought it back from the brink again, Liam," she said, and handed him the bill she pulled out of her back pocket before taking the seat he offered. "But it's on life support. You're going to need a new one soon."

He grinned, then glanced at the bill and winced. "I know," he said, lifting his gaze to hers. "But there's always a more important use for the money. And Connor's promised to rebuild the engine when he gets a chance, so I'll wait him out."

Connor.

The very man she wanted to talk about. But now that she was here, she really didn't know what to say. How could she tell a *priest* that she wanted to kill his brother?

"Something wrong?" Liam asked, sitting down across from her and leaning forward, elbows braced on his knees.

"What makes you ask that?"

He smiled. "Because the minute I said the name Connor, your face froze and your eyes caught fire."

"I guess poker's not my game, huh?"

"No." He shook his head, reached out, tapped the back of one of her hands and asked, "So, want to talk?"

Emma opened her mouth, but they were interrupted. She wasn't sure if that was a good thing or not.

"Tea, Father," Mrs. Hannigan announced as she bustled into the room carrying a wide tray loaded with a pitcher of a murky brown liquid, two tall glasses filled with ice and a plate of cookies.

"Oh," Liam said with heartfelt sincerity, "you really didn't have to do that, Mrs. Hannigan."

"No trouble." She set down the tray, dusted her palms together, then turned on her heel and marched out of the room with near military precision.

"We have to drink it," Liam said on a sigh as he reached for the pitcher.

"I know." Emma braced herself as she watched him pour what looked like mud into the glasses.

"She's a good woman," Liam said, lifting his own glass and eyeing it dubiously. "Though I can't imagine why the concept of tea escapes her."

Emma decided to get it over with and took a hearty swig. She gulped it down before it could stick in her throat, then set the glass back on the tray and coughed a little before speaking again. "So about Connor..."

"Right." Liam gagged a little at the tea, set the glass down and shuddered. "What'd he do?"

Intrigued, Emma asked, "How did you know he did anything?"

"Something put that flash of anger in your eyes, Emma."

"Okay, yeah. You're right." She jumped up from the chair that was big enough and soft enough to swallow her whole and started walking. Nowhere in particular, she just felt as though she needed to move. "He did do something, well, *said* something and it made me so mad, Liam, I almost punched him and then I thought he wouldn't even understand why I was hitting him and then *that* made me even more mad, which even I could hardly believe, because honestly I was never so mad in my life and he didn't even have a clue. You know?"

She was walking in circles, and Liam kept his head swiveling, to keep up with her, following her progress around the room and trying to keep up with the rambling fury of her words.

"So, would you hate me, too, if I said I don't have the slightest idea what you're talking about?"

Emma blew out a breath and stopped in front of the wide windows overlooking the shady front lawn. The scent of the roses in the cold hearth mingled with the homey scent of lemon oil clinging to the gleaming woodwork. Outside, a slight wind tugged at the leaves of the magnolias and two kids, oblivious to the heat, raced past the church, baseball bats on their shoulders.

"He's an idiot." Emma turned and looked at him. "Connor, I mean."

"True," Liam admitted and gave her a smile that took the edge off her anger. "In fact, all of my brothers are idiots—" he caught himself and corrected "—maybe not Brian anymore since he wised up in time to keep Tina in his life. But Connor and Aidan?" He nodded. "Idiots. Still, in their defense, they're under a lot of...*pressure,* right now."

"You mean the bet?" Emma asked.

Liam blinked. "You know about it?"

"It's practically all Connor's talked about for the last month."

"Is that right?" Liam smiled again, wider this time. "Driving him crazy, is it?"

Emma grinned at him, despite the bubbles of anger still simmering inside her. "You're really enjoying this, aren't you?"

"I shouldn't be, should I?"

"I don't know," Emma said, her smile fading just a little, "okay, you're a priest, but you *are* still a Reilly."

"Guilty as charged," Liam admitted. "And this Reilly wants to know what Connor did that upset you so much."

"He dismissed me."

"Excuse me?"

Emma shrugged, as if she could shift what felt like a load off her shoulders, then shoved both hands into the pockets of her jeans. Blowing out a breath, she realized that it was just a little harder than she'd thought it would be to talk about this. Saying it all out loud only made it harsher and made her remember the stupid smile in Connor's eyes when he told her she was a "pal."

Gritting her teeth, Emma got a grip on her anger and muttered thickly, "He actually told me that he didn't want me, so I was safe to be around."

Liam groaned. "He really is an idiot."

"Yeah, well." Feeling the sting of Connor's words again, Emma turned her head and looked out the window, focusing on the gnarled trunk of the closest magnolia tree. She should just be mad, but there was an undeniable sting of hurt jabbing at her, too. And it was that niggling pain that bothered her the most. She hadn't let a man close enough to actually *hurt* her in three years. The fact that Connor could do it without even trying infuriated her.

"He's going to be sorry," she whispered, more as a solemn promise to herself than to Liam.

"Emma?"

She wouldn't look at him. How could she? She heard the concern in his voice, and though she appreciated it, she didn't need it. She'd be fine. Just as she'd always been. And once Connor had been taught a *very* costly lesson, things would go back to the way they should be. "I'm going to see to it he loses that bet, Liam."

He sighed and she heard him stand up and walk toward her. "Not that I wouldn't be pleased if the church got a new roof," Liam said when he stopped beside her. "But I feel I ought to caution you."

"About?" She slanted him a look.

Shaking his head, Liam said softly, "Sometimes the best-laid traps can backfire, Emma. They can spring shut on the one who set the trap in the first place."

Not if the trapper was careful.

"Don't worry about me, Liam," she said firmly. "I'll be fine."

"Uh-huh," he said, and reached out to turn her face toward him. "But you and Connor have been friends for a long time."

"So?" She didn't mean to sound so much like a cranky child. But she couldn't seem to help it. The fact that they *had* been friends was the very thing that had made this whole situation so infuriating.

"So," he said, "it's not that far a fall from friendship to love."

Emma laughed and shook her head. "Sorry for laughing, Liam. But trust me, there's no chance of that."

Number one, she wasn't interested in loving anybody. She'd tried that once and she still had the emotional bruises to prove it. And Connor wasn't looking for love either. Heck, if anything, he was trying to avoid women altogether. And clearly, she told herself, her spine straightening and her chin lifting, if he *were* to go looking for love…he wouldn't be looking at her. Nope. No danger here.

Still chuckling, she turned and headed for the door. "I've got to get back to the garage," she said. "And don't worry about giving me a ride back. It's only a few blocks. I could use the walk."

At the door, she stopped and turned back to look at him again. Father Liam was watching her with a concerned expression on his handsome face.

"Don't look so worried," she quipped. "I'm going to help you get that new roof."

"A new roof's not worth a broken heart, Emma."

If something inside her shivered, she ignored it. He meant well, but he didn't understand. This wasn't about making Connor love her. This was about making Connor want her, and then leaving him flat.

This was about payback.

"Hearts are *not* involved here, Liam."

Still worried, Liam watched her go. "For your sake, I hope you're right."

Two days later Connor couldn't stand his own company any longer.

He'd been avoiding his usual hangouts—except for Jacobsen's Garage—but Emma hadn't had much time to talk to him in the last couple of days. He might have thought that she was avoiding him, but that didn't make any sense at all.

To fill his time, he'd spent a few hours working in his mother's garden, played basketball with Liam and had even mooched a meal from Brian and Tina. But, Connor thought, as good a cook as his sister-in-law was, he just couldn't take another evening over there. Not with the way Brian and Tina were all over each other.

It was hell to be jealous of a married man.

But there it was.

"I think going without sex is killing off brain cells," he muttered, and shut off his car's engine. Instantly the air conditioner died and the temperature in the car started to climb.

Summer nights weren't much cooler than summer days and the humidity was enough to make a grown man weep. He stared through the windshield at the Off Duty Bar and told himself if he was smart, he'd fire up the engine, turn the car around and drive back to his empty apartment.

But damn it, temptation of women or not, Connor wanted a couple of hours of listening to music, drinking a beer and talking to his friends.

"I can do this," he assured himself as he opened the car door and stepped out into the sultry summer air. Music, loud but muffled, floated to him on the way-too-slight breeze and the scent of jasmine, coming from the bushes growing at the edge of the parking lot, was thick and sweet.

Connor slammed the car door, punched the alarm button until the car horn beeped, then headed for the front door. As he walked closer, a couple left the building, the man's arm wrapped tightly around his woman's shoulders as he dropped a kiss on her hair.

Connor groaned and seriously considered turning back while there was still time. But the lure of air-conditioning, cold beer and some conversation was just too strong. He grabbed the silver bar in the center of the door and gave it a yank. The door flew open, music slapped at him, and the scent of perfume, beer and cigarette smoke welcomed him.

He stepped into the dimly lit room and nodded greetings as he made his way to the bar. Signaling the bartender, Connor said, "Beer. Draft." He slapped a bill on the bar top and when his drink was ready, he lifted it and took a long pull.

The icy froth soothed him as it slid down his throat, and he shifted his gaze to take in the room. The bar itself was old. Probably fifty years at least. The walls were painted battleship gray and the furniture was scarred. From the open, beamed ceiling, hung memorabilia of the corps. Vintage helmets, bayonets in frayed scabbards, and even a ceremonial sword, belonging to the current owner, a retired Sergeant Major. The whole place was designed to make a military man feel welcome. A Marine, most of all.

There were pool tables at one end of the main room, and on the opposite end, a dozen round tables were lined up in a wide circle, so that the middle of the ring could be used for dancing. The jukebox, which looked older than Connor, blasted out current rock along with some of the classics.

Most of the regulars at the Off Duty were Marines. Winding down after a day of work or just stopping in for a cold one before going home. Of course, there were also a few civilians and more than a few women.

Not that Connor was noticing.

Then the crowd shifted. His hand tightened on the glass of beer. Through the gap in the people milling

around the bar, he had an all-too-clear view of a tall
blonde in a skirt short enough to be just barely legal.

She was bending over the pool table, lining up a shot.

Connor's mouth went dry.

Her long, blond hair hung in a honey-colored curtain down to the middle of her back. As she tipped her
head to one side, that fall of hair shifted, off her shoulders and his gaze was caught by the way the overhead
light picked out streaks of sun-kissed hair, brighter
than the rest. She wore a pale-blue tank top that looked
as if it had been glued onto her body, and the tiny denim
skirt, just covering her behind, hitched even higher as
she leaned farther over the pool table. Her shapely legs
looked smooth and tanned and about three miles long.
She wore black, sky-high heels on her small feet, and
her ankles looked as fragile as her thighs looked sexy.

Sexy?

The woman *oozed* sex.

His fingers squeezed the glass of beer until he
wouldn't have been surprised to feel it shatter like
spun sugar in his grasp. Scraping one hand across his
face, he inhaled sharply and watched, spellbound, as
she lifted her right foot and rubbed it slowly against
her left calf.

Need spiked.

His body went instantly hard.

His breath shuddered and his heartbeat staggered.

He watched one of the guys closest to her, lean in
and whisper something, and Connor wanted to grab
the guy and pitch him through a window.

Okay, *breathe.*

He sucked in air and told himself that he was only reacting like this because of his recent dry spell.

But it was more.

There was something about her.

Something that called to him from all the way across the room. Something that made a man want to toss her over his shoulder and carry her off to a cave where he could have her, over and over again. Where he could listen to her moan and taste her sighs.

He took another gulp of beer, hoping the icy drink would put out some of the fire. But he knew better. Damn it, he never should have come in here.

The blonde straightened up slowly, then hitched one hip higher than the other as she laughed. That tight, short skirt of hers hugged her behind. She shook her long blond hair back from her face, and Connor was captivated, watching the thick, wavy fall of blond shift and dance around her.

He swallowed hard.

Then she tipped her head back and playfully patted the other guy's chest.

Connor dropped his beer.

The glass shattered at his feet, splashing ice cold beer on everyone close by.

He didn't notice.

He couldn't take his eyes off the blond with the body made for sex.

"Emma?"

Three

Even over the pounding rhythm of the jukebox, Emma heard the glass shatter.

But then, her ears were attuned to everything. She'd seen Connor walk into the bar—which was exactly why she'd maneuvered herself to the end of the pool table. She'd even opted to take a *lousy* shot, because she knew *exactly* what kind of picture she'd make, leaning over the pool table.

Nerves hit her hard and fast. Her stomach spun, and the edges of her vision got a little foggy, but she could deal with that. Had to deal with it. Too late now to change her plan.

Smiling up at the guy she'd just beaten at pool, she ignored the sensation of Connor's gaze boring into her back. "That's twenty bucks you owe me, Mike. Want to go double or nothing?"

The tall Marine smiled down at her as he handed over a twenty-dollar bill. "How about you let me buy you a drink instead?"

"How about you take off?" Connor's voice was nothing more than a low growl.

Emma shifted a look at him and had to force herself not to smile at the stunned-to-his-toes expression on his face. Good. She definitely had his attention.

"Connor," she said, in mock surprise. "I didn't see you come in."

Viciously he rubbed the back of his neck, then let his hand drop to his side. "Yeah, well. I sure as hell saw *you*."

"Friend of yours?"

Emma glanced back at the man she'd just beaten twice at pool. Tall and good-looking, any other night she just might be interested. Tonight, though, every thought was centered on Connor. But Mike didn't look too pleased at the idea of sharing.

They were attracting a small crowd, drawn no doubt by the bristling testosterone in the air. Emma wanted to shake her head at the ridiculousness of it, but there was a small part of her enjoying the whole show.

After all, she spent most of her time being just what Connor had called her. One of the guys. A pal. Well, she'd been underestimated most of her life. True, she'd probably played into it by never bothering to dress the part of "female." But she'd always figured she shouldn't have to. A woman who was a successful business owner should be accepted on her own terms without having to stand in killer high heels and skirts so short she felt a breeze *way* too high up.

"Emma," Mike said, bringing her up out of her thoughts with a jerk. "You know this guy?"

"Oh, yes," she said, sending another look to Connor and really enjoying seeing him watch the other guy through narrowed eyes. "Connor and I are old *friends.*"

"And we need to talk," Connor said, not bothering to take the warning out of his voice as he faced the other Marine. "So why don't you get lost?"

"Yeah?" Mike snarled. "I don't remember inviting you over."

Connor's chin went up, Mike stiffened and curled his hands into fists, and Emma suddenly felt as though she were in the middle of a special on that cable channel about animals. The men were like two bull elephants about to butt heads.

And in spite of the anger she still felt toward Connor, a purely female spurt of delight shot through her—which she quickly shot down. Seriously, two men go caveman and woman reverts right along with them. Must be contagious.

Stepping in between them, Emma smiled up at Mike Whatever-his-last-name-was and said, "It's okay. I do need to talk to Connor so…" She let her sentence trail off and shrugged an apology.

He didn't like it, but he moved away, rejoining his

friends at the bar. Connor glared after him, then shifted his gaze back to Emma.

With a calm she wasn't quite feeling, she folded the twenty-dollar bill she'd just won and tucked it into her bra—the push-up kind that gave her more cleavage than God had ever gifted her with. And she didn't miss Connor's gaze following the action.

A swirl of something hot and thick simmered within, and she told herself it was purely a female re-action to a male stare of appreciation. Although, she hadn't exactly been panting when Mike was giving her the once-over.

Doesn't matter.

All that mattered was that her plan was working.

She smiled to herself and rubbed the tip of her cue stick with a square of chalk. Then, setting it aside, she pursed her lips and blew gently on the tip. Con-nor swallowed hard.

This is just *fun,* Emma thought.

"So," she said, tipping her head to one side so that her hair fell around her like a gold curtain, "what'd you want to talk about?"

He snorted and swept his gaze up and down her. "You're kidding, right?"

She leaned one hip against the pool table, while she idly stroked her fingers up and down the cue stick. "Is there a problem?"

"A *problem?*" Connor's eyes bugged out and his mouth worked a time or two, as if he was trying to speak but just couldn't convince the words to cooperate. Finally he got a grip on himself, leaned in toward her and said in a strained hush, "Damn it, Emma, *look* at you. When you were bent over that pool table, I could see clear to—"

She raised one eyebrow and hid the delighted smile she felt inside. "Clear to *where,* Connor?"

He straightened up. "Doesn't matter." He inhaled sharply. "What *does* matter is that every guy in here is looking, too."

Okay, there was just a tiny stirring of uneasiness. She'd *wanted* Connor to get an eyeful, and she'd known going in that she might attract some attention from other guys. But the thought of a roomful of Marines scoping her out gave her a chill that wasn't quite the thrill she might have guessed. If anything, she felt a little…*outnumbered.*

But she wasn't going to let Connor know it.

"And how is this any of your business?" she asked.

"Well," he started, then stammered to a stop. He glanced around, giving the evil eye to one guy sidling a little too close for his comfort, then shifted a glare back at her. "We're *friends,* Em," he said. "I'm just trying to look out for you. That's all."

"That's the only reason you came over here, then?" She didn't believe him for a minute. There was a flash of something dark and dangerous in his eyes and it didn't have a thing to do with feelings for his *pal.*

"Why else?"

Okay, fine. They'd play this out. She could go

along. In fact, this worked out better for her. The longer he tried to hold out against her, the harder she'd make it for him.

Pushing away from the pool table, she picked up her cue stick, then ran the tips of her fingers along the top edge of her tank top, as if she were hot. She didn't miss Connor's gaze snapping right to where she wanted him to be looking.

"Well, thanks, Connor," she said, licking her lips slowly, provocatively. "I appreciate the concern."

He gritted his teeth, and she watched a muscle in his jaw tick.

"No problem. In fact," he added, "if you're ready to leave, I'll just take you home. Make sure you're okay."

Emma smiled up at him despite the urge to smack him over the head with her cue stick. Instead she laid one hand on his chest and felt the drumbeat of his heart beneath her palm. "That's so sweet," she said softly. "But no, thanks, I'm not ready to leave yet."

"You're not—"

"Tell you what," she said, sliding past him in a move that put her between his rock-hard body and the edge of the pool table. As she moved, she heard him hiss in a breath. Good. "Now that you've scared off my playing partner, you ready to take me on instead?"

He scowled. "Take you on?"

She snapped her fingers in front of his glassy eyes. "Pool, Reilly. You want to play me a game of pool?"

"Right. Pool. Sure." He scrubbed both hands over his face, then looked at her again and blinked as if trying to clear blurry vision. "It'd be better if we just left and—"

"Oh, you go ahead," she said, letting her gaze slide around the room, as if she were considering picking a different challenger from the men in the bar. "I can find someone else to play."

"I'll bet," he muttered darkly. "Look, Emma, I just don't think you should be hanging out here—not tonight. Not the way you look—"

One blond eyebrow lifted again, and slowly she hitched one hip higher than the other and tapped the toe of her shoe against the floor. Around them, people laughed and talked and a handful of couples danced on a small square of unoccupied floor. She paid no attention to any of it.

"What?" she asked. "I look what, exactly? Good? Bad?"

He scowled at her. "Different."

She turned to hide her smile and offered herself a small internal *whoop* of congratulation. Mission accomplished. Connor Reilly had taken notice. In fact, if he'd noticed any harder, he'd be standing in a puddle of drool. A sense of power swept through her, and Emma hugged it close.

A heady sensation for a *pal*.

She picked up the triangle-shaped rack hanging on the side of the pool table, then set it down in position on the green felt. Not even looking at him, she said, "I wasn't born in coveralls, you know."

"Sure. I know that," he said, and reached into the

corner pocket to pull out a handful of the striped and solid balls. "It's just…"

Emma sighed and muttered under her breath. Okay, she'd thought to surprise him, but this was ridiculous. It was as if he were staring at a dog who'd suddenly learned to talk. How was she going to seduce the man—make him lose that stupid bet—if she couldn't get him to move past *stunned* into *hunger?*

She straightened up and moved closer to him. His gaze went right to the top of her scoop-necked tank top and stayed there. Her breasts looked high and full, thanks to the "miracle" bra that was currently strangling her. And Connor was certainly appreciating the view.

And that's what she'd wanted, right?

"Look," she said, "I want to play pool. If you don't want to, I'll just ask Mike, or one of these other guys, if he wants to go another round and—"

"Leave him and anybody else out of this," Connor muttered thickly, lifting his gaze to hers. "I'll play."

Now, a girl could take that one of two ways. Play *what* exactly? Pool? Or something else, entirely? For the moment, she'd go with pool. "Twenty bucks a round. Eight ball."

"You're on."

"Then," she said, walking past him to circle the table and head for the opposite end, "as the challenger, you rack 'em."

"Yes, ma'am."

* * *

Connor couldn't take his eyes off her.

Damn it, who would have guessed that little Emma Jacobsen was packing concealed weapons?

And man, she had weapons to spare.

The tops of her breasts pushed teasingly against the edge of her tiny tank top. Her hips swayed when she walked and the hem of that incredibly short skirt just barely managed to cover the gateway to paradise. And her legs. God, her legs.

He dropped one of the billiard balls and had to bend down to snatch it up off the floor. Which gave him much too good a view of those amazing legs as she walked away from him. And why had he never noticed the sweet curve of her behind?

How could he have missed it?

His whole body was stiff as a board. He felt hot and eager and pushed to the very edge of self-control. Damn it, it had been a mistake to come here. He'd known it before and he was sure of it now. But if he hadn't, he might never have seen this side of Emma.

The very side that was making it an effort to walk. He suddenly wished that his jeans were a hell of a lot baggier.

And even as he thought it, he straightened up, his grip on the fallen billiard ball tight enough to crush it to dust. *This is Emma,* he reminded himself. *Good old Emma.*

Pal.

Buddy.

He shifted his gaze to her and felt his throat close

up. Her blue eyes looked wider tonight. Her mouth looked edible. Her tanned, smooth skin was the color of warm honey and looked just as lickable.

Oh, man.

She was watching him with a curious expression on her face and he really couldn't blame her. Hell, they'd been hanging out together for a couple of years now and he'd never stuttered around her before. Just like he'd never taken the time to notice that her breasts were just the right size to fill a man's palm.

Damn it.

She held her cue stick in her left hand. Idly, she slid her fingers up and down the slim, polished wood, trailing her touch delicately enough to drive him insane by wondering how those fingers would feel on *him*.

"Man, get a grip, Reilly." His voice was thick and his muttered whisper was soft enough to be buried beneath the onslaught of rock music pouring into the room. At least, he hoped it had been.

He really didn't want Emma knowing that he was getting hard just watching her.

It's just the bet.

That's all it was.

He was hard up.

Frustrated.

Walking the fine edge of sanity.

But man, she looked good.

"How long's it take to rack some balls?" she asked.

Connor winced and shot her a quick look. "A little patience goes a long way."

She laughed and the deep, throaty, full sound of it, rippled over the conversations in the bar and danced to the rhythm of the music. It seemed to reach for him and grab him by the throat.

"You?" she asked. "Patient?"

Her fingers were still caressing the cue stick and he had to force himself to look away. But meeting her gaze wasn't much safer. Had her eyes always been that color of blue? Sort of summer skyish? He gritted his teeth.

"I can be patient when I have to be," he countered. Like now. It had been a long month. The stupid bet with his brothers was making him crazy. But he was patient—even if Emma didn't think so. And he'd make it through the next two months.

As long as she didn't bend over again.

"Yeah?" She tilted her head, and that fall of hair swung out past her shoulders. "How are you at pool?"

He lifted the rack off the triangle of balls, hung it on the hook at the end of the table and forced a nonchalant shrug. "Take your best shot and let's find out."

She nodded slowly. "Twenty bucks a game."

"High stakes."

"What's the matter?" she asked, a smile tugging at the corners of her mouth. "Scared?"

Well, that helped. His dignity won out over his hormones. "Hell, no. I can take you."

"Really?" she said softly. "And just *where* did you plan on taking me?"

She didn't wait for a reply. Instead, she bent over

the table, lined up her cue stick and drew it back and forth between her fingers while she aimed her shot.

Unfortunately, this gave Connor *way* too much time to appreciate the view of her breasts, practically spilling out of her tank top.

His body went to DefCon 2.

And he suddenly knew *just* where he'd like to take her.

A back room.

A flat surface.

On the damn pool table.

Crap. He rubbed his face and damn near slapped himself. He wanted *Emma.* Now. More than he could ever remember wanting anything else in his life.

The only thing that stopped him was he was pretty sure it wouldn't have worked. Just because he was acting like a slobbering horn dog didn't mean she was feeling the same thing. And the only thing worse than falling off the wagon and losing the bet would be trying to lose the bet and having Emma tell him thanks but no thanks.

She took her shot, and the triangle of balls scattered across the green felt surface. She looked up at him and grinned, and Connor's breath caught in his throat.

"You sure you're willing to risk the twenty bucks?" she asked, her voice teasing.

"I'm not afraid of a challenge," he countered, leaning both hands on the cherry wood edge of the table. "How about you?"

"Oh, don't you worry about me, Connor. Trust me, I'm up to the challenge."

"Yeah?" he asked. "And after I've won your twenty bucks, then what'll we play for?"

Emma lined up her next shot, then paused to slant him a look. "Oh, I'm sure we'll think of something."

Four

Emma Jacobsen was driving him over the edge and damned if she didn't seem to be enjoying the ride.

Connor lost two games of pool and couldn't even resent the laughter from the handful of people gathered around to watch the competition. How could he? Hell, if he'd been watching, he'd have been laughing his butt off at the poor guy getting worked by the petite woman in the tank top.

But damned if he could help himself.

How was a man supposed to concentrate on a game when he kept getting distracted by a woman's breasts? Or her legs? Or her laughter? Or the way she walked?

Damn it.

Emma crossed to the wall and set her cue stick into the rack before slowly maneuvering through the crowd to his side. Holding out her hand, she waited for him to hand over his last twenty.

"You were using secret weapons," he said and dropped the bill into her hand, too wary of actually *touching* her. Though the thought of his fingers brushing her palm sent a jolt of heat darting through him, he figured he shouldn't risk it. Hell, he wasn't sure he'd be able to *stop* touching her if he got started.

"Is that right?" she asked, and grinned up at him. Her smile packed a hell of a punch. Something else he'd never noticed. Emma had smiled at him maybe hundreds of times over the past couple of years. Why had it never hit him just what a great mouth she had? What…had he been going through his life blind or something?

"Oh, yeah." Connor forced the words past the hard knot in his throat. "Trust me when I say you weren't fighting fair."

Shaking her head, she laughed and said, "And here I thought I just played way better than you."

"Another match another time," he promised. As long as she was wrapped up in an Eskimo jacket.

"I'm always ready for a challenge." She smiled and tucked the twenty-dollar bill into the dip of her cleavage. He watched it disappear and his mouth went dry.

Behind them, a couple of guys moved in to take over the pool table. Emma stared up at him for a long minute or two, and Connor's brain tried to kick into gear. He had to say something. Something to convince—if not her, then at least himself—that he wasn't a slobbering moron.

But apparently his mind was taking the night off.

In those sky-high heels of hers, she was taller than usual. Her mouth was close enough to kiss and tempting enough to make him want to risk it. He could almost taste her and that thought splintered inside him until he had to curl his hands into fists to keep from reaching for her.

Damn it.

This was *Emma*.

Has to be the bet, he told himself.

Then she spoke and he listened up. Her voice was soft, so he had to strain to hear her over the clash of music and conversation. Not to mention the thunderous pounding of his own heart.

"You're staring at me."

"No, I'm not." Stupid.

"Okay," she allowed, a smirk curving her lips. "You're staring at the wall behind me and I'm just in the way?"

He scraped one hand over his face, hoping to stir himself out of the sexual coma he'd slipped into. Didn't help much. "Sorry. Thinking."

Yeah, thinking about tossing her onto the pool table and peeling her out of that tank top and skirt. Geez, he could almost feel her amazing legs wrapped around his hips.

DefCon 1.

He was definitely in too deep here.

"Uh-huh," Emma said, with a shake of her head that told him she wasn't buying the whole "lost in thought" excuse. Already turning, she said, "Well, it's been fun, Connor, but I've gotta be going."

She was leaving.

He should be grateful.

He wasn't.

"What's your hurry?" he asked, voice tight.

She stopped and looked up at him.

He mentally scrambled for something to say. Something that would convince her to stay for a while. He wasn't finished torturing himself. Wasn't finished being amazed by the surprise that was Emma.

Blowing out a breath, he said, "I'd offer to buy you a beer, but somebody just won all my cash."

A quicksilver grin flashed across her face and was gone again in an instant. "So if I was a good sport, I'd buy *you* a beer?"

"Something like that." Anything, he told himself. He just wasn't ready yet for this time with her to be over. Wasn't even sure why, but he knew he wanted to be with her. Even over all the other scents colliding in the air of the bar, he could almost taste the scent clinging to her alone. It was fresh and citrusy and reminded him of long summer nights under star-filled skies.

And he couldn't quite believe it was Emma Jacobsen making him feel all these things. Maybe that was why he didn't want her to leave yet, he told himself, grasping for a reason, *any* reason. Maybe he had to prove to himself that it wasn't Emma herself affecting him. That it could have been any woman at this point in the bet. That he was just a hormone-plagued, needy Marine, and any good-looking woman could have been the last straw on this particular camel's back.

No doubt about it, either, she was real good-looking. Up, down or sideways, Emma had something that was making him reel.

"Sorry," she was saying. "Work tomorrow, so I'm heading out."

She turned and weaved through the crowd, moving for the front door. Guys she passed craned their necks for a better view. Connor was surprised there wasn't a river of drool running through the bar. As he watched them watch her, he felt the sudden, driving urge to slam all their heads together and let them fall.

Where the hell did they get off watching Emma?

A couple of long seconds ticked by before he reacted. But then he was moving fast, pushing past the people in his way, as if they were deliberately trying to separate him from Emma. He caught up with her just outside.

The scent of jasmine was thick and sweet in the hot summer air. The silence, after the door swung closed behind him, was almost startling after the prolonged exposure to blaring music. And in the relative quiet, he heard her steps, crunching in the gravel of the parking lot. Instinctively he followed.

She spun around, right hand raised and fisted, with keys jutting out from between her fingers.

"Whoa!" Connor held both hands up in mock surrender.

Emma sighed and let her hand fall. "Darn it, Connor, you *scared* me."

"Sorry, sorry." He hadn't thought about it. Hadn't considered the fact that she might get a little spooked having someone chase her into the parking lot.

In fact he'd *never* stopped to think about Emma that way and suddenly, he realized that she must cross lots of dark parking lots. What about at night, when she closed up her shop and she was alone? And he wondered why he suddenly felt as though he wanted to be the guy protecting her.

Oh, man.

This just kept getting worse and worse.

"What do you want, Connor?"

He lifted her right hand, ignoring the heat that spread from her hand to his and up his arm. Silently he examined the keys she held primed between her fingers. "You were ready for trouble, weren't you?"

"Uh, *yeah*." She pulled her hand free and released her tight grip on the keys. "A smart woman pays attention and doesn't take chances. So, why'd you follow me out here, Connor? Forget to tell me something?"

"No," he blurted, and took her elbow in a firm

grip. She felt warm and soft and, damn it, way too good. "I just thought I'd walk you to your car."

She glanced down at his hand on her arm and he wondered if she felt the same sweeping sensation of warmth that had jolted through him at first contact.

"That's not necessary," she assured him, pointing off to her left. "My car's right there."

He glanced in that direction and spotted her small, two-door, silver sedan about thirty feet away, parked directly beneath one of the light poles. Smart, he thought. Emma'd always been smart.

Then he shifted his gaze back to the sky-blue eyes still watching him. "Fine. You don't need me to do this. But it's necessary for me."

"I can take care of myself, Connor. I always have."

"I know." He'd never thought about it until tonight, but now he wondered why the hell he hadn't. Emma'd always been his friend. Someone he could shoot the breeze with as easily as he could one of the guys on base. He'd never really stopped to think of her as being female.

But looking at her tonight, he couldn't imagine thinking of her as anything else ever again.

"Humor me."

"Why should I?"

He smiled. This was the Emma he knew. Stubborn, ready to argue at the drop of a hat, unwilling to accept help if she figured she could handle something—and she *always* figured she could handle anything.

"Because," he said, smoothing his fingers over

her elbow, enjoying the slide of skin to skin, "you just beat me into the ground in front of about a hundred witnesses. Every Marine I know is going to be giving me hell about losing a game of pool to you."

"*Three* games, but who's counting," she corrected.

"*Two*," he said and leaned closer, "and *I'm* counting."

"Of course you are." Connor'd always been competitive. Which was why he'd gotten himself involved in that silly bet in the first place.

The bet.

The reason she was here, dressed like...well, she didn't really want to think about what she was dressed like. She'd spent most of the evening feeling *really* exposed. At least, until Connor had arrived. Then she'd pretty much just felt warm.

Emma inhaled slowly, deeply and told herself to get a grip. But it wasn't easy. The feel of Connor's hand at her elbow was swamping her brain with way too many emotions and too few clear thoughts.

She'd thought this was going to be easy.

Work him into a frenzy, seduce him, then tell him how she'd tricked him into losing the bet with his brothers.

She hadn't expected that *she* would be having trouble keeping focused.

But having his heated gaze locked on her body for the past two hours had churned her up so much that it was hard to remember to breathe. In fact, she hadn't taken an easy breath at all until the minute she'd stepped out of the bar and started across the parking lot.

Connor coming up behind her and scaring her out of five years of her life hadn't helped anything, either. But now he was here. So close. Close enough that she could look up into his eyes and see her own reflection staring back at her.

"So, are you going to let me play white knight?" he asked softly, "Or are you going to force me to follow you at a distance to make sure you're safe?"

Something inside her softened and then toughened up again. Sure, it was nice having someone care enough to make sure she got to her car safely. But if she'd wanted, or needed, an escort, one of the bouncers would have walked her out. The fact that Connor was all of a sudden acting like Sir Walter Raleigh or something was both flattering and infuriating.

She hadn't missed the fact that he'd only treated her like a girl when she was dressed as *he* thought a girl should be. If she was smart, she'd play along, keep reeling him into the fact that for the night, she was a soft, helpless female type.

But she just couldn't do it.

"First tell me something."

"What?"

"How come you never offered to walk me to my car before tonight?"

"You know," he admitted, lifting one hand to brush the side of his head, "I was just asking myself the same thing."

She watched him, admiring the strain of his black USMC T-shirt across his broad, muscled chest. "And did you get an answer?"

He straightened up again, and looked down into her eyes, pinning her gaze with his until Emma saw that his deep, ocean-blue eyes were churning with emotions she'd never expected to see.

"Only one," he muttered, taking a firmer grip on her elbow and steering her across the dark lot. The lights rimming the lot shimmered in pools of brightness splashed across the shadows.

"Which was?" She hurried her steps to keep up with his much-longer legs.

He stopped and looked at her. "I'm an idiot."

She smiled. "I can accept that."

Standing in one of the pools of light thrown from overhead, Connor's face was in shadow, but she felt him watching her anyway.

"You surprised me tonight, Em," he said, and his voice sounded softer than the breeze that drifted past them.

Her stomach did a slow spin. "Why's that?"

He shrugged. "I just never thought of you as—"

If he came right out and said, "I never thought of you as a girl," again, Emma might just have to punch him.

"As what?"

He paused, then seemed to catch himself. He took a step back, shook his head and muttered, "A pool player."

Disappointment curled in the pit of her stomach. He could have said, sexy, or hot stuff or gorgeous. But, no. Apparently, the shock was still too much for him. Well, fine. So she wouldn't be seducing him on the first try. She had time. She'd get him into bed yet.

"Live and learn," she said, and stepped past him to open her car door. She slid inside, rolled down the window and looked up at him. "See you, Connor."

"Right. See you."

She put the car in Reverse and pulled out of her parking space. As she slipped the gear shift into Drive, she looked in the rearview mirror to see Connor, standing where she'd left him, still watching after her.

The fact that she really wanted to go back and kiss him meant absolutely nothing.

"It's *Emma*, for crying out loud." Connor snatched the basketball thrown at him, then dribbled it absentmindedly.

"You gonna play or what?" Aidan ran up to him, grabbed the ball away from him, turned and made a jump shot, sending the basketball through the hoop.

"Maybe he's got something else on his mind," Brian said, wiping sweat off his face with his forearm.

"What about Emma?" Liam asked, grabbing the ball in rebound and bouncing it back down the driveway behind the rectory.

Connor looked at his older brother and wondered how in the hell he could explain what had happened to him two nights ago. Hell, he still couldn't figure it out for himself.

But since the moment Emma'd hopped into her car and driven away, he hadn't been able to think of anything else but her. And that was just way too weird.

"I saw her the other night," he said, and instantly a vivid image of Emma in that short, tight skirt leaped into his mind and hovered there to torment him.

"So?" Aidan moved in closer, taking the beer from Brian's hand and draining it.

"Hey!" Brian complained.

"Get another one, geez," Aidan sniped.

Sunshine poured down on the concrete driveway and bounced off the cement surface to surround the brothers in steamy summer heat. Hardly a breath moved through the trees and there wasn't a cloud in sight. But they'd made plans to play basketball today and come hell or dehydration, they were going to play.

Brian snapped the top on another beer and held it far away from Aidan's reach. Taking a drink, he glanced from Connor to Liam and winked. "Hey, looks like you've got another brother about to topple."

Connor straightened up and scowled at him. "No way. I can make it. Unlike *some* people."

Brian just laughed. "Hey, I don't get the money, but I *do* get laid. *Often.*"

"Bastard," Aidan muttered, then added, "can't understand why a woman as great as Tina would put up with you."

"She wanted the best," Brian assured him.

"Yeah, yeah." Aidan threw the ball at him, Brian caught it and sent it toward the hoop.

As they moved off, Liam stepped up to Connor and slapped him on the back. "So, anything you'd like to share with your friendly neighborhood brother slash priest?"

Connor shook his head. "You're in no position to give advice on women, Liam. I may be out of the game for two more months, but you're in it for life."

Liam shrugged, reached down into the open cooler beside him and pulled out two cans of beer. Tossing one to Connor, he opened one for himself and said, "I wasn't born into the priesthood, you know."

"Yeah, I remember."

"So? Feel like talking?"

"No." Connor took a long gulp of the beer and felt the icy froth race down his throat and send a welcome chill throughout his body. But it wouldn't help for long, he knew. Ever since seeing Emma at the Off Duty, he'd been hot and hadn't been able to cool off. Thoughts of her plagued him. Memories of the way she moved, the way she smiled, the way she smelled, were becoming a part of him.

Which was exactly why he'd stayed away from her garage the past couple of days. He needed space. Time. He needed to figure out just what the hell had happened to him the other night. And until he did, it wasn't safe for him to be around Emma.

Going into his second month of forced celibacy, Connor was balancing precariously on a razor's edge of control. One little push either way, and he was a goner.

And the way Emma had looked the other night, she was just the one to give him that push.

"That's it?" Liam asked. "Just *no?*"

"Liam, the day I need a priest's advice on women, is the day you can shave my head and send me to Okinawa."

"You're a Marine, moron," Liam reminded him, setting down his beer and moving back to the top of the basketball court, where Aidan and Brian were dueling it out. "Your head's already shaved and you've *been* to Okinawa."

Connor scowled at him.

Hell, maybe he *did* need advice from a priest.

Five

"**H**e hasn't been back, Mary Alice." Emma leaned back in the office chair that had once belonged to her father and was now all hers.

"You expected him to come running right over?"

"Well, *yeah.*" She twirled the coiled telephone cord around her index finger so tightly her skin turned bluish purple. Quickly she unwound it again. "If you could have seen him drooling all over me, you would have thought so, too."

"Uh-huh," Mary Alice said, "and what were you doing while he was drooling?"

"You mean besides falling out of my top?"

"Yeah. Were you drooling back?"

"A little maybe." Okay, *a lot.* But she couldn't

very well admit that to Mary Alice, could she? Not when her friend had warned her going in that this was a bad idea? Oh, maybe it *had* been a bad idea.

For two days now Emma'd been doing little else but think about Connor. Which was weird. He'd been a part of her life for two years, but until this week, she'd never once imagined him naked in bed with her. And, oh, boy, her imagination was *really* good.

"I knew it," the voice on the phone said, disgusted. "I knew you'd be setting yourself up again. Honestly, Em…"

"This is different," Emma protested, not sure if she was trying to reassure her friend or herself. Memories of three years ago and a broken engagement darted through her mind and were just as quickly extinguished. "I'm not looking for forever," she said. "Just a little right now."

"Uh-huh."

Emma scowled at the phone. "You don't have to sound so unconvinced."

"Please, Em. You are *so* not the one-night-stand kind of woman."

She stiffened. "I could be."

"Yeah, and I could be a runway model, if not for the extra twenty pounds."

"Funny."

"I'm not trying to be funny," Mary Alice said. "I'm *trying* to make you come to your senses before you get in so deep with this guy that your heart gets broken again."

"Wow. First Father Liam warns me about the dangers of seduction turning into love and now you." Emma blew out a breath. "My heart is perfectly safe. It's my hormones that are getting the work out."

Well, that set Mary Alice off. A floodgate of warnings poured from her, and she barely paused for breath.

While she listened to her friend's worries pouring through the receiver, Emma glanced around the tiny Jacobsen "empire."

The office was filled with potted plants, and flowering vines fell from baskets hanging in the corners of the room. The wide glass windows gleamed in the sunlight and gave Emma a bird's-eye view of the flower beds lining the front of the shop. Zinnias and petunias added color and scent to the shop and welcomed customers with unexpected beauty.

Her father had started the business more than thirty years ago and had never really concerned himself with making the place "pretty." He'd built a reputation based on honesty and fair prices and when he passed away five years before, he'd left that business in Emma's capable hands.

She knew her way around an engine—hard to grow up the only child of a mechanic and *not* learn—but as she'd helped the business grow, Emma had found herself spending more time lately on paperwork than on actual engines. Though there was still nothing she loved better than restoring classic cars.

The two mechanics she had working for her were

good at their jobs and didn't have a problem taking orders from a woman—especially one who could do a tune-up in less than thirty minutes.

"Hello? Earth to Emma."

"Huh? What?" Emma shook her head, sighed deeply and said, "Sorry. Zoned out there for a minute."

"I'm giving you all this great advice and you're not listening?"

"I didn't say that. I heard you. I just think you're going a little overboard."

"No such thing. You're not experienced enough with guys to know how to protect yourself."

"Gee, *Mom,* thanks."

"You *did* call me to talk about this, remember?"

"Yeah," she paused and pushed a long strand of blond hair behind her ear. She'd given in to a weak moment and called her best friend in the world because Emma was getting a little nervous. This wasn't working out quite the way she'd planned it. She was supposed to be driving Connor insane with desire—not herself. "I remember."

"So, talk to me."

"I already told you about the other night at the bar."

"Yeah," Mary Alice said with a sigh. "Wish I could have seen you balancing on those heels while playing pool."

"Hey, I'm better at it than I used to be." She grinned, though, remembering how many times she'd fallen on her behind when Mary Alice had coached her through actually *walking* in high heels. That had only been four years ago. When she'd first decided to remake herself in the hopes of falling in love. Back before she realized that love only really mattered if the guy was in love with the *real* Emma.

"God, I should hope so," she chuckled, then continued, "so you said Connor was all droolly, right?"

"Like a starving man looking at a steak."

"This is a good thing."

"Yes, but I haven't seen him since." Damn it. Emma'd thought for sure that Connor would come by the garage the day after their pool match. The way he'd stared at her breasts and her legs, she'd have bet money on him being completely hooked.

She would have lost.

"Figure he's avoiding you on purpose?"

"Seems like that's the case."

"Then you must have worried him."

Emma smiled, dropped her feet from the desk and sat up. "Hey...I hadn't really thought about it like that."

"If he doesn't trust himself around you, I'd say you're close to getting him to lose the bet."

"Good point." She'd been so busy being annoyed that Connor was keeping his distance, Emma'd never really asked herself *why* he was suddenly so determined to avoid her. Maybe he wasn't thinking of her as a pal anymore, and that had him worried. Maybe her too-tight skirt and too-small shirt had done the deed after all.

But then why didn't he come over for another look, damn it?

She stood up and walked around the edge of the desk, stretching the coiled phone cord as far as it would go. Outside, the summer sun blasted down on the city streets, heat shimmering in the air, giving Baywater the wavering look of a mirage. On the main street traffic bumped along, and as she watched, a black SUV made the turn into the garage's driveway.

A chill swept instantly down her spine, and Emma tried to tell herself it was just the icy breeze from the air conditioner affecting her. But she knew better.

She licked suddenly dry lips. "He's here."

"What?"

"Connor," Emma said, her fingers tightening on the receiver. She watched him step out of his car and wince as the heat slapped at him. Oh, he looked way too good. Despite the summer heat, he wore faded jeans that clung to his long legs. His white T-shirt strained across his broad chest, and his jaw was tight and set as he stuffed his keys into his pocket and headed for the office—and her.

A jolt of pure anticipation lit up her insides and made her mouth water.

"What's he look like?" Mary Alice demanded.

"Dessert," Emma groaned. "Gotta go." She hung up while her friend was still talking, then eased one hip against the corner of her desk and tried to look nonchalant. Not at all easy when your stomach is spinning and your heartbeat is crashing in your ears.

Emma couldn't take her gaze off him, and she wondered just when this little game she'd started had turned on her. He was the one who was supposed to be going all gooey-eyed, not *her.* But here she stood, watching his long legs move across the parking lot and wishing he'd turn around so she could get a glimpse of his very nice behind.

Her stomach took another nosedive, and she slapped one hand against it as he opened the door and stepped inside. Instantly her small office felt darn near claustrophobic.

Connor ground his back teeth together as he looked at her. Big mistake coming here. After leaving his brothers, he'd gone home to take a shower, but hadn't been able to sit still. Thoughts of Emma had plagued him as they had been for the past two days, and he'd finally decided there was only one thing to do about it.

If he hoped to keep his friendship with her, then he needed to stay the hell away from her for the duration of this stupid bet.

He wasn't about to risk his nice, easy relationship with Emma just because he was so damn horny he could hardly see straight. Emma was his *friend.* The bet was the only reason he was acting like a moron around her now. And damn it, he wouldn't give in to it. He was no teenager stuck on the first girl to smile at him.

He was a Marine.

He was tough.

He was hard.

And getting harder by the second.

His gaze swept over her quickly, thoroughly. She was wearing a pair of pale-green coverall shorts that displayed miles of smooth, tanned leg. And under the bibbed coverall, was a dark-pink tank top edged with lace. Her blond hair was pulled into a high ponytail and then braided into a thick rope that lay across her right shoulder. And his fingers itched to touch it. He wanted to undo the tight braid and rake his hands through the softness.

Whoa.

He stiffened slightly, instinctively shifting into a *braced for battle* position. Feet wide apart, arms crossed over his chest. Ordering himself to stand down, he knew, more than ever, that he'd done the right thing in coming here. He had to explain to her that he wouldn't be seeing her for the next couple of months. Had to tell her—what?

That he didn't trust himself around her?

That he all of a sudden was spending way too much time thinking about her trim little body?

That he wanted to sink his teeth into her shoulders and then lick his way down the length of her?

Oh, yeah. That'd be real smart.

"Emma, we have to talk." The words came out a little harder than he'd planned, but then, his jaw was clenched so tight every word was an effort of will.

"Really?" She smiled and edged off the corner of the desk.

Her sandals were white with little daisies on the top strap. Her toenails were painted the same dark shade of pink as her tank top, and she wore a gold toe ring that winked and sparkled in the sunlight. Damn it. Mechanics don't wear jewelry on their feet.

He frowned. "Since when do you wear a toe ring?"

She looked down, then up at him. "Since three years ago."

"Oh." He scraped one hand across his face. Something else he'd never noticed. Or if he had, it had been ignored, because Emma was his friend. His buddy. But that was then, and this was now. "Look, Emma, about the other night—"

"What about it?" She moved a little closer and he got a whiff of her perfume.

The soft, haunting scent reached for his throat and squeezed. This was risky. Being this close to her. He should have called her. Should have kept his distance. But he hadn't wanted to, and at least he could admit that much to himself.

Hell, he couldn't figure out why this was happening to him at all. He'd never spent much time fantasizing about one particular woman. To Connor, women were like candy. You never wanted to stick with one too long, because you'd just get tired of it. He was a big believer in the "variety is the spice of life" theory on romance.

But since seeing Emma at the bar the other night, she'd been right up at the forefront of his mind. He hadn't been able to shake her. Hell, he hadn't been able to make himself *try.*

"You surprised me," he said.

She stepped closer, and her scent moved in for the

kill. Damn it, she was wrapped around him now and he couldn't breathe without taking a piece of her inside him.

"Yeah, you said that already."

"Right." He had said it. Outside in the parking lot. When he'd tried to convince her *and* himself that he'd been surprised by her pool-playing abilities. He frowned, shook his head and looked down at her. Her summer-sky eyes were wide and incredibly blue. A man could lose himself just staring into those depths. And he didn't want to be lost.

"Look," he blurted, taking a hasty step back, hopefully out of range of her force field. "You want to go get some lunch or something?"

Her blond eyebrows lifted high on her forehead. "You're asking me to lunch?"

"Something wrong with that?" he demanded, as he silently cursed himself. For God's sake, you don't get over a woman by asking her out to eat. "Can't two friends share a meal together without making a big deal out of it?"

Her lips twitched, then her mouth slowly curved and he felt a tug of reaction deep inside him.

"Who's making a big deal about anything?"

"Nobody," he said, nodding as if trying to convince himself. "Not a big deal. Just lunch." He frowned. "So? You interested?"

"Sure. Just let me tell the guys I'm leaving."

She walked through the connecting door to the garage bay and God help him, Connor watched her go.

Man. Short coveralls had never looked so good. There was nothing "friendly" in the way his gaze locked onto her—and he knew he was digging himself an even deeper hole.

Delilah's Diner was relaxed and casual.

Tourists and locals mingled together and the low hum of activity echoed throughout the place. Booths lined one wall by the window overlooking Pine Avenue. A dozen or more round tables were dotted around the rest of the room, with a long lunch counter sweeping around the back. Waitresses moved through the crowd with dazzling speed and the "order ready" bell rang out with regularity.

Emma leaned back against the white Naugahyde booth seat and folded her arms on the scrubbed red vinyl tabletop. Connor hadn't spoken to her at all since leaving the shop, and now he looked as if he'd rather be anywhere but here.

How was a girl supposed to take that?

While they waited for their order, she reached for her glass of water and took a long sip before asking, "So are you going to be silent all through lunch?"

"Huh?"

"You said you wanted to talk, but you haven't even opened your mouth since we left the garage."

"Miss the sound of my voice?"

He grinned, and the quick smile jolted something deep inside her. Emma took a long drink of water in an attempt to drown it.

"What's going on, Connor?"

"Nothing, it's just that—"

Their waitress chose just that moment to arrive with their meals. She slid Emma's chef salad across the table then carefully placed Connor's hamburger and fries directly in front of him. Emma rolled her eyes and watched, half amused, half irritated as the woman did everything but coo and stroke Connor's chest.

"Thanks," he said, smiling up at the redhead.

"You bet," the woman said on a sigh, barely sparing a glance for Emma. "If there's anything else you need—" she paused meaningfully "—anything at all, you just call me. I'm Rebecca."

"Thanks, Rebecca," Emma spoke up, startling the waitress out of her flirtatious mood. "We'll call if we need you."

The woman flashed her a frown, then shot Connor another smile before reluctantly wandering off.

"Amazing," Emma said, shaking her head in disgust.

"What?"

"You didn't notice?"

He picked up his hamburger and took a bite. Shrugging, he chewed and repeated, "Notice what?"

"Unbelievable. But then why would you?" Emma asked, not really expecting an answer. "You've probably affected women like that your whole life."

"What the hell are you talking about?"

"The redheaded waitress?" Emma coaxed. "The one who wants to have your child—here on the table?"

He laughed and picked up a French fry. "Don't you think you're exaggerating a little?"

She stabbed a forkful of lettuce and chicken and really considered stabbing him in the hand just for the heck of it. No wonder he'd never paid attention to her. He had women crawling all over him all the time. The man was a babe magnet. Any female between the ages of fifteen and fifty would turn for another look at him. "No, I'm not."

Connor shrugged. "She probably thinks I'm Aidan. He eats in here a lot."

She just stared at him. She'd never had any trouble at all telling the triplets apart. Sure, they were identical, but there was a little something different about each of them that made all the difference. With Connor, it was the way the right corner of his mouth lifted when he didn't really want to smile but couldn't help himself.

"What was it like?" she asked. "Growing up with two other people who look just like you?"

His mouth curved, just the way she liked it.

"Fun. We had a great time, the three of us. And Liam, too, before he went into the seminary." He paused and looked at her. "I can't imagine growing up like you did. An only child."

She lifted one shoulder and took another bite of her salad. "It was okay. My dad and I got along fine, just the two of us."

"Yeah, I bet you did. But you didn't have somebody to trade places with at exam time."

"You didn't."

"Sure we did." Connor laughed and his eyes flashed with memories. "Aidan's the brain. So come chemistry finals—he took all of our tests."

Emma laughed and shook her head. "I can't believe you got away with that."

"We did. For the first two years of high school. After that the teacher wised up. Noticed that all three of us answered every question the same way."

"What happened when you got caught?"

He winced, then winked at her. "Let's just say our mother is more than a match for her sons. None of us saw the outside world for a solid month."

"Even Liam?" Emma reached for her ice tea. "He was innocent."

"Yeah, but he was the oldest. Mom figured he should have kept us out of trouble."

While Connor talked about his brothers, Emma watched him and tried to remember that she wasn't supposed to be getting more deeply involved in his life. This was just a seduction. Pure and simple. A plot to get him to lose a bet and be sorry he'd ever dismissed her.

But he smiled and she forgot about her plan. He laughed and she just enjoyed the loud, rolling sound of it pouring over her. Beneath the table, his foot brushed her leg, and she felt the punch of electrical awareness dance up her calf, past her thigh to simmer in a spot that was already too hot for comfort.

He felt it, too; she sensed it.

His gaze locked with hers across the table, and the humor in his eyes faded slowly away to be replaced by a slow burn of hunger that scorched her, even at a distance. "What're we doing, Emma?"

"Having lunch?" she asked, swallowing hard and trying to steady her breathing.

"What else?"

"Is there something else, Connor?"

"I didn't want there to be, but it's damn hard to ignore."

A spurt of disappointment shot through her but didn't do a thing toward cooling the fires within. "Well, that was flattering."

"Emma, we're friends." He leaned across the table and took her hand in his. His thumb scraped her palm until the tingles of sensation speared through her.

She blew out a breath, but didn't let go of his hand. She liked the feel of his fingers entwined with hers. Liked the heat she found pulsing in him and the flames awakening in herself. "And friends don't see each other naked?"

"Not usually," he admitted, through gritted teeth.

She nodded slowly and, just as slowly, reluctantly, pulled her hand free of his. "Then we'll just have to stop being friends, won't we, Connor?"

Six

Stop being friends?

Emma's words hit Connor like a fist to the gut.

"That's exactly what I'm trying to avoid," he muttered, his hand tingling with emptiness now that she'd let go of him. He rubbed the tips of his fingers together, as if he could still feel the silky slide of her skin on his. Damn it. He didn't have so many close friends that he was willing to lose one. Especially *this* one. He and Emma always had a good time together. They could talk about anything. He could laugh with her. Tell her what he was thinking.

When the new recruits in his charge were starting to drive him up the wall with frustration, Connor knew he could go to Emma's and forget about the world for a while. When his brothers made him nuts, she laughed with him about it. When the rest of the world looked less than warm and welcoming, Emma's smile set it right.

And he wasn't ready or willing to give that up.

"You can't always get what you want," she said with a little shrug that nudged the strap of her coveralls down her left shoulder.

He scowled at her. What was *that* supposed to mean? Did she *want* to end their friendship and try something different? Or was she trying to tell him that she wasn't interested in sex with him?

Why couldn't women be as clear as men?

"Don't start quoting song lyrics at me."

"A little touchy, aren't we?" she asked.

"Not touchy, just surprised you're so damn willing to toss our friendship for a quick roll in the hay."

"I didn't say *that,* either."

He actually *felt* his scowl deepen. "Then just what the hell are you saying?"

"Not much," she said, and her voice was cool, amused, even. "Just that if you want to go to bed, we'll stop being friends. If you don't, we won't."

"Oh, so it's all up to me?" He didn't believe that for a damn minute. There wasn't a woman alive who wasn't completely at the wheel of any relationship. And all men knew it. They just pretended otherwise to hang on to their pride.

Which was *precisely* why he'd always avoided commitment like the plague. Once a woman got a good hold on you, things changed. Your life wasn't your own anymore. You were going to chick movies regularly and worrying about putting coasters under your bottle of beer.

Not worth the effort. Leave the married life for people like Brian. For Connor, it was love 'em and leave 'em—quick.

She shook her head, and he watched that thick, honey-gold braid swing from side to side like a pendulum. "Up entirely to you? Not a chance. Look, you just said yourself you didn't *want* there to be anything else between us."

"Yeah, but—" Not fair to use a man's own words against him.

"So, there's no problem, right?"

He scraped one hand over his face. Something was wrong. Somewhere or other he'd lost the thread of this conversation, and he wasn't sure any more which side he should be defending. Damn it, a man needed a battle plan to deal with a woman. Any woman.

Especially, it seemed, *this* woman.

Emma grinned, tilted her head to one side to stare at him, and her thick, blond braid swung over her right shoulder. He wanted to reach across the table, undo the rubber band at the end of it and comb her hair free, burying his fingers in it.

"Do I make you nervous, Connor?"

"No." The answer came sharp and swift, and he had to wonder if he was trying to convince Emma or himself. Dismissing the idea entirely, he picked up his hamburger, took a bite and chewed like a man on a mission. However he'd lost control of this conversation, he could still get it back.

After he swallowed, he said, "I'm not *nervous.*"

"Then what's the problem?"

Problem? Where to start? How about sitting across from his friend in a lunch diner and knowing he'd need about twenty minutes before he could stand up and walk out of there without embarrassing himself? How about the fact that he could smell her perfume—something a little different today, flowers and…lemons, but just as intoxicating.

He couldn't tell her any of that. Just as he couldn't tell her that he'd been lying awake at nights imagining her *naked.* That would damage the very friendship he was fighting so hard not to lose.

This was all his brothers' faults. Every last one of 'em. Brian being so happily married now—and delighting in telling Connor and Aidan about all the sex he was currently enjoying. Aidan being so determined to being the last man standing. And even Liam, standing on the sidelines, laughing at all of them as they tried to do for three months what he'd committed to for a lifetime.

He never should have made the stupid bet.

It'd been a pain in the butt from the get-go.

And it was only getting worse.

"Damn it, Em," he muttered thickly, fighting past the knot of need lodged in his throat, "it's the bet. You know that's what's behind all of this."

"Uh-huh."

He frowned at her less-than-convinced reply. When she took another bite of salad, then delicately licked a drop of dressing off her bottom lip, every cell in Connor's body lit up like a fireworks show. Inwardly groaning, he squashed the lightninglike flash of need bursting to life inside him.

"Look," he said, leaning toward her and lowering his voice to be sure none of the other diners could overhear, "we both know this bet is making me nuts. We both know that we're *friends*, nothing more."

She nodded and smiled. "You bet."

He inhaled sharply, deeply. His stomach knotted and he glanced down at his hamburger in sudden distaste. He couldn't force a bite down his tight throat now if someone had a gun to his head. Pushing the plate aside, he leaned both forearms on the table and held her gaze with his own. "I *like* you, Emma."

"Thanks, Connor," she said, daintily picking a piece of chicken out of her salad and popping it into her mouth. "I like you, too."

"Exactly!" He slapped one hand against the tabletop with enough force to make the iced tea glasses jump and shudder.

Several people turned to look at him, and Emma laughed. He didn't care.

"That's my point." He glanced around warily, then lowered his voice again. He felt like a secret agent in a bad movie. "We *like* each other too much to climb into bed together."

"Okay."

He sat back, stunned. *"Okay?"*

She shrugged again and this time the tiny spaghetti strap of her little tank top slid off her shoulder to join the strap of her coveralls. Connor gritted his teeth.

"Sure," she was saying, and he blinked away the haze of pure, one-hundred-proof lust clouding his mind so he could listen. "I mean it's no biggie to me. If you'd rather not, then fine."

"Just like that."

She smiled. "Did you expect me to throw myself across the table and plead with you to *take me now, big boy?*"

Maybe a little, he admitted silently. He'd thought sure she was feeling what he was feeling. That she'd wanted him as much as he had her. But apparently not. And why didn't that make him feel better?

"Sorry to disappoint you, Connor," she said, and idly lifted both straps off her upper arm to slide them into place. "But I'll survive if we don't hit the sheets together."

"I know that," he said, and wondered how in the hell this had all turned around. When had he set himself up to be turned down? When had *she* become the one to say no?

"Good." She took another bite of her salad and if she hadn't just a second ago told him she wasn't disappointed by the thought of not going to bed with him—Connor would have thought she was licking her lip deliberately. She did it slowly—tantalizingly slowly—and his body, still at DefCon 1 lit up like a demilitarized zone during a night landing.

She picked up her iced tea, took a long drink, and Connor's gaze fixed on the line of her throat. His vision blurred.

Then she set her glass down, glanced at her watch and said, "Oops! Gotta run."

"Now? You're leaving now?"

"I really have to," she explained, gathering up her brown leather purse and slinging it over her left shoulder. "But you go ahead and stay. The shop's only a block away. I'll walk it."

When he didn't say anything, she stopped scooting toward the edge of the booth. "Connor? Was there something else you wanted to talk about?"

"No," he grumbled. "Nothing at all."

"Okay, good." She leaned toward him and smiled. "I've got a bad carburetor coming into the shop in twenty minutes, so I have to be there."

"Right." He grabbed his own iced tea glass and cradled it between his palms, letting the cold seep into his skin, his bones.

She stood up and flashed him another smile as he looked up at her. Then she dropped one hand onto his shoulder and he swore he could feel the warmth of her skin right through the fabric of his shirt.

"I'll see you later, okay? And thanks for lunch."

"Right. Later." He nodded and swallowed hard.

She walked away and he couldn't help himself. He turned on the booth seat to watch her go and groaned

as his gaze locked onto the curve of her behind.
Grumbling under his breath, he turned back around
and squirmed uncomfortably on the bench seat.

Rebecca, the friendly waitress, hustled right over
and asked, "Can I get you anything else?"

He didn't even meet her eyes this time. Instead he
drained his iced tea, then handed her the empty glass.
He wasn't going anywhere until his body cooled
down. Shouldn't take more than an hour—and since
he couldn't very well take a cold shower, he'd have
to settle for cold drinks. And maybe he should just
pour the next one in his lap where it would do the
most good.

"Bring me another one of these, would you? And
make it a large."

She frowned, but he didn't notice.

Or care.

Later that evening Connor drove from his apartment to the base. Sick of his own company, he'd decided to check in with his assistant drill sergeant.
Now, watching the young troops trying to settle into
life as Marines, he at least had something else to
think about besides himself.

And they *were* young.

Most of them still in their teens, they were
driven to the recruit depot at Parris Island at night.
Brought across the long road winding into the base
past swamp water and marsh grasses in the dark.
Deliberately. Not to disorient, but to have them

connect to *this* world almost instantly. To remind
them that they and their fellow recruits were now
a team. A family. That they'd become a part of
something much bigger than they'd ever known
before, and that the life they left behind had no
place here.

Standing in the corner of the barracks, Connor
watched DI Jeff McDonald striding up and down the
aisle separating two long rows of bunks. Each new
recruit stood in front of their beds, heads newly
shaved, narrow shoulders thrown back and chins jutted out.

"Boy," McDonald shouted, stopping in front of a
tall, thin kid, "did I just see you *smile?*"

"Sir! No, sir!"

Connor smothered a grin and watched as McDonald feigned disgust.

"You think you're going to a party, recruit?"

"Sir! No, sir!"

McDonald leaned in closer, his nose just a hair's
breadth from the kid's. He pointed to the chevrons
on his sleeve. "Then you better stop smiling recruit,
or I'm gonna think you think I'm funny lookin.'"

The kid looked horrified by the idea.

"Do you think I'm funny lookin,' recruit?"

"Sir! No, sir!"

Connor watched from the shadows and silently
approved. McDonald was good at his job. He'd in-
timidate the recruits, teach them what they needed to
know to survive, and in the end he'd have their re-

spect. And he would have turned out a new company of Marines.

Smiling, Connor told himself the kid would learn. They all would. Or they wouldn't make the grade. But most of them would. They were here because they wanted something more and, generally, were willing to work for it.

Connor shook his head, shoved his hands into his pockets and slipped out the side door. The summer night was warm, the air felt thick with the scent of the South and the humidity that was such a part of life here.

He stopped and tilted his head back to stare up at the black, star-studded sky. Things were running as they should be here. He wasn't needed. McDonald didn't have time to talk, and he wasn't in the mood to hunt down any of his other friends.

He still had days to go on his leave time. Hell, he should be *itching* to get into town. To grab a beer. Play some pool at the Off Duty.

Connor winced. He had the distinct feeling he'd never again be able to stroll into that bar without his brain replaying the image of Emma bent over the pool table, taking a shot. He scrubbed both hands over his face and shook himself like a big dog climbing out of a lake.

They'd settled *nothing* at lunch.

If anything, he'd only walked away more confused than he had been before.

So the only way to get this clear in his mind was

to go and see Emma. Talk to her. Figure out what the hell it was that was driving him and then find a way to end it.

And if a small, rational voice in the back of his mind was warning him to steer clear of Emma Jacobsen—he wasn't listening.

Emma sat on her back porch, staring up at the sky.

Star Jasmine flavored the warm, moist air and stirred in the gentle breeze that swept through the yard, then disappeared again. Sighing, she leaned against a porch post and stretched her legs out, down the steps leading to the grassy yard. She reached for the frosty margarita sitting beside her and lifted it for a sip.

Ordinarily she didn't drink much.

But after her lunch with Connor, and a long, dreary day of rebuilding a carburetor and then the depressing conversation with Mrs. Harrison, she'd felt she'd earned a drink or two.

Mrs. Florence Harrison, a widow who lived just outside of town had been disappointing Emma for two years now. All because of a '58 Corvette currently rusting in Mrs. Harrison's barn. The car had once belonged to the woman's son, now dead forty years. Emma had lusted after the 'Vette ever since the moment she'd first seen it. She longed to bring it into the garage and restore it to its full glory.

But Mrs. Harrison flatly refused to part with her late son's "baby."

"Ah, well," Emma said, and took a long, deep

drink of the frothy concoction in her glass. She let the icy stream wash down her throat and send chills to every corner of her body. "What's one more *no* in the grand scheme of things, anyway?"

Connor didn't want her enough to lose the bet, and Mrs. Harrison was clutching that Corvette to her bosom like a long-lost child.

Pushing off the top step, Emma stood up and walked down the stairs and across the lawn. The damp grass felt cool and lush beneath her bare feet as she wandered aimlessly through the shadows. From down the street, she heard snatches of sound, letting her know her neighbors were also enjoying the cool relief of the summer night. Children laughed, dogs barked and the faint sound of a radio playing caught the air and hung on it.

When the wind kicked up suddenly, it swept through her hair, lifting it off her neck into a wild, brief dance. At the side of the house, the wind chimes tinkled merrily, and she smiled at the sound, in spite of everything.

"What're you thinking?"

The deep, familiar voice came from somewhere close beside her, and Emma's stomach jumped as she turned to face Connor. "You scared me," she said, though that wasn't strictly true.

Startled, yes. But scared? Nope. Much closer to a rush of hunger than a rush of fear. Funny how she'd never noticed before now just what kind of effect his voice had on her. Just when exactly had *that* started happening?

"Sorry. Didn't mean to sneak up on you," he said, and took a step closer. "But you looked like you were thinking serious thoughts—then you smiled. Intrigued me."

Still in the USMC T-shirt and jeans he'd been wearing earlier, Connor looked good enough to fuel dozens of dreams. At the thought she clutched her margarita glass a little tighter and took a sip, even as she acknowledged that it was false courage. "I, um, just liked the sound of the wind chimes."

As if awaiting a cue, the wind breathed past them again, and the chimes sounded out like fairy bells.

"Pretty," he said.

"Yeah, they are."

"Not them," he said. *"You."*

Whoa.

Head rush.

It wasn't the margarita. She hadn't had enough of that to matter. It was Connor. Plain and simple. In the moonlit darkness, he looked impossibly handsome. His strong jaw worked as though his teeth were clenched. His eyes were as dark as sapphires, and the reflection of stars danced in them. His mouth was tightened into a grim slash that made him look as though he regretted saying those words.

Well, too bad if he did.

He *had* said them and there was no going back now.

"Thank you."

"Emma…"

"Connor," she interrupted him neatly and took another sip of her drink to stall for a precious second or two. "If you're here to tell me again what a great pal I am and how you don't want to lose me—" she stopped and took a breath. "You don't have to bother. I get it. Understood. Go. Be happy. Fly free."

He glanced around the empty yard, and she knew he wasn't noticing the lushly crowded flower beds or the sweet smelling jasmine vines clinging to the fence wrapping around her property. He was waiting, thinking, maybe having as difficult a time as she was with whatever it was that lay between them.

And for one brief moment Emma wondered if she'd done the right thing in setting this ball in motion. But there was no turning back. No avoiding whatever was coming.

Finally he looked at her and she read a decision in his eyes. She lifted her chin and braced herself for whatever was coming next.

"This isn't about our friendship, Em," he said softly. "This is about what's making me crazy."

"And what's that?" Oh, man. She held her breath and felt the sense of waiting all through her body.

"If I don't kiss you in the next ten seconds, I think I'm gonna lose what's left of my mind."

All of the air left her body and fire replaced it. She felt tongues of flame working their way through her insides. Her body went hot and ready and eager. Her mind clicked off and her emotions charged to the surface. But her voice was steady as she smiled up at him. "Time's awastin' then."

He grabbed her.

She dropped the acrylic margarita glass to the ground, spilling the icy drink across the grass.

He pulled her hard against him, stared deeply into her eyes for one heart-stoppingly long moment.

And then he kissed her.

Seven

Connor hung on to Emma as if it meant his life.

And in that moment maybe it did.

For the past several days, she'd filled his mind. Every thought, every dream was stamped with her image.

She fit against him as if she was the missing piece to his puzzle. And though one corner of his brain clanged out a warning bell, he refused to listen.

His arms wrapped around her, pulling her close, closer. His hands swept up and down her back, aligning her body with his, until he felt every inch of her pressed to him tightly enough that he felt her heartbeat fluttering wildly. His mouth took hers, his tongue tangling with hers in an erotic dance that fired his system with a need unlike anything he'd ever known before.

She sighed into his mouth, and he swallowed her breath, taking it inside and holding it. Her arms linked at the back of his neck, and she pressed herself even more fully against him.

He felt the pressure of her pebbled nipples pressing into his chest, branding his skin with heat that seared him right down to his soul. Connor groaned, and his arms tightened around her, lifting her feet clean off the ground.

Again and again their tongues tangled in a dance as old as time and as new as sunrise. She tasted of her icy drink and tantalizing secrets. He couldn't get enough of her.

Somewhere in the back of his mind, a voice shouted, *This is Emma.* His pal.

His buddy.

And right now the only thing in his life he desperately wanted.

Tearing his mouth from hers, he gasped for air like a wild man. Blindly, Connor stared down at her and saw her familiar features through a bristling red haze of passion. Her mouth was swollen from his kiss. Her summer-blue eyes were glazed with the same desire blasting through him. Her breath labored in and out of her lungs, and he wondered if her heart was thundering in her chest—as his was.

"Wow." She blinked up at him and smiled with all the wonder of a kid at Christmas, unwrapping a gift she hadn't even been aware of wanting.

Connor knew just how she felt. "Yeah," he said, "I think that just about covers it."

"Who would have guessed?"

He set her back onto her feet and released his viselike hold on her. Still, though, he was reluctant to break all contact. He lifted one hand and stroked her cheek with his fingertips. Her skin was as warm as sunlight and as soft as velvet.

Emma turned her face into his touch and closed her eyes as he caressed her face. She sighed a little, opened her eyes again and said, "Why *did* you come here tonight, Connor?"

Good question. He wasn't entirely sure he had an answer for her. Shaking his head, he said simply, "I don't really know. I just drove here. Didn't actually stop and think about it. Didn't plan it. Just followed my instincts and they led me here."

"Instincts, huh?"

He nodded and shoved one hand along the side of his head. Hard to admit, even to himself, that it was pure gut reflex that had brought him to Emma's door. But there it was. As a Marine, he'd learned long ago to trust the impulses that drove him. He didn't question, didn't doubt. He just *did*. That confidence in his own subconscious had saved his butt more than once.

And tonight those instincts had brought him here. To Emma.

"What are they telling you to do now?"

If he told her that, she'd probably run for the hills. Because it was taking all of his self-control to keep from tearing her clothes off and tossing her onto the cool, damp grass. He wanted her naked. He wanted her beneath him. Over him. Astride him. He wanted her in every possible way, and as they stood there in the starlit shadows, that want continued to pulse and grow. "You don't wanna know."

She stepped up close, close enough that he could feel the heat of her body radiating out around her. "Yes, I do."

Her scent lifted into the air and filled his mind. The taste of her still lingered on his tongue. His blood raced, his body tightened until the pain of waiting was almost as fierce as the desire gnawing at him.

He hadn't meant to start this. To light a match to the stick of dynamite lying between them. But now that the first, most difficult, step had been taken, now that the lit fuse was lying there sparking and sizzling, there was no going back. Though his brain shouted at him to think about what he was doing, what he was thinking, his body wasn't listening.

His mouth hungered for another taste. His hands burned to touch her, to sweep along her skin, define every inch of the compact, curvy body that had been plaguing him.

"If you don't want this to happen," he managed to grind out, "say so now."

She was breathing as heavily as he was. Even in the pearly moonlight, he saw the flush on her cheeks and the glitter in her eyes. And he prayed—desperately—that when she made her decision it would be one he could live with. One that wouldn't haunt them both. Even as he thought it, though, he realized that the hell of it was, no matter what she said, they would be haunted.

Because after *this* night, nothing between them would ever be the same—whatever happened.

"If I didn't want this," she pointed out, "you would have known about it when you kissed me."

"Be sure," he said, and wasn't entirely sure himself why he was giving her this out. Why he was practically daring her to call a halt to this. Because if she did say no—it was going to kill him.

"I'm sure, Connor. Are you?"

"Decision made, babe." He grabbed her again, filling his hands with the thin fabric of her tank top. He pulled her close again and dipped his head to take her mouth with his. To drown in the taste of her. She sighed into him, and Connor's blood raced through his veins, thick and hot. He groaned, broke the kiss and stared down at her for a long second, before picking her up and tossing her over his shoulder.

"Hey!" She braced her palms against his lower back, pushed herself up and shouted, "What the hell are you doing?"

"I'm through wasting time, Em." He slapped his palm against her butt, and when she yelped, he grinned.

"What are you, a caveman?"

"Caveman, Marine…you tell me."

"I will if you'll put me down."

"Not a chance." He marched across the moonlit backyard, took the five steps to the back porch at a dead run, then yanked open the screen door and stepped into her kitchen.

He paid no attention to the homey room with its glass-fronted cabinets. He glanced at the blender full of margaritas, then kept walking, out of the kitchen to the bottom of the stairs. He'd been to her house before. He knew his way around the ground floor— but he'd never been upstairs. Never been into her bedroom. Never even considered it until tonight. But that was then—this was now.

"Damn it, Connor," she said, slamming her fist against his back, "I mean it. Put me down."

"As soon as I see a bed. Trust me. I'll put me down. Where'm I headed?"

She sighed, then laughed, and the magic of it floated in the air like soap bubbles on a summer wind. "Upstairs, you Neanderthal. First door on the left."

"Got it." He took the stairs two at a time, his long legs making short work of the trip. Emma's slight yet curvy body hooked over his shoulder didn't slow him down one bit. It did, though, fill him with a fierce and frantic need to reach her bed—hell, *any* bed.

The first door on the left stood open in invitation and he rushed through it. Connor hardly noticed the room itself. All he saw was the double bed with the wrought iron head and foot rails. A colorful, flower-splashed quilt was spread over the mattress and a half dozen throw pillows in different colors and shapes were piled against the bigger bed pillows.

Every cell in his body urged him to hurry. To grab her, take her, fill himself with the taste and touch of her. Giving in to that urge, Connor flipped Emma over his shoulder and onto the mattress. She bounced a couple times and laughed even harder than she had downstairs.

"You're crazy," she said, grinning up at him in the moonlight pouring through the bedroom window overlooking the backyard.

"Been said before," he agreed, planting one knee on the edge of the bed and leaning over her.

She reached up and caught his face between her palms. Her gaze locked with his, and he felt as if she were trying to see all the way through him, down to his soul. And a part of him wondered what she'd find there.

Then philosophical questions faded from his mind as he slid one hand beneath the soft fabric of her tank top. At the first touch of her skin against his, he swallowed hard, and she hissed in a breath and let her eyes slide closed.

"Have to have you, Emma," he murmured, and bent his head to take one kiss, then two.

"Have to have each other," she answered, and snatched a kiss for herself as his hand slid higher, up her rib cage to cup her breast.

"No bra." The words slipped from him on a grateful sigh. His thumb and forefinger tweaked her pebbled nipple, and she arched into his touch, her breath sliding in and out of her lungs in hungry gasps.

Her skin was magic.

Warm silk.

He moved to straddle her body, his knees at her hips. He stared down at her as he pushed her tank top up and over her head, tearing it off and tossing it over his shoulder to land on the floor. A spill of moonlight lay across the bed and bathed Emma in a wash of pale light that almost made her skin glow.

He looked his fill and knew it would never be enough. He cupped her breasts in his hands and felt a hum of appreciation rush through him. Her nipples hardened at his touch. She reached up and ran her palms up and down his forearms, and he felt every stroke of her fingers like a live match against his skin.

Bending low, Connor indulged himself with a taste of her. He took first one nipple, then the other into his mouth, his tongue and teeth nibbling, pulling, teasing at her flesh until Emma was twisting and writhing beneath him.

Every move she made inflamed him. Every sigh that escaped her fed the flames engulfing him. Every touch made him want more. His eyes blurred, his brain shut down and his body took over. All he could think about was burying himself deep inside her. Feeling her damp heat surround him. Feeling her body quiver in climax.

He growled against her flesh and suckled her deeply. Emma's back bowed and she groaned his name as she clutched at his shoulders. "Connor, Connor don't stop. Don't stop doing that."

"Not a problem," he mumbled, surrendering to the hunger clawing at his insides. His mouth drew at her nipples again and again, feeling her need build, feeling his own desire ratchet up past the boil-over point, and still he wanted more.

Sliding down her body, he unzipped her shorts and as he moved, he skimmed them and the white lace panties beneath them, down and off her legs. In the moonlight, he saw the tan lines marking her body and felt his heart jump at the narrow strips of pale flesh over her breasts and at the juncture of her thighs. Why the thought of her in a tiny bikini could inflame him even while he was staring at her nudity, he couldn't figure out and didn't much care.

Everything he wanted in the world was there, at his fingertips. And he meant to enjoy it.

Emma felt him watching her and thought she might just burn to ashes under that heated gaze. But instead her body lit up like a fireworks display. His hands on her legs, as he caressed her from her ankles to her thighs and…oh, boy—even higher, felt hot, heavy, rough and so damn sensual, she couldn't imagine how she'd lived so long without having him touch her.

Her blood was bubbling inside. That had to be the reason why her whole body felt so twitchy. She wasn't a virgin. She'd had sex before.

But she'd never had sex like this before.

Not when she felt as though the top of her head was going to fly off into space—as though her insides were so jumbled with an intensifying need, that she might never feel normal again.

Connor's lips replaced his hands on her legs, and she felt the warmth of his breath dusting her skin as he moved to the insides of her thighs, kissing, nibbling, licking.

Her breath rushed in and out of her lungs. She heard herself panting. She felt herself writhing and couldn't stop. Didn't want to stop. All she wanted was more. More of *him*.

Then his mouth covered her center. "Connor!"

Thank heaven he didn't stop at her shout. She parted her thighs wider, inviting him closer. She planted her feet on the mattress and lifted her hips, rocking with the soul-shattering rhythm that he'd set with his lips and tongue. He tasted her intimately, sending showers of sparks throughout her body. Emma felt the world around her tremble as anticipation built within.

She opened her eyes and looked at him, watched him taste her, watched as he learned the secrets of her body, and she felt a rush of something hot and primal burst into life inside her.

His hands cupped her bottom and squeezed. She licked dry lips and kept her gaze locked on him as her body strained toward the shattering point that was now so close she could feel it.

Reaching down, she cupped the back of his head

and held him to her. Her fingers pushed through his silky black hair and she groaned as he nibbled at her. "Connor, I feel—I need—"

He growled.

No other word for it.

He seemed to know exactly what she needed. He growled against her body, lifted her hips in his strong hands, and as she dangled helplessly above the bed, he pushed her over the edge into a chasm so full of sparkling lights and colors, it nearly blinded her.

"Connor!" She shouted his name, heard the wildness in her own voice and reveled in it as she rode a climax unlike anything she'd ever known before.

As the last tremor rocked her body, he left her, and she wanted to weep for the loss. Her eyes closed to better savor the incredible wash of satisfaction sliding through her, she heard foil tearing and then he was there, somehow already gloriously naked, over her, filling her.

She arched her hips and took him inside. His body pushed into hers and the moment she felt his length within, she came again, trembling anew, riding fresh waves of pleasure that tore at her and left her gasping for air.

"Beautiful," he whispered, his voice a hush of sound in her ear. "So damn beautiful."

She *felt* beautiful. Emma grabbed him, holding him, her arms wrapped around him, her hands splayed against his back, pulling him tighter, closer.

She lifted her legs and hooked them around his waist, tilting her hips to take him even deeper.

He groaned as his hips rocked against hers in an age-old rhythm that sent flutters of brand-new need pulsing at the core of her. She met him, stroke for stroke, and enjoyed the feel of his body covering hers. The solid, heavy weight of him, pushing her down into the mattress. The ripple of muscles straining across his back.

Again and again he withdrew, then pushed himself home. Sweet friction escalated inside her, and Emma ran with it, eager to reach that peak one more time. The heady sound of flesh on flesh filled the room and became an intimate symphony.

He lifted his head to look down at her, and she gasped at the hunger glittering in his eyes. He looked like a warrior. Like the caveman he had pretended to be. He was intent. On *her*. On the breathless craving that had them both wrapped in a tight fist.

In the moonlight his broad, tanned chest looked delectable. She swept her hands around from his back and caressed his skin with her fingertips. At his flat nipples, she flicked the pebbled surface with her nails and watched as his eyes narrowed and his mouth flattened into a harsh line.

He grabbed her right hand, linked his fingers with hers and braced them both on the mattress. Staring down at her, he muttered thickly, "Come again, Em. Come with me this time."

As if his words alone had been enough to ignite

new flames, her body erupted, and bubbles of expectancy churned inside her. She moved with him again, feeling every sweep of his body against the so-tender flesh at the heart of her.

Again and again he staked his claim on her. Then he dipped his head and took her mouth with his. His tongue swept aside her defenses and claimed all that she was. His breath mingled with hers until she didn't know where she began and he ended and didn't care, either.

She tasted his need.

She shared his greed.

And this time when the world around them tottered and fell, they were together as they took the leap and together still when they fell.

Eight

Connor's weight pressed Emma into the mattress, making each breath an adventure. But she didn't mind. In fact, she loved the feel of him lying atop her.

She loved the hum still vibrating inside her body. She loved how he made her feel when he touched her. She loved touching him and seeing his response flicker in his eyes.

And she was using the word love way too many times.

She put a mental stop to that real fast. Opening her eyes, Emma stared blindly up at the ceiling and tried to get a grip on the emotions churning through her. But it wasn't easy. Connor's breath labored in her ear and his heartbeat raced in tandem with her own. And she wondered if his stomach was suddenly doing a weird little pitch and roll.

Probably not.

Guys didn't spend a lot of time thinking about the repercussions of sex. Guys only thought about *getting* sex, and then once they'd had it, they worried about getting it *again*. Life was simpler for the Y chromosome set.

But as far as Emma was concerned, things had just gotten really complicated.

"I'm smashing you."

"Only a little." Stupid. She shouldn't have said that. Should have said, Yes, you are. Move over. But she hadn't wanted him to move and what did that say? Oh, God, she wasn't sure she wanted to know what that said.

Instantly the memory of Father Liam's warning came crashing back at her, echoing over and over again in her mind. Something about "being careful because sometimes even the best-laid traps snapped shut on the wrong target."

She squeezed her eyes shut and deliberately shut down the memory. Her trap had worked fine. Just as she'd planned. She'd gotten him into bed, hadn't she? She'd proven to Connor that she was as female as the next woman and she'd made sure he'd lost that stupid bet with his brothers.

No problem.

She squelched a groan. So if everything was so great, why wasn't she celebrating?

Connor lifted his head and, poised above her, he blocked her view of the ceiling and forced her to meet his gaze. She stared up at him and her heart gave a slow jolt that shuddered through her body like ripples on the surface of a pond.

Oh, boy.

"Damn, Emma..." His voice trailed off as he brushed a stray lock of blond hair off her forehead.

His features were stamped with an expression of stunned surprise, and Emma wasn't sure whether to be flattered or insulted. And did it really matter?

"That was—" he stopped and grinned "—amazing."

Oh, yeah, it had been, she thought, feeling the power of his smile slam into her. Amazing, earth-shattering, completely befuddling. Emma squelched a groan that was building deep inside her. She didn't want to put hearts and flowers on this night. That wasn't what this had been about.

She wasn't in love with Connor Reilly.

Didn't *want* to be in love with him.

That wasn't in the plan.

She'd set out to make him lose that bet for being so damn insulting, and she'd succeeded. That's all she had to remember here. That her scheme had worked. She'd brought him to his knees—figuratively speaking—and okay, she thought as she remembered him kneeling between her thighs, literally, too. But that was it. It was over.

And she'd be doing herself a huge favor to keep that in mind.

In an attempt to do just that, she forced a smile she didn't really feel and gave his back a friendly slap. "So, guess I'm not just 'one of the guys' after all, am I?"

He frowned down at her and levered himself up onto his elbows, taking most of his weight off her. Emma would rather have curled up and died than admit she missed the feel of his body pressed onto hers.

"One of the guys?" he echoed.

"You remember," she prodded, reminding herself as well as him. "A week or so ago we were talking about the bet and you said I was 'safe to hang out with'?"

"I did?" The frown on his face deepened and he shifted position slightly.

Emma swallowed another groan that erupted when his body, still locked within hers, stirred into life again.

Keep your mind on the conversation at hand, she warned herself. Keep remembering that, until about twenty minutes ago he hadn't really considered you a woman. "Yeah. You did."

He moved one hand to fiddle with the rubber band at the end of her braid. But she refused to be distracted.

"And," Emma said, her breath hitching as his hips rocked against her, "you actually said, 'you're not a woman, Em…you're a *mechanic.'*"

"Huh."

She reminded him of the most humiliating moment of her life and all he had to say was "*huh?*"

His fingers undid her long, blond braid, and a part

of her brain focused on the soft tug as he freed her hair. But mostly she kept reminding herself that she'd won a victory here. A victory for every woman—heck, every *girl*—who was just a little bit different from the rest of the crowd.

"Don't you remember?" she demanded.

"Not really."

"But you said it," Emma insisted, determined now to ignore the stirring of her body as he shifted position over her again.

"If you say so."

"If *I* say so?" She blinked up at him and paid no attention when he pulled her now-loosened hair across her shoulders and dipped his head to bury his face in the thick mass. "Seriously, you don't remember saying that?"

"Vaguely," he said, and moved again, this time trailing warm, damp kisses along the line of her throat.

"Vaguely?"

"Do you really want to talk right now?" he mumbled, his words muffled against her neck.

No, she didn't want to talk. Didn't want to think. Didn't want to do anything except revel in the soft slide of his tongue along the length of her throat. She arched into him, despite her best efforts, and tilted her head to one side, giving him easier access. He smiled against her skin.

A sigh of a breeze drifted through the partially opened window and carried the scent of summer roses with it. The night was soft, quiet, as if she and Connor were the only two people in the world. It was as if they were wrapped together in a cocoon of sensation.

He was distracting her.

And doing a damn fine job of it, too. But they were getting off subject. She was trying to tell him that she'd tricked him into losing his precious bet, and he was too busy stirring her body up again to listen.

Determined now, Emma put both hands on his shoulders and shoved. He lifted his head and looked down at her, one corner of his mouth tugging into a half smile that did some incredible things to her insides. But Emma fought that reaction down and met his gaze steadily.

"What's wrong now?" he asked, and his deep voice rolled through the room like summer thunder.

"Nothing's *wrong*," she said tightly. "It's just—" How was she supposed to have a conversation with a man whose body was even now swelling to fill hers again? Concentrate, she thought. It was the only way. "Connor, I'm trying to tell you that I got you into bed deliberately. I *tricked* you."

"Yeah?" He smiled again and gave her a wink. "Then, thanks." Dipping his head, he took one of her nipples into his mouth and suckled it briefly.

She hissed in a breath as white-hot sensation shot through her bloodstream like skyrockets. Her vision blurred, her breath went soft and hazy, and she had to fight to come up for air again. When she did, she gave his broad, muscled shoulders another shove for good measure. "You're not listening to me."

"I'd rather kiss you," he admitted as he reluctantly lifted his head to stare down at her. "I'd rather taste you again. Why the sudden need for chitchat?"

His eyes seemed to glisten with a new urgency. And as he spoke, Emma felt her own heartbeat quicken in anticipation. But before they indulged themselves again, there were a few things that had to be said.

"Don't you get it, Connor?" she said, capturing his face between her palms. "I deliberately trapped you. Set you up, then knocked you down."

A short, sharp laugh shot from his throat. "Am I supposed to be sorry?"

"You lost the bet," she reminded him.

He frowned. "Oh, yeah…"

"I *wanted* you to lose the bet."

"Why?"

"To teach you a lesson," she said, and slid her hands from his cheeks, to his neck, to his shoulders, skimming over the hard, warm muscles and loving the feel of his skin beneath her palms. "To show you that just because I'm a mechanic doesn't make me less of a female."

He stared at her for a long moment, then slowly, a deep throated chuckle rumbled from his throat. "Well, you sure as hell proved your point, Em. I'm convinced," he said, still smiling as he dipped his head for a quick, hard kiss.

"Aren't you mad?"

"Should I be?" In one smooth move, he flipped onto his back, bringing her with him as he rolled over the mattress.

"You lost the bet."

"Seems like."

"I tricked you."

"Did an excellent job of it, too."

Straddling him now, Emma felt the thick, solid length of him pulsing within her. Unconsciously she rocked her hips and smiled when he hissed in air through clenched teeth. Watching him, she looked for signs of anger in his expression, but there was nothing there. He wasn't angry about losing the bet. Wasn't mad about being tricked.

What he *was,* was insatiable.

Thank heaven.

"But the money, Connor," she persisted. "It was down to just you and Aidan."

He reached up and covered her breasts with his hands, squeezing, rubbing, tweaking at her sensitized nipples until Emma moaned and let her head fall back.

"You think I give a damn about the bet now?"

Breathing hard, she lifted her head again and looked at him. "You don't?"

Shaking his head, he said, "I never would've made it, Em." He grinned. "Not hanging around you, anyway. And hell, it's hard to mind losing a bet when losing's this much fun."

She shrugged, and her hair slid over her skin like golden silk. "There is that."

He lifted his hips and Emma gasped as she rose up high, like a bronc rider astride a wild mustang. Except this felt *much* better. Her brain went on automatic pilot, and every inch of her body was already alert and screaming for attention.

Still, though, she couldn't leave things as they were. She had to know one more thing.

"Connor, where do we go from here?"

He stopped moving beneath her and locked his gaze with hers. His hands dropped to her hips and held her tightly, every finger pressing into her skin as if somehow branding her—however temporarily.

"Why do we have to go anywhere?" His voice was low, soft and she had to strain to hear him over the thundering crash of her own heartbeat. "Why does this have to be more than one night of amazing sex?"

If there was a part of her that was disappointed in his reaction, she buried it. After all, she hadn't been looking for a commitment. She hadn't been looking for *love*. She'd already tried love once and that had turned into a disaster of near epic proportions.

She'd never planned on having more than this one night with him. Her imagination hadn't taken her quite so far as that.

So Emma told herself to be grateful that Connor was who he was. A friend. A friend who happened to have the ability to turn her blood into steam…but a friend, first and foremost.

"It doesn't," she said, and deliberately twisted her hips, grinding her center against him, taking his body deeper, higher within her own. Her whole system shivered and she shook with the force of it. When she could speak again, she said, "One night, right? We have this one night and then go back to the way we were?"

He sucked in a gulp of air, his eyes fired in the shadows and then he nodded. "We stay friends."

"Friends," she agreed, and went up on her knees, feeling his body slide free of hers before she sank on him again, enjoying the rich feel of his hard length invading her heat.

Connor watched her as she moved over him and lost himself in the glory of the moment. How the hell could he think about where they went from here? How could he possibly worry about losing that stupid bet when Emma was riding him in slow, sensuous movements?

Her hair, loose and free, streamed over her shoulders and across her breasts, her rigid nipples peeking through the golden strands to tempt him. She was more beautiful than he could have imagined. She was more *everything* than he had ever guessed.

Her body was hot and tight, surrounding his with a velvety grip that drove him to the edge of oblivion with every move she made. He bit back a groan and choked off the urge to surrender to the climax crashing within. He wanted this to last. Wanted to stretch out their time together, to make the most of every second he spent here in her room.

Tomorrow he'd confess to his brothers that he'd lost the bet. Tomorrow things would go back to the way they'd always been between him and Emma. They'd be friends, because her friendship was something he didn't want to lose. But tonight they were different. Tonight they were lovers, and he for damn sure meant to enjoy every minute of it.

She arched her back and moaned, a soft sigh of sound that shook him down to his bones. He tightened his grip on her hips and increased the rhythm sparking between them. Over and over again, she pulled free of his body only to capture him again with a nearly hypnotic effect.

Moonlight danced on her naked flesh and she let her head fall back again as she rode him. He felt his own release building and knew he wouldn't be able to hold out much longer. His breath staggered from heaving lungs. His brain was short-circuiting. His body felt electrified—surging with a power he'd never known before.

And Connor knew he wanted to take Emma with him when his body exploded. Dropping one hand to the spot where their bodies joined, he stroked her damp heat. Rubbed the one spot on her body that he knew would send her tumbling wildly over the edge.

"Connor…" She said his name on a throaty groan of need and passion.

He continued to stroke her, watching as her features shifted with the churning emotions slashing at her. She moved faster, rocking her hips with him in a timeless rhythm that swept both of them up in a frantic rush toward completion.

And when her body splintered, he caught her and held on as he let himself follow after.

"I'm out." Connor slid onto the bench seat at the Lighthouse Diner and shrugged when all three of his brothers just stared at him.

He hadn't been looking forward to this. Facing his brothers and admitting that he hadn't been able to last the full three months of their bet was humiliating. Even though, he thought, with a small inner smile, losing the bet had been the best time of his life.

When that thought crowded into his brain, Connor frowned and pushed it back out.

"You're kidding, right?" Aidan, sitting right beside him asked, with an elbow jab to his ribs.

"Ow." Connor looked from Aidan to Brian and finally to Liam. "Nope. Not kidding. I'm out. Fit me for the coconut bra."

"Woo-hoo!" Aidan hooted gleefully and signaled the waitress to bring another round of beers to the table. Shifting his gaze back to his brothers, he grinned and said, "This round's on me. In celebration."

"Hey," Connor reminded him, "just because I lost, doesn't mean *you* won."

"He's right," Brian chimed in. "We're out of the running, but you signed on for three whole months of no sex. You've still got another six weeks to go, man."

"Piece o' cake," Aidan said, reaching for the bowl of tortilla chips in the center of the table. "I'll show you guys how it's done."

"Right," Liam said, sarcasm dripping from his tone. "You're in complete control."

"Totally," Aidan boasted.

"Liar," Brian said, taking a sip of his beer.

"Hey," Aidan took exception. "Shouldn't you guys be ragging on Connor? *He's* the one who lost the bet, y'know."

"Thanks," Connor said, and absently smiled at the waitress as she brought them each a tall, frosty glass of beer. He took a long drink and let the icy, foamy drink slide through him, cooling him off.

It had been a long, hot day.

And every time his thoughts had returned to the night before, spent in Emma's arms, the temperature had only climbed.

"So," Liam asked in the sudden silence, "do we get to know who?"

Connor glanced up from his drink and found all three of his brothers watching him. Well, hell. Only a few weeks ago he'd sat in this very booth and laughed his tail off as Brian had confessed to dropping out of the bet. Funny, it had seemed hilarious at the time. Now...not so much.

"Emma," he said tightly.

"The mechanic?" Aidan's voice hitched in surprise.

A flicker of something hot and dangerous sparked into life inside Connor. He swiveled his head to stare at the brother sitting alongside him through narrowed eyes. "You've got a problem with Emma?" he asked tightly. "Something wrong with her?"

Aidan's eyes widened as he lifted both hands in mock surrender and shook his head. "Nope, not a thing. I was just surprised is all. Chill out, man."

"A little touchy aren't you?" Brian asked.

"And your point is…" Connor demanded, sparing the man opposite him a quelling look.

"No point, just an observation."

"Emma's a sweetheart," Liam's quiet voice spoke up, and the three men looked at him. Liam shrugged. "Hey, she fixes my car and I think she's cute."

Brian lifted one eyebrow and chuckled. "You *are* a priest, remember?"

"I'm a priest, I'm not dead." Liam shook his head and then turned to focus on Connor. "So you and Emma are together now?"

Panic reared up inside Connor. He leaned back into the booth, as if to distance himself as much as possible from that question. "Together? No. We're not a couple or anything. We're just friends."

"*Naked* friends," Aidan said on a laugh.

"Best kind." Brian lifted his beer in salute.

"Friendships change," Liam mused quietly.

Connor slanted him a wary glance. It didn't help at all that he himself had been thinking the same damn thing all day. His friendship with Emma was important to him. They got along great, shared a love of cars and old movies and thunderstorms. They could talk about anything, and he trusted her as he trusted few other people in his life.

Connor's friends were important to him.

And Emma was a *friend*.

"Whatever you're thinking," he grumbled, "just forget about it. I'm not looking to get married like poor ol' Bri here."

"Hey," Brian objected. "It's not like I'm caught in a trap trying to chew my leg off to get free, you know."

"I didn't say that," Connor snapped. "I just said that it wasn't for me." Never had been, never would be. He didn't want to be married. Didn't want to have anyone depending on him. Didn't want to change who he was to accommodate someone else.

He liked his life just the way it was. Hot and cold running women streaming in and out of his life in a constantly shifting smorgasbord of femininity.

Emma was a great woman—but she wasn't going to be the *only* woman.

That's not what he was looking for.

Connor waved Brian off and concentrated on his brother the priest. "Don't start thinking that just because Emma and I heated up the sheets that it's going to be anything more than that, Liam."

"I don't know, bro," Aidan pointed out, helping himself to another chip, "you *did* give up a shot at ten thousand bucks for her."

Connor scraped one hand across his face and wished to hell he'd been born an only child. "It was just sex."

"You sure?" Liam asked quietly.

"Of course I'm sure." Connor picked up his beer and took a long swallow. As the conversation between his brothers went on without him, he fought down the stray thought niggling in the back of his mind.

The one that claimed he wasn't as sure as he was pretending to be.

Nine

"Mrs. Harrison," Emma said as she stalked around the confines of her small office, tethered by the coiled phone cord. "If you'd just reconsider, I could make you a very good offer for the car."

The woman on the other end of the phone line sighed, then said, in a soft, Southern drawl, "I know it seems silly to you, Emma dear, but I just can't bear to part with Sonny's car. He loved it so."

"But that's my point, Mrs. Harrison," Emma plunked down on the one uncluttered corner of her desk and stared off through the front windows at Main Street. "If Sonny loved the car so much, wouldn't he want to see it restored to all its former glory?"

"Well…"

While the older woman thought about that, Emma stared out at Baywater. Summer traffic was still as thick as the humid air. Even at sunset, tourists crowded the sidewalks and cars backed up at the streetlights. Horns blasted, people shouted, and kids, apparently immune to the heat, dashed along sidewalks on skateboards, dogs nipping and yelping at their sides.

A typical, ordinary, summer evening.

So why did everything feel so different?

Because *she* was different.

Emma sighed and told herself to get over it. To get past it. But how could she? For hours the night before, she and Connor had made love. It was as if neither of them could bear to stop touching the other. He'd stayed with her until sunrise, leaving only when the first streaks of crimson splashed the horizon.

She'd walked him to the door and watched him stride to his car and then drive away and she hadn't once given in to the urge to call him back.

But it had been there.

A crouched, needy thing deep inside her. She'd fought it back and made herself remember the promise they'd made to each other after their first bout of soul-shattering sex.

Friends.

They'd vowed to remain friends and she wanted that. Absolutely. But she also wanted him in her bed. And just how was she supposed to get past that?

Oh, things were fast getting more complicated instead of easier.

"I don't know, dear," Mrs. Harrison said, dragging Emma gratefully away from her thoughts. "It just doesn't seem quite right to me somehow."

Emma sighed, but she wasn't really surprised. She spoke to Mrs. Harrison at least once a month, hoping to get the woman to part with that old Corvette. Sonny Harrison had been dead for forty years, but his mother still wasn't ready to let his car—all she had left of him—go. So Emma would give up today and try again in a month.

"I understand," she said, and a part of her really did. It had to be hard, losing the one last link to a past that felt more real than the present. It was pretty much how she'd felt the day she'd packed up all of her girly clothes after her ex-fiancé, Tony Demarco, had shown his true colors. But she'd gotten over the death of her dreams, and one of these days maybe Mrs. Harrison would, too. "I hope you don't mind if I keep trying to convince you, though."

"Not at all, honey. You call again real soon."

When they hung up, Emma smiled. She had a feeling that the elderly woman would never sell her that car—mainly because then she'd lose the fun of Emma's phone calls and visits.

The phone rang again almost instantly, and for one brief shining moment, Emma thought that maybe Mrs. Harrison had changed her mind. "Hello? Jacobsen's Garage."

"You haven't called me with an update."

"Mary Alice?"

"Who else?"

Emma smiled, walked around the edge of her desk and sat down in her chair. Kicking her feet up, she crossed her legs at the ankle on top of a stack of papers at the edge of the desk and said, "I've been meaning to call you."

"Uh-huh," her friend said, "and I've been meaning to go on a diet."

"Another one?" Emma grinned.

"Let's not get off track here," Mary Alice said quickly. "This isn't about *me.* I want details. When last I heard, Mr. Gorgeous Reilly was walking up to your office looking like dessert."

"Oh, wow…"

"I'm guessing that this is going to be a long story?"

"You have no idea." She'd meant to call Mary Alice. She really had. But she'd gotten so involved with her own plans and preparations for snapping a trap shut on Connor, that Emma'd completely forgotten about everything but the task at hand.

And after the night before, she thought, her insides curdling into a warm puddle of something sticky, she was lucky she could think at all.

"So talk."

"Where do you want me to start?" Emma asked, "With the first time or the last time?"

Mary Alice sucked in a breath that was audible

even from three thousand miles away. "How many in between?"

"Three." Connor, Emma had learned during the long night, was a pretty amazing man. In stamina alone, the Marines were lucky to have him.

And so was she.

Whoops. A minor mental slip there.

She didn't actually *have* him, now did she?

"Oh, boy." A heavy sigh drifted through the phone line. "Hold on a sec."

A lot more than one second ticked past before Mary Alice spoke again. "Okay," she said. "I'm back. I needed a glass of wine for this. Start talking and re-member to linger over the details."

Emma laughed and silently thanked her friend for calling when she most needed her. "God I love you."

"Ditto. Now spill your guts."

Connor'd had every intention of staying away.

He'd reassured himself all day long that there'd be no problem in keeping his distance. It was for the best, anyway. For both of them. Last night had been amazing, but it was one night out of their lives.

Emma was his friend. That she was also the woman who'd nearly set his hair on fire the night be-fore, wasn't important. The friendship *was*. So with that thought firmly in mind, he'd made a solemn vow to himself that he'd steer clear of her for at least the next few days.

Give them both a little breathing room.

Make the memory of last night a little dimmer before they spent time together again.

After dinner with his brothers, he'd even driven halfway home before he'd found himself turning around and heading back to Emma's house. The disappointment he'd felt at seeing the house dark and empty wasn't something he wanted to think about. And what he should have done was take her absence as a sign from above. Someone up there was looking out for him. Steering him away from Emma even when he was trying to hunt her down.

Instead though, he'd driven to the garage.

Over the past two years, there had been plenty of times when he'd worked late with her, helping her with a stubborn oil change or just sitting in the office talking. In fact, he hadn't really noticed—until he started trying to stay away from her—just how much time he actually spent with Emma.

Somehow or other, when he wasn't looking, she'd become an integral part of his day. She was usually the one he complained to about whichever new recruit was giving him fits. She was the one he laughed with over the stories Aidan told. She was the one who listened to him grouse about his dates, his job, his life.

Emma was more than a friend.

She was his *best* friend.

"And now you know what she looks like naked." He groaned tightly and told himself to shut that thought off fast. No way could he concentrate on driving if his brain was filled with images of Emma's smooth skin in the moonlight.

Beside him at the stoplight, a carload of teenagers were whooping and hollering. The girls looked shiny bright and the boys were busy trying to be cool. Music blasted through their open windows and into Connor's, shattering his thoughts. He smiled to himself as the light changed and the car sped off with a squeal of rubber on asphalt. He almost envied them.

Summer nights were made for long drives and laughter. For stolen kisses and slow walks. For sighs and whispers and the promise of more.

And damn it, he *wanted* more.

More of Emma.

"You're in bad shape," he muttered grimly as he steered the car toward the garage. His fingers clenched the steering wheel until his knuckles were white. His stomach jumped and his brain was shouting at him to stay the hell away from Emma.

But he wasn't listening.

He couldn't.

Besides, he thought, staying away from her was probably not the answer. *Not* seeing her only made him think about her more. Maybe *seeing* her would help him keep this whole business in perspective.

That thought made him feel a little better about the whole situation. Slapping the steering wheel with the flat of his hand, he nodded and said, "Exactly. She's your friend. So going to see her is just proving to both of you that you can deal."

If a small voice in the back of his mind whispered that he was just making excuses…he ignored it.

He pulled into the parking lot in front of Jacobsen's Garage and noticed that the office was dark but that lights were on in the garage bay. The oversize garage door was closed, but the half-moon-shaped windows above the door shone with soft lamplight.

Turning the engine off, he set the brake, clenched his jaw and realized that for the first time in his life, he felt like retreating.

That thought alone was enough to get him out of the car and moving toward the shop. The hot summer night closed in around him as he stalked across the parking lot like a man on a mission.

Emma'd always liked working late. She liked being here alone. Having time to think, she called it, and Connor wondered what she was thinking about tonight.

Opening the office door, which she should have had locked, damn it, Connor scowled and closed it behind him, turning the lock for good measure. What the hell was she thinking, working late and leaving the door open for just anybody to stroll inside? His stomach fisted as the thought of "what might have beens" rushed through his brain.

Idiotic, he knew. Baywater was a safe, tiny community and no doubt there was nothing to worry about. But he suddenly didn't like the idea of Emma working here late at night, all alone. He suddenly didn't like the idea of her *being* alone. And what the hell did *that* mean? It hadn't bothered him last week or last month or last year. Oh, man—

Shaking his head, Connor stepped into the air-conditioned office and headed for the connecting door to the garage. A wave of hot, steamy air rushed at him. The garage was not air-conditioned, since it would have been impractical, with the door wide-open all day. There were fans whirring in every corner, but they didn't do much to reduce the ovenlike effect.

Connor didn't care, though. He stepped into the heat and closed the door to the office behind him. He heard the music first, and smiled in spite of the thoughts churning in his mind. Classic rock and roll, and if he knew Emma, she was singing along, safe in the knowledge that there was no one to hear her.

He paused in the shadows, giving himself time to simply admire the view.

She hadn't heard him come in—not surprising since the radio volume was set at just under ear shattering. She wore coverall—standard, gray coverall that before wouldn't have given him a moment's pause. Today, though, he wasn't fooled. Today he knew what kind of weapons she was hiding beneath the too-baggy work uniform. And his body went hard just thinking about it.

She did a quick little sidestep, her hips swaying to the rhythm pounding out around her and her blond ponytail swung with her movements. She kept time with the rhythm even as her small, capable hands worked on the carburetor lying in pieces on the workbench.

He grinned when she picked up a wrench and, holding it as if it were a microphone, sang into it along with the voice pouring from the radio. Even though she had more enthusiasm than talent, Emma poured her heart into the song of love and loss, and something inside Connor twisted as he watched her.

Beautiful.

Even in the ugly gray coverall, she was beautiful.

Sure, he thought. *Friends*. No problem here.

Scraping one hand across his face, Connor breathed deeply, hoping to ease the instinct clamoring within. The one that was prompting him to march across the garage, grab her up and bury himself inside her as fast as he could. Every cell in his body was on high alert.

Coming here had been a lousy idea.

But he couldn't have left if it had meant his life.

When she lifted both arms high and did a spin to coincide with the end of the song, she spotted him. Stopping dead, she squeaked out a half-choked-off scream and slapped one hand to her chest.

"Connor!" She took a deep, steadying breath, then blew it out in an exasperated rush. Reaching across the workbench, she hit the volume button on the radio and cranked it down to background level. "Geez, you scared me half to death. Do you have to be all stealthy?"

Stealthy? Hell, he was surprised she hadn't heard

his heart pounding over the blast of the radio. "Sorry. Didn't mean to surprise you."

"Next time say something."

"Like?"

"Like, hello?" Still agitated, she dropped the wrench onto the work surface, then rubbed her palms together. "How tough is that?"

Right now, he thought, pretty damn hard. Hard to talk at all past the knot of need lodged in his throat. But he forced a smile and said, "Fine. Hello, Emma."

She smiled, tipped her head to one side and studied him. "Something wrong?"

Hell, yes. He'd been thinking all day about getting his best friend naked again. That was wrong in so many ways.

But all he said was, "No."

"Didn't think I'd be seeing you today."

She wiped her hands on a clean rag, then tossed it onto the bench behind her. From the radio came a soft rush of guitars and drums, pulsing out around them.

"Yeah, me, neither."

She shoved her hands into the pockets of the coveralls. "So why are you here?"

Good question.

"Because we said we'd stay friends, Em. Because if I stay away from you because of last night, we'd lose that."

"True."

"And," he admitted, "I wanted to prove to myself

that I could come here—see you—and not want to take you to bed again."

She frowned at him and he could have sworn the temperature in the garage dropped a few degrees. "Gee, that just makes me feel all warm and fuzzy."

"That probably came out wrong," he muttered.

"You think?"

"Damn it, Emma." He started across the garage toward her. He closed the distance between them with four long strides that took him around the front end of the sleek little convertible waiting to be serviced. When he was right on top of her, he stared down into her eyes. "This is new territory for me, ya know? I generally don't spend a lot of time thinking about getting my friends naked."

She grinned, and he felt the power of that smile reach in and grab his throat.

"Good to know."

"The point is," he said, letting his gaze slide across her features, from her tiny, straight nose to the curve of her mouth and back up to the depths of her eyes. He inhaled and blew the air out again in a rush. "The point is, I *am* thinking about getting you naked. And I'm thinking about it *way* too much."

She shivered and he fisted his hands at his sides to keep from reaching for her. If he touched her now, that would be it. No going back, no reining in, no turning away.

"So stop," she said, lifting her chin.

"Easier said than done."

"Yeah," she said on a sigh, "I know."

The tight, cold fist around his lungs eased back a little. "You, too?"

"Only every other minute or so." She backed up from him, as if just talking about this was getting a little too difficult. "But it'll pass. Right?"

"Shown no signs so far." He kept pace with her, taking one step forward for each of her backward steps. "Only been a day."

"A *whole* day," he said.

"Right." She glanced around the shop as if looking for the nearest exit, then caught herself and stopped at the front end of the red sports car. "Twenty-four whole hours."

He nodded and moved in closer. "Thousands of minutes."

"Uh-huh." She licked her lips and stared up at him. "We're gonna do it again, aren't we?"

"Oh, yeah." He wanted her with everything in him. He'd never known such all-consuming hunger before, and a part of him wondered if it would always be this way. Was there no going back to the way things had been between him and Emma? Did he really *want* to go back?

Hell, no.

But at the same time Connor was forced to admit that if they couldn't go back, they'd have to go forward. There was no standing still.

Though maybe there *could* be. Just for tonight. Tomorrow was soon enough to think about the repercussions. Tonight all he wanted to do was recapture those hours he'd had with her the night before. Wanted to lose himself in the taste of her, surround himself with her heat and watch as her eyes glazed over with pleasure.

Everything else could just wait.

He bent, grabbed her up and kissed her, long and hard and deep. His tongue swept into her warmth and claimed another piece of her soul. Her breath mingled with his. Her tongue teased his. Her heartbeat shuddered in time with his own and when she arched into him, Connor's mind emptied of everything but the raging need pounding inside him.

Desperate to touch her, to have her, he reached for the zipper at the front of her coveralls and whispered, "I've gotta know what you're wearing under this thing."

Her eyes went wide. She grabbed his hands and held them still.

"What?" He met her gaze and saw embarrassment dart across the surface of her eyes. "What's wrong?"

"Nothing," she hedged, and lowered her gaze, still keeping a tight grip on his hands. "It's just…"

"Tell me."

She took a deep breath and forced herself to look up at him. "Fine. When I shut the garage bay doors, it was really hot in here and—well, I was all alone and—you know," she pointed out, "the shop was closed…"

"Will you just spit it out?"

Emma let go of his hands and huffed out a breath. "Fine. It's hot in here, so…"

"So?" Impatience clawed at him.

"So, I'm not wearing *anything* under it."

Connor's blood rushed through his veins. His body went hard and tight and eager. His breath staggered in his lungs. Looking down into her flushed face, he smiled and took hold of the zipper again. Giving it a tug, he stared at her lusciously delectable, completely naked body beneath those ugly gray coveralls and smiled as he whispered, "It's Christmas."

Emma laughed, but the sound ended abruptly as his hands covered her breasts. Thumbs and forefingers squeezed, tweaked and pulled at her nipples. She gasped and felt the drawing sensation right down to the soles of her feet.

From the corners of the room, fans pushed hot air at them, and still Emma felt as though she couldn't catch her breath. His hands. She'd been daydreaming about his hands all day and now suddenly, they were here, on her, driving her up that wild, slippery slope that led to an amazing reward.

"Gotta have you, Em," he murmured thickly as he leaned over her, pushing her back, back, until she lay atop the hood of the red convertible.

"Need you, Connor. Right now. Oh, please," she whispered as his mouth closed over one of her nipples, *"right now."*

His right hand dipped down her body, sliding

across her abdomen, past the nest of tight curls at her center until he touched the heart of her. Light, skimming strokes pushed her higher, faster, than she'd ever been before. And still it wasn't enough.

"Now, Connor," she begged and even hearing the pleading in her own voice couldn't stop her from begging again. "I want you inside me. Now."

"Right now, baby." He lifted his head, pulled his hand free of her heat and reached for the shoulders of her coveralls. In one slick move, he'd scooped the fabric off her shoulders, down the length of her body and off. Then he was laying her back against the hood of the car and all she could think was, the metal still felt cool against her skin. Despite the hot air and the heat he created within her, the metal was cool and slick beneath her body.

Emma opened her eyes and watched him as he quickly undid his jeans and stepped out of them. Pulling his shirt off, he came to her, strong, muscular, tanned and ready. Emma's hands itched to touch him, to scrape her fingernails down his back and over the curve of his behind. She wanted to feel him atop her. Feel him fill her until all the lonely, empty spaces inside were quiet.

She licked her lips as if awaiting a treat, and he caught the motion and gave her a slow smile. Grabbing a condom from his wallet, he tore the paper open, smoothed the fragile rubber over himself and came to her. She lifted her legs, parting them wide in welcome and held her breath as he entered her on a sigh.

The radio played, a fast, pulsing tune that gave them the rhythm they both needed. Fast, hard, hungry. Again and again, they parted and rejoined as he plunged within her and each time was harder, stronger, more relentless than the last.

And as the end crashed down around them, Connor looked down into her eyes, and Emma lost herself in his dark-blue gaze. She cried out his name as the heat swallowed them and bound them even more tightly together.

Ten

"Okay," Emma said as soon as she was able to talk without her voice quavering, "this was a mistake."

"Hard to look at it like that when you're in my position," Connor quipped and grinned down at her.

That grin was such a potent weapon. And with his body still pressed to hers, still intimately invading hers, she could hardly argue the point. *However*, one of them had to make a stand—even if she was lying down when she did it.

"Get up, Connor."

"What's your hurry?" He nibbled at her throat, then deliberately ran his tongue across her skin.

Bubbles of fresh anticipation frothed to life inside her. She could almost hear her blood boiling. Every inch of her body felt alert, awake, *alive*—all because of him. How had they managed to know each other for two years and never discover the chemistry that lay sizzling between them? And how could they get back to where they'd been, now that they *had* discovered it?

Emma's stomach jittered at the thought that maybe they wouldn't be able to go back. Maybe by finding something special, they'd lost something equally important. She closed her eyes and bit back a groan. Then, gritting her teeth, she said, "I mean it, Connor," and slapped one hand against his back for emphasis. "Get up."

"Bossy little thing, aren't you?" he asked, lifting his head to look down at her again. A self-satisfied half smile curved his mouth, and it was all she could do to keep from reaching up and defining that curve with her fingertips.

"How come I never noticed that about you before?"

"There are a lot of things you didn't notice."

"Yeah," he wiggled his eyebrows and leered at her. "But I'm catching on quick."

He rocked his hips against her, and her bones melted—along with what little resolve she'd been able to muster. Before she succumbed completely, though, she ordered, "Connor..."

"I'm moving, I'm moving."

He did. Slowly, tantalizingly. As if he were tormenting her for ending this little...*session.*

Emma stifled a groan and bit down on her bottom

lip to keep from asking him to stay. To make love to her again. Oh, she had to be out of her mind. Here she had a gorgeous, talented lover at her disposal and she was telling him thanks but no thanks?

Her brain screamed at her to be rational, and her body was shouting just as loudly to stop thinking and just feel. She wasn't sure which of them was the stronger at the moment, so as soon as she could, Emma slid off the hood of the car and quickly grabbed up her coveralls. With clothing, might come clear thinking. Heaven knew it wasn't there when she was naked.

The fans blew a constant stream of heated air against her sweat-dampened skin, and chills rippled along her spine. She shivered and kept moving.

Stepping into her clothes again, Emma kept her back to Connor until she was dressed, with the zipper pulled up to her throat. Stupid, since he'd already seen her naked, but hey, she needed all the armor she could get at the moment. Shoving the oversize sleeves up to her elbows, she took a deep breath, ignored the hum still reverberating throughout her body and turned around to face him.

He had his jeans on, but he was still bare-chested, and a more tempting sight Emma couldn't imagine. Her mouth watered and she felt her resistance melting like ice in a warm drink. Oh, she'd really opened up a huge can of worms by starting all this. And if she could have figured out how to do it, she would have kicked her own behind.

They'd been happy. Fine. Good friends. Then she'd let herself get all huffy and offended, and now see where they'd landed. Up a creek without even a boat—let alone a paddle. And she had absolutely no idea how to undo it.

Or even if she wanted to.

And that one thought worried her.

Because she was slipping.

She could feel it.

Her heart ached, just looking at him. If the situation were different—if *she* were different, she might have allowed herself a little dreaming. Might have let what she already felt for him blossom. Might have indulged in the hopes and fantasies that she'd once believed in.

But fantasies were fragile, and dreams were tricks your mind played on you. She knew that. She'd learned her lesson the hard way. So she ached at the knowledge that nothing would ever be the same between Connor and her again.

Their easy friendship was gone, burned in a fire she hadn't expected to find.

"Whatever you're thinking," he said softly, "it looks serious."

"What?"

"Should I be worried?" He yanked his dark-red T-shirt over his head and shoved his arms through the sleeves.

"One of us should be," she murmured. Then louder she said, "We can't keep doing this."

He grinned again. "Give me five minutes, I think I could change your mind."

No doubt he could. But that wasn't the point. "Connor, I'm trying to do the right thing, here."

"Well, cut it out." Scowling, he reached over and flipped off the radio. With the music suddenly cut off, the whir of the fans was the only sound as they faced each other.

Emma could have sworn she could actually *see* electricity flashing back and forth between them. Heaven knew she felt the heat. But she closed her heart to it. Sighing, she said, "Last night was a bump in the road."

"More than one," he commented wryly.

She ignored it. "But tonight just proves that this is getting out of hand."

Scowling, he said, "Okay, I admit, things got a little out of hand tonight—"

"Yeah, just a little."

He shook his head and folded his arms over his chest. He braced his long legs in a wide apart, battle stance and Emma wondered idly who he was preparing to fight? Her? Or himself?

"You should know this isn't why I came here tonight."

Of course she knew that. After all, no one would *plan* to have sex on the hood of a car. She sighed again. "I know, it's just—"

"I came to talk since I couldn't find you at home," he continued, cutting her off neatly. "And, hey—" he broke off and glared down at her "—by the way, lock the damn door when you're here alone, Emma."

"Excuse me?"

"The door to the shop. It was unlocked. For God's sake, anybody could have come in."

"Anybody did," she said, stiffening in self-defense.

"Yeah, but you *know* me."

"I used to think so."

"What's *that* supposed to mean?" he demanded.

Temper flared into life inside her, and Emma clung to it desperately. Anger was easier to deal with than whatever it was she was feeling for Connor at the moment. "It means that whether or not I lock my doors is up to *me*."

"Who the hell said it wasn't?" He unfolded his arms and threw his hands high as if trying to catch the threads of the argument that were quickly spiraling out of his control.

"You did," she snapped, folding her own arms across her chest and glaring back at him. This was comfort. This was safety. An argument with Connor she could handle. Tenderness from him left her wary and unsure of herself. "I'm perfectly safe here."

He frowned at her, his dark-blue eyes getting nearly frosty. "Probably," he admitted. "But it's stupid to take chances, Emma."

"I'm not stupid, and I don't need you to tell me what to do."

He gaped at her. "I didn't say you were stupid."

"You did, too, just a minute ago."

"I said it was stupid not to lock the door."

"And since I didn't, I'm stupid."

"What the hell's going on with you, Emma?" His voice growled out with the strength and ferocity of a grizzly bear coming out of winter hibernation, looking for a meal.

She didn't *know.* God help her, she just didn't know. Thoughts, emotions, feelings, splintered inside her and the slippery shards were too fragile…too many to identify. All she knew for sure was that she needed to be alone. She needed to think. Desperately she fought to control the rising sense of panic clawing at her insides. "I don't like being ordered around."

He sucked in a huge gulp of air, swallowed it and paused, as if silently counting to ten. Or twenty. Emma could have told him it wouldn't help. She'd already tried it.

Finally he spoke again, keeping his voice low and even. "I'm not *telling* you what to do. I'm just saying I was worried when I saw you were vulnerable and—"

Oh, she was plenty vulnerable. But not in the way he meant. Everything inside her was a churning, dazzling swirl of need and fury. She wanted him and couldn't have him. Needed him and didn't want to. Loved him and—

Oh, God.

She staggered back a step.

Felt the blood drain from her head until the room tilted ominously.

She loved Connor Reilly.

Air rushed in and out of her lungs in short, sharp gasps. The edges of her vision sparkled with white and blue dots, and she wondered absently if this is what an out-of-body experience felt like. For a second or two she worried that she might faint. Then the thought of waking up and having to explain to Connor just what had prompted the faint quickly slapped her back into shape.

Heat pulsed inside her, then was rapidly replaced by an icy chill that made her shiver reflexively.

Love?

OhGodohGodohGod.

Trouble. Big trouble.

No way out.

She slapped one hand to her forehead and rubbed at the sudden throbbing of a massive headache. But it wasn't going anywhere. Her brain felt as if it were about to explode. Her mouth was dry, it hurt to swallow and still she had to speak. Had to say something to keep him from noticing that she was currently in the middle of a minor nervous breakdown.

She pulled in a shaky breath and blew it out before trying to speak. "I'm not *yours* to worry about Connor."

How did the man go from smoldering lover to scolding big brother in ten seconds flat? And for pity's sake, how could she *love* him for it?

"I-didn't-say-that." Each word was bitten off as if it tasted bitter. "All I said was—"

She held up one hand and tried not to notice that it was shaking. Then, curling her fingers into her palm, she said, "I heard you the first time. But whether or not I lock the door is no concern of yours."

He was right, though, and that only made her madder. She never worked late without locking herself in the garage. Baywater was safe, she knew, but she didn't take foolish chances. And if she *had* locked the stupid door, then Connor couldn't have sneaked up on her, they wouldn't have made love again and *she* wouldn't have had to face the completely startling fact that she'd gone and fallen in love.

"Now I can't worry about you?"

She shot him a hard look, fired by the anger rippling through her at her own stupidity. "Did you worry *before* we went to bed together?"

He started to speak, then closed his mouth again. But then, she didn't need to hear his answer. She already knew what it was.

"No, you didn't," she said for him. Fury pulsed wildly inside her, like a living, breathing creature, completely separate from her. He was just like Tony, she thought frantically. This was déjà vu and she didn't want to go back there. Didn't want to remember the pain, the disappointment, the regret of having loved someone who couldn't or wouldn't understand her.

Like Tony, Connor wasn't seeing the *real* her.

"When we were just friends," she said hotly, "you

assumed I could take care of myself. Now that we've been naked together, apparently I've lost a few brain cells."

"Damn it, Em," he took a step toward her, then stopped dead. "I didn't say that, either."

"You didn't have to," she snapped. "I can see it in your face. God, Connor, it's practically stamped on your forehead."

"What're you talking about?"

"You. Me. *This.*" She waved one hand at the car where they'd just made love and nearly shivered. But she stiffened her spine instead. "I've been down this road before, Connor. Trust me, I'm not going to do it again."

"What's that mean?"

"You're just like Tony."

He threw his hands high. "Who the hell's *Tony?*"

"I was engaged to him three years ago."

He blinked at her. His expression was thunderstruck. He looked like a man who'd just been pummeled with a two by four and wasn't sure whether to stagger or fall down.

"Engaged?" He repeated after a moment or two. "You were *engaged? Why* didn't I know about this?"

"You never asked."

He opened his mouth, then snapped it shut again.

She shook her head and stared up at him, too wound up to be quiet now, even if that might have been the better thing to do. "You're just like him, I swear. He never noticed me until I wore girly clothes.

Just like you, Connor. And when I was just *me,* he wasn't interested. He even wanted me to sell the garage. Become the perfect little wife who baked cookies and drove in car pools. Well, there's nothing wrong with that, but it's not *me.*"

"And I'm like that moron exactly *how?*"

"Oh, please," she said, on a roll now and unwilling to quit. "You never looked twice at me until that night at the bar."

"That doesn't—"

She cut him off, unwilling to listen to lame-ass excuses. "When I'm a woman, you want to protect me. When I'm *me,* that all changes. Well, guess what, Connor? I'm the same person. Whether I'm in a skirt or these coveralls."

"I know that—"

"I don't think you do. I think you're all hot and bothered over the girly Emma. Well, that's not who I am, Connor." She waved a hand at the grease-spattered coveralls. "*This* is me. The real me. And she's not someone you'd go for. Face it."

"So now you read minds?"

She choked out a laugh. "Yours isn't that hard to read."

Darn it, everything was falling apart. Just like she'd known it would. She never should have let this get started. Never should have tried to set him up, because in doing so, she'd knocked the earth out from under her own feet and now she was on shaky ground.

And the fact that a part of her almost wished she

were the girly-girl type—the kind of woman that Connor would want—really irritated her.

"So you've got this all figured out," he said tightly.

"You bet."

"You get engaged to a jerk and then figure every other guy is just like him?"

"Not every guy."

"Just me."

She nodded, not trusting herself to speak.

"The man was an idiot."

"Yeah," Emma said, "but at least he was honest about what he wanted. You're not being honest, Connor. Not with me. Not with yourself."

"That's just perfect," he muttered, shoving both hands along the sides of his head as if trying to keep his skull from exploding.

Well, she knew just how he felt. Funny how the warm, delicious buzz she'd been feeling only a few moments ago had completely faded away. Now all that was left was a sense of loss.

And just a touch of mind-numbing panic.

"You should probably just go, Connor."

"Not till we talk about this."

She laughed and the sound of it was shrill, even to her. "We've been talking, Connor. And we're going in circles. What's left to talk about?"

"Us. What's going on. Where we go from here."

"We did that last night. We decided to remain *friends*—" God, that word sounded empty "—remember?"

"Yeah," he said with a glance at the car's hood, "that seems to be working real well."

"Well it would have if you hadn't come over," she snapped.

"Ah." Connor nodded slowly, his deep-blue eyes hazy with an emotion she couldn't quite read and wasn't sure she wanted to. "So the secret to us handling this is to stay the hell away from each other?"

"Apparently."

"And our friendship?"

Emma looked up at him and felt her defenses crumbling. If he stayed much longer, she just might do something totally idiotic, like throw herself into his arms and say to hell with doing the smart thing. But that wouldn't solve anything. It would only serve to make this harder eventually. Because she knew that Connor wasn't looking for love.

Heck, he never dated the same woman more than three times.

He wasn't a man to build fantasies around, even if she was still into daydreaming. Which she most certainly was *not*. She'd learned her lesson about love. And this time she'd take her lumps in private. Connor would never know that she was hurt. She wouldn't let him close enough to see that he had the power to crush her—whether he wanted it or not.

Tony Demarco's betrayal had hurt her.

When Connor did the same thing, it would kill her.

Nope.

She wouldn't let that happen.

"I'm not going to lose what we have," Connor said, when she didn't answer him. He stepped close enough to drop both hands onto her shoulders and squeeze. "Damn it, Emma, I *like* you. The *real* you. I like spending time with you and I don't want to lose that."

He *liked* her and she was in *love*. Oh, yeah. Fate had a twisted sense of humor.

"We've already lost it, Connor."

His hands tightened on her shoulders. "What's that supposed to mean?"

She swallowed hard, yanked free of his grip and turned her back on him, headed for the office. He caught up with her in a few long strides, grabbed her upper arm and turned her around to face him. His grip on her arm felt strong and warm. And the thought of never feeling his hands on her again made her want to whimper.

But because she was feeling just a little shaky, she straightened her spine, lifted her chin and met his gaze squarely. "You know just what it means. How are we supposed to pretend nothing's changed when everything has changed?"

"There's a way," he said.

"Well, when you find it, you let me know."

Connor's brain scrambled, trying to keep up with Emma. Wasn't easy, either. Not when his blood was still pumping and his body was still hot and eager.

But looking into her eyes now made Connor *want* to say the right thing. Somehow or other, he'd lost control of whatever it was between them. Not that he'd ever really had control.

Damn it, she'd been *engaged*. To some clown who'd hurt her. And now he was hurting her, too. The one thing he hadn't wanted to do, he'd ended up doing, just the same. Really pissed him off. And left him with a helpless feeling that he wasn't used to experiencing.

"I think you should just go, Connor."

Her voice, small and quiet, snapped him out of his thoughts and back to the moment.

Instinctively he reached for her again. She stepped back, avoiding his touch, and he felt the sting of it jab at him. His hand fisted on emptiness and dropped to his side. Something dark and cold settled in his gut, and Connor had the distinct impression that it was there to stay.

"Emma—"

"Just go. Please."

He blinked at her, too surprised to speak. Momentarily. "You're telling me to leave?"

She gave him a sad smile. "I'm *asking* you to leave."

He swallowed hard and battled a growing sense of desperation. In all the time they'd known each other, they'd never been so far apart. And even though she was just an arm's reach away, Connor had the feeling that with every passing second, she drifted even further from him.

She sighed and lifted one hand to rub at her forehead again. Guilt zapped him. Damn it, he hadn't meant to make her feel bad. Hadn't meant to start an argument that had no beginning and no end. Hadn't meant to *hurt* her.

Hadn't even meant to come here tonight.

Just like he didn't want to leave her now. Not when nothing had been settled. Not when she looked so damn...*sad*. But if he stayed, he'd only make this worse. She didn't want him here, fine.

He'd go.

For now.

Nodding, he choked back his own wants and said. "Okay, I'll go."

She gave him a smile that was so small, it was hardly worth the effort. But he appreciated it just the same.

"Thanks."

"This isn't over," he said before he stepped past her and opened the door. He stopped on the flower-bedecked porch and felt the warm summer air wrap itself around him. Looking back over his shoulder at her, he worked up a half-assed smile and said softly, "Please lock the door, Emma."

Eleven

Emma buried herself in work.

For the past three days, she'd done tune-ups and oil changes and rebuilt two carburetors. She gave her mechanics a few days off and handled everything herself to make sure she kept busy. For three days she concentrated solely on the garage, and when she ran out of cars to work on, she replanted the flower beds.

Anything to keep from thinking about Connor.

And still it didn't help.

Mary Alice had sympathized and even offered to send her husband out to beat up Connor. But Emma didn't want him bruised—she wanted him to love her. Which wasn't going to happen.

Standing in the garage bay, she glanced toward where the car they'd made love on had been parked. And though the car was gone now, the memories remained.

Every touch, every sigh, every whisper was as fresh and clear in her mind as if it had just happened. She remembered his smile, the shine in his eyes and the feel of his hands on her skin. Her body ached for him and her heart just plain *ached.*

"Oh, man…" She set the torque wrench down and rubbed her eyes with the tips of her fingers. She hadn't slept more than a few hours in the past three days. Up at dawn, she worked late at the shop, trying to avoid sleep because every time she closed her eyes, Connor appeared in living color.

She'd done this to herself, she knew. She'd walked into this with her eyes wide-open—and her heart undefended. But she hadn't ever considered that it would be in danger. How could she have guessed that the love she used to dream about would be found in the arms of her best friend?

"And the worst part," she said, picking up the wrench again and squeezing it tightly, "is that I can't talk to my *best friend* about any of it. And darn it, Connor, I *miss* you."

The sun was bright, the sky clear and the ocean calm. In short, it was the perfect day for some saltwater fishing. A couple of times a season, Brian borrowed a little sport fisher boat from one of his pilot buddies, and the four Reilly brothers had a long day at sea—away from phones and work. Ordinarily Connor would have enjoyed the day out with his brothers.

Today he was forcing himself just to pay attention. Disgusted, Connor shifted his gaze from the frothing sea to the deck, where his brothers gathered around an open cooler.

"I'm telling you," Aidan said, pausing to take a sip of beer, "the wind was so high, the chopper was rocking back and forth like somebody was trying to shake us out. J.T. had hold of the stick with both hands, fighting to keep us steady. Right under us, the Sunday sailor's clinging to the upended bottom of his boat and he's holding on for dear life."

"Probably glad to see you then, huh?" Brian smiled and snapped his right wrist back, then forward, casting his line out into the ocean. Then he stuck the bottom of his rod into the pole holder on the side of the boat and set the bale on the reel. Leaning back, he watched Aidan and waited for the rest of the story.

"See that's the deal," Aidan went on, looking from one brother to the next with mock outrage. "There I am, jumping out of a chopper into storm surf—the waves were seven, maybe ten feet high—just to save this guy's ungrateful butt and does he thank me? Hell no, he takes a swing at me when I try to get him into the rescue basket."

"What?" Liam sounded incredulous, but Aidan's

story didn't surprise Connor. People always reacted weird in a panic situation. Which is why Marines came in so handy during a disaster. Cool heads.

And God knew Aidan needed a cool head doing his job. Working on the USMC sea rescue team, they were the guys called out to help stranded boaters or pick up pilots after they'd ditched their planes in the sea. The job was hard, dangerous and right up his brother's alley.

Aidan laughed. "No shit. The guy's panicked. Won't let go of the hull of his boat. Water's slapping at him, wind's howling, and he won't let go of the damn boat. Finally, he pries one hand off to take that swing at me, tells me he's afraid of heights and he wants us to send a ship out for him."

"A ship?" Liam asked laughing. "You mean like the one that sunk out from under him?"

"Exactly." Aidan leaned back against the side of the boat and drew both knees up, resting his forearms atop them.

"So how'd you get him in the basket?" Connor asked, drawn into the story in spite of the turmoil racing in his mind.

Aidan laughed. "I climbed into the basket myself and said, 'see ya.' The guy was so stunned that I'd leave him out there, he let go of the hull and jumped at the basket. I got out, got him in and Monk hoisted him up." He shook his head and sighed fondly. "Hell of a ride."

"Yeah, yeah, Mr. Hero," Brian teased and walked toward the hatch leading to the galley below deck.

"Come on, hero. Help me carry up that mountain of sandwiches Tina made for us."

"Tina made food?" Aidan asked, clearly worried. "Is it safe?"

"Hey," Brian complained as he started down the short flight of steps. "She's getting better."

Aidan groaned and muttered, "She couldn't get any worse without killing us."

"Yeah, well," Brian said, chuckling, "Tina's not real fond of you, so maybe you should watch what you eat."

"What d'you mean she's not fond of me?" Aidan's voice was outraged. "I'm the *fun* one!"

But he followed Brian out of the sunshine into the galley, leaving Liam and Connor alone on deck. The screech of the seagulls sounded weird and otherworldly in the silence. Off in the distance a sailboat caught the wind and flew across the ocean's surface, its red sails bellied, as it raced toward the horizon. Overhead, clouds scuttled across a deep-blue sky and briefly blotted out the sun's heat.

Connor sighed and focused his gaze on the distant spot where sky and sea met, blurring the lines of both. In the quiet, the gentle smack of the water against the hull was soothing, but didn't seem to help the thoughts churning in his mind.

He probably shouldn't have gone along with his brothers today. But if he'd tried to get out of it, he'd have had to come up with explanations he wasn't ready to make.

"Want to tell me what's going on?" Liam asked and sat perched on the edge of the boat's stern. He braced his hands on his knees and waited.

Connor flicked him a glance, then shifted his gaze back to the horizon's edge. "Nope."

Liam nodded, reached out and fiddled with the reel on Connor's fishing rod.

"What're you doing?"

"The bale was locked. Anything nibbles at your line, you lose the rod."

Connor sighed. Hell, he hadn't made that mistake since he was a kid and their father had taken them all out on the half-day fishing boats. "Thanks."

"You're welcome."

Liam fell into silence, gaze fixed on Connor until he shifted uneasily under that steady stare. "What're you looking at?"

"A man with a problem."

Major understatement, Connor thought, but kept his mouth shut. He just wasn't the kind of guy who needed to "vent" his feelings. He'd never wanted to hug and cry and learn and grow. He didn't mind listening to his friends' problems when they needed someone to talk to. But his own problems remained just that. His own.

"Knock it off, Liam."

"Hey, just sitting here."

"Well, sit somewhere else."

"It's a small boat," his brother said, shrugging.

"Getting smaller every damn minute," Connor

muttered. He lifted his right foot and braced it on the stern. "Don't you have a rosary to say or something?"

Liam grinned, unoffended. "I'm taking the day off."

"Lucky me."

"True."

"What?"

Liam smiled again. "You are lucky, Connor. You have a career you love, a family willing to put up with you and a beautiful day to do some fishing. So, you want to tell me why you look like a man who just lost his best friend?"

That last, stray statement hit a little close to home, and Connor winced. He stood up, walked to the edge of the boat and braced both hands on the gleaming wood railing. He shot Liam a quick look, then shifted his gaze back to the unending, rolling sea. "I think I *have* lost my best friend."

"Ahh…"

Connor snorted in disgust. "Don't give me Father Liam's patented, generic, sympathetic sigh."

"You want more specific sympathy, tell me what's going on."

"It's Emma."

"I figured that much out already." When Connor looked at him again, Liam shrugged. "Not that hard to work out, Connor. You lost the bet to her and now I'm thinking you lost something else to her as well."

"Like?"

"Your heart?"

Connor jerked up straight, as if he'd been shot. He

viciously rubbed the back of his neck, then pushed that hand into the pocket of his jeans shorts. "Nobody said anything about love."

"Until now," Liam mused.

"You know," Connor pointed out with a sidelong glare, "you can be pretty damn annoying for a brother, *Father.*"

"So I've heard." Liam stood up, too, and faced his younger brother. "Talk to me, Connor."

With a quick glance at the galley steps to make sure Brian and Aidan were still out of earshot, Connor blurted, "I think I'm losing my mind." Then he glared at his older brother. "And it's all your fault. The stupid bet. That's what started all this."

"Ahh…" Liam turned his face away to hide his smile. He wasn't entirely successful.

Connor muttered, "That's great. Laugh at your own brother's misery."

"What's a brother for?"

The boat rocked, sea spray drifted with the breeze and, overhead, seagulls kept watch, looking for supper.

"What's making you miserable?" Liam asked.

"Emma."

"This is getting better."

"Damn it, Liam." Connor stalked to the corner of the boat, then turned around and came back again. "Something's wrong."

Liam frowned. "With Emma? Is she okay?"

"*She's* okay. I'm the one in trouble."

"Oh."

Connor blew out a breath and viciously rubbed his face with both hands before dropping them to his sides. He couldn't believe this was happening. Not to him. Not to the man who'd firmly believed that the reason God had created so many beautiful women was to make love and marriage unnecessary.

All his life, one woman had been pretty much like the next. He'd figured if he lost one, there'd be another one right around the corner. Now? Now the only woman he wanted, didn't want *him*.

It had been three long days since the night he'd left Emma in her shop. Three days and three even-longer nights.

He'd tried everything he knew to keep his mind off her. He'd thought about asking some other woman out, but he just couldn't work up any interest in someone who wasn't Emma. He'd gone to his favorite hangout, but every time he saw that pool table, he saw Emma, stretched across it, her perfect legs tormenting him. Hell, he couldn't even work on his car without thinking about her.

His dreams were full of her image and every waking thought eventually wandered back to her. His chest felt tight every time he realized that she just might not want to see him again. Unconsciously he rubbed his chest with one hand and looked at Liam. "She won't talk to me."

"Does she have a reason?"

"Maybe." Remembering the look on her face when she'd told him about the idiot Tony, Connor winced. He hadn't been looking for a relationship. Hadn't wanted one. Hadn't expected to find one.

He'd lived his life pretty much on his own terms and had never considered changing. So *why,* he wanted to know, did the fact that Emma wouldn't talk to him, hurt him badly enough to make his whole insides ache with it?

Love?

Inwardly he reared back from the thought. Love? *Him?* Panic chewed on him.

He didn't *do* love.

"Hell," Connor muttered, still trying to get over the shock of what he might be feeling, "I really don't know anything anymore."

"Never thought I'd hear *you* say something like that."

"What?" Connor asked wryly, "a priest doesn't believe in miracles?"

"Good point." Liam leaned against the stern, crossed his arms over his chest and stared at him. "What are you going to do about this, Connor?"

He shook his head. "I think I've done enough already." Hell, he'd made his best friend throw him out of her place. He'd fixed it so she wouldn't talk to him. So she couldn't stand the sight of him. Oh, yeah. His work was done.

"So you're gonna quit? Walk away?"

Connor fixed him with an evil look. "You're manipulating me."

"No kidding."

"And who said anything about quitting?"

"Then, what's the plan?"

"If I knew that, would I be standing here being insulted by you?"

Liam grinned. "Okay, but aren't you the guy who said, and I think I'm quoting here, 'the day I need advice on women from a priest is the day they can shave my head and send me to Okinawa'?"

Man, the hits just kept on coming. Blowing out a breath, Connor grumbled, "Fine. I'm an idiot. I need advice."

Liam slapped one hand on his brother's shoulder. "Then here it is. You've already opened your eyes about Emma—maybe it's time you opened your heart."

"That's it?" he asked. "That's all you've got?"

Liam laughed. "Think about it, grasshopper. The answers will come."

"*Before* I'm old and gray?"

Probably." Liam bent and opened the cooler. "Want a beer?"

"Open my heart." Connor snorted and stepped out of his car into the humid night air. Liam's words echoed in his mind as they had all day. He looked at the garage, the light gleaming behind the windows and knew Emma was in there. His stomach fisted like he was about to tiptoe through a minefield.

Love?

Was he in love with Emma? He still didn't know the answer to that one.

He *liked* her. More than he ever had anyone else. It bothered hell out of him that they weren't speaking. That she didn't want to see him. And it really bothered hell out of him that he couldn't think about anything *but* Emma.

"But that's all going to change now," he murmured. It had taken him most of the day to figure out what Liam's advice had meant. Then it had finally hit him.

Stop treating Emma like his *friend* and start treating her like a *woman*.

He smiled to himself as he reached into the car and pulled out the white-tissue-paper-wrapped bouquet of red roses. Their scent was heavy, cloying and just right. Still smiling, he held the flowers in his left hand and grabbed up the gold foil box of expensive chocolates.

Finally. He felt in control.

This he knew.

"*This* I'm good at." Hell, he could write a how-to book for guys on how to smooth talk a woman out of being mad. Flowers, chocolate and a few kisses had bailed him out of trouble with women more times than he could count.

All he had to do was show her that he appreciated her. Show her that what they'd found was more than a one-night—or two-night—stand. Then, once she was softened up, they could find a way to deal with the changes in their relationship.

He straightened up, kicked the car door closed

and headed for the garage. Automatically he tried the doorknob and was pleased to find she'd locked it. "At least she listened about that."

Clutching the box of candy, he rapped the door with his knuckles and waited what felt like forever for her to answer. When she did, she opened the door only a few inches and peered out at him.

Through that narrow opening, he could see only one of her beautiful eyes and the tips of her fingers wrapped around the edge of the door. Partially hidden as if protecting herself, she was wearing the gray coveralls again, and a part of him wondered if she was naked beneath it. But then his body stirred and his mouth went dry, so he attempted to steer his brain away from the roller-coaster ride it was headed for.

"Connor. What're you doing here?"

"I needed to see you, Em," he said, and lifted the roses and candy, just in case she hadn't spotted them. "And I wanted to bring you these."

"Roses."

He smiled and took a step closer. "And candy."

She laughed shortly, a harsh, stiff sound that held no humor, and pushed the door a bit more closed. "You still don't get it."

Confused, he frowned and stared at her. "Get what? I'm just trying to be nice, here. What's going on, Emma?"

She looked at him for a long, silent minute. Connor could have sworn he could actually *hear* his own heartbeat in the deafening quiet. Then at last she opened the door wider and stepped out from behind it. Folding her arms across her chest, she shook her head and stared up at him.

Only then did he see the sheen of emotion glistening in her eyes. And he knew, instinctively, that he'd done something wrong. But for the life of him, he couldn't figure out *what*.

"You brought me roses."

"So?"

"I hate roses."

Something clicked in the back of his brain and he wanted to kick himself. He'd *known* that, damn it. Known that Emma's favorite flowers were carnations. His left hand squeezed the bouquet tightly as if he were hoping he could just make the damn flowers disappear. But he couldn't, so he said, "You're right. I didn't think. I—"

Emma lifted her chin and stared into his eyes. To Connor's horror, those beautiful eyes of hers filled with tears, and he prayed like hell they wouldn't spill over.

"No, you didn't think," she said sadly. "Not about *me*. You bought me your traditional make-up present and figured that would do it."

"Emma..." This wasn't going the way he'd planned. Nothing was working out. He was getting in deeper and felt the quicksand beneath his feet sucking at him.

Desperation clawed at him as he realized that by trying to make things better between them, he'd only made them worse.

"I told you three days ago, Connor," she said, her voice still just a low, disappointed hush, "the foo-foo girl thing is *not* me. The me you were with before doesn't exist. Not really. And the me I really am, you don't want."

His insides trembled, and he scrambled to find the right words to say. But nothing was coming to him. The one time he needed the ability to smooth talk, he was coming up empty.

He'd hurt her again.

And that knowledge delivered a pain to his soul like nothing he'd ever known before.

Suddenly it was more important than it had been to get through to her. He felt as though he was sliding down a rocky cliff, trying to grab something to stop his fall. But there was nothing there. "Emma, I know I did this wrong..." He let his hands, still holding the offerings she hadn't wanted, fall to his sides. "I just wanted us to be friends again."

"I don't want to be your *friend,* Connor."

Her voice was too small, too hushed, too full of pain, and every word she spoke fell like a rock into the bottom of his heart. "Why the hell not?"

"Because I love you, Connor."

"Emma—"

"Don't say anything, okay?" She held one hand up for quiet. "Please." She choked out a laugh that sounded as though it had scraped her throat. "This is my fault and I'll get over it—*trust me.*" She inhaled sharply, deeply, then blew it all out again, lifting one hand to swipe at a single, stray tear glistening on her cheek.

Connor's chest tightened as though he were in a giant vise and some unseen hand was forcing it closed around him. He couldn't breathe. His heart hurt, his hands ached to hold her and he *knew,* without a doubt, that if he tried to reach for her, Emma would turn him away. And he didn't know if he could take that.

So instead he stood there like an idiot while the woman who meant so much to him battled silent tears.

"I can't be your lover anymore, Connor," she said and he swallowed hard at the calm steadiness in her eyes. "It would kill me to have you and yet never have you—you know? And I can't be your friend anymore, either—"

She gulped in air and kept talking, her words rushing from her in a flood of emotion that was thick enough to choke both of them.

"Emma—"

"No. I can't be your buddy and listen to you complain about the women in your life. I don't want to hear about the date of the week or the hot brunette who caught your eye."

Guilt raged inside him and battled with another, stronger feeling that was suddenly so real, so desperate, he trembled with the force of it.

For the first time in his life, Connor felt helpless. And he didn't like it one damn bit.

"Go away, Connor," she said as another tear slid

down her cheek. Stepping back from the doorway, she pushed the door closed. As she did, she said softly, "And do us both a favor, okay? This time when you go? Stay away."

Then the door closed, and Connor, the damn roses in one hand and a box of chocolates in the other, was left standing alone in the growing darkness.

Despite the hot summer night, he felt cold to the bone.

Twelve

The next morning Emma had a pickup truck that needed a new timing belt, an SUV with bad brakes and a headache that wouldn't quit.

Too many tears and not enough sleep.

And the way she was feeling, she didn't see things changing anytime soon.

For most of the night she'd agonized over blurting out her love to Connor. *Why* hadn't she just kept her big mouth shut? Bracing her elbows on her desktop, she cupped her face in her hands and tried desperately to forget the look on his face when she'd said the three little words designed to inspire panic in the hearts of men everywhere.

"Oh, God." She swallowed hard and took a deep

breath. "Emma, you idiot. You never should have said it. Now he *knows*. Now he's probably feeling *sorry* for you. Oh, man…"

She jumped up from the desk, started for the door to the garage bay, then changed her mind and whipped around, walking toward the bank of windows instead. She couldn't go into the garage. She didn't want to talk to the guys. Didn't want them wondering why her eyes were all red. Didn't want anyone else knowing that she'd allowed her heart to be flattened by an emotional sledgehammer.

"Maybe I could sell the shop," she whispered. "Leave town—no, leave the state." Then she caught herself and muttered, "Great. Panic. Good move."

She wasn't going to leave. Wasn't going to hide.

What she *was* going to do, was live her life. Pretend everything was normal and good until eventually, it *would* be. Positive mental attitude. That was the key. She'd just keep her thoughts positive and her tears private.

Everything would work out.

Everything would be good again.

"God, I'm such a liar." Sighing, Emma thought about going home, but that wouldn't solve anything. At least here, in the shop, she had things to concentrate on. She could catch up on paperwork.

Of course, what she wanted to do was lie down somewhere in the dark and go to sleep. Then hopefully, when she woke up again, her heart would be healed and she'd be able to think of Connor without wanting to either hug him or slug him.

But it wouldn't be that easy, she knew.

She was going to have to deal with Connor—at least until he was transferred to another base or deployed overseas or something. She'd have to find a way to learn to live with what had happened between them. Learn to survive with her heart breaking.

Shouldn't take her more than ten or twenty years. "Piece of cake."

A florist's van pulled into the driveway off Main Street and Emma nearly groaned. Oh, God, more flowers. Last night he'd brought the "Gee, I'm sorry, please forgive me" bouquet. What was up today? she wondered. Maybe a little something from the "Too bad you're in love and I'm not" sympathy line?

"This just keeps getting more and more humiliating," she said as she hit the front door and marched across the parking lot to head off the delivery guy.

The sun was hot, the air was stifling, and even the asphalt beneath her feet felt as if it was on fire. All around her, Baywater was going about its business. Behind her in the garage bay, she heard the whir of the air compressor. Kids played, moms shopped, guys cruised in their cool cars, looking for a girl to spend some time with.

And here, in this one little corner of town, Emma

prepared to take a stand. She didn't want Connor's pity bouquets. She didn't want his guilt.

All she wanted now was to speed up time so that this whole mess could be safely in her past.

"Emma Jacobsen?" The delivery driver shouted as he jumped down from the van, holding a long, white box, tied with a bright purple ribbon.

"Yes," she said, remembering that the flowers weren't *this* guy's fault. He was just doing his job. "But if those are for me, you can just take them right back."

"Huh?" He was just a kid. Couldn't have been more than eighteen. His almost-white blond hair stood up in spikes at the top of his head, and he pulled his sunglasses down to peer at her over the rim. "You don't *want* 'em?"

"No, I don't." Be strong, she told herself. Be firm. Be *positive*.

He laughed and shoved his glasses back up his nose. "He *said* you'd say that, but I didn't believe him. I never had anybody say no before."

"Happy to be your first," she snarled, really annoyed that Connor had *predicted* that she wouldn't want his latest attempt at reconciliation. Turning sharply, she headed back for the shop, but the kid's voice stopped her.

"Hey, wait a minute. He told me to tell you something if you said no."

She shouldn't care.

But damn it, she *did*.

"Fine." Emma squared her shoulders and turned back to glare at him. "What?"

"Sheesh, lady, don't shoot the messenger."

"Sorry." She inhaled sharply, then let the air slide from her lungs in an attempt to cool down. "What?"

"The guy said to say—" he screwed up his face trying to remember every word "—are you too chicken to even look?"

"Chicken?" she repeated, amazed. "He actually said *chicken?* What? Is he in fifth grade or something?" She frowned at the kid. "You're sure he said 'chicken'?"

"Yeah." The kid shrugged, still holding the long white box crooked easily in one arm. "So. Are you? Chicken, I mean? No offense."

"None taken," she said, then stomped toward him. "Fine. I'll take them." Even though she *knew* Connor was manipulating her into it. He'd known darn well that she'd respond to a dare. Her heart twisted a bit. How could he know her so well *and* so little?

"Sign here."

She did, then took the box, which was a lot heavier than she expected it to be. She shot the kid a quizzical look.

He shrugged. "You got me, lady. I just deliver 'em." Then with a wave he jumped back into the van and pulled out of the lot.

Emma carried the box back to the office and set it on top of the desk. Her fingers danced across the lid, as she decided whether or not to open it. The ribbon felt cool and slick and the gold seal beneath the ribbon read Scentsabilities, the exclusive flower and gift shop at the outskirts of town.

"Fine," she muttered, glaring at the box as if it were a personal challenge—which, she admitted, it *was*. "I'll look. That doesn't mean I'll *keep*."

She pulled the ribbon off, lifted the lid and then poked through several layers of pale-blue and green tissue paper. She stopped and stared. Her breath caught. Hot tears filled her eyes, and her lower lip trembled as she smiled and reached into the box.

A single white carnation lay atop a collection of brand-new, top-of-the-line, *socket wrenches*.

"Oh, Connor," she said, running her fingertips over the cool, stainless-steel tools. "You wonderful nut."

He'd touched her, damn it. He'd known just how to do it and he'd touched her heart again. Why? Why was he doing it? What did it mean? And how could she keep her heart from jumping to dangerous conclusions?

"What're you doing, Connor? And why're you doing it?" She dropped into her desk chair, holding the single carnation close to her heart—and tried desperately not to read too much into this.

Connor had a plan.

He'd spent most of the night coming up with it, and now all he had to do was wait and see if it would work.

Leaving Emma the night before had been the hardest thing he'd ever done. Forget boot camp. Forget active duty in a war zone. They were nothing.

Walking away from a woman you'd hurt was immeasurably worse. Especially when that woman meant more to you than you'd ever realized. Why is it that you never really knew how important someone was until you'd lost them?

He'd been up all night, figuring out what to do, figuring out just what he *wanted* to do.

At first, he hadn't been able to think beyond the memory of Emma's tear-stained face and heartbroken voice. He'd stalled and relived that moment over and over again before it had dawned on him what the answer was to the situation.

And once he'd faced the truth, the solution was blindingly simple.

The answer was *Emma.*

Always *Emma.*

He couldn't imagine his life without her in it.

For two years they'd laughed together and worked together and talked about anything and everything. She'd been the center of most of his days, and he'd never picked up on it. Then finally, because of that stupid bet... The nights he'd spent with her in his arms were the most perfect he'd ever experienced. He'd found magic with Emma. A magic that had slipped up on him. Magic he'd almost lost through his own stupidity.

Now all he had to do was convince Emma that he was smart enough to recognize the best thing that had ever happened to him.

Bright and early the next morning, Emma stumbled into the dimly lit kitchen, looking for coffee. She pushed her hair out of her eyes and tossed a glance at the still-silent phone.

She'd expected Connor to call her last night.

Naturally, he hadn't.

"The man never does what you expect," she murmured and grabbed a blue ceramic coffee cup out of the cupboard and turned for the coffeepot. She poured herself a cupful, then headed to the back porch to drink it.

She stepped into the early-morning cool and sighed as a soft breeze caressed her bare legs. Soon enough, the summer heat would start simmering Baywater in its own juices. But now, in the minutes before dawn, the air was fresh and sweet and still-damp with dew.

Swinging her long hair back over her shoulders, she sat down on the top step and cradled her cup between her palms. The rich coffee scent stirred her mind and opened her eyes. She took a sip and felt the liquid caffeine hit her system like a blessing.

Thoughts of Connor had again kept her up most of the night, but this time there'd been fewer tears and more questions. The socket wrenches had been a balm to her bruised heart. He'd seen *her*. Paid attention to *her*.

"That's something, isn't it?" she wondered aloud.

"Talking to yourself's a bad sign."

She sucked in a breath and whipped her head around. "Connor? What're you doing here?"

"Wishing I had some of that coffee, for starters," he said, and walked through the garden gate off the driveway. He wore jeans and a dark-blue T-shirt that hugged every rippling muscle of his chest.

She watched him come closer and wished to high heaven she'd taken the time to at least brush her hair. Or get dressed. Good God, she was wearing her summer pj's—a pair of men's boxers and a dark-pink tank top with a teddy bear on the front. Curling up smaller on the step, she flashed Connor a frown. "You shouldn't be here."

"I had to be here," he said and reached out to grab her coffee cup. Taking a sip, he sighed, then smiled and handed it back. "You look beautiful."

"Oh, yeah. Right."

"I'm the one doing the looking, aren't I?"

His gaze drifted over her in a lazy perusal, and Emma felt her blood begin to boil. Her skin felt hot and tingly. Her breath was strangled in her throat, and her heart pounded like a bass drum in a Fourth of July parade.

She scooped her hair back from her face and blew out a fast breath. "Why are you here?"

"To show you something."

"More wrenches?"

He grinned and her heart sped up. "You liked 'em?"

"Yes," she said, lips twitching. "Thank you."

"You're welcome." He held out one hand toward her. "Now, come with me."

"Connor..." She lifted her gaze from his outstretched hand to his eyes. "You don't have to—"

He grabbed her hand and pulled her to her feet with such strength she flew at him, her chest slamming into his. He wrapped one arm around her waist, looked down into her eyes and said, "Just trust me, Em. This one time, will you just trust me?"

Emma would have agreed to anything while his body was pressed to hers. She felt his heartbeat thundering in time with hers, and shockwaves of sensation rocketed through her. Despite how good it felt to be close to him again though, Emma had to at least attempt to protect herself. Pulling back, she looked up at him and nodded. "Okay. Five minutes. Then I'm going inside and you're going home."

He smiled and lifted one hand, running the tips of his fingers along her jawline. "Five minutes, then."

He tightened his grip on her hand and dragged her behind him as he stalked across the yard toward the gate. A wooden lattice arch rose over the garden gate, and deep-blue morning glories spread their beauty and scent along the rungs. He drew her under the arch and through the gate, saying, "Close your eyes."

"Connor..."

"Five minutes, Em."

"Fine." She closed her eyes and stumbled barefoot

behind him. The dewy grass became river stone pavers and then the already-warming asphalt of the driveway. Emma held on to Connor's hand, and in a corner of her mind she told herself to enjoy this. The feel of his hand on hers. The joy of seeing him first thing in the morning. The sparkle in his eyes and the warmth of his smile.

Then he came to a stop and announced, "Open your eyes, Emma."

She did and immediately gasped aloud. Dropping her hold on his hand, she walked toward the banged-up, rusted, completely ruined hulk of a '58 Corvette. Its red paint had oxidized, the chrome bumpers were peeling and crumpled, the leather seats were cracked and springing out in tufts of cotton batting.

And it was the most beautiful thing she'd ever seen.

Whirling around to face him, she said, "How? How did you get Mrs. Harrison to part with Sonny's car?"

"You like it?"

"*Duh*." She glanced over her shoulder at the car, as if to make sure it hadn't disappeared in the last moment or two. "But how? And how'd you get it here?"

He shoved his hands into his jeans pockets. "I went to see her yesterday," he said. "I convinced her that Sonny's car deserved to be everything it was *meant* to be."

"You did?"

"Yep." He smiled proudly and she couldn't blame him for it. "As to getting it here, Aidan has a friend with a tow truck. We unhooked it at the end of your street and pushed it up your driveway so we wouldn't wake you up." He rolled his eyes. "Surprised you didn't wake up, anyway, with all of Aidan's whining about it. Almost gagged him."

"I can't believe you did this," she whispered, looking from him, to the car and back again.

He shrugged and added, "I also promised Mrs. Harrison that once we'd restored the 'Vette to its former glory, that we'd come out and take her for the first ride."

"*We?*"

"Caught that, did you?" he smiled, and took a step toward her.

She took a deep, steadying breath. "Connor, no one's ever done anything like this for me before. I don't even know what to say."

"Good," he said quickly, stepping forward and grabbing her shoulders. "Speechless. That means I've got a shot to have my say."

"Now just a darn—"

"Too late," he said, talking over her, his drill sergeant's voice drowning her out with no problem at all. "My turn, Em." He slid his right hand from her shoulder to her neck and up, to cup her cheek. "I see *you,* Emma. The *real* you."

His thumb traced her cheekbone with long, gentle strokes, and he silently prayed that for once in his life, he'd find the right words. The words he needed to win this woman—because without her his life looked long and lonely.

"Last night, when you closed the door and sent me away," he said, shaking his head slowly, as if unable to bear the remembered pain of being shut out, "I finally *knew*."

"What?"

"I love you, Emma Jacobsen."

"Oh, Connor," she whispered, "no, you don't."

"Yeah. I do."

His voice was steely and every word stood on its own, loud and proud. Her eyes went wide and filled with tears, but she blinked them away, for which he was grateful.

"Hey, surprised me, too," he said, a strained, half laugh choking him. "I'd always thought that I didn't need love. That my life was fine, just the way it was. But the only reason it *was* fine, is because *you* were in it." He cupped her face between his palms and stared directly into her eyes. "When something good happens, *you're* the one I want to share it with. When I feel like hell and nothing's going right, I head right here—to talk to *you*."

She reached up and covered his hands with hers. "Connor, I..."

"Without you, Em, there's no laughter." He shook his head and smiled down at her. "There's no warmth. There's only emptiness. And I don't want to live like that. I want to live with *you*. I want to marry you. Have babies with you. Build a *future* with you."

"You what?" She dropped her coffee cup, and it landed with a solid crash on the asphalt, spilling hot coffee as it went.

Instantly Connor scooped her into his arms and held her cradled close to his chest. "You okay?" he asked. "Burned? Cut?"

"I'm fine," she said on a whisper, lifting one hand to stroke his face. "Unless of course, I'm dreaming, in which case I'm really going to be disappointed when I wake up."

He smiled down at her, then bent his head and stole a quick kiss. "Not dreaming. In fact, I feel like I'm just waking up."

"I do love you," she said softly.

"I love you, too, Em," Connor said, smile gone and gaze steady on hers. "I want us to be like that old car. I want us to be what we *deserve* to be. Together."

Her heart felt full enough to explode, and her eyes blurred with tears of happiness so thick she could hardly see. And yet there he was, in all his blurry glory. He'd been her friend, then her lover and now, finally and forever, he would be her husband.

Emma blinked away her tears, because she wanted this moment to be clear in her memory. "I'll marry you, Connor. I'll have a family with you. And I promise I will love you forever."

"That's all I'll ever ask, Em," he said, and carried her beneath the arch of morning glories into the shade-dappled yard.

"That's all?" she teased.

"Well," he hedged, "that and a cup of coffee. I've been up all night, waiting for you to wake up."

"Then let's forget about the coffee," she said, reaching up to hook her arms around his neck, "and head right to bed."

Connor grinned. "You know, I think I'm gonna like being married."

Emma laughed aloud and hung on for dear life as she and her best friend started their new life together in the first sweet hush of dawn.

* * * * *

THE LAST
REILLY STANDING

One

Aidan Reilly was so close to winning, he could almost taste the celebratory champagne. Okay, beer.

The longest three months of his *life* were coming to an end. Only three more weeks to go and he'd be the winner of the bet he and his brothers had entered into so grudgingly at the beginning of the summer.

He shuddered thinking about it, even now. Ninety days of no sex and the winner received the whole ten thousand dollars left to the Reilly triplets by their great-uncle. It was all their older brother, Father Liam Reilly's fault. He'd waved the red flag of challenge at them, insisting that priests were *way* tougher than Marines—since he'd had to give up sex for *life*. Well, no self-respecting Reilly ever turned down a challenge. Though this one had been tougher to survive than any of them had thought.

Brian and Connor had already folded—which left Aidan alone to hold up the family honor—and make sure their older brother, Father Liam, couldn't laugh his ass off at all of them.

It wasn't even about the money anymore, Aidan thought, staring across their table at the Lighthouse restaurant at Liam. Their older brother wanted them all to lose the bet so *he* could use the money for a new roof on his church. Well, Aidan wasn't about to tell him yet, but once he won this bet and had all of his brothers admitting that *he* was the strongest of the bunch then he planned on giving the money to Liam anyway.

He didn't need it. Being a single Marine, he made enough money to support himself and that was all he cared about. He'd never entered the bet for the *money*.

What he wanted was to *win*.

He leaned back on the bench seat and avoided letting his gaze drift around the crowded restaurant. The Lighthouse was a spot favored by families, so he was pretty safe. The only women he had to worry about in here were the waitresses—and they looked too damn good for his well-being. And at that thought, he shifted his gaze back to the surface of his drink.

"Worried?" Brian muttered, lifting his glass to take a sip of beer.

"Hell no—I'm closing in on the finish line."

"Yeah, well. You haven't won yet."

"Only a matter of time." Aidan smiled, while keeping his gaze fixed on his glass of beer.

"Gotta say," Connor admitted, leaning forward to brace his forearms on the table. "I'm impressed. Didn't think you'd last this long."

"I did," Liam said, taking a drink of his own beer.

"Yeah?" Aidan lifted his gaze and grinned at his older brother, ignoring the other two—identical replicas of himself. "Because I'm the strongest, right?" he spared a quick look at his fellow triplets and sneered. "Hah."

"Actually," Liam said smiling, "it's because you've always been the most stubborn."

Beside him, Connor laughed and Aidan gave him a quick elbow jab. "I'll take what I can get," he said.

"You've still got three weeks to go," Brian reminded him from his seat beside Liam. "And while Connor and I are getting regular sex from our lovely wives, you're a man *alone*."

There was that. Aidan scowled as he took a sip of his beer and made a point of keeping his gaze locked on the three men sitting with him. One glimpse of some gorgeous blonde or a curvy redhead or God help him, a pretty brunette and he'd have to go home and take yet another cold shower. Hell, he'd spent so much time in icy water lately between the showers and his work as a USMC rescue diver, he felt like a damn penguin.

"I can make it," he said tightly.

"Three weeks is a long time," Connor pointed out.

"I've already made it through *nine* weeks," Aidan reminded them. Nine long, miserable weeks. But the worst was over now. He was on the downhill slide. He'd make it. Damned if he wouldn't.

"Yeah," Liam said with a knowing smile, "but everyone knows the *last* mile of the race is always the most difficult."

"Thanks a lot."

"Twenty-one whole days," Liam said, making the three weeks sound even longer.

"How many *hours* is that?" Brian wondered.

"Man, you guys are cruel."

"What're brothers for?" Connor asked.

Aidan shook his head and kicked back on the bench seat. Ignoring Liam and smirking at his identical brothers, he said, "Do I have to remind you two what wusses you both were? How you both caved so easily?"

Brian grimaced and Connor shifted in his seat.

"Nope," Aidan muttered, smiling to himself, "guess not."

Bright and early the next morning, Terry Evans took a long look around the Frog House bookstore and told herself this would be a snap. A good change of pace. An interesting bump in the long, straight highway of her life.

Then a five-year-old boy grabbed a book away from a three-year-old girl, resulting in a howl rarely heard outside of the nature channel on TV during a documentary on coyotes.

Terry winced and smiled at the harried moms as they raced to snatch up their respective children. Oh, yeah, she thought, suddenly rethinking her generous offer to help out a friend. A snap.

There were kids all over the bookstore. No big surprise there, since the shop catered to those ten and under. Not to mention their moms.

Frog House was filled with pillow-stuffed nooks and crannies, where kids could curl up with a book while their mothers sat at the small round tables, sipping fresh coffee. The kids had a great time, exploring a place where everything was "hands on" and the moms could relax, knowing that their children couldn't possibly get into trouble here.

Donna had wanted a kid-friendly store and she'd built a child's fantasy. Murals of fairy tales covered the walls, and bookshelves were low enough that even the top shelf was within reach of tiny hands. There was a coloring corner, with child-size tables littered with coloring books and every color crayon imaginable. During story hour, every day at four o'clock, at least twenty kids sat on the bright rugs, listening with rapt attention to the designated reader.

Terry sighed a little and smiled as the squabbling kids settled down again, each with their own book this time. If her gaze lingered on the five-year-old boy a moment or two longer, she told herself no one but she would notice.

Her heart ached, but it was an old pain now, more familiar than startling. She'd learned to live with it. Learned that it would never really go away.

And if truth were told, she didn't want to lose that pain. Because if she did, she would have to lose the memories that caused it and she would never allow herself to do *that*.

"Excuse me?"

She turned her gaze from the kids at the "play time" table that was littered with discarded coloring books and half-eaten crayons, to face...*A MAN*.

At first sight of him, she immediately thought of him in Capital Letters. As her temperature climbed, she took a second or two to check him out completely. Tall, easily over six feet, he wore a black T-shirt with USMC stamped on the left side of his impressive chest.

Not surprising to find a Marine standing in the shop. After all, Baywater, South Carolina, was just a short drive down the road from Parris Island, the Marine Corps Recruit Depot—not to mention the Marine Corps Air Station in Beaufort.

But *this* Marine had her complete attention.

The Man's muscles rippled beneath the soft, worn fabric of his shirt and when he folded his arms across his chest, she nearly applauded the move. His waist was narrow, hips nonexistent and his long legs were hugged by worn, threadbare jeans. The hem of those jeans stacked up on the top of his battered cowboy boots.

Oh, my.

She lifted her gaze to his face and felt her internal temperature spike another ten points. Black hair, unfortunately militarily short, ice-blue eyes, a squared off jaw and a straight nose that could have come off a Roman coin. Then he smiled and she saw gorgeous white teeth and a dimple, God help her, in his right cheek.

Did it suddenly get hot in there?

"Hello?" He lifted one hand and snapped his fingers in front of her face. "You okay?"

Minor meltdown, she wanted to say, but for a change, Terry wisely kept her mouth shut. For a second. "Sorry. What can I do for you?"

He gave her a slow smile that notched up the heat in her southern regions and she groaned inwardly. She'd walked into that one. Figured he was a man who could take a simple statement and make it sound like an invitation to sweaty sheets.

"Can I help you?" She shook her head. This wasn't getting any better.

Finally, though, he quit smiling, stepped up closer to her and looked around the bookstore as if searching for something in particular. "Can you tell me where Donna Fletcher is?" he asked, shifting his gaze back to hers.

Terry checked her wristwatch, then looked up at him again. "Right now, she's about halfway to Hawaii."

"Already?" He looked stunned. "She didn't tell me she was leaving early."

One of Terry's perfectly arched, dark blond eyebrows lifted. "Was there some special reason she *should?"*

He scraped one hand across his square jaw. "Suppose not," he admitted, then blew out a breath. "It's just that I'm supposed to be doing a project for her and—"

Realization dawned. Actually, Terry felt as if she were in a cartoon and someone had just penciled in a lightbulb over her head. "You're Aidan Reilly."

His gaze snapped to hers. "How'd you know that?"

She smiled, shook her hair back and told herself that she was going to have to have a long conversation with Donna one of these days.

Her very best friend had told her all about the bet that Aidan had entered into with his brothers—and that she, Donna, had offered Aidan the bookstore as a safe place to hide out from women. In exchange, of course, for Aidan agreeing to build a "reading castle" for the kids. But, she'd never mentioned that Aidan Reilly looked like a walking billboard for good sex.

Actually, *exceptional* sex.

Maybe even *amazing, incredible, earthshaking* sex.

Terry was beginning to suspect a setup.

Donna, a romantic at heart, had decided that what

Terry needed was a permanent man. Someone to love. Someone to love *her*. The fact that Terry wasn't interested in anything more permanent than a long weekend, didn't really enter into Donna's plans.

Aidan Reilly, it seemed, was the latest salvo fired in an ongoing battle.

And though Terry still wasn't interested, she had to admit that Donna was using some first-class ammunition.

He was snapping his fingers in her face again. She reached up and swatted his hand away. "You keep doing that. It's annoying."

"You keep zoning out," he said. "Even more annoying."

Good point. "Sorry. I'm a little tired. Got in late last night and had to open the shop first thing this morning."

"Fascinating," Aidan replied. "Still doesn't tell me how you know my name and why Donna didn't tell me she was leaving three days early."

"Donna told me your name, and by the way, I'm Terry Evans," she said and smiled at a woman who walked up and handed her a book ready for purchase. Walking around behind the counter, Terry rang up the sale, bagged the book and handled the credit card transaction. When she'd finished, she wished the woman a good day, turned back to face Mr. Tall, Dark and Gorgeous and picked up right where she left off. "And I'm guessing she didn't tell you she was leaving early because she didn't think it was any of your business."

He scowled at her and strangely enough, she found *that* expression even more intriguing than the flash of dimple when he smiled.

"I told her I'd take her and the kids to the airport," he muttered. "But she wasn't supposed to leave until Friday."

"She got an earlier flight and grabbed it," Terry explained with a shrug. "I took her and the kids to the airport," she added, remembering the warm little hugs and the sticky kisses she'd received last night as the Fletcher family set off for their vacation.

He blew out a breath. "Probably good. She could use the break."

"Yes," Terry said. "She really can. Her folks live on Maui, you know and they're dying to see the kids and with—"

"—Tony deployed overseas," Aldan finished for her, "she needed to get away."

"Yeah. Worry takes a lot out of you." Heck, Terry wasn't even married to Tony Fletcher and she worried about his safety. She couldn't imagine what it was like for a Marine wife. Having to run the house, keep sane, deal with kids, all while keeping one corner of your brain saying a constant stream of prayers for your husband.

"So I'm told."

"But," Terry said, waggling her index finger in a

"follow me" signal, "Donna told me all about your 'problem' before she left."

"Is that right?"

She nodded as she stepped behind the glass case containing fresh muffins, brownies and cookies. Grabbing a tall paper cup from the stack near the espresso machine, she added, "And she told me how you like your coffee."

He smiled again, and Terry told herself to ignore the wildly fluctuating heat barometer inside her. Seriously, though, the man was like a lightning rod. He channeled hormones and turned them into heat that simmered just under a woman's skin. Pretty potent stuff.

"The day's looking a little better already."

She smiled, glanced at him, then looked away quickly—watching Aidan Reilly was *not* conducive to concentration. And running the complicated machine with dials and steamers and nozzles and whatchamacallits required concentration. While the steamer hissed, she risked another quick glance at him and noted that he was now leaning on the glass countertop, watching her closely.

His eyes were blue enough to swim in, she thought idly and wondered just how many women had taken that particular plunge.

"So what did Donna say, exactly?" he asked.

Clearing her throat noisily, she said, "She told me about the silly bet you and your brothers made."

"Silly?"

"Completely." She pulled the stainless steel pitcher of frothing milk free of the heating bars, then wiped them down with a damp towel. As she poured the hot milk into the cup, she kept talking. "She told me that she'd offered you the use of the bookstore as a sort of demilitarized zone and in return, you're going to build a castle for the kids."

That was how Donna had put it, anyway. She remembered the brief explanation she'd gotten only the night before.

Aidan's a sweetie, Donna told her, *packing up the last of the kids' stuff. But he's determined to win this stupid bet. So I told him he could hang out at the bookstore when he's off base. It's pretty safe there since not many single women come to the shop. And in return, he's promised to build a "reading castle" for my littlest customers.*

And I'm supposed to protect him from women? Terry asked.

Please, honey, Donna said laughing. *He doesn't need protecting. He just needs a safe zone to wait out the rest of the bet.*

And you're being so accommodating, why?

Donna closed the suitcase, then spotted a ragged blanket with more holes than fabric, sighed and opened the suitcase again to stuff Mr. Blankie inside. When she was finished, she sat on the bed and looked up at Terry. Because he's been a good friend while Tony's been deployed. He comes over here if I need the sink fixed or if the car takes a dump. He and Tony went through boot camp together. They're like best friends and Aidan's...family.

Which was why, Terry told herself, she was standing here staring into a pair of blue eyes that shone with all kinds of exciting sparks.

"Demilitarized zone, huh?" he asked. "Well, that's one way of putting it."

She smiled and spooned on a layer of foam before snapping a plastic lid on the coffee cup and handing it over. "Donna says you spend your time off from the base here, hiding out because most of her customers are young married moms—and therefore *safe*."

He took a sip of coffee, lifted both eyebrows and nodded. "Not bad."

"Thank you."

"And I don't consider it hiding out."

"Really? What do you call it?"

"Strategic maneuvering."

Terry smiled. "Whatever helps. So, you've got to last three more weeks without sex to win the bet."

"That's about the size of it."

Now it was her turn to lift her brows and smile at him.

Took Aidan a minute, to catch the joke playing out in her eyes, but finally he grinned in appreciation. Not only was she gorgeous, but she had a quick, wicked mind. Normally he liked that in a woman.

But this wasn't "normal." This was a time when

he had to stay stronger than he ever had before. And having Terry around for the next few weeks wasn't going to make life easier.

She was still watching him, a playful smirk on her mouth. "This isn't about size."

"It's *always* about size," she retorted and stepped out from behind the espresso machine. "This time, it's just about the size of your ego."

He followed her as she walked to the kids play table and idly straightened up the mess. He tried not to notice the fall of her pale blond hair against her porcelain cheek. Just like he tried to ignore the curve of her hip or the way the hem of her skirt lifted in back as she bent over the scattered books. And he *really* tried not to notice her legs.

What the hell had Donna been thinking? Bringing in Terry Evans to help him stay away from sex was like lighting a fire to prevent heat.

Oh, yeah.

This was gonna work out just fine.

Scowling slightly, he said, "You don't know me well enough to know I have an ego."

"Please." She gave a short laugh and looked at him over her shoulder. "Look at you. Of course you do."

"I think that was a compliment."

"See?" she pointed out. "Ego."

"Touché."

She gave him a brief, elegant nod.

He watched while she wiped up a crayon mess and

when she straightened and tossed her hair back from her face, he said, "So you're going to help me win the bet, huh?"

"You got it."

"How?"

She smiled and he felt the powerful slam of it hit him like a sledgehammer.

"Why, First Sergeant Reilly, if some gorgeous woman shows up, I'll just throw myself on you like you were a live grenade."

He looked her up and down slowly, completely. Then he shook his head. "Terry Evans...*that* kind of help and I'm a dead man."

Two

Summer in South Carolina could bring a grown man—even a *Marine*—to his knees weeping.

And September, though technically the beginning of fall, was actually summer's last chance to drum every citizen of the South into the dirt. Today, summer was doing a hell of a job of it.

Aidan paused, tipped his head back and stared up at the sweeping expanse of blue sky, looking for a cloud. *Any* cloud. But there was nothing to blot the heat of the sun and no shade nearby in the alley behind the bookstore.

He could have worked inside, but being out in the heat, away from Terry Evans made him feel just a little *safer*. Not that he was generally a man who ran for cover. Actually he was just the opposite. He liked the thrill of a risk. The punch of adrenaline when it raced through him. The sensation of balancing on the fine edge between life and death.

And he was smart enough to know that it wasn't adrenaline he felt when he looked at Donna's friend Terry. It was heat, pure and simple. The kind of heat he had to avoid for three more long, agonizing weeks.

"Donna," he muttered, "what in the hell were you thinking?"

He got no answer, of course, so he focused instead on the pile of wooden planks in front of him. "Just do the job, idiot."

Aidan had learned early the importance of focusing on the task at hand, despite the distractions around him. In the Corps, that focus could mean the difference between life and death.

And God knew, Terry Evans was a distraction.

The woman's laugh rang out a little too often. And her voice, when she spoke to the kids streaming in and out of the specialty bookstore, was soft and dreamy. Just the kind of voice a man liked to hear coming from the pillow beside his.

"Yeah. Concentrating." Aidan muttered the words as he slammed a hammer down onto a nail head. The solid slam against the wood jolted up his arm and hopefully, would shake thoughts of Terry out of his mind.

He couldn't believe his miserable luck. He'd

thought riding out the last three weeks of this bet would be easy, as long as he was here, in the bookstore. Actually he'd thought for sure that Donna would be closing the place while she was gone. Giving him a peaceful place to work and keep his head down until the bet was over.

But, no. Instead of peace and quiet, he got a Dolly Parton lookalike. Good thing he preferred brunettes—or he'd be a dead man already.

"How's it going?"

Her voice, from too close by, startled him, and Aidan slammed the hammer down onto his thumb. Pain streaked through him and stars danced in front of his closed eyes as he grabbed his injured thumb and squeezed. He clenched his jaw, trapping every cuss word he'd ever learned—and there were *many* of them—locked inside him.

Shifting a look at her, he nearly groaned again. Not from pain, this time. But from the absolute misery of having to look at a gorgeous woman and realize that he couldn't do what he'd normally do. Which was, offer to buy her a drink. Turn on the Reilly charm. Work his magic until he had her right where he wanted her.

In the dark.

In his bed.

Naked.

Oh, yeah, Aidan thought, his gaze locking on her sharp green eyes. The next three weeks were going to be a nightmare.

His thumb throbbed in time with the steady thud of his heart. While he stared at her, she cocked her hip, folded her arms beneath her truly impressive breasts and watched him with a benign look that told him she knew exactly what he'd been thinking.

"You know," she said finally, shaking her hair back from her face as a soft sea wind darted down the alley. "If you keep looking at women like that, you'll never last another three weeks."

He grinned and the pain in his thumb eased up a little. "Yeah? Irresistible, am I?"

She moved to the next step down from the porch, then sat down, her skirt hiking up, giving Aidan a better glimpse of her legs.

"Oh, I think I'll be able to restrain myself."

"Good to know."

"Besides," she pointed out, "you're not really interested in me."

"I'm not?" Intrigued, he forgot about his aching thumb. Hooking the claw tip of his hammer through a belt loop on his jeans, he planted one hand on the back wall of the bookstore, crossed one foot over the other and looked down at her.

"Nope." She smoothed her palms over her dark green skirt and demurely slid both legs to the side, crossing her feet neatly at the ankles.

A *demure* Dolly Parton.

Great.

"Face it, Aidan—I can call you Aidan, right?"

"That's my name."

"Well, face it, Aidan, you're a starving man and I'm a hamburger."

He snorted, looked her up and down thoroughly, then lifted his gaze back to hers. "Darlin', you're no hamburger. You're a steak."

She smiled. "Well, thanks. But like I said, you're a starving man. A man like you? No sex for nine weeks?" She shook her head slowly, still smiling. "I'm thinking that even hamburger would start looking like filet mignon."

"You have looked into a mirror lately, right?"

"Every day."

"And you see hamburger."

"I see eyes that are too big, a mouth that's too wide, a nose that turns up at the end, a scar on my eyebrow and a chin that has a stupid dent in it."

Amazing, Aidan thought. He'd been with enough women to know when one of them was fishing for compliments. And to be honest, most of them never had to fish around him. He was always the first to compliment a woman on her hair, her shoes, her smile…but this woman wasn't fishing.

"You know what I see?" He pushed away from the wall, hooked his thumbs into the back pockets of his jeans and looked down at her with a critical eye.

"Steak?"

"Grass-green eyes, a wide, luscious mouth, a pixie nose, an intriguing little blip in a perfectly curved eyebrow and a lickable dimple in a softly rounded chin."

She tipped her head to one side, studied him for a long moment, then blew out a breath. "Oh, you're very good."

"Yeah. And you're quite the filet yourself."

She held out one hand to him and Aidan took it. His fingers closed around hers and he could have sworn he felt the zing of something hot and lusty shoot straight from her fingertips to the area of his body most neglected lately.

When she was standing, Terry let go of his hand and rubbed her fingers together to dissipate the lingering heat she felt on her skin. "You know, it's a wonder you've lasted nine weeks," she said.

"Is that right?"

Forcing a laugh she didn't quite feel, she pointed out, "Hello? You just made a move on the woman who's supposed to be helping you *win* the stupid bet."

He scowled a bit.

"Seriously. You just can't help yourself, can you?"

"Excuse me?"

"Flirting." She absently brushed off the seat of her skirt with both hands, then stepped up onto the porch again. Grabbing hold of the doorknob, she gave it a twist, then turned to look at Aidan Reilly again. "Flirting is like breathing to you. You do it without even thinking about it."

"I wasn't flirting," he argued, grabbing the hammer off his belt loop.

"Please. 'Grass-green eyes? Lickable dimple?'"

"I was just—"

"Making a move," she finished for him and shook her head slowly. "And really? It was *so* blatant. Not subtle at all."

"Is that right?"

"Oh, yeah," Terry said and opened the door. "Does that kind of thing usually work for you? I mean, are women really that gullible? That easy to maneuver?"

He frowned up at her and Terry smiled inwardly. The man had more than enough confidence. She hadn't shattered him any. Maybe a couple of dings in a healthy ego, but she was pretty sure he could take it. Besides, if he ever found out how his words had hit her—about the fires still licking at her insides—well, let's just say, he wouldn't be winning any bets.

And Terry wasn't here for the scenery.

She wasn't here to get lucky with a Marine, either.

She was here to help out her dearest friend.

Then she'd be going back home.

"I don't 'maneuver' women," he said tightly.

"Sure you do," Terry quipped. "You just don't usually get caught doing it."

"You're not an easy woman, are you?"

"Depends on what you mean by *easy*."

"Not what you think I mean," he countered.

"I guess we'll see, won't we? In the next few weeks, that is."

He inhaled sharply, deeply and his scowl went just a little darker. "Exactly why did you come out here, anyway? Just to get a few digs in?"

"Actually," she said, pushing the door open, "I came to see if you wanted some iced tea."

"Oh." He balanced the hammer in one palm and slapped it rhythmically against his hand. "Well then, that'd be great. Thanks."

"It's in the fridge. Help yourself whenever you want it." She took a step inside, then stopped when he spoke up again.

"You're not going to bring it out here?"

Shaking her head again, Terry smiled. "Apparently you're used to women who fetch and carry. Sorry to disappoint you."

He gave her a slow smile. "I'll let you know when I'm disappointed, darlin'."

Terry sucked in a gulp of air, squared her shoulders and stepped into the air-conditioned haven of the small kitchen at the back of the store. She closed the door behind her, leaned against it and stared up at the ceiling. "Damn it, Donna. What have you gotten me into?"

The next couple of days were...*interesting.* If Terry could have looked at them objectively, she might have considered them an excellent exercise in self-control.

Instead she was just a little on edge and wondering how she was going to get through the next three weeks. Not only was Aidan Reilly an incredibly sexy man, but he was also a sexually starved man. As for Terry…she couldn't remember her last orgasm.

She'd done her share of dating—God, she hated that word—in the last few years. But being willing to go to dinner and a play with a man was a far cry from wanting him in her bed. She was picky, and she was the first to admit it. She didn't do one-night stands, and she couldn't bring herself to invest in a long-term relationship, so that pretty much left her out of the bedroom Olympics.

Which didn't really bother her most of the time. She kept busy. She was on more charitable boards than she could count, her fund-raising abilities were legendary and because of her gift with numbers, she'd been handed the reins of her family's financial empire three years ago.

This was the first "vacation" she'd had in years. Most people wouldn't consider working in a small-town bookstore a holiday. But for Terry, it was a treat.

Well, except for Aidan Reilly.

This whole situation just went to prove that Fate had a sense of humor. Putting a woman who'd been too long without sex in the position of keeping the world's sexiest man from *having* sex, had to be a cosmic joke.

Aidan cringed as he stepped into the blissfully

cool store and stopped in the open doorway leading from the kitchen to the main shop. Kids cried and shouted and laughed. Their mothers chitchatted, oblivious to the racket and he stood there, silently wishing he were out at sea.

He'd never really understood the draw of having children. To him, they looked like tiny anchors on long, heavy chains, designed to drag a man down. Besides, they were too damn loud.

He'd only come inside because he had the main structure of the reading castle finished and needed Terry to take a look at it. He laughed inwardly. Hell, he didn't really need her opinion. He'd gone over the plans and the basic idea with Donna, who'd already approved the whole thing.

What he really wanted was another look at the woman whose face had been invading his dreams for the last couple of nights. Self-preservation instincts told him to keep his distance—but the instinct that continuously prodded him to volunteer for dangerous missions was stronger. Which explained why he was now knee-deep in kids, waiting for a glimpse of Terry Evans.

Then there she was, moving through the sea of children like a sleek sailboat through choppy seas. Dipping and swaying with an instinctive elegance, she had a smile for each of the noisy kids and seemed completely unflustered by the racket.

She took a seat in a splash of afternoon sunlight,

as the children gathered on the floor in front of her. They quieted down slowly, giggles and grumbles fading into silence as Terry picked up a book and began to read. Her voice lifted and fell with the rhythm of the story, and Aidan, like the kids, couldn't take his gaze off her.

Terry held the colorful book up every now and then, to show the pictures and the kids laughed along with her as she acted out the different voices of the characters.

She was really something, Aidan thought. Even while a part of him really appreciated the picture she made—a larger part of him was shouting out *warning!*

If he had any sense he'd leave. He'd made it through nine long weeks of temptation and he wasn't about to lose the bet now, just because of a curvy blonde with hypnotic eyes.

He snorted. *"Hypnotic?"*

Man. He was in bad shape.

The kids laughed at something in the story and with an effort, he shook himself out of the stupor he'd slipped into. Screw having her check over his work. Screw hanging around this magnet for kiddies. He'd just go back outside, move the skeleton of the castle into the storage shed and get the hell outta Dodge.

He'd no sooner planned his escape than the cell phone he kept jammed in his jeans pocket let out a muffled ring. Digging for it, he checked the number, flipped the phone open and answered it while he headed for the back door.

"Get your butt back here, boy. We gotta move." J.T., the chopper pilot Aidan worked with, spoke fast. "Sport boat capsized about five miles out."

"On my way." Instantly, every thought but work raced out of his mind.

Aidan snapped the phone closed, jammed it into his pocket and headed out. He glanced back over his shoulder as he hit the doorway leading to the kitchen and the back door beyond. Terry's gaze slammed into his and he read a question in her eyes.

Just one more good reason to keep his distance, he told himself as he turned and stalked out. He wasn't a man who liked having to explain himself.

Having no one but himself to answer to kept life simple.

If he was lonely sometimes, that could be solved with friends or with a willing woman who knew not to expect any tomorrows out of him.

Terry Evans was not that kind of woman.

She had *tomorrows* written all over her.

Which should be enough to keep Aidan the hell away from her.

Three

The sea swallowed him.

In that one instant, when his head slipped below the cold water, Aidan wondered, as he always did, with just a small corner of his mind, if this might be the time the sea would keep him. Hold him, drag him down to the darkest water, where sunlight never touched. Where fish never swam. Where the cold was as deep as the darkness.

And just as quickly as it came, that thought disappeared, pushed aside so that he could do the job he'd trained for. He gave a couple of hard, powerful kicks, tipped his head back and breached the surface of the water. Cloud-dappled sunlight welcomed him, and he took a moment to find his bearings. Glancing to his left, he spotted the capsized sport boat about ten feet away, then shifted his gaze to the helicopter, hovering loudly about ten feet over head. The blades whipped the air, churning the already choppy water into a white foamed froth. The noise was tremendous. He lifted one arm, waved to Monk, hanging out the side of the chopper, then struck out swimming toward the boat and the two men perched on top of the upended hull.

"Man," the older one of the two shouted as he got nearer, "are we glad to see you guys."

Aidan grinned. Grabbing hold of the boat, he looked up at the men. They looked like father and son. The younger of the two couldn't have been more than seventeen. He looked scared and cold. Couldn't hardly blame him. Couldn't be easy to have your boat flip over on you.

He slapped the side of the boat. "You two need a ride?"

The helicopter came closer, dragging the orange steel cage basket through the water, skimming the surface, splashing through the whitecaps.

"Hell, yes," the older man shouted and slapped his son on the back. "Take Danny first."

Aidan shook his head as the basket came closer. Grabbing hold of it, he kept kicking, keeping his head above water and spitting out mouthfuls of it as it slapped him in the face. "No need. Basket's big enough. We all go."

The kid looked a little dubious and who could blame him? But to give him his due, he bit back on his own fears and slid down the side of the hull into the water. Aidan was ready for him, grabbing one arm with his free hand and tugging him closer. Over his radio, he heard Monk muttering.

"Move it along, will you, Reilly?"

"I'm getting there. Hold your horses."

"Who you talking to?" The kid shouted as he scrambled, with Aidan's help, into the basket and then inched to one side of it, with a two fisted, white knuckle grip on the rail.

"Them!" Aidan shouted and pointed skyward toward the hovering chopper. Then turning his gaze on the older man, he yelled, "Let's go!"

The man slid down and got into the basket with less trouble than his son had had. Then Aidan climbed in, and shouted, "Take us home, J.T."

While the chopper pilot moved off, the basket swung lazily into the air, like some amusement park ride. Monk operated the winch, raising the basket to the open door of the chopper, then when it was close enough, he grabbed hold and pulled it aboard.

"Everybody okay?" he shouted to be heard over the roar of the helicopter's engine.

"Fine." The older man climbed out, then reached

a hand to his son, to help him into the belly of the chopper. "Thanks for dropping by."

Monk draped the two guys in blankets while Aidan grinned and clambered out of the basket wiping water out of his face. "Always a pleasure," he yelled, feeling the adrenaline still pumping inside. "What happened to your boat?"

The man shook his head and leaned back against the shell of the chopper. "Damn thing started taking on water. Almost before we'd finished radioing for help, she got bottom heavy and did a roll, pitching us into the drink."

"Don't like boats," Monk shouted to no one in particular as he grabbed hold of one of the straps hanging from the roof of the chopper. "If God wanted us in the water, he would have given us gills."

Aidan laughed at his friend's solemn voice. The man hated water. Strange that he'd ended up in Search and Rescue. "But flying's okay?" he prodded, knowing the answer even before he asked the question.

"Hell, yes. It's *safer.* You ever see a tidal wave in the sky?"

While the man and his son relaxed to enjoy the ride, Aidan laughed at Monk and told himself he was a lucky man—jumping out of helicopters for a living—did it get any better than that?

By the next afternoon, Terry was ready for a break. She'd spent the last several days either in the bookstore, or tucked away in Donna's tiny, cottage-style house. She didn't know anyone in town—except for Aidan Reilly—and she hadn't seen him since he'd rushed out of the bookstore the previous afternoon.

Not that she *wanted* to see him, of course.

But spending too much time on her own only gave her too much time to think. Not necessarily a good thing.

Still, just because she was alone in a strange city, didn't mean she couldn't get out and mingle. Which was why she was spending her lunch hour walking along a crowded boardwalk, disinterestedly peering into the shop windows as she passed.

Although now, she was rethinking the whole, "get out and see some of Baywater" idea. The September sun beamed down from a brassy sky and simmered on the sidewalk before radiating back up to snarl at the pedestrians.

Even in a tank top and linen shorts, she felt the heat sizzling around her and realized that South Carolina muggy was *way* different than Manhattan muggy. She lifted her hair off her neck and let the soft ocean wind kiss her sweat dampened skin. One brief moment of coolness was her reward, but it was over almost before she could enjoy it.

All around her, families laughed and talked together. Kids with zinc oxide on their noses bounced in their tennies, eager to hit the beach. Young couples snuggled and held hands and the sound of cameras clicking was almost musical.

She came to the corner and stood on the sidewalk, watching the cars stream past along Main street. Well, "stream" was subjective. They were moving faster than she could walk, but traffic was pretty impressive for such a small town. When the light changed, she jumped off the curb and hurried across the street, unerringly headed for the dock and the ocean beyond. The nearer she got to the water, the brisker the wind felt and the ocean spray on her face was cool and welcome.

Boats lined the dock. Everything from small skiffs and dinky rowboats to huge pleasure crafts and mini yachts, bumped alongside each other like close friends at a cocktail party. Fishermen littered the pier, their poles and lines dangling over the weather beaten railings. A couple of skateboarders whizzed through the crowds, weaving in and out of the mob of people like dancers exhibiting precision steps. A balloon slipped free of a little girl's grasp and while her mother consoled her, the wind carried the bright splotch of red high into the sky.

Terry smiled to herself and kept walking. The scent of hot dogs and suntan lotion filled the air and as she passed a vendor, she stopped, giving in to hunger. She bought a hot dog and a soda, then carried them down a steep set of stairs to the rocks and the narrow beach below. Close enough to the pier that she heard the crowd, but far enough away that she felt just a touch of solitude.

Perching on a rock, she brought her knees up, took a bite of her hot dog and only half listened to the sounds around her as she focused her gaze on a couple of surfers, riding a low wave toward shore. Close to the sea, the temperature was easier to take.

"Still, strange to be sitting on a beach in the middle of the day," she murmured, then glanced around quickly. Talking to yourself was the first sign of a wandering mind. She sure as heck didn't want witnesses.

If she were back home right now, she'd be rushing down Fifth Avenue, clutching her purse to her side and walking fast enough to keep up with the incredible pulse and rhythm of New York City. She'd be racing from one meeting to the next, lining up volunteers and donations for whichever charitable organization she was working for at the time. There would be luncheons and brunches and coffee-fueled meetings at trendy restaurants.

Busy days and empty nights.

She shivered, took another bite of the hot dog and told herself that her life was full. She did good work—important work. In the grand scheme of things did it really matter that at some point in the last five years, she'd actually stopped *living* her life?

"Great," she muttered, rolling up her napkin and taking a swallow of her soda. "Self-pity party at the pier. Bring your own *whine*."

She pushed off the rock and started for the shoreline where the water edged in across the sand, staining it dark and shining. Terry smiled, kicked off her sandals and let the cool, wet sand slide around her feet. The ocean rippled close and lapped over her skin and she kicked at it idly, sending spray into the air.

When her cell phone rang, she almost ignored it. Then sighing, she reached into her shorts pocket, pulled out her phone and glanced at the number before answering.

"Donna. How's Hawaii?"

"God, it's good to be home for a while," her friend said with a sigh of contentment. Then she added quickly, "Jamie, don't hit your brother with the sand shovel."

Terry chuckled and started walking slowly along the edge of the ocean. The tide rolled in and out again with comforting regularity and the shouts of the children on the beach played a nice counterpoint.

"How's it going there?" Donna asked as soon as the Jamie situation was settled.

"Fine. Business is good."

"And Aidan?"

Terry pulled the phone away from her ear and smirked at it. "You are completely shameless."

"Gee, don't know what you mean."

"Right." Terry laughed. "You're impossible."

"I'm a romantic."

"Who's wasting her time."

"Come on," Donna wheedled. "You've got to admit he's gorgeous."

"He is," Terry admitted with a sigh as an image of Aidan Reilly rose in her mind. "I give you that. But the man swore off sex, remember?"

"Uh-huh. And trust me," Donna said. "He's a man on the edge. Wouldn't take much effort to push him over."

"I thought you were supposed to be *helping* him."

"I'm *trying* to help both of you."

"And it seems so much like interfering."

"To the suspicious mind…"

"Not interested," Terry said firmly and half wondered if she was trying to convince Donna or herself. Then she said it again, just for good measure. "Seriously. Not interested."

"Fine, fine," Donna agreed. "I can see you're going to be stubborn, so forget I said anything."

"Already working on it," Terry assured her and swished one foot through a rush of cold seawater.

From a distance, a shout floated to her and she looked up in time to see a man jump off the pier and drop, feet first, into the ocean below. "What an idiot."

"What? Who are you talking about?"

Shaking her head, Terry said, "Some moron just jumped off the pier."

"That's nuts," Donna screeched. "That close to shore, there are rocks and sandbars and—"

"Now he's swimming to shore, so apparently he survived."

"You know what they say," Donna said, "God protects fools and drunks—Jamie, don't hit your brother with the sand pail, either!"

"Whether he's a fool or drunk is still a mystery," Terry murmured, only half listening to her friend as she kept her gaze locked on the idiot swimming through the waves. "But he's a good swimmer."

When he finally hit shore, he stood up and turned toward her. His dark T-shirt clung to his muscular chest and his sodden cutoff jeans shorts hung from his narrow hips. As she watched, he came closer, grinning now and Terry's stomach fluttered weirdly as she whispered, "I don't believe it."

"What?"

"It's him. Aidan."

"The moron who jumped off the pier?"

"The very one and he's headed this way," Terry said, trying to ignore the stutter of her heart and the jolt in the pit of her stomach.

"Well, well, well," Donna said, laughing, "isn't this fascinating?"

"Go save Danny from Jamie," Terry muttered and hung up while Donna was still laughing.

Stuffing the phone back into her pocket, she gripped her sandals tightly in one fist and waited as Aidan came closer. If she had any sense at all, she'd turn around and head back the way she'd come. Take the stairs up to Main Street and get back to the bookstore.

But simple pride kept her in place.

No way was she going to run away from him. Give him the satisfaction of knowing that he could get to her without even an effort.

"Come here often?" Aidan asked.

"Are you insane?"

His grin widened and her heart did a fast two-step. Ridiculous how this man could jitter her equilibrium.

"Not legally," he said and swiped the water from his face with one tanned, long fingered hand.

His soaking wet shorts hung low across his narrow hips. His legs were long and tan and his feet were bare. He looked athletic, rugged and way too good.

"You jumped off the pier."

"Yeah." He half turned and waved one arm over his head.

Two men on the pier waved back.

"Your keepers?" she asked.

Aidan laughed and turned back to look at her. "My brothers. Well, two of 'em."

Staring at Terry, he could see she was annoyed and damned if she still wasn't an amazing looking woman. Her green eyes flashed at him and disapproval radiated off of her. But there was something else, too…something like excitement. And that made the jump off the pier and the swim to shore more than worthwhile.

He could still hear Connor's and Brian's hoots of glee when he'd spotted Terry and told them to take his fishing gear home for him. No doubt they were already planning to make room for him in the convertible they'd be riding around base come Battle Color Day. But hell with that, Aidan told himself. No way was he going to be seen in public wearing a grass skirt and a coconut bra like his bet-losing brothers.

Nope.

Instead he planned on having a front row seat for the spectacle—cheering them on while basking in the glow of their envy—for him having won the bet.

"The other two thirds of your set of triplets?"

One of his eyebrows lifted. "Donna tell you lots about me or what?"

"Just the basics," Terry said and walked a little further into the ankle deep water. "She never mentioned your death wish."

He threw his head back and laughed. "Death wish? From jumping off that short pier? Babe, that little jump was like rolling off the couch to me."

"What about the rocks? Sandbars?"

He waved her points away and joined her in the froth of water sluicing up over the sand. "From the fourth pylon to the sixth, there's a trench, deeper water. We've been jumping off that stupid pier since we were kids."

"So you've always been crazy."

"Pretty much."

"You grew up here?"

"Ah, so Donna did leave out a few details."

Terry chuckled, glanced at him and gave him a half shrug. "There's that ego again. Contrary to what you may believe, Donna and I didn't really discuss you in great depth."

He laughed again. Something about the way she could quickly go from fury to prickly to laughing really got to him. Nothing like a woman whose moods you couldn't predict to keep a man on his toes.

Not to mention her lushly packed body. It hadn't been hard to spot her from the pier. Her profile was tough to miss. She had more dangerous curves than the Indy 500 and her shoulder-length blond hair flew out around her in the sea wind like a starting flag. Probably every male within miles had already started their engines.

God knew *his* was up and running.

He brushed that thought aside, though. He wasn't some hormone driven teenager with his first case of lust. He could control himself. He could talk to her without drooling all over her. And he'd damn well prove that to both himself and the brothers he *knew* were still watching from the pier.

"Well then," he said and walked closer to her, dragging his feet through the icy froth of water, "let me regale you with tales of the Reilly brothers."

She smiled and shook her head. "So this is a comedy?"

"With us? Damn straight." He shifted his gaze from hers to the endless stretch of ocean laid out in front of them.

The sunlight glittered on the surface of the water, like a spotlight on diamonds. A few sailboats skimmed close to shore, their sails bellied in the wind. Surfers lazily rode the minor swells in toward shore and overhead, seagulls danced and screeched. A couple of kids with swim floats raced in and out of the water while their parents watched from a blanket and from not too far away, came the tinny sound of country music sliding from a radio.

"We moved to Baywater when we were thirteen. Liam was fifteen. Our dad was a Marine, so up until then, we'd traveled all over the damn place." He smiled when he said it, remembering all the moves with a lot more fondness than his mother felt for them. "We were stationed in Germany, Okinawa, California and even a quick stint in Hawaii."

"All before you were thirteen?"

"Yep." The water was cold, the sun was hot and a gorgeous woman was standing beside him. Days just didn't get any better than this. "Anyway, when he was assigned to MCAS Beaufort—"

"MCAS?"

He grinned. "Sorry. Marines tend to talk in acronyms. MCAS. Marine Corps Air Station."

"Ah…" She nodded.

"When he was assigned there, we followed just like always. He made every move seem like an adventure. New town, new friends, new school."

She was quiet for a minute or two, then looked up at him with eyes that looked deep. "Must have been hard."

"Could have been," he admitted, caught for a moment or two by the empathy in her eyes. But he didn't need her sympathy. "Probably was for other Marine brats. But we always had each other. So we'd go into a new school with built-in friends."

"Handy."

More than handy, he thought. The Reilly brothers had stuck together through thick and thin. Even when they were battling—which was pretty damn often—there was a bond between the four of them that had been stronger than any outside pressure.

"Hey, there's a lot to be said for having a big family. Always someone to hang with."

"Or fight with?"

"Oh, yeah. We had some great ones. Still do on occasion. You have brothers and sisters?"

"One," she said. "Brother. Older. We're not close."

There was a story there that she wasn't telling. He could see it in the way she shifted slightly away from him. Her body language said a hell of a lot more than she was. "Why not?"

She stiffened a little further, lifted her chin as if

preparing for a battle that she was used to fighting. Then she said, "Lots of reasons. But we weren't talking about me, remember?"

Shut down. Neatly. Politely. Completely. Okay. He'd let it go, he thought. Come back to it another time. He wanted to know why her green eyes looked shadowed. Why her brow furrowed at mention of her family. And yet…he really didn't want to explore *why* he wanted to know.

So he was happy enough to turn the talk back to him and his family.

For now.

"Right." He blew out a breath, focused on the sea again and started talking. "Anyway, Mom handled everything, as usual. Dad made it an adventure, Mom made it all work. She handled the packing, the bills, the requisitions, the dealing with the movers…everything. Basically all us guys had to do was show up."

"Your mother's crazy, too," she said, though her words were filled with more than a little admiration.

He laughed shortly. "She'd be the first to agree with that." He shrugged and stared hard at the horizon, where sea met sky and both blended, becoming a part of each other. "But, everything changed when we moved here. Mom loved it. Said she felt a 'connection' to this place. She loved everything about Beaufort, the south, the people. When she found Baywater on a shopping trip, she told my dad that here is where they'd be staying."

"Could he do that? Just opt to stop being deployed?"

"Not easy, but, yeah. Ask for an assignment to a company that doesn't deploy and you're pretty safe. But Mom wouldn't let him do that. She knew how much he enjoyed the deployments."

"But what about when he was reassigned to live somewhere else for a year or two? That happens, doesn't it?"

"You bet. Mom just told him 'happy trails' and that she'd be right here, letting us go to school and have some stability." He shoved both hands into his jeans pockets and winced as he realized he'd dived into the water still carrying his wallet. Damn it. But he hadn't been thinking. He'd taken one look at Terry and jumped off the pier.

He shook his head. "Mom wanted us to be able to finish out high school in the same place."

"So she stayed here with you guys and let him go?"

"Yep." He smiled to himself. "Dad would head off for six months and Mom would be right here, running the show until he got back. She told him this was home and she wasn't leaving it again."

"Strong woman."

"You have *no* idea." He laughed, remembering how his mother had managed to ride herd on four teenage sons and make it all look easy. "Dad lasted another year or two, then wangled an assignment back to MCAS and they've been here ever since. He retired not long after that—"

"Now?"

Aidan sighed. "He died a few years back."

"I'm sorry."

He looked at her. "Thanks. Mom's still in their house here in Baywater and loving the fact that all three of her sons are stationed close enough for her to irritate whenever she wants to."

"And you're all nuts about her."

He shrugged. "Hard not to be."

"And your other brother?"

"Ah, Liam. *Father* Liam." Aidan looked down at her, then lifted one hand to tuck a long strand of silky blond hair behind her ear. "Every Irish woman's dream is to be able to say, 'my son the priest.' Liam's church, St. Sebastian's, is here in town, too, so Mom lucked out. For a while anyway. Until one of us is transferred out."

"Even apart, though, you'll still have each other."

He studied her and noticed the shadows were back, haunting her eyes. Something inside him wanted to reassure her. To wipe away the shadows and make her smile.

And that worried the hell out of him.

Four

By late afternoon, the wind had picked up, the sky was crowded with clouds and Terry was still trying to convince herself that Aidan wasn't getting to her.

But he was.

"Damn it."

She closed the shop, locked the door behind her and stepped out onto the sidewalk. Tilting her head back, she watched the slate-gray clouds colliding into each other like bumper cars gone amuck.

"Storm coming." A soft voice, female, with just a touch of humor in it.

Terry turned, smiling, to face Selma Wyatt. At least seventy years old, Selma's blue eyes sparkled with a kind of vitality that Terry envied. The woman's long, silver hair hung in one thick, neat braid, across the shoulder of her gauzy, pale yellow, ankle skimming dress. The toes of her purple sneakers peeked from beneath the hem.

"Yeah," Terry said with another quick look skyward. "Sure looks like it."

Selma shook her head until that thick braid swung out like a pendulum. "Not the storm I'm talking about, honey."

"Ah…" Terry nodded sagely and didn't bother to hide her smile. "See something interesting in your cards?"

The older woman ran the spirit shop/palm reader emporium next door. And though Terry had never been one to believe in the whole "mystic" thing, she figured Selma must be good at what she did, because there was an almost constant stream of customers coming and going from the Spirit Shop all day long.

In the few days Terry had been in town, Selma had pretty much adopted her. She'd taken her out to lunch, introduced her to the noontime crowd at Delilah's diner and pretty much elected herself friend and watchdog. She'd even offered to give Terry a "reading," but she'd declined, since, if her future was anything like her past…Terry really didn't want to know.

"Heck no, honey," Selma said. "Didn't need the cards for this one. It's in the air. Can't you feel it?"

A slight chill danced up Terry's spine before she shook it off, telling herself that Selma'd been staring into her crystal ball too long. "The only storm I feel is the one blowing in off the ocean."

Selma smiled patiently—the same kind of smile an adult gave a two-year-old who insists on tying his own shoe even though he can't quite manage it. "Of course, dear. Pay no attention to me." Then she paused, cocked her head and said, "Oh. There it is. Wait for it."

A little impatient now and feeling just a bit uneasy, Terry inhaled sharply and asked, "Wait for what?"

Then she heard it.

A low rumble of sound.

Like distant thunder, it growled and roared as it came closer. The fine hairs at the back of Terry's neck lifted and she turned her head toward the sound.

Overhead, lightning shimmered behind the clouds, just a warning. A hint of bigger things to come.

But she forgot all about the storm as she watched a huge motorcycle slink to the curb and stop. In the dim light of dusk, the spotless chrome sparkled and shone and the black paint gleamed like fresh sin.

And speaking of sin…

Aidan Reilly sat astride the motorcycle and dropped both booted feet to the ground to steady the bike while he looked at her.

"Now *that's* a storm, honey," Selma murmured. "A big one."

Terry hardly heard her. Her breath came fast and short. Her heartbeat jittered unsteadily and every cell in her body caught fire at once.

He wore faded jeans and the battered cowboy boots he'd had on the first day she met him. His black T-shirt was strained across his chest, looking about two sizes too small—not that she was complaining. He wore dark glasses that hid his eyes from her, but no helmet and he looked...*dangerous*.

Her stomach fisted and she swallowed hard against the gigantic knot of something hot and needy lodged in her throat.

Then he smiled and Terry felt her toes curl.

Oh, this couldn't be good.

"Evening, Ms. Wyatt," he said, his voice as low and rumbly as the engine of the machine vibrating beneath him.

"Aidan," Selma said with a nod and a smile. "Come to have your fortune read?"

He grinned. "Now, Ms. Wyatt, you know I like surprises."

"Then I'll leave you to them," she said and headed off down the sidewalk.

Terry barely registered the fact that the woman was gone. All she could think was, it just wasn't fair for a man to look that good.

And why did he have to have a motorcycle?

"Terry!"

She blinked her way out of a very interesting daydream and realized that he must have been calling her name for a couple of minutes. How embarrassing was *that*?

Burying her own jittery reaction to him under a snarl of much more comfortable indignation, she snapped, "What're you doing here, Aidan?"

He glanced at the sky just as a grumble of thunder rolled out, long and low, and filled with the promise of coming rain. Then he glanced back at her. "Just thought maybe you could use a ride back to Donna's house."

"I can walk," she said, turning to put action to the words. The faster she got some distance between she and Aidan, the better, all the way around. "Thanks anyway."

He kept pace with her, rolling the bike and walking it down the side of the street with his long legs. "Gonna rain any time now," he pointed out.

"Then I'd better hurry," she countered, telling herself to put one foot in front of the other. To keep moving. To for heaven's sake, don't *look* at him.

He chuckled. "You're so stubborn you'd rather get wet than accept a ride from me?"

She chanced a quick glance at him. "Hello? On a motorcycle, I'd get wet anyway."

"Yeah," he pointed out with a quick grin that showed off the dimple she'd been spending too much time thinking about, "but you'd be moving faster. Having more fun."

"Slow can be fun, too," she said tightly and wondered why she suddenly sounded like a ninety-year-old librarian.

"I grant you. In some things, slow is *way* better."

She stumbled when the images *that* remark blossomed in full, glorious color in her brain. Oh, God. Did his voice just drop another notch, or was she simply going deaf from the pounding of her own heartbeat? Swallowing hard, she demanded, "Don't you have to be somewhere?"

"I'm right where I want to be."

"And what about the bet?" she asked hotly, stopping short to face him.

He lifted one eyebrow, took off his dark glasses and hooked them in the collar of his shirt. "Babe. I asked you to ride the motorcycle—didn't ask you to ride *me*."

A quick rush of heat swamped Terry and she wondered if everyone was seeing those little black dots now fluttering in her vision—or if it was just her. Probably just her. Which couldn't be a good sign.

Taking a deep breath, she got a good tight hold on suddenly rampaging hormones and told herself to get over it. She wasn't looking for a fling and if she were, she wouldn't be looking at Aidan Reilly. The man had sworn off the very thing she was suddenly hungry for. So what point was there in getting herself whipped up into a frenzy?

None.

So okay, she could do this. She could be a grown-up. And besides…a fat, solitary raindrop splattered on top of her head. He had a point. If he took her home on that rolling sex machine, then she'd be in out of the rain a lot faster than she would be if she was stubborn and insisted on walking.

This was purely an act of necessity.

Nothing out of the ordinary to accept a ride from a friend of a friend.

He was just doing her a favor.

Not the favor she secretly *wanted,* but he didn't have to know that.

"Okay," she said, trying to shut up the internal argument she was having with herself. "I'll take the ride. Thanks."

He gave her a slow smile that set fire to the soles of her feet, but she refused to feel the flames. As the rain spattered around her, she walked to the bike. He reached back and unstrapped a shiny black helmet from the tall, chrome backrest bar.

"Good," he said, handing it to her. "Put this on."

"Why do I have to wear a helmet and you don't?" she asked, taking the darn thing.

"Because my head's a lot harder than yours."

"Don't bet on it," she muttered, but yanked the helmet on and fixed the strap under her chin.

"Looks good on you."

"Oh, I'm sure," she said and swung her left leg over the seat as she climbed aboard. Good thing she'd worn linen shorts to work today instead of a skirt.

He half turned to look at her. "Grab hold of my waist and hang on."

Oh, boy.

Beneath her, the powerful engine throbbed and purred as he gunned the motor. The resulting vibrations of the bike set up a series of trembling quivers inside her that took her to the brink of something really interesting.

And she hadn't even touched him yet.

"Are you going to hang on or what?"

She gritted her teeth and grabbed hold of his waist. She didn't have to wrap her arms around him or anything. A simple handhold would be enough, she told herself and fought the rush of something hot and dark and sweet as he revved the engine again and eased the bike onto the street.

The stoplight at the corner was red, so they didn't go far.

She heard the smile in his voice as he glanced back over his shoulder and said, "You're gonna have to get a better grip on me than *that.*"

"I'm fine," she insisted, trying not to think about her thighs aligned along his or the powerful engine vibrating beneath her.

"What's wrong, babe? I *worry* you?"

"Not at all. Why don't you just take care of driving and I'll take care of me."

"Your call." He shrugged, turned his face forward again and when the light blinked to green, he took off like the hounds of hell were right behind them.

"Hey!" She shrieked and instinctively wrapped both arms around his middle.

He chuckled and she felt his body shake with silent laughter.

Let him laugh, she thought. She was more interested in keeping her perch on the bike than she was in pretending to be aloof.

He steered the bike down Main street, threading between the cars chugging lazily along the road. As they picked up speed, the wind slapped at her, raindrops pelted her like tiny bullets of ice and Terry relaxed enough to smile, enjoying the rush of air, the sense of freedom and the small, tingling sensation of danger.

It had been so long.

Before her life had become one charitable function after another, she had sought out things like this. Motorcycles, paragliding, deep sea dives, rock climbing.

She hadn't always been adventurous—but when her world collapsed, Terry had stopped caring. She'd gone out of her way to *live* every moment. She'd sought out the most exciting, the most heart pounding, risky activities she could find and then lost herself—and her pain—in the adrenaline rush.

Until five years ago.

When she'd awakened in a hospital one morning, to find herself lying there with a broken arm and leg. And she'd finally realized that chasing death wasn't living. That burying her pain didn't make it disappear. And that the only way to make that pain livable was to help people however she could.

Since that morning, she'd become a champion of causes. Terry Evans became the "go to" girl for most charitable foundations in and around Manhattan. She arranged flashy fund-raisers, was able to browbeat bazillionaires into contributions they'd never had any intention of making and could turn a celebrity auction into the event of the year. And she did it all with a calm, cool smile that managed to hide the *real* Terry from almost everyone.

She had legions of acquaintances, but very few *friends*. And the friends she *did* have, were more her family than those she was related to by blood.

Which was how she'd ended up in Baywater, South Carolina, sitting behind a hunk in jeans, riding a motorcycle in the rain.

Because of Donna.

Since that awful moment twelve years ago, when Terry's world dropped out from under her, Donna had been there for her. She'd cried with her, hugged her and supported her when Terry had taken her stand against her family. Donna Fletcher was the one link to her past that Terry treasured.

"How you doin' back there?"

Aidan's shout cut into her thoughts and Terry inhaled sharply, reminding herself that the past was long gone. "I'm fine," she called back, to be heard over the roar of the engine.

Rain still spattered, as if the storm just couldn't work up the energy to get serious. As they roared along the road, streetlights winked into life and the few raindrops falling were spotlighted in the glow.

A car whizzed past, its radio blaring, tires spitting up water in its wake. Terry ducked her head behind Aidan's shoulder and stared out to one side as the storefronts gave way to houses and those to trees lining the coast road.

The throb of the engine beneath her, the rush of wind all around her, her arms around Aidan's hard middle and the cool splat of rain against her skin, was mesmerizing. Which was why it took her an extra minute or two to notice something.

"Hey!" she shouted, lifting her head. "You missed the turn to Donna's street."

"No, I didn't."

"You passed it."

"Yes, but I didn't *miss* it."

She squeezed her arms tight around him and he grunted. "What're you up to?"

"Can't you just enjoy the ride?" he asked.

"Not until you tell me what's going on." Damn it. She'd relaxed her guard. She never should have taken this ride from him. She'd known it was a mistake the minute she climbed onto the bike. But what red-blooded woman would have been able to say "no" to a Marine cowboy biker?

"Aidan…"

"Relax, babe—"

"Stop calling me *babe*."

He laughed. She felt it shake through him and it made her grit her teeth even harder. The minute he stopped this bike, she was jumping off and *walking* if she had to, back to Donna's house.

The magic of the ride was gone as she simmered quietly in a temper that flashed and flared inside her. By the time he finally *did* stop the bike, Terry didn't even pause to see where they were before she leapt off her perch, snatched off her helmet and glared at him.

"You really *are* nuts, aren't you?"

He grinned at her and she realized that sexy or not, that smile could get really irritating.

"Thought you might like to take a little sightseeing tour."

"In the *rain?*"

He held out one hand palm up and shrugged. "We drove out of the rain a few minutes ago."

Frowning, Terry lifted her face to the sky and saw that he was right. They'd driven far enough out of Baywater that they'd left the brief summer storm behind them. Now, she took a minute and glanced around. She stood on a cliff road, the ocean far below them. The road behind them was nearly deserted and lined by towering trees that dipped and swayed in the wind as if dancing to a tune only they could hear.

When she finally turned to look at Aidan again, she found him standing beside her, staring out over the black water. Moonlight peeked out from behind the clouds, darting in and out of shadows, like a child playing hide-and-seek.

"Worth the ride?" he asked.

She shifted her gaze to the view and had to admit, it was gorgeous. Moonlight danced on the water, then winked out of existence when the clouds scudded across the surface of the moon. Whitecaps dazzled with phosphorescence that looked ghostly in the darkness.

"It's beautiful."

"One of my favorite spots," he said, walking closer to the edge of the cliff, until he could curl his hands around the top bar of the iron guard rail. "I come up here when I need to get away from people for a while."

She joined him, taking slow, almost reluctant steps. "Then you really shouldn't bring *people* with you."

He glanced at her and shrugged. "Usually don't."

Idly she swung the helmet in her left hand, slapping it gently against her thigh. "So why me?"

"Interesting question."

"That's not an answer."

He turned his back on the view and faced her, leaning against the railing and crossing his arms over his chest. "Don't have one," he admitted after a long moment.

His blue eyes fixed on her, Terry had to force herself to stand still beneath his steady regard. She didn't want to think about the subtle licks of warmth invading the pit of her stomach. She *did* want to hold onto her temper, but it was already fading.

"I just wanted to see you again."

"Why?"

He laughed shortly. "Beats the hell outta me."

"Aidan," she said on a sigh, "this isn't a good idea."

"Which idea is that?"

"This," she said, waving one arm even as she gripped the helmet in one tight fist. *"Us.* You. Me."

"Well that about covers everything," he said, still smiling, "except for what I feel when I'm around you."

"Aidan…"

"You feel it, too."

Oh, boy howdy.

But that wasn't the point.

"Doesn't really matter what we feel, does it?" She tipped her chin up and stared at him, unwilling to let him know just how close she was to losing control.

"Why not?"

"Because whatever it is, it's based on hormones."

"And your problem with that is…?"

"For heaven's sake, Aidan, we're not high school kids."

"What's that got to do with anything?"

Think, she told herself. But all the urging in the world wasn't quite enough to kick-start her brain when her body was obviously in charge, here.

Shaking his head, Aidan spoke again. "There's something here, Terry. Between us."

"There can't be," she said.

He laughed and the low, throaty sound rolled over her with a warmth that dispelled the chill wind. "Why the hell not?"

"Your stupid *bet,* for one thing."

He blew that off with a wave of his hand. "I'm not talking about sex."

That stopped her.

"You're not?"

"Was that disappointment I heard in your voice?" he asked.

"Of course not," she covered quickly. "Just…confusion."

His eyebrows wiggled. "Well, let me clear things up for you. I haven't forgotten about the bet. A little less than three weeks to go and I'm the champion Reilly."

"And that's important to you?"

"Damn straight. I want to be able to lord it over my brothers forever."

"That's mature."

He shrugged and smiled. "*Anyway,* I wasn't talking about sex before, Terry. Though it appears I am now, and can I just say, I'm happy to hear you bring it up?"

"Cut it out," she said and tossed the helmet to him. He caught it neatly. "You don't want to lose a bet and I'm not looking for a summer fling."

"Oh, I'm not going to lose the bet," he said and

pushed away from the rail to walk toward her. "And I'm not looking to be your 'fling,' either."

"Good."

"But…"

"No buts…"

"*But…*" He repeated as he walked closer, keeping pace even as she inched back warily. "There's lots of things two people can do without actually having sex."

"This is *so* not a conversation I want to have."

"Then we're on the same page after all."

"What?" The wind raced past her, tossing her hair across her eyes and Terry frantically reached up to push it away. Wouldn't pay to take her gaze off him. He was just too smooth to *not* keep an eye on.

He tossed the helmet toward the bike and watched it roll until it came to a stop on the ground beside the front wheel. Then he shifted his gaze back to her, stepped up close and grabbed her hips in a hard, two-fisted grip.

"Aidan…"

"Terry…" He bent his head, smiled and whispered, "Shut up," just before he kissed her.

Five

He groaned as his mouth came down over hers.

Aidan hadn't planned to kiss her.

Hell, if it came to that, he hadn't planned to *see* her tonight. When he left the base, he'd headed straight for the Off Duty, a local bar that catered to Marines. He'd had a beer, and shot a game of pool with a First Sergeant who had more money than pool playing ability. He'd joked around with a few of his friends, bought a round of drinks for a gunnery sergeant about to be deployed—and then he left. Hadn't been able to sit there talking shop with the guys because his mind was somewhere else.

With Terry Evans.

The damn woman had been in his brain all day. Her face had haunted him. Her smile had tempted him. Her temper intrigued him. Since earlier that afternoon, when he'd jumped off the pier to see her—she'd been with him. And he hadn't been able to shake her, despite his efforts.

Now, with his mouth on hers, Aidan felt her slip even deeper inside him.

The taste of her, the feel of her against him, swamped him with more sensations than he'd ever experienced before.

And he wanted more.

He held her tighter to him, wrapping his arms around her middle, sliding his hands up and down her back, following the line of her spine, cupping the curve of her behind.

Her mouth opened under his and his tongue swept within, exploring, defining, discovering her secrets, reveling in the rush of sensations rippling through him.

She sighed into his mouth and her breath filled him. He swallowed it and demanded more. His arms tightened around her further, squeezing until she moaned against him and he could have sworn he felt the imprint of her body on his.

And still it wasn't enough.

Too many weeks of celibacy, he thought wildly, while he tore his mouth from hers to run his lips and tongue along the column of her throat. Too long without the taste of a woman, without the feel of her heat. That's all this was. A reaction to deprivation.

"No," he murmured, running the tip of his tongue across her skin until she shivered and grabbed at his shoulders. That wasn't all. He'd been horny before. He'd been needy before. And he'd never known such an all encompassing hunger. He didn't just *want*.

He wanted *her*.

"Aidan…"

He barely heard her whisper over the roaring in his ears. His heartbeat thundered in his chest and his blood pumped with a blinding passion that left him breathless.

"Aidan…"

Groggily, like a man waking up from a three-day drunk, Aidan lifted his head and stared down at her. "Terry—" He touched her face, running his fingertips down her cheek. She closed her eyes and shuddered in an unsteady breath.

"This is *not* good," she finally said, in a voice so soft, a freshening wind nearly carried it away.

He forced a short laugh. "I don't know. I thought it was *damn* good."

"That's not what I meant," she said and stepped back, away from him.

His hand fell to his side and he fisted it, as if to capture the feel of her skin on his fingertips. Already, he wanted to be touching her again. Already, he missed the taste of her. Warning bells clanged in the back of his brain, but Aidan ignored them. His heart-beat was still racing and his breathing way less than steady.

From below them, came the thunderous, pulsing roar of the ocean as breakers smashed into the rocks. Out on the highway, a solitary car streamed by, its en-gine whining briefly before disappearing into the darkness. And here on the cliff's edge, an icy wind swept past them, around them,

Drawing them together and at the same time, holding them apart.

"Look, Aidan," she said, lifting both hands to shove her wind-tousled hair back from her face, "I just think that this is...*dangerous.*"

He gave her a quick grin. "Nothing wrong with a little danger. It spices things up."

A quick, harsh laugh shot from her throat. "Oh, man," she said, turning away from him to stare out over the ocean, "it's probably a good thing we didn't meet five years ago."

Intrigued, he stepped up beside her and tried not to notice when she inched away from him. "Why five years ago?"

She glanced at him and in the pale wash of moon-light, her blue eyes shone. "Back then," she said softly, "I'd have given you a run for your money, dangerwise."

"Yeah?" He smiled down at her, even as her fea-tures shuttered and her own smile faded.

She shifted her gaze back to the water and took the step or two that brought her close to the iron guardrail. She closed her hands over the top rung, lifted her face into the wind and said, "Yeah. Para-sailing, deep sea dives, mountain climbing…"

"You? Danger girl?" He grinned as he stared at her, trying to imagine her racing through life look-ing for an adrenaline rush. Nope. He just couldn't picture it.

"It was a long time ago."

"Sounds like fun."

"It was. For a while."

Aidan leaned one hip against the top railing, folded his arms over his chest and watched her, thoughtfully now. "What changed?"

She leaned forward, straining toward the ocean as if trying to escape the conversation. "*I* changed."

"A shame."

Glancing at him, she smiled briefly. "You *would* think so."

He shrugged. "Nothing wrong with chasing life at high speed."

"I suppose," she said softly. "Unless it's not about chasing as much as it is about running."

"From what?"

He wanted to know, even though a part of him wondered how this conversation had taken such a turn. A minute ago, he'd held her in his arms, tasted her breath, captured her sighs, felt her tremble in his grasp. Now, she was standing just inches from him and yet, it felt as though she were miles away.

"Life?" One word, more of a question than a statement.

Misery etched itself onto her features and even in the dim light of a nearly cloud covered moon, Aidan saw the shadows crouched in her eyes. He wanted to reach for her, but something told him she wouldn't welcome the contact.

Not now.

"You want to talk about it?"

She looked at him again, seemed to consider it, then said, "No. I don't."

Disappointment rose up inside him and surprised the hell out of Aidan. He'd wanted to know what put the shadows in her eyes. What it was that had such power over her that years later, just the memory of it could bring pain strong enough to make her shudder with it.

Always before, he'd kept his relationships on a superficial level. It was, he'd always assured himself, where he felt most comfortable. He wasn't looking to find a happily ever after. He wasn't looking for Ms. Right—more like Ms. Right *Now*.

He'd never really bought into the whole concept of being married to one person for*ever*. There were just too many women and not enough time as far as Aidan was concerned. He liked his action hot and his women temporary. And that outlook on life had served him well so far.

Didn't matter that his brothers—fellow triplets—had just lately fallen into the cozy clutches of two great women. Hell, he didn't mind being the last Reilly standing. He'd go through life proudly carrying the Bachelor banner.

So why then, did he suddenly want to know Terry Evans's secrets? Why did he *care* about whatever it was making her sad? It wasn't any of his business. Shouldn't affect him.

And yet…

"I really think you should take me home, now," she said, splintering his thoughts with the effectiveness of a hand grenade.

Probably best, he thought, but heard himself ask, "Still running?"

She stiffened and narrowed her eyes.

Well, great. Way to go, Aidan. Nice job.

He held up both hands and gave her a smile. "Never mind. Stupid thing to say."

"Fine. Can we go now?"

"Sure." He pushed away from the railing, took her elbow in a firm grip and steered her the few steps toward the bike. Bending down, he scooped up the helmet, then handed it to her.

She took it in both hands, and staring at it as if she'd never seen it before, she said, "Look, Aidan, about that kiss…"

He swung his left leg over the bike and settled onto the seat. Looking up at her, he gave her a smile he figured she needed about now. "Just a kiss, babe. Not a world ender."

"Right," she said and pulled the helmet on. She buckled the strap, then climbed onto the bike behind him.

"Just a kiss."

Her thighs aligned along his.

Her arms came around his waist.

Her breasts pressed into his back.

Aidan fired up the engine and revved it hard, gritting his teeth as he steered the bike out onto the road and back toward the storm hovering over Baywater.

Oh, yeah.

Just a kiss.

No problem.

"So what's the problem?"

Aidan glared at his older brother, then threw the basketball at him. "Haven't you been listening?"

Liam laughed, took the ball and bounced it idly, keeping one eye on the ball and one eye on his brother. "You mean to the rambling story you've been telling me for the last hour and a half? Yes. I was listening."

Aidan muttered a curse, bent down and snatched up a water bottle from the side of the driveway behind St. Sebastian's church. Uncapping it, he took a long drink, hoping the still cold water would put out some of the fires that had been with him since he dropped Terry off at Donna's house the night before.

It didn't.

And the weather wasn't helping any, either. Hot. Hot and humid, with the air so damn thick, it felt as though you should chew it before inhaling. Roiling gray clouds moved sluggishly across the sky and a hot wind occasionally kicked up out of nowhere. Hurricane season in the south.

Aidan exhaled sharply and narrowed his eyes on the sky. He had a feeling in his bones that the hurricane even now building up in the ocean would be headed their way all too soon. Which meant that the Search and Rescue unit would be on high alert twenty-four hours a day—not just for sea rescues, but working with the local police as well. In times of emergency, people didn't care *who* saved them—as long as they got saved.

Ordinarily the Coast Guard would take up a lot of the slack when it came to disaster time. But here, just outside Beaufort, the closest Coast Guard unit was stationed in Savannah and no one was going to sit around and wait for help. He squinted as the sun briefly peeped out from behind a bank of clouds and thought about the last hurricane that had blown through just a month ago.

Baywater was lucky that time around. Got plenty of rain and enough wind to snatch off shutters and toss old trees. But nothing as devastating as the outer banks had seen. He hoped their luck would hold.

"Worried about the storm?" Liam asked, drawing Aidan out of his thoughts.

"A little," he said, shrugging. "Weather report says it's going to skip us this time, hit in North Carolina. But my bones tell me different."

Liam nodded and glanced skyward. "I hate hoping for disaster to visit someone else."

"You're not. You're just doing what everyone else is doing and hoping it skips *us*."

Aidan recapped the water bottle, tossed it onto the grass under the shade of an oak tree and snapped another look at Liam. "So back to the point…where's the advice, *Father*? You're a priest, for God's sake. Say something meaningful."

Liam chuckled, turned on one heel and jumped, firing the basketball at the hoop tacked up over the garage behind the rectory. *Swish*. The ball swept through the net without ever touching the rim of the basket. Grinning, he trotted up to retrieve the ball, then tossed it back to his brother. "What kind of advice did you have in mind, Aidan?"

"Something *comforting*, damn it."

Liam laughed again. "Since when do you need comfort on the subject of women?"

This couldn't get much more humiliating, so he spilled his guts. "Since a few days ago, all right?" Hadn't he just spent the last hour or so explaining all of this?

"Donna's friend Terry is getting to you."

"I didn't say that."

"Sure you did."

No. He deliberately had *not* said that. In fact, he'd talked circles around himself in an effort to stay far away from such a statement. Apparently, though, Liam was good enough at reading his brothers that he didn't need a flat out admission.

"What do you want me to say, Aidan?"

"I don't know. You're the priest. Come up with something."

Liam laughed, bounced the basketball a couple of times, then shot it at his brother. Aidan snatched it and held on to it with a viselike grip.

All night, he'd thought about Terry. About that kiss. About the way she'd looked up at him in the moonlight. About those damn shadows in her eyes. And all night, he'd kicked himself for not staying with her. For not digging out what it was she didn't want to talk about.

Which was just so unusual for him, he'd shown up at the church at the crack of dawn for a little sympathy from the family priest. So far, he hadn't gotten much more than his butt kicked in a game of Horse.

Liam walked to where he'd dropped his own bottle of cold water, grabbed it and glugged down half of it before speaking again. "Aidan, you're just shook up because you've never been interested in a woman beyond getting her into your bed before."

Aidan stared at him. "That's it? That's the best you've got? They teach you that at priest school?"

"You're not mad at me, you know," Liam said, capping the bottle again and tossing it to the lawn.

"Really? Cause I think I am."

"You're mad at *you*."

"That's brilliant. For this I got up early and came over here." Nodding, he tossed the ball back to Liam, then bent to snatch up his T-shirt. Dragging it over his head, he shoved his arms through the sleeves and glared at his older brother again.

"Don't you want to know *why* you're mad at yourself?"

"Enlighten me."

"Because you care about her. And you don't want to."

That was a little close to home, but he wasn't going to give Liam the satisfaction of admitting it. "Don't build this up into some hearts-and-flowers deal. I've only known her a few days."

Liam shrugged and used the hem of his sleeveless jersey to wipe sweat off his forehead. "There's a time limit?"

He snorted. "You're way off base here."

"Sure."

"Seriously." Aidan bounced the basketball again, listening to the solid slap of the ball against the pavement, concentrating on the smack of the ball against his palms. "There's nothing going on between us."

Beyond some amazing sexual chemistry and some curiosity on his part.

"So why're you here?"

"Believe me, I'm kicking myself for coming."

Liam grinned. "You want to know what I think as long as its what you *want* me to think."

"You know," Aidan snarled with a shake of his head, "why we come to you for advice on women is beyond me, anyway. You haven't had a date in fifteen years."

"And you've never been a priest, yet you always feel free to complain about the church."

"Good point."

"But, whether you want this advice or not, I'm going to give it to you." Liam came closer, took the ball from Aidan and bounced it a couple of times while he gathered his thoughts.

Finally he looked at his brother and said, "You've got an opportunity here, Aidan."

"And what's that?"

"You've got the chance to get to know a woman *outside* your bed. Who knows? Maybe you'll like her."

"I do like her." He scowled slightly as those words shot from him before he could keep them bottled up inside where they belonged.

Liam smiled. "Maybe there's hope for you yet, Aidan."

"Yeah, yeah," he muttered and grabbed the ball back from his brother, bouncing it idly a few times while he tried to figure out just when he'd started *liking* Terry Evans.

"So. You gonna last the rest of the bet?"

He snapped his gaze up to meet Liam's. "Damn straight I am."

"Uh-huh." Liam caught the ball on a bounce and backed up, still dribbling. "But just so you know, I picked up Connor's and Brian's grass skirts and coconut bras the other day."

Well that cheered him right up. Aidan laughed, picturing his brothers, mortified, driving around in a convertible while every Marine in the south was free to laugh their asses off at the Reilly brothers. "Excellent."

"And just in case," Liam said, taking a shot for the hoop, "I picked up a set for *you,* too."

He stiffened. "Not a chance, Liam. No way is that going to happen."

"We'll see about that, won't we? Still have a couple of weeks to go…"

Before Aidan could argue, thunder rolled, grimly, determinedly and the leaves on the trees rattled as a sharp wind blasted through. Aidan glanced up at the sky, watched the gray clouds gathering.

"What do you think?"

"I think we might not get lucky this time."

"Could be days yet before we know."

"Yeah."

"You on call?" Liam asked, teasing forgotten.

"Hurricane season? Always." Hopefully the hurricane would burn itself out before reaching them, but even if the full brunt of the storm didn't hit Baywater, the accompanying winds and drenching rain could do plenty of damage.

"Hard to believe anyone would want to take a boat out in weather like this," Liam was saying.

But Aidan knew differently. Folks never figured that bad things would happen to *them*. It was always the "other" guy who ended up with his picture in the paper.

"Oh, there's always some idiot who thinks a storm warning is for everybody *else* in the city." He grabbed the ball back from Liam and ran three long strides before leaping at the hoop and dunking the ball.

Liam caught the rebound and made a jump of his own as Aidan said, "I guarantee you, right now, there's some guy out on the ocean who never should have left his house."

Six

She should never have left the house.

"Damn it!" Terry turned the ignition key again and listened with disgust to the pitiful whinewhinewhine of an engine trying to start—and failing.

She slammed one fist onto the dash, then gripped the wheel with both hands, squeezing it tightly instead of tearing her own hair out. "I don't believe this," she muttered, lifting her gaze to stare out over the wind-whipped ocean.

She scooped her hair back out of her eyes and stared off in the direction of Baywater. She couldn't see land. A sinking sensation opened up in the pit of her stomach—and she only hoped the boat wouldn't start feeling the same thing. The stupid boat *had* managed to get a few miles out to sea before the engine gave up and sputtered an ugly death. Now she could only pray that the hull of the damn thing was in better shape than its motor.

"What were you thinking?" Good question, but she didn't have a good answer.

She'd been up all night, trying to sleep but unable to close her eyes without being sucked back into the vortex of emotions that Aidan Reilly had stirred inside her. It had all started with the roar and grumble of that damned motorcycle. And sitting behind him, pressed close to his hard, warm body hadn't helped anything.

It had been so long since she'd experienced that flash of awareness, that spark of...*adventure*. She'd believed herself past the need or the desire for those feelings, but once awakened, she hadn't been able to put them to rest again.

She wanted to curse him for it.

But a part of her was grateful.

And then there was that *kiss*. She closed her eyes now and let herself feel it again. That amazing, soul-stirring, heart-crashing, bone-melting kiss. Every inch of her body had jumped to attention and clamored for more. He'd stirred something within her even more intriguing than that quest for adventure. Aidan Reilly had made her remember just how long it had been since she'd felt...*anything*.

She opened her eyes again and sighed as she scanned the ocean, unsuccessfully, for a hint of another boat. Someone she could wave down for assistance. She was, however, *alone*.

And it was all Aidan Reilly's fault.

Just before dawn, Terry had given up on sleep and surrendered to the urge driving her to get up and do something. She'd made her way down to the harbor, found a boat rental place and slapped down enough cash to allow her to steer her own course for a few hours.

That's all she'd wanted. To get out onto the ocean. To feel the wind in her face, the salt spray against her skin. To feel...*free*.

"Of course, it would have helped if the stupid boat would run." Muttering curses, she flipped the radio on, picked up the handset and said, "Mayday, mayday." She let up on the button and listened. Nothing. Not even static. She switched channels, spinning the dial as if it were a wheel of fortune.

Still nothing.

Why she was surprised, she couldn't say. If the engine didn't run, why should the radio work?

Oh, she really was an idiot. She hadn't thought this through. Hadn't checked the boat over before setting out. Hadn't done a damn thing to help herself.

Then she remembered her cell phone. Giving up on the radio, she rummaged in her brown leather shoulder bag and came up with a tiny, flip-top phone.

Sighing, she did the only thing she could do and dialed nine-one-one.

"911, what's the nature of your emergency?"

God, it felt good to hear a voice that wasn't her own. "Hi. This is Terry Evans. I'm stranded in the ocean, a few miles outside Baywater. I'm stalled. Engine won't turn over and the sea—" she glanced out over the frothing waves and blistering wind "—is getting bad."

"Name of the boat?"

Wet Noodle," Terry said, cringing at the ridiculous name for the rusting pile of flotsam. "If you could just call the Coast Guard for me—"

"No Coast Guard around here, ma'am," the operator said, a low country accent drawing out her words until they were a soothing lullaby of sound. Comforting, soothing. "But we'll get someone right out to help you. You just hang on a bit, all right?"

Lowering to admit, but she did need help. Soon. She should have checked the weather before setting out this morning. Should have checked out the boat, but that would have been too smart. Too logical. And she hadn't been feeling logical this morning.

She'd been feeling...*restless.*

"That's good. Thanks." She nodded, as if the operator could see her. "Could you get them to hurry, though?"

Then the voice was gone and Terry was alone again. She dumped the phone back into her purse and braced her feet wide apart, to help keep her balance as the choppy waves crashed against the rusted hull of the boat from hell.

Hang on?

What else could she do but hang on?

"One of Bucky's boats," Monk shouted, despite the mic he wore on his helmet. "The poor fool that rented it, couldn't even use the radio to call for help—didn't work—had to do it on a cell phone."

Disgusted, Aidan said, "I'm surprised any of Bucky's boats are still floating. The man's a menace."

Monk nodded. "Someone should put that old coot out of business."

"Yeah, but without Bucky renting out those rust buckets of his, who the hell would we have to rescue?"

Monk shook his head somberly. A bear of a man at six-four and about two hundred fifty pounds, Monk took up a lot of space and always managed to look as though he'd just lost his best friend. He leaned out and stared down at the ocean as it whizzed past beneath them, he said, "Things're getting ugly down there, Reilly."

Monk's voice came through the earpiece he wore, despite the thunderous noise of the Marine helicopter as it sliced through the air about twenty feet above the surface of the water.

Aidan looked out for himself and noticed the froth of whitecaps and the choppy sea. Storm was brewing out in the Atlantic and it was getting closer. Hell, he could feel the chopper pushing hard against a headwind. Another couple of days, that hurricane just might hit landfall and then they were in for a hell of a ride.

"Looks bad, man," Monk said, still shaking his head.

"Relax, Monk. You don't have to dive in, remember?"

"Damn right I remember," the big man said, glancing at him. "No way in hell do I go swimming in a fish's dining room. You divers are nuts."

"You know most people are afraid of flying."

"There's no figuring people," Monk said and pulled a stick of gum out of the pocket of his flight suit. Unwrapping it, he added, "They'll go swimming with sharks, or sit out on a puny little boat to wave to whales, but they're afraid of a plane—precision aeronautics." Shaking his head, he popped the gum into his mouth and chewed. "Makes no sense."

"Almost on 'em," J.T. said over the mic from the pilot's seat. "E.T.A. two minutes."

Monk grabbed hold of one of the chicken straps and leaned far out of the chopper, more at home in the air than most people were on land. "Yep. There it is. Hell, whoever's on it's lucky it hasn't sunk yet. Damn that Bucky to hell and back. Prob'ly a couple hungry sharks down there right now."

"Jeez, Monk," J.T. complained. "Let it go, will ya?"

Aidan laughed as he geared up, checking his dive

suit and adjusting his mask. "Just be ready with the basket. We'll bring up the passengers and leave the boat. Let Bucky worry about hauling it back in."

"Now that's justice," Monk muttered, "send the old bastard out in one of his own boats."

Aidan smiled and stepped to the open hatchway. J.T. brought the chopper in low and hovered steadily, despite the wind trying to push them back toward shore. Glancing down into the boiling surf, Aidan shot a quick look at the small boat rocking wildly with the waves, then lifted a hand to Monk, held on to his face mask and jumped.

That first second out of the chopper was the biggest rush he knew. For that one moment, he was flying. Free and easy, the wind whipping around him, tethered to neither land nor ship, and Aidan felt...*alive* in a way he never could if he were stuck in a nine to five job.

Then he hit the water and the icy slap of it jolted him just like always. Darkness grabbed at him with cold hands and held him briefly in the shadowy quiet. Then he was kicking for the surface again and breaching, just ten feet or so from the boat that looked as if it was going to rock itself to pieces any second.

Being one of Bucky's Bombs, it probably would.

He struck out with strong strokes and in a few seconds was grabbing hold of the side of the boat. Someone on board grabbed his hands and when he tipped his face up to say hello, his grin died.

"Terry?"

"For God's sake," she complained. *"You?"*

"Just what I was thinking, damn it."

Aidan shook his head, then waved to Monk, still hanging out of the chopper. In another second, the man had the rescue basket swung out into the wind and was winching it down carefully, one hand on the cable.

Turning his gaze back on Terry, Aidan hooked his arms over the side of the boat and said, "What the hell were you thinking coming out now?"

She pushed windblown hair out of her eyes and glared at him. Not much of a welcome for the guy who'd come to save her.

Her lips pinched together as if she really didn't want to answer. But she did. "I just wanted to go out on the water for a couple of hours."

"Been watching any news lately?"

"No."

"Guess not. Ever heard of Hurricane Igor?"

"Hurricane?" She shouted to be heard over the wake of the chopper.

Torn between amazement and fury at the astonishment on her features, Aidan snapped, "Get your stuff, we're taking you out of here."

"What about the boat?"

"We'll radio it in. Bucky can come get his own damn boat this time."

She stared at him. "How'd you know I rented it—"

His back teeth ground together. "It's rusty as hell

and it's dead as Moses. Has to be one of Bucky's. Now let's get going, huh?"

Terry had already turned away, though, gathering up her purse and a small thermos.

"You ready?" he shouted as the rescue basket dragged through the water toward him.

"As ready as I'll ever be."

"Swing your legs over the side." He called out and reached to steady her as she did what she was told. With one hand, he grabbed the basket, hauling it closer, then looked up at her. "You're gonna get wet."

For the first time since he'd arrived, she smiled and threw her head back, tossing her hair out of her face again. "Not as wet as I *thought* I was going to get."

Admiration roared through him like an F-18. Amazing woman. No hysterics. No whining about the situation. No fear. Just calm acceptance and simple obedience to his orders.

Aidan laughed while he held the basket steady for her. She slipped off the edge of the boat and landed inelegantly in the basket. Ocean water sloshed over the edges and surged up through the iron grillwork to soak her pale green shorts and halfway up her T-shirt. "Whoa!" she shouted as the cold gave her a solid jolt.

She held her purse aloft to keep it dry and clutched the iron railing with her free hand. Once she was in, Aidan climbed aboard, too, then waved to Monk. The winch cranked and the basket left the water, swinging wildly in the wind, turning, spinning, while Terry's grip on the rail tightened until her knuckles were white.

Aidan watched her, noted the excitement in her eyes, dusted with a healthy dose of fear, and he felt…*something*. His heart hadn't been steady since the moment he'd looked up into her green eyes. Finding her out here, in rough weather, all alone, had, for one moment, scared the tar out of him. But now, watching her take the wild ride with the enthusiasm of a kid at an amusement park, he felt something completely different.

Something deeper.

Something warmer.

Something dangerous.

By the time they reached the base, she was shivering despite the blanket Monk had provided. She didn't argue when Aidan told her he'd drive her home and she was damn quiet on the trip.

But then, so was he. Too busy trying to figure out just what he was feeling to speak, he concentrated on driving—though he indulged himself more than once with quick, sidelong glances at his passenger.

They were more than halfway home when the storm jumped into high gear. Lightning sliced the gray clouds open like a knife puncturing a water balloon and rain poured out in a blinding slash.

"Glad I'm not still on the boat," she muttered, clutching the blanket a little more tightly around her.

Her voice, quiet, was almost lost in the pounding of the rain on the roof of Aidan's SUV. He gripped the steering wheel with both fists and asked, "Why the hell were you out there at all?"

She sighed and let her head drop to the seat back. "I just wanted to be out on the ocean for a while. To just...*be*."

"And you decided to wait for hurricane weather for this outing?"

"I didn't know about the hurricane."

"Most people check the weather before they head out in a boat."

"Well, I'm not most people, I guess then, am I?"

"Already knew that," he muttered, remembering that stab of shock he'd felt when he'd seen her, sitting in that damn rust bucket. "And why the hell did you rent a boat from Bucky of all damn people?"

"He was the only one open."

He slapped one hand against the wheel and squinted into the driving rain. It was like trying to drive through a carwash. "Well, that should have told you something right there. Nobody in their right mind is renting out boats with a hurricane coming in."

"I didn't know about the hurricane. I already told you."

He blew out a breath and took one hand off the wheel long enough to scrape it across his face. "Fine. Fine. Not going to argue that one again."

"Gee, thanks." She turned her head on the seat

back to look at him. "Not that I don't appreciate the rescue, but I could do without the lecture."

"Yeah, probably." But damn it, if they hadn't been able to get to her, then what? She'd have been stranded in the middle of the damn ocean with a hurricane headed her way. In one of Bucky's boats, for God's sake. Which was about as safe as taking a cruise in a colander.

"Shook me a little, seeing you out there," he admitted finally.

"Shook me, too," she said. "Been awhile since I've been in a situation like that."

"You've done this before?" he asked, and made a left off the main highway into a subdivision of tidy homes and narrow streets. The trees lining Elmwood Drive were dancing and swaying with the punch of the wind and experience told him that if Igor didn't change directions mighty damn soon, most of those trees were going to be pulled up by the roots and tossed like sticks.

"Last time," she said, capturing his attention again, "it was on the Gulf Coast. Took a hired boat out and a friend of mine ran it across a sand bar. Ripped the bottom out and we were treading water for what felt like days."

He shook his head. Sounded like something he and his buddies would get into. Why it bothered him to think of *Terry* being in that situation, he didn't want to acknowledge.

"It's your fault anyway," she said suddenly, her tone shifting from memory to fury.

"Yeah?" He snorted an astonished laugh as he pulled into Donna's driveway. Throwing the gearshift into Park, he yanked up on the brake hard enough to spring the damn thing, then turned to face the woman beside him. "How d'you figure?"

"Last night." She waved one hand at him accusingly. "That motorcycle ride. That—" She snapped her mouth shut, shook her head, and opened the car door to a blast of wind and rain that swamped her the moment she stepped out. She slammed the door hard enough to rock the car, then stalked around the front end and headed for the porch.

Aidan was just a heartbeat behind her. Damned if he'd let her say something halfway and then stop. He joined her on the narrow porch and was grateful for the slight overhang that kept most of the punishing rain from slamming their heads. The wind pushed at them though and slanted the rain in at them sideways. Her hands were shaking. So Aidan took the key from her and opened the door.

She stepped into the foyer of Donna Fletcher's bungalow and Aidan stepped in after her, before she could close the door on him. He swung the door closed behind him, then turned to face her.

"Thanks for the ride home," she said tightly, lifting her chin in an age old gesture of defiance. "Bye."

Terry's insides were jumping. She'd been stranded

on a storm-tossed ocean, picked up in an iron basket and helicoptered to a Marine base. She'd had rain and wind and noise all before she'd had two cups of coffee.

But none of that accounted for what she was feeling at the moment. She felt as though she were balanced on the very edge of a cliff, with rocks below and no guardrail above. And it wasn't the rescue at sea doing it to her, damn it.

It was *Aidan*.

She swallowed hard, pushed past him and marched through the small, neat living room to the kitchen beyond. She hit the light switch on the wall and kept walking, straight through the bright yellow room to the service porch.

Aidan was right behind her.

She heard his heavy steps, but would have *felt* his presence even if she couldn't hear him.

She hadn't really expected him to leave, but oh, how she'd hoped he would. At the moment, her emotions were as tangled as her wind-tossed hair and spending more time with Aidan wasn't going to help any.

For heaven's sake, he'd jumped out of a helicopter to ride to her rescue. She leaned on the gleaming white washing machine, closed her eyes and she could still see him, jumping out of that chopper, hitting the water and disappearing beneath the surface. Even before she'd known it was Aidan, she'd been caught up in the...*heroics* of the diver.

Then, when she'd seen him grinning up at her, her heart had jumped in her chest. The man affected her in ways no one else ever had.

And, damn it, she didn't know what to do about that.

"Finish," Aidan said, taking hold of her arm and turning her around to face him.

She ignored the blistering sensation of heat that snaked up her arm from where his skin met hers. "Finish what?"

"What you were saying. The motorcycle—and the—" he prompted.

She inhaled sharply, blew it out and tapped the toe of her soaking wet shoe against the floor. Glancing up at him, she demanded, "You're not going to let this go, are you?"

"Nope."

Another breath. Another stall. She shifted her gaze from his to the window over the back door. Rain pelted against the glass. Though it was barely noon, it looked like dusk outside. Wind rattled the window glass and howled under the eaves of the house, sounding like lost souls looking for a way out.

Well hell. She knew just how they felt.

She needed a way out of this situation and she didn't think she was going to get one. Aidan's hand tightened on her arm.

Finally she turned to meet his gaze again. "Fine. The *kiss,* all right? Happy now?"

"Delirious."

"Good. Now go away."

"Not likely."

"Seriously, Aidan." She kept her voice steady, which was no small task, considering the way her heart was thumping in her chest, "I think you should leave."

"Probably should," he admitted, sliding his hand up her arm. "But not about to."

"This is so not a good idea," she muttered, already leaning toward him, lifting her face.

"I hear that."

"But we're going to anyway," she said and ended with a hopeful, "aren't we?"

"Oh, yeah."

Seven

Terry sighed into him as Aidan pulled her close. His arms came around her and Terry lost herself in his eyes. Blue. Deeper than the sky, wilder than the sea.

Then his mouth took hers, her own eyes closed and stars exploded behind her shuttered lids. Every square inch of her body lit up and flashed like a neon sign at midnight. Tingles of awareness skittered through her and she forgot to breathe.

But then, air was overrated anyway.

He parted her lips and her tongue tangled with his in a frenzied, twisting dance of rocketing desire. Her heartbeat ratcheted into a fierce pounding that nearly deafened her. Her blood raced, her mind went blissfully blank and she gave herself up to the incredible sensation of taking and being taken.

His hands swept up and down her back and finally settled on her behind. She felt the imprint of each of his fingers against the cold, damp fabric of her shorts and he heated her so that she wouldn't have been surprised to see steam rising up around them.

She reached for him, linking her arms around his neck and pulling him closer, tighter, to her. Mouths meshed, breath mingling, sighs humming in the air, she felt him surround her with the kind of heat she'd never known before.

This was new.

This was amazing.

This was terrifying.

One small corner of her brain remained oddly rational despite the rush of hunger leaving her dazzled and breathless. And when he pulled his mouth from hers to run his tongue down the length of her throat, Terry tipped her head back, stared at the ceiling and tried to listen to that rationality.

She knew this was a mistake. Knew that there could be nothing between her and this man. And *knew,* without a doubt, that if he stopped touching her, she'd simply dissolve into a sticky, gooey puddle of unresolved want.

A low, deep tingle started just south of the pit of her stomach. She twisted against him, rocking her hips instinctively against his, pressing close, needing…needing…

"You're killing me," Aidan whispered, his breath brushing her skin until goose bumps raced gleefully up and down her spine.

"Trust me," she managed to say, "I don't want you *dead*."

He chuckled and she felt the low vibration of his laughter move through his body. Her hands swept across his back, tracing muscles barely hidden beneath the soft fabric of his T-shirt. And oh, she wanted his skin beneath her hands. She wanted to define every inch of his sculpted chest and back with her fingertips. She wanted to trail her hands down his body slowly, watching his eyes flash and spark as she took his length in her hands.

"Oh, boy," she whispered brokenly as her own thoughts fired her need to a fever pitch that left her nearly breathless.

"Yeah," he murmured, nibbling at the base of her throat, "just what I was thinking. Need to touch you."

"Oh, yeah. Now. Please now," she said, shutting down that small rational voice in her head. She didn't want reason. She didn't want to think.

She wanted an orgasm, damn it.

His hands moved, sliding between their bodies to the waistband of her shorts. Her breath came fast and furious as she felt him fumble with the button and zipper. Silently she cried, *Now, now, now. Hurry, hurry, hurry.*

She was so close.

It had been so long.

Too long since she'd felt a man's hands on her.

And even then, it hadn't been like this.

It had *never* been like this.

Terry fought for air. Fought to stand still. Fought to not knock his hands out of the way and undo her shorts herself.

Finally, *finally,* she felt the button give and the zipper slide down and she groaned as he slid one hand across her abdomen. "Aidan…"

"Have to touch you, Terry. Have to feel your heat. Now. Now."

"Now," she agreed and kept a tight grip on his shoulders as his hand slipped beneath the elastic band of her silk and lace panties and down, further, further until his fingertips touched her core and she jolted in his arms. "Aidan!"

He bit her neck gently, lightly, then stroked her skin with his tongue as his fingers worked their magic. He dipped first one finger and then two into her depths and she rocked against him, wanting more, wanting to feel him deeper, wanting to feel a *different* part of him, full and deep within her body.

She shifted her position, widening her stance, welcoming him higher, closer, and still it wasn't enough.

"Oh…my…*Aidan…*"

"More," he murmured and before she knew what was happening, he'd pulled his hand free, then tugged her shorts and panties down and off. Grabbing her at the waist, he lifted her, then plopped her down onto the washing machine.

The cold metal bit into her skin, but nothing could stop the flames consuming her. Terry didn't think about what they were doing. Didn't stop to care that he was still dressed while she was mostly naked on her friend's service porch.

The rain hammered at the roof and windows. The wind shrieked and slammed into the house. It was as if even nature had been pushed farther than it could take and had been forced to surrender itself to the moment.

Terry ran her hands over his face, smoothing her thumbs over his mouth, his cheekbones. Her vision was blurred with want. Her breathing staggered in and out of her lungs.

He leaned in and kissed her hungrily, desperately, grinding his mouth against hers in a fierce assault that left her trembling and starving for more. But he pulled away, despite her clinging hands, despite her soft moans of protest.

His big, strong hands grabbed her hips and pulled her close to the edge of the steel machine and then he parted her thighs, pushing her legs apart with gentle determination.

"Aidan…" she whispered and heard the plea in her

own voice and couldn't be embarrassed by it. She was too far gone. Too far along the road of no return. She knew only need. Knew only the hunger that had her in its grasp and wouldn't let go. "Touch me."

He cupped her cheek in the palm of one hand, bent to kiss her briefly, then moved back to stare into her eyes while he dipped his fingers into her heat again. In and out, his fingers built a rhythm that she felt right down to her bones.

"I've never wanted *anyone* the way I want you. Never."

She laughed. Shortly, harshly, desperately. "Then take me, already."

He grinned and that dimple of his shot a flame of something sweet and sharp into her heart. Grabbing her hips with both hands again, he dropped to one knee in front of her and Terry's breath stopped. She knew what he was going to do. Knew it, felt it and wanted it with a passion more fierce than anything she'd ever felt before.

His strong hands gripped her hips, holding her in place. Her heart stopped—hell, the *world* stopped— as she watched him lean in to take her in the most intimate way possible.

His mouth covered her and she groaned aloud, rocking into him. Leaning back, she braced her hands on the washing machine, searching for purchase in a suddenly spinning universe. But Aidan's hands on her hips kept her centered even when she felt herself falling, falling, into a chasm filled with spikes of pleasure and whirlpools of almost delirious need.

He tasted her, his tongue stroking, licking, tasting. His breath dusted her heat, pumping her even higher, faster. Again and again, he dipped into her center, his tongue defining every line, every curve, every inner most secret.

And Terry watched him, unable to look away. Unable to take her gaze from him. Her body rocked in his grasp as she rode the crest of a wave that had been too long banked inside her. She felt herself spiraling, flying faster. A blissful sort of tension gripped her and tightened almost painfully. Her goal was close, and getting closer with every passing second.

She lifted one hand and cupped the back of his head. His short, black hair felt soft beneath her palm. His tongue stroked her core again, in a long, stroking caress that sent her rushing forward toward the fireworks she knew were waiting.

"Aidan!" She shouted his name as the first spasm shattered what was left of her control. Holding him tightly to her, she concentrated solely on the feel of him so intimately joined to her. Her body trembled, her heart ached.

And when the fireworks finally exploded within, she called his name again.

This time in a broken whisper.

When the last of her climax had passed, Aidan stood up and pulled her into the circle of his arms.

She melted into him, locking her legs around his middle and drawing him in close.

She staggered him.

His own heart pounded in tandem with hers. He'd felt her release in every cell of his body. He'd felt the joy, experienced the pleasure and shared the hunger.

And now he wanted more.

Sweeping his hands up, he bracketed her face in his palms and stared into eyes gone glassy with unleashed passion.

"Aidan," she said, struggling to catch her breath, "that was…"

"…just a warm-up," he finished for her and kissed her, swallowing her sigh. Her arms came around him and she scooted closer to him on the stupid washing machine. "I want you," he said when he could manage to tear himself off her mouth. "I want you really bad."

"I'm so glad," she said, giving him a quick smile that shattered something inside him. She leaned in to kiss him again, then stopped, holding him at arm's length as she looked deeply into his eyes. "But what about the bet?"

The bet.

Aidan's already fogged over brain started clicking. If he gave in to what he wanted, he'd lose that stupid bet and end up in a grass skirt and a coconut bra. And what was worse, he'd have to listen to his brothers ragging on him the way he'd been hassling *them* for the last few weeks.

He looked at Terry. Felt the slim strength of her legs locked around his hips. Noted the full, luscious lips just a breath away from his.

Didn't take long to make up his mind.

"Screw the bet."

"I was so hoping you'd say that," Terry whispered, and dropped her hands to the waistband of his jeans.

The backs of her fingers brushed against his abdomen and Aidan's body tightened even further. If he didn't have her soon, he was a dead man. And he wouldn't be dying happy.

"Right there with you, babe," he muttered, dropping a kiss on the top of her head, the curve of her shoulder.

"This is crazy."

"Oh, yeah, no doubt.

"And *so* necessary," she whispered on a choked off laugh.

"Right again. Love a woman who's right so often."

"Unusual man," she murmured as she finally worked the last button of his fly free.

"I like to think so," he managed to say through clenched teeth.

"No underwear," she whispered, sliding her hand down, down, *bingo*.

"Too confining." He hissed in another breath as she stroked him.

"So are your jeans."

"Good point." He let go of her long enough to shove at his jeans—and his cell phone rang. "Damn it."

"Don't answer it," she urged, scraping her palms up now, under his shirt, across his chest.

"Have to. I'm on call," he muttered grimly, already digging for the damn thing out of his jeans pocket. He flipped it open, checked the number and cursed again, viciously. He glanced at her. "It's the base."

Stepping away from her reluctantly, he answered it. "What?"

"Hey, boy, we got another call. Get your ass back here."

J.T.'s voice sounded almost cheerful—for that alone, Aidan wanted to wring his neck. Shoving one hand through his hair, he muttered, "What's up?"

"Some guy fell off a charter fishing boat. Nobody noticed till they got back to the dock." J.T. snorted. "Apparently the guy was a real idiot and people were so grateful that he was 'quiet,' they never questioned it."

"Who the hell would go fishing in this weather?"

"Got enough money to convince the captain, a charter boat's gonna give it a go. You coming or what?"

"Yeah. Be there in fifteen." Aidan flipped the phone closed, heaved a sigh and buttoned up his jeans. Then bending down, he grabbed Terry's shorts and tossed them to her.

"You're leaving."

"Have to."

"So," she said, giving him a smile he knew she wasn't feeling. "I'm not the only idiot out on the water today."

"Looks that way." He watched her and everything in him wanted to ignore the call to duty. For the first time...*ever*, he wanted to blow it all off. To stay here. To lose himself in a woman he'd known less than a week.

That shocked the hell out of him.

He scraped one hand across his face, shoved the phone back into his pocket and stepped up close to her, still perched on the edge of the washing machine. A buzz of passion, excitement, still coursed through him. He reached out and took her face between his palms. Kissing her once, twice, he pulled back and looked into her eyes for a long minute before speaking again.

"Do me a favor?"

She licked her lips and sent a white-hot blast of need shooting right through him.

"What?"

Aidan inhaled slowly, deeply, and let the air slide from his lungs. "Stay home today. Keep the shop closed."

"Aidan, I—"

"Trust me," he interrupted neatly. "Nobody's going to be out shopping today. They'll all be hunkering down, waiting for the hurricane."

She sighed. "If the hurricane *is* coming, then I need to go to the shop. Board up the windows. Donna told me where everything is and—"

"I'll do it."

She bristled. "I'm not helpless, Aidan. I can do it."

"Didn't say you were helpless," he muttered, wondering where the soft buzz of sexual electricity had gone. "Just—*wait* for me, all right? I'll help when I'm off-duty. You want to start boarding up here, okay by me. Just watch yourself."

For a second or two, he thought she might argue. Then she nodded.

"I will."

He kissed her again, one last, lingering kiss filled with promise and disappointment and regret. Then he took a step back and turned for the doorway to the kitchen. "Gotta go."

"Aidan?"

He stopped to look at her.

"Be careful out there."

A slow, wicked smile curved his mouth. "I'm *always* careful, babe."

And then he was gone.

Eight

The neighbors helped.

It seemed when hurricane season rolled around, there were *no* strangers.

Rain slashed at Baywater, coming in so fast and so furiously that it was hard to see as far as across the street. The wind whipped through the trees and tore loose shingles off houses that shuddered with the force of the pre-hurricane gusts.

Donna had been prepared, Terry gave her friend points for that. All of the wood used for boarding up the windows and glass topped doors was stacked neatly in the garage and clearly labeled, telling Terry exactly where each piece went. With the help of a couple of neighbors, Donna's house was as protected as it was going to get in just a couple of hours.

Then there was nothing to do but wait.

Making herself a cup of coffee, Terry winced as she listened to the slam of hammering rain crashing against the house. She kept the TV on, as one of Donna's neighbors had warned her to listen for evacuation notices.

Her stomach churned and her nerves were stretched to the breaking point. She cradled the coffee cup between her palms and tried not to notice the howl and shriek of the wind as it whipped past the house.

"Okay, adventure is one thing," she muttered, glancing at the ceiling as though she would be able to look through it to the storm-tossed sky above. "This is nuts."

And Aidan was out in it.

It had been hours since he'd left her to go on another rescue mission. Hours since she'd taken an easy breath. She shouldn't be worried. This was what he did. The man was trained. And good at his job. She'd seen that for herself only that morning. Though listening to the weather now, she still couldn't believe she'd been dumb enough to go out on a boat today.

But it didn't seem to matter that she knew Aidan was well trained and very capable. She felt a cold, tight fist close around her heart as her mind drew images of him leaping out of that helicopter into the churning mass of the sea. She pictured him swimming toward that lost fisherman and getting swallowed by an ocean that was determined to not give up its prize.

As those images and more raced through her brain, Terry shivered, set the coffee cup down on the kitchen counter and walked out of the room. She crossed the living room, dark now, despite the lamps turned on to keep the shadows at bay. With the boarded up windows, she felt as though she were in a coffin.

Alone.

Afraid.

Shaking her head, she grabbed the doorknob, gave it a turn and opened the door. Instantly wind whipped rain slashed at her, sweeping through the screen door into the foyer as if it had been perched on the porch, just waiting for its chance.

The world was wild.

Trees bobbed and swayed, like desperate sinners, pleading for forgiveness. Rain sluiced out of a gunmetal-gray sky. Houses were boarded up. No one was on the street. People were locked up, shut in and praying that the heaviest part of the storm would pass them by.

Terry walked to the edge of the porch, dipping her head into the wind, forcing herself forward, though it was like trying to run in a swimming pool. Her fingers curled over the rail at the edge of the porch and she squinted into the rain still slashing at her.

Stupid. She should be inside. Warm. Dry.

But inside, she was too alone. Inside, she was reminded that she was a woman apart from the rest of this tiny town at the edge of a storm. Everyone else was with their families. With people they loved or cared about.

Terry had no one.

She'd wanted it that way, of course. For years, she'd done everything she could to keep her distance from anyone or anything that might claim an attachment. She'd loved once and she'd lost and promised herself then that she wouldn't risk that kind of pain again.

Well, it had worked, she told herself now, clinging to the porch railing and watching a watery world of roaring noise and vicious winds. She'd successfully isolated herself.

And she'd never felt more alone.

The family was safe.

Aidan steered his car cautiously down the street, windshield wipers doing their best to keep up with a steady downpour, he looked at the world through a veil of water. Images were blurred, wind whipped, but his mind was clear. Focused.

He'd checked on the rest of the Reilly's. His mom was with Tina and Brian, helping Tina's nana get her house ready. And Connor and Emma were at the church, helping Liam's parishioners batten down the hatches at Saint Sebastian's.

Which left Aidan free to do what his heart was telling him to do.

Go to Terry.

After getting back to base, with a very wet, very angry fisherman, sputtering about lawsuits, he'd headed straight to the Frog House bookstore. With the help of the other local businessmen, he'd managed to board up Donna's place and help Selma tie her shop down as well. Now, they'd done all they could and all they could do was wait.

And there was nowhere he'd rather wait than with Terry.

She'd been there, in the back of his mind, all day. Throughout the rescue calls, throughout all the hurricane preparations, she'd been there, lurking in the shadows of his mind. Reminding him that he had more now to think about than himself. More to take care of than his family.

"Which was damned weird when you think about it," he muttered, steering his SUV around a downed tree and cautiously inching forward, on the lookout for fallen electrical wires.

He hadn't *asked* to care about anyone.

Hadn't *wanted* to be worried about a curvy blonde with a smart mouth.

And yet…instead of hanging around the base as he would have normally—in case they were called out again—he was driving through hell just so he could see her. Reassure himself that she was all right. He'd tried calling her, but the phone lines were down. No surprise. They were usually the first to go in a big storm.

But this was the first time in memory that not being able to make a phone call had turned his insides to jelly.

His fists tightened around the steering wheel as the car was buffeted by wind. He bent his head to look up through the windshield and winced as he watched trees leaning precariously over the street, shimmying as leaves were whipped free, sailing through the air like tiny green missiles.

Aidan made the turn on Elmwood and barely noticed the boarded-up houses and the abandoned look of the normally cozy, kid-filled street.

His gaze locked on one house. He headed toward it as if drawn by a powerful force he had no intention of fighting.

Then he saw her.

Standing on the porch, clutching the railing that shuddered in the wind as if it were a lifeline. His heart thundered in his chest as he watched her blond hair whipping around her head. She lifted one hand to shield her eyes as he got closer and he saw the brief flash of welcome dart across her features as he pulled into the driveway.

He drove as close to the garage as he could, where the car would be protected on one side at least, by the house itself. Then he parked, shut off the engine, set the brake and opened the door.

The wind grabbed it from him, wrenching it wildly out of his grasp and he had to fight to get it closed again.

Once he had, he bolted for the house, long legs striding through the mud and standing water, rain pounding him, wind pushing at him, as if deliberately trying to keep him from her.

But nothing could.

He hit the porch, grabbed Terry and pulled her into the house. When the door was closed and locked behind them, he pulled her into his arms and simply held her, enjoying the feel of her cold, wet body plastered against his.

"What were you doing out there?"

"I couldn't stand it in here anymore," she admitted, holding on to him with a grip as strong as his own. "It felt so…*empty* in here. So quiet."

He laughed shortly and lifted his head, hearing the wind, the rain and the low-pitched voice of the weatherman on the television. *"Quiet?"*

She looked up at him and blew out a long breath. "I felt…alone. And I couldn't take it anymore."

"You're not alone now," he pointed out.

"No." She smiled. "And boy am I glad to see you."

He shifted one hand to touch her cheek, sliding his fingertips across her smooth, pale skin. "Same here."

Her hands moved, from his back to his front, skimming up the front of his now soaking wet T-shirt. Yet, he felt the heat of her touch right down to his bones.

"You were gone a long time."

He sucked in air. "The lost fisherman wasn't easy to find."

"But you did."

"Yeah." He slid one hand along her spine, noted her shiver and moved his hand lower, lower, until he could caress the curve of her behind. His gaze searched hers, for what, he wasn't sure. "J.T. flew all over the damn place. Monk and I were hanging out the hatch and Monk spotted the guy's orange vest."

She inhaled sharply as his hand on her behind pulled her tight against him. Licking her lips, she closed her eyes briefly and whispered, "So he's okay?"

"Yeah. Ungrateful bastard, though." Aidan smiled. "Already talking about suing the charter boat captain and maybe *us*."

"For what?" she asked, clearly stunned.

"He wrenched his neck climbing into the rescue basket."

"Idiot."

"That about covers it." He moved his hand again, this time to the waistband of her shorts. Then he dipped beneath the fabric and scraped his palm over her damp, chilled skin. He sucked in air. "You didn't put your underwear back on?"

She shook her head and closed her eyes again as his fingers kneaded the soft flesh of her behind. "Forgot about it. Got busy…ohhh…"

"You're killing me again."

She smiled lazily. "I don't think so."

He cupped the back of her head with his free hand and threading his fingers through her hair, tipped her face up to his. He bent and gave her a kiss. And another. "I have a feeling this is going somewhere."

"Feels like it to me, too," she managed to say and then swallowed hard.

"So before we get started, you should know I already boarded up the store."

"Oh, good. Thank you."

He grinned quickly. "No arguments? No *'you should have taken me with you'?"*

"Nope," she murmured.

The wind howled again, and the front door rattled loudly as if trying to hold its own against a ravening beast fighting to gain entry.

"We're trapped here, you know. Can't leave in this."

She opened her eyes and looked up at him. "Who wants to leave?"

"Not me, babe."

"You've got to stop calling me 'babe.'"

He grinned again. "I'll work on it. Later."

"Oh, yeah. *Later.*"

Swooping in, he took her mouth with his and showed her just how much he wanted her. How much he'd been thinking of her. How thoughts of her had been haunting him throughout the day.

She opened her mouth to his and when her tongue met his, Aidan sucked in air like a dying man hoping for just another minute or two of life. He tasted her, explored every inch of her warmth, drawing her heat into himself and holding it close, letting it feed the fires licking at his insides.

This.

This is what had kept him going through the long, hard day. The promise of touching her, exploring her, having her beneath him, over him.

His hand on her butt tightened, squeezing, and she moaned into his mouth, squirming closer to him, brushing her hardened nipples against his chest until Aidan was sure she'd left an imprint on his skin right through his shirt.

"Flat surface," he muttered, tearing his mouth from hers.

"Now," she agreed and stepped out of his embrace. Taking his hand, she led him on a quick march through the living room to the hallway and the bedrooms beyond.

Aidan had been in Donna's house before. He knew the layout and he knew when Terry made a right turn, they were headed for the master bedroom. He grabbed her up, unwilling to wait another moment before touching her, feeling her.

She yelped in surprise, then settled against him, running her hands beneath the collar of his T-shirt, splaying her palms against his shoulders, his back. Heat. Incredible heat, speared through him, nearly stopping him in his tracks.

He dropped his head to hers and kissed her again, hungrily, desperately, a man on the edge and ready to jump feetfirst into the abyss.

Then they were in the bedroom and Terry leaned down from her perch in his arms to grab the edge of the handmade quilt covering the mattress and toss it to the foot of the bed. Lacy pillowcases covered the plump pillows and fresh white sheets looked like heaven, even in the gloom.

With the windows boarded up, the room was like a cave, dimly lit, sheltered, tucked away from the storm-tossed world outside.

An island of seclusion.

"Turn on a light," he murmured, swinging her down onto her own two feet. "I want to see you."

A long breath shuddered into her lungs, but she nodded as she crossed the room to turn on a small desk light covered by a Tiffany style lampshade. Pale, ghostly colors danced suddenly around the room, gleaming through the stained-glass shade.

Terry just stared at him. There was no turning back now. And maybe there never had been. Maybe they'd been destined to reach this moment from the instant they'd met. Hadn't she been drawn to him, in spite of her best efforts? Hadn't she felt the magic of his touch in quick, near electrical jolts of awareness every time he was near?

Hadn't she spent the last several hours remembering that incredible orgasm he'd given her and wanting *more?*

While he watched her, she took another steadying breath and quietly, soundlessly, lifted the hem of her dark green shirt up and over her head. He sucked in a breath and she felt his hungry gaze fasten on her breasts, still hidden from him behind their shield of lace.

Slowly, teasingly, daringly, she lifted her hands to the front closure and snapped it open. Then she shrugged out of the lacy fabric and let it fall to the floor behind her.

"Terry…"

She threw her shoulders back and with his gaze locked on her every move, slowly undid the button and zipper of her wet shorts. Then she let them go and they slid down her legs to puddle at her feet.

"If I don't have you in the next couple of minutes," he said, his voice a rumble of sound lower, more demanding and insistent than the thunder outside, "I swear I'm a dead man."

She smiled, feeling a rush of feminine power swamp her, rushing through her blood, making her limbs tremble and her brain shut down. "You're wearing too many clothes again."

He gave her a quick smile that sent a bolt of something delicious straight down to the core of her.

"Guess I am." In seconds, he'd peeled off his shirt, unhooked his jeans and shucked them and his shoes and socks. He let her look her fill, just as he had.

And Terry wanted to *whistle*.

She'd never seen a more gorgeous man in her life. Every inch of him was tanned to a golden-brown and every muscle rippling across his arms and chest and abdomen were sharply defined. And as for the rest of him, his....

"Oh, my."

He grinned and stalked toward her, grabbing her tightly to him, pressing her naked body along the length of his. Hard to soft, heat to heat. She felt the hard, jutting strength of him poking at her and everything inside her went to damp neediness. Her breasts crushed against his chest, her nipples tingled in anticipation even as he took her mouth with his, tangling his tongue with her, tasting, taking, giving.

Her mind whirled.

Her blood raced.

Her body quickened as it had only hours ago, only this time, it was more. More, because she'd had a part of him and wanted all of him.

"Fill me," she murmured, breaking the kiss and nibbling at his neck. "Fill me completely."

Thunder rolled, rain pounded and the wind groaned. The house shimmied, boarded windows rattled and the world seemed to take a breath.

Then he lifted her, as if she weighed nothing. Two big hands at her hips and she was airborne, clutching at his shoulders for balance, looking down into his hungry eyes. She read the passion, the untamed fury and felt a matching need rise in her. His strength cradled her as he lowered her slowly onto the hardened length of him.

"Aidan…" she whispered his name as he entered her, pushing into her depths with a steady determination. Her damp heat welcomed him, and her body adjusted, making room, taking him deeper.

She locked her legs around his middle and leaned back, trusting his strength, letting her head fall and her hair swing wild and wet from her head in a dripping blond curtain.

"Deeper," she crooned, using her legs, hooked over his hips, to pull him closer. "*Deeper,* Aidan. I need to feel *all* of you."

An inferno of need rose up around them, trapping them, drawing them both deeper into the gaping canyon of desire.

He dipped his head to take one of her nipples into his mouth and as his lips and tongue and teeth worked the sensitive tip, a moan slipped from Terry that left her whimpering in its wake.

Every inch of her felt alive, tingling, *desperate.* When he suckled her, she felt the drawing power of him clear to her toes and still, it wasn't *enough.*

Aidan heard that moan and it triggered something inside him that pushed him over the brink of control into the whirlwind of passion. He'd never known need so fierce, so all consuming.

Never tasted passion tinged with desperation.

Never felt anything like this woman he held so intimately.

He tightened his grip on her hips and pulled her down harder onto his length, pushing the whole of him into her depths, savoring the feel of being surrounded by her heat. Lifting his head, he took pleasure in watching the play of emotions on her face. Watching her teeth bite into her full bottom lip. Hearing the whispered breaths and edgy sighs.

Arms straining, muscles screaming, he used every ounce of his strength to set a rhythm designed to drive them both wild. He watched the play of emerald, green and gold light dazzle her pale, creamy skin and lost himself in the wonder of the moment. Her fingernails dug into his shoulders and she lifted her hips in his grasp and then lowered herself onto him again, grinding her body against his as if she couldn't take him deep enough. Hold him tight enough.

His brain short-circuited.

His heart hammered in his chest.

His mouth went dry and his vision blurred until Terry was his whole world. The universe, wrapped up in pale, jewel toned light, sighing, writhing, moaning.

"It's…coming…Aidan…" Whispered, broken words, trembling from her lips as she twisted on him, like a live butterfly on a pin.

"Let it come, Terry," he murmured, tightening his grasp on her hips, plunging himself deeper, higher, inside her. "There'll be another one. Let this one come."

She lifted her head and looked at him through glassy eyes. "Come with me," she ordered, licking her lips, breath coming in short, hard gasps.

Then linking one arm around his neck, she stretched out her other hand, reached beneath the spot where their bodies joined and cupped him, her fingers exploring, rubbing, stroking.

Lights exploded behind his eyes.

Aidan held her tight.

He heard her groan.

Felt her body implode.

And finally allowed his to follow.

Nine

Outside, Mother Nature shrieked.

Inside, Mother Nature celebrated.

Even before the last of the tremors had eased from him, Aidan wanted Terry again, with, if possible, a deeper need than before.

He'd never experienced anything like this. Never known need that couldn't be satisfied, desire that couldn't be quenched. Even now, still buried inside her, his body stirred, eager for another bout. Another surging race through madness to completion.

"That was—" Terry's head dropped to his shoulder "—*amazing.*"

He smiled into her wet hair, kissed her head and murmured, "And I don't do my best work standing up."

"Could've fooled me." She lifted her head to look at him. Their gazes locked and he watched as new hunger lit up in her eyes, chasing away the shadows that had first intrigued him.

She moved on him, lifting her hips slightly, only to lower herself again and his body reacted in a heartbeat.

"Again?" she whispered, nibbling at his neck, tonguing his skin, leaving a damp, warm trail against already fevered flesh.

"And again and again," Aidan promised, already moving toward the bed.

One part of his tortured brain heard the howl and cry of the wind, the hammering of the rain. But he paid no attention.

They were warm.

They were safe.

They were stranded.

Here.

Together.

That was enough.

He pulled free of her body long enough to lay her down on the crisp white sheets that smelled of lavender. He'd only uncoupled from her so that he could feel the rush of entering her again. Otherwise, he would have been happy to stay locked within her depths for the rest of eternity.

She moved on the bed, scooting back, sliding her feet on the sheets until her knees lifted and her thighs parted. He looked his fill of her and knew it would never be enough. Reaching out, he touched her center, smoothing his fingertips over swollen, damp flesh, and watched her eyes—those incredible grass-green eyes—glaze over in a mindless daze.

"Aidan…I want you again. Now."

His heart quickened, drumming so loudly in his chest as to be deafening. Every nerve ending in his body sizzled in eager enthusiasm. But this time, he was in no rush. This time, he wanted to draw the experience out—for both of them.

He slipped first one finger and then two inside her, playing with her, stroking her, exploring her. And he watched her move against him, lifting her hips, rocking into his hand while her own hands fisted on the sheet beneath her. Her head tossed from side to side. She licked dry lips and whispered broken, half-hearted pleas as he continued to stroke her body into a firestorm of *need*.

And with every stroke of his fingers, his own body tightened until he felt rock-hard and aching for want of her. Seconds ticked past, and Aidan realized he wouldn't be able to draw this time out much longer than he had the first. Not when need crouched in his chest and hammered at him to bury himself inside her. Not when hunger roared through him and danced on each of her sighs.

Levering himself over her, he slid his hands up, up, her body, over her curves, defining every line of her with fingertips careful as he would be while caressing fragile shards of crystal.

Her back bowed as she arched into him and he dipped his head to taste her. He took first one pebbled nipple and then the other into his mouth, rolling his tongue across them, nibbling with the edges of his teeth. She lifted small hands and cupped the back of his head, holding him to her as he gently tormented her.

"Feels so good," she whispered in a harshly strained voice.

"Tastes even better," he assured her, smiling against her body as he suckled her, pulling on her flesh, trying to draw her essence inside him.

"Aidan!"

His name in a quiet cry of nerves, stretched tight, shuddered through him and he moved to cover her. To push himself home, deep within her. He knelt between her legs and as she parted her thighs in welcome and held her arms wide to draw him in, he slid into her heat again.

Diving deep, he drove himself home with a hunger that grabbed him by the throat and wouldn't let go. He rocked wildly, furiously, in and out of her body, loving the slow slide to heaven enough to put up with having to leave her with every stroke.

She moved with him, instinctively following his rhythm, then setting one of her own. Hands fisted, breaths mingled, sighs twisted in the still, jewel-colored air. She took him, all of him, and held him deeply.

He looked into her eyes and felt himself falling into their depths and knew he didn't want to save himself. Everything he wanted, needed, was right here. In this bed in the middle of a storm that was tearing at the city.

But he wanted to see her, too, so he rolled onto his back, taking her with him, astride him.

She straddled him in the soft light and smiled down at him as she continued the rhythm he'd set, moving, rocking her hips, swiveling her body against his.

She rode him with a quiet power and a tender fury. Flesh slapped against flesh. Heat burrowed into heat. He lifted his hands, covered her breasts with his palms and sucked in a frantic gulp of air when she covered his hands with her own.

Terry looked down at him and felt herself drowning in eyes the color of a stormy sea. She felt the build in her body, knew a climax was shuddering close and felt the rush of expectation tingle through her.

He pulled his hands out from under hers and let them slide down her body, fingertips dancing fluidly over her skin until she could have sworn she felt him touching her on the *inside*.

She kept her hands on her own breasts, squeezing, tweaking her nipples, tugging at them, while he watched her and his eyes went gray and cloudy. A fierce smile curved her mouth as she rocked her hips against him, taking him in as deeply as she could.

Then he dropped one hand to the spot where their bodies joined and touched the very core of her. That one supersensitive nubbin of flesh. He stroked her, once, twice—and her body exploded into a showery storm of brightly colored lights. Her head fell back as she screamed his name into the fury of the storm.

Then he flipped her onto her back and before the last trembling shiver coursed through her body, he'd claimed his own release, whispering her name just before collapsing on top of her.

What could have been minutes—or hours—later, Aidan turned his head on the pillow and looked at the woman lying beside him. In the dim light, she looked like something mystical. Something not quite of this world.

Even as he thought it, he smiled to himself, silently acknowledging that the Irish in him was coming out. With her fair hair and pale, smooth skin, she looked as though she'd been carved from alabaster by a talented, generous sculptor.

But she was real—as he was here to testify.

She turned her head on the pillow and her gaze met his. She smiled. "Well, I guess you've really lost that bet now."

He winced, but couldn't bring himself to mind very much. "Guess you could say that. Man, my brothers will never let me hear the end of this."

She rolled to her side and went up on one elbow to look at him. "Why'd you do it? Why'd you throw away the bet when you were so close to winning?"

He thought about that for a moment. Didn't have to spend much time thinking about it now, as he'd done plenty of thinking about it earlier today. In fact, *all* of today, when he'd been away from her. When he'd had just a small taste of her and was still—as he was now—eager for another. Rolling to his right side, he, too, propped himself up on one elbow and watched her as he reached out to stroke a single fingertip across the tops of her breasts.

She hissed in a breath and sighed it out.

"Because," he said, still shaken by the knowledge, "I wanted *you* more than I wanted to *win*."

"I think that's a compliment."

"Damn straight," he said. "Believe me."

She caught his hand in hers and folded their fingers together. "Why did you want to win that silly bet so badly anyway?"

"To be the best," he answered, without hesitation. "To be the last Reilly standing."

"And now?"

He grinned. "Well, now…Liam will get the ten thousand bucks and he can start getting that new roof for the church." He paused and listened to the still screaming wind and the battering fists of rain. "And judging by this storm, he's going to need a new one. Soon."

"That's good, isn't it?"

"Sure it's good. Hell, I was going to give him the money anyway," he admitted, and realized that she was the only person he'd confessed that small truth to. And he wondered why it was he felt comfortable talking to Terry about his life—his family—everything that was important to him. Then he pushed that question to the back of his mind to be examined later. Much later. "I just wanted to *win*."

"Important, is it?"

"In *my* family? Yeah."

"But you gave it up." She rubbed the edge of her thumbnail against his palm and it was his turn to hiss in a breath.

"And I would again," he assured her.

"For an afternoon like this one," she said, "so would I."

"Glad to hear it."

She laughed, a low, throaty chuckle that set up a reaction that swept through him, carrying new heat, new need.

"Please," she said. "I'm sure you know just what a good time I had today."

"Day's not over."

"Glad to hear *that*," she said and inched a little closer to him. Tipping her head back, she confessed, "Today has been…special, I guess is the right word. I haven't been with anyone in a long time."

He'd guessed that, but he was damn happy to hear it said aloud. He didn't want to think about Terry with anyone else. Also didn't want to think that in a couple of weeks she'd be gone from his life.

So he smiled. "Well, it's been awhile for me, too."

"Poor baby."

"Sarcasm from a naked woman. I like it."

He shifted position, rolling her onto her back and dipping his head to kiss her middle. His tongue dipped in and out of her belly button and slid lower.

She combed her fingers through his short hair, her long nails gently scraping against his skull.

"The reason I told you that it had been a long time for me was that I wanted you to know that I'm not usually this kind of woman."

"What kind is that?"

"You know," she said, sighing as his breath dusted her skin and his tongue swept warm, damp caresses across her abdomen. "The fling type. I'm…more complicated than that." She paused. "Although, after today, you might not believe it."

He laughed against her flat belly. "Babe, believe me, I already knew you were complicated. But thanks for the warning."

Thunder crackled overhead and the wind slammed against the board covered windows. Terry jerked beneath Aidan and he used his hands and mouth to soothe her.

After a minute or two, she started talking again. "There've only been three men in my life. One I loved…one I thought I loved, which is pretty much the same thing." She paused. "And then there's you."

He stilled, even his heartbeat went soft and quiet. Outside, the storm blasted at the windows and doors, searching for a way in. But here in this room, another storm raged. This one in Aidan's heart. Love? Who'd said anything about love?

She laughed. "Don't look so panicked, Aidan. I wasn't proposing."

He gave her a smile he didn't feel.

"I'm just saying," she continued, pushing pillows beneath her head so she could see him clearly, "That this…*means* something to me."

He lifted his head to meet her gaze. And in all honesty, he could say, "It means something to me, too. I don't know what, Terry. Can't tell you that. But it means *something*."

"Thanks."

"For what?"

"For not trying to lie your way out of a tricky situation. For not pretending to be the love of my life. For respecting me enough to give me the truth."

"I'll always give you that, babe."

She smiled. "You know, it's interesting. I'm starting to like hearing you call me that."

"Happy to oblige." He kissed her belly again and moved a little lower.

She sighed. "I'm not looking for love anyway, Aidan. Not again."

That caught his attention. The sorrow, the pain in her voice and he knew that if he looked into her eyes, he'd see those shadows again. The ones that had haunted him from the moment they met.

And he couldn't help himself.

He looked.

Saw the pain and ached for her.

"Who was he?"

She sighed again and this simple release of pent-up breath rattled him right down to his soul.

"His name was Eric."

Aidan hated him already. No doubt tall, muscle-bound and too stupid to know what he'd had when he'd had it. "What happened to him?"

She closed her eyes. "He died."

Damn. Empathy welled up inside him. "God, Terry. I'm sorry."

"It was a long time ago."

"How long?" he wondered, because the shadows in her eyes looked fresh enough to have been born the day before. The pain was obviously still sharp.

She glanced at him and ran her fingertips along the side of his face. "Twelve years."

He blinked. She couldn't be more than thirty now. "You were a kid."

"Not for long." She moved beneath him, arching her body up to his as if to remind him that he'd been kissing her a minute or two ago and she wouldn't mind having him start back up. "I don't want to talk about it now, okay?"

"Sure. Okay," he said, mind spinning, even while his body urged him back to the business at hand.

He dipped his head again, trailing his lips and

tongue across her belly, lower, lower, until just above
the triangle of soft blond curls, he noticed the thin
sliver of an old scar.

He ran his finger across the faint, silvery line
and kept his voice even, as he asked a question he
was pretty sure he already knew the answer to.
"What's this?"

She closed her eyes, let her hand fall from his
head and said, "I had an operation."

"Yeah I get that. What kind?"

She blew out a breath. "Caesarean section."

"You had a baby."

"Yes."

"When you were a kid."

"Yes."

"Eric," he said, feeling his heart sink for her.

"Yes. Eric. My son." Terry's eyes filled with tears
and she blinked frantically, trying to keep them at
bay. Stupid. She shouldn't have started talking.
Opening up a conversation that would inevitably lead
them down this path.

"What happened?" Aidan asked and a part of her
was surprised that she could hear his soft, low-
pitched voice at all, over the freight train of sound
just outside the house.

Staring up at the ceiling, she concentrated on the
colored shadows tossed from the stained-glass lamp.
"Why do you want to know?"

He slid back up the length of her body, flesh

brushing against flesh, hard to soft, warmth to warmth and she was so damned grateful for that *connection,* her eyes filled again. It had been a long time since she'd felt connected to anyone. And that she would find such a feeling in the middle of a hurricane with a virtual stranger, was like a gift.

When his face was directly over hers, his mouth just a kiss away from hers, he looked into her eyes and said, "Because I see shadows in your pretty eyes, Terry." He kissed her. "Have from the first time I saw you. And I want to know what caused them." He dropped another brief, gentle kiss on her lips.

Nodding, she stared up into his deep blue eyes and fell into memory. Fell into the past that she kept too close and yet at a distance.

Running one hand idly up and down his rib cage, she spoke softly, quietly, words tumbling from her in a rush, as if they'd been banked up inside her for too long. "My family's rich. *Really* rich."

"Okay…"

"My older brother was the heir apparent. I was the princess. The debutante, the good girl who did everything right."

He kissed her again as encouragement.

"Until I was seventeen. I fell in love. With the son of my father's friend."

"You got pregnant."

"I did." And she clearly remembered the panic. The fear. The excitement and terror of knowing that she carried a child. Mistakes like unplanned pregnancies just didn't happen in the Evans family. There, everything was planned, thought out, arranged. Babies were neither expected nor wanted.

"The baby's father was scared."

"And you weren't?"

She smiled and patted his back in thanks for his solidarity. "Terrified," she assured him. "When I told my parents, they hit the eighteen-foot ceilings. They told me that I was a disappointment, but that they would take care of this 'episode' for me so no one would know."

Amazing, but her heart could still ache over that long-ago night. Scared, she'd faced her parents, knowing they'd be upset, but secretly hoping for support. Understanding.

She'd received neither.

"They arranged for an abortion. They couldn't have an unwed teenage mother in the family and they didn't want me to marry Randolph."

He snorted. "Randolph. Weenie name."

She laughed, surprising herself. "Randolph *was* a weenie. Didn't mean to be. But he'd been bred to it. And, he was young, too. Anyway…" She shook her head, jostling herself back on track. "I refused the abortion so they agreed to send me to Paris. To stay with my aunt until the baby was born. Then I would give him up for adoption."

"But you couldn't."

A single tear spilled from the corner of her eyes. "I couldn't. He was born and he came out and looked at me as if he knew me. He smiled. And he was *mine*."

Aidan kissed her again and swiped that tear from her cheek with his thumb.

"I told my parents that I was keeping him. They told me I couldn't come home. So I stayed. In Paris with my aunt for a while, then I used my inheritance from my grandmother. Got an apartment and loved my son."

They were heady days. Filled with love and laughter and a sprinkle of fear for the future. But she wouldn't have traded a moment with Eric. Not one second. He was *love*. More love than she'd ever known before. She hadn't realized that she could feel so deeply, so profoundly.

Eric was a tiny, helpless package of love who touched her in ways she had never known existed before him. He was her world. Until…

"Terry?" His voice came, a murmur of sympathy and comfort, whispered close by her ear. "What happened?"

She closed her eyes, steeling herself against the memory, but closing her eyes only made the pictures stronger, sharper. "He was five months old. One morning, he didn't wake me up. I slept until nine and woke up thinking, *Great. He's finally sleeping through the night. Won't this make life easier?*" She bit down hard on her bottom lip, looked him in the eyes again and said, "I went in and said 'Good morning, sleepy boy' and I touched him." She was back in that sun-washed apartment. She could feel the soft breeze slipping in through the partially opened window in Eric's nursery. She heard the gentle tinkle of the wind chimes she'd hung on the terrace. She *saw* her baby. "He didn't move. Didn't stir."

"Ah, God…"

She swallowed the knot in her throat. "I remember thinking. *That's strange.* And I bent over to kiss him awake. He was cold."

"Terry…"

She brought herself up out of the past with a jerk. She couldn't stay there. Couldn't relive the rest of it. The hysterical tears, the screams for help, the sirens and the firemen and the policemen and her neighbors…all looking at her with sympathy. With tears on their faces and dread in their eyes.

"The doctor said it was SIDS. Nothing could have been done. He just…slipped away in the night."

"Jesus, Terry, I'm *so sorry.*"

"I know…"

He kissed her and tasted her tears. She felt his heat, his comfort, his need and let it swamp her, bring her from the past into a present filled with hunger and passion and *life.*

Then he went deathly still, lifted his head and looked at her through horrified eyes.

"What is it?"

"I can't believe I did this…*we* did this. Never happened to me before, I swear."

"What?"

"Talking about Eric made me think of it. Protection, Terry. We didn't use protection. Either time." His features screwed up into a mask of misery. "And now, knowing what I know, I can't believe I let you risk…"

"Hush." She laid her fingertips on his mouth, silencing him. Her own heart was pounding. She hadn't thought once about protection, either, and she of all people should have known better. But it didn't matter. As long as he was healthy, it didn't matter.

"I take the pill. To regulate my periods."

His forehead dropped to hers. "That's good." Then he rose again to look into her eyes. "I'm healthy. Don't worry about that. I'm a careful man."

"That's good to know," she said softly, catching his face between her palms. His deep blue eyes flashed with emotions she was too wrung-out to try to decipher. And right now, it wasn't important. Right now, she wanted to feel that rush of life pulsing through her again. Feel her own heartbeat race. Feel Aidan's body moving on hers.

"I'm healthy, too," she assured him, then stroked his cheekbones with her thumbs. "Now, I want you to make love with me again. And, Aidan…"

"Yeah?"

"Don't be careful of me."

Ten

The next few days passed in a blur of activity. The brunt of the hurricane skipped Baywater, moving along the coast, drenching them in high winds and torrential rain, but sparing the little town what could have been disastrous damage.

Yet, there was a lot of cleanup to do. Aidan's team was kept busy, helping the local police and fire department on several calls. He called to check on his family's safety, but didn't have time to actually get together with his brothers. Until tonight. Between his regular duties on the base and the SAR runs his team was making, he was kept pretty much at a run.

And whatever down time he *did* have, he spent with Terry.

He couldn't seem to get enough of her. Since that first night of the storm, they'd been together every night. Making love, talking, laughing, arguing. He'd never spent so much time with a woman before without feeling the need to bolt.

Always, before Terry, Aidan had kept his distance—at least emotionally. He'd never wanted to *know* a woman beyond the superficial level that allowed them both to enjoy each other. Now though, there was more.

It had sneaked up on him and he wasn't entirely sure what to do about it. Drawn to her time and again, he felt himself being pulled deeper into her life, her world. A corner of his brain continually warned him to back off. To remember that his life was here, hers was in New York. That a former debutante had *nothing* in common with a career Marine.

And mostly, to remember that he wasn't *looking* for forever. That he didn't *want* love.

But that small voice in his mind was getting fainter—harder to hear.

He walked into the Lighthouse restaurant and paused just inside the entrance. He hooked his sunglasses on the open vee neck of his dark blue pullover shirt and let his gaze sweep the crowded restaurant. Families dotted the round, wooden tables, celebrating being together. Celebrating surviving the hurricane.

He spotted his brothers at a back table and braced

himself for the ragging he knew was coming his way. He'd been riding Connor and Brian hard for the last few weeks, so he fully expected to take his share of crap.

Stalking across the crowded room, he stepped up to the table and told Brian, "Move over."

When he did, Aidan dropped onto the bench seat. Shifting his gaze from Brian beside him to Connor and Liam across from him, he took a breath and said, "I'm out."

Whoops and delighted laughter rolled out from the other three men and got loud enough that people at the other tables turned to stare.

Aidan hunched his shoulders. "Jeez. Keep it down, will ya?"

"This is great," Connor said, still laughing.

Brian held up one hand and leaned across the table. Connor slapped that hand hard and they whooped again, just for the hell of it. Liam grinned and rubbed his own palms together as if he were already getting ready to count the money he and the church had just won.

"So what happened?" Brian demanded, giving Aidan a hard elbow to the ribs.

"What? You need a picture? You know damn well what happened."

"Yeah, but what happened to all your big talk about outlasting us?"

"I *did* outlast you two losers," Aidan reminded him quickly. He might not have won the bet, but he'd sure as hell beat out the other two members of the Reilly triplets.

"Yeah, man," Connor said, folding his arms on the table top. "But you only had two weeks to go. I really thought you were gonna pull it off."

"Not me," Brian muttered.

"Terry?" Liam asked quietly.

Aidan just nodded.

"Terry?" Connor repeated, straightening up and looking around the table like a man who's the only one not in on a joke. "Who the hell's Terry?"

"Yeah," Brian added, glaring at Liam. "How is it *you* know about this chick and we don't?"

"You guys don't know everything," Aidan muttered, sliding down in his seat.

"Here you go, guys," a woman's voice said cheerfully, "four draft beers."

The Reilly brothers shut up fast while the waitress delivered their drinks and didn't start talking again until after she was gone.

Aidan reached for his beer and took a long, deep swig. The icy froth hit the back of his throat and eased down the knot of irritation lodged there.

"So spill," Connor demanded. "Who's the new babe?"

"She's not a 'babe,'" Aidan told him, wincing slightly, since he called Terry "babe" all the damn time.

"Where'd you meet her? The Off Duty?" Brian laughed.

He had a right to laugh, Aidan supposed. Usually the women he met *did* hang out at the bar that catered to Marines.

He took another drink, then explained how he'd met Terry. And in telling his brothers, he relived it all. He didn't notice, but his voice softened, his eyes shone and his features lit with warmth.

"She sounds…special," Liam said when Aidan stopped talking.

Snapping his gaze to his older brother, Aidan fought down a sudden, near-overpowering flash of panic. Glancing from Liam to Brian and finally to Connor, he shook his head. "Don't start with me, you guys. Don't make more of this than there is."

"I didn't say anything," Connor pointed out, lifting both hands in mock surrender.

"You didn't have to. I can see it on your face."

"You ought to be looking at *your* face," Brian pointed out and took a drink of his own beer.

"What's that supposed to mean?" Aidan argued.

"Hell, man," Brian said, "holster it. Loving a woman's nothing to be ashamed of." He grinned. "Well, except for Liam."

"Funny," their older brother said and leaned across the table to slap Brian upside the head.

"Hey!"

"Stand down," Aidan told all of them, his voice low pitched but steady and firm. "Nobody said anything about *love* for God's sake. All I'm admitting to is losing the stupid bet."

"Relax, man," Connor said, picking up his beer and gesturing with it. "We've all been there—except for Liam."

"I have to take this from you, too?" Liam growled.

Connor shrugged.

"Seriously," Aidan said, feeling the snaky, cold tentacles of panic tighten just a bit around his insides, "shut the hell up about love. I'm not in love. Don't plan to be in love. You guys can have it."

"You make it sound like a disease or something," Brian said.

"Isn't it?" Aidan countered.

"What crawled up your ass and died?" Connor grumbled.

"Yeah," Liam asked, his voice quieter, more thoughtful. "What's got you so scared, Aidan?"

Instantly he bristled. "Didn't say I was scared, for God's sake. Just said I wasn't interested."

"Don't know why the hell not," Brian said. "Hell, can't imagine not being married to Tina."

"Oh, yeah," Aidan sniped. "You liked marriage to Tina so much, you divorced her *then* remarried her."

"You want to go a round with me?" his brother snarled.

"He's just itchy," Connor cut in, breaking up the tension before it could spiral into one of the Reilly brothers' world famous knock-down-drag-out fights.

"Hell, I remember how it felt. I love Emma, but damned if I wanted to admit it—even to myself."

"Now you're both married," Aidan grumbled. "And what'd it get you?"

"Happiness?" Liam offered.

"No offense, Liam," Aidan said, snapping him a look. "But priests don't get a vote in this."

An angry flush swept up his older brother's face, then faded again almost instantly. "I may be a priest, Aidan, but I'm also a man. *And* your brother."

"*And,* you know jack about women." Aidan took another long drink, set his beer down onto the table and cupped the frosty glass between his palms. Staring at the pale gold liquid, he muttered, "These two at least have a position to argue from. You don't. You don't know what it is to—" he caught himself before uttering the 'L' word "—*care* about someone. To know she matters and also know that you can't let her matter too much."

"Got you there, Liam," Brian pointed out.

"Too true," Connor added. "You lucked out. Didn't have to worry about pissing a woman off and living with the results."

"Who the hell do you three think you're talking to?" Liam demanded, but focused on Aidan, leaning across the table, forcing Connor back in his seat, a surprised expression on his face. "Do you think I was *born* wearing this collar?" he tapped at the white circlet at his throat. "I was your brother first. I was a man first. Do you really believe I never loved anyone? That I don't know what it feels like to *want?*"

Aidan just blinked at him. It had been years since he'd seen that flash fire of fury in Liam's eyes.

"Take it easy, Liam," Brian urged, shooting a glance at the table closest to them and glaring the nosy woman sitting there a narrowed glance.

"You shut up," Liam growled. "This is between me and the moron."

"Hey."

"My turn, idiot. You shut up and listen." Liam pointed one finger at Aidan, took a breath and lowered his voice. "I was in love once."

"What?" All three triplets said it at once.

Liam's eyes didn't flicker. His gaze didn't shift. Just held Aidan's steadily.

"Her name was Ailish."

"Whoa," Connor murmured.

"I thought priests *heard* confessions…" Brian said softly.

"I met her in Ireland," Liam continued as if none of them had spoken. "That last summer before I went into the seminary."

Aidan thought back, remembering the trip Liam had taken while trying to decide if he was really cut out for a life in the priesthood. He'd stayed in their grandparents' house outside Galway and toured Ireland for a summer. He'd never really talked about those three months, and the rest of them had let it go, assuming that Liam had spent those months in quiet reflection and prayer.

Apparently, they were wrong.

Aidan kept his gaze locked with Liam's, unable to look away. "What happened, Liam? If you loved her so damn much, why'd you let her go?"

Liam's breath hissed in and out of him in rapid succession. His eyes glimmered brightly, then darkened in memory. Slowly, he eased back into his seat, still staring at Aidan. "She died."

"Ah, Liam." Connor murmured.

"Damn, Liam…" Brian winced in sympathy.

Aidan held his breath. Sure there was more. He watched his older brother relive old pain and wondered how they'd drifted into this minefield of emotion.

"She drove into Galway city to meet her sister for some shopping," Liam said softly. "An American tourist got confused, drove on the wrong side of the road. Hit her head-on. She was killed instantly."

God.

"I'm sorry, Liam," Aidan said, stunned to his soul. In all these years, his brother had never hinted at the tragedy that must haunt him still. And Aidan finally realized that Marines weren't the only people with courage.

Anger gone now, Liam smiled sadly. "It was a long time ago, Aidan. And I'm only telling you guys now because I want you to know I *do* understand. I know what it is to love a woman so much that she's all you can see of tomorrow."

Silence dropped on the four of them like an old quilt. Each of them lost in their own thoughts, none of them wanted to be the first to speak.

Naturally enough, it was Connor who finally shattered the quiet.

"So, if Ailish had lived," he asked, slanting a glance at Liam, "would you still have become a priest? Or would you have walked away from her?"

Liam's hand fisted around his glass of beer. He lifted it, took a long sip and set it back down again before answering. "I've asked myself that a thousand times over the years," he admitted, then looked from one brother to the other, each in turn. "The honest answer is, no. I wouldn't have. When I met her, it was as if God had sent me a sign, telling me that He didn't want me in the priesthood after all." He sighed again, wistfully. "We planned to be married in the local church. Get a house near Lough Mask. Then when she was gone…"

"Married?" Aidan's voice was a whisper, carrying the stunned surprise all of them felt.

It took another moment or two before Liam smiled again. "I still believe there's a reason for everything—though I've yet to find the reason for her death. But maybe meeting Ailish, *loving* Ailish was supposed to help me be a better priest."

"I don't know what to say," Brian looked at their oldest brother.

"You don't have to say anything," Liam told them all.

An uneasy silence dropped over them. All of them aware now of Liam's private little hell—none of them quite sure how to handle this new side to a brother they thought they'd known.

Finally Brian spoke up again and, thank God, changed the subject. "You are a good priest, you know."

Liam glanced at him. "Thanks. I think."

"No, I mean it," Brian said and took a drink of his own beer. "Which means, I can probably use a few of those super prayers you've got in your stash."

"What's going on?" Connor asked the question they were all thinking.

"I'm shipping out." Brian looked at each of them in turn, then shrugged and grinned. "Next month. Middle East."

Growing up with a Marine father had taught them all that sudden moves were to be expected. Growing up a *family* made them all feel that instant quiver of worry.

"Have you told Tina yet?" Liam asked.

"Nope," Brian admitted. "I'm going home to do that now. That's why I thought I'd ask for those prayers." He grinned again. "Combat's dangerous, but fighting with Tina can be deadly."

"But you'll still be here for our joint humiliation, right?" Connor asked.

"Oh, yeah. Battle Color day. Convertible. Hula

skirt, coconut bra. I'll be there." He gave Aidan a shove. "Slide out, will you?"

"I'll walk out with you," Connor said, "Gotta be getting home or Emma'll hunt me down like a dog."

Aidan snorted a laugh. "See? This is what married gets you. A woman ready to tear your lungs out."

Brian shook his head. "You really *are* an idiot, aren't you?" Then he punched one fist into Aidan's shoulder. "Move."

Aidan got to his feet and Brian slid across the bench seat and stood up beside him. Pulling a couple of bills from his pocket, he tossed them onto the table and said, "See you guys later."

Then he and Connor headed out and Aidan sat back down. "Tina's not going to be happy about this."

Liam shrugged. "She's strong. She'll worry about him, but she'll handle it."

"I suppose." But Aidan wasn't really thinking about his sister-in-law, or even about Brian, soon to be deploying into a combat situation.

Instead he was thinking about his older brother and the love he'd lost so long ago. Looking at Liam, he asked, "Why'd you tell us about her?"

Liam sighed and leaned back in his seat. "I don't know. Maybe I was just tired of hearing about how I don't know jack about women."

Aidan smiled briefly and nodded. "Okay. I can get that."

This news was still too fresh to make much sense

of. He'd always thought of Liam as a quiet, reflective man. Born for the priesthood. Now, to discover there'd been dreams born and lost along the way was a little…disquieting.

"What was she like?"

"Ailish?"

"*Yes.*"

Liam smiled sadly. "Beautiful. Warm. Funny. Stubborn." His voice softened in memory. "She was an artist, too. Damn good one. Landscapes mostly."

A lightbulb clicked on in Aidan's brain. "The painting in your room. The one of the standing stones."

"Yeah. That's one of hers."

Aidan had always liked that painting. Had even tried to buy it from Liam once. Now he knew why his brother had refused to part with it. A simple scene of a circle of standing stones, a dance, as the Irish called them, it had a mystical quality, with soft gray mist spilling across the emerald green grass and twining itself up around the stones like loving hands.

"She was good."

Liam smiled. "I don't need you to feel sorry for me, Aidan."

"What am I supposed to feel, then?"

Liam leaned across the table and smiled patiently. "I just want you to *think*." He pulled money from his pocket, tossed it onto the table and said, "Think about what you've found. What you *could* have. And think hard before you let yourself lose it."

Then he left.

And Aidan sat alone, not sure of anything anymore.

Eleven

"**I** can come home early."

"You don't have to do that," Terry said, clutching the phone receiver as she walked around the kitchen, pouring herself some iced tea. "Honestly, Donna, everything's fine."

"No damage to the store? The house?"

Terry sighed. She'd already reassured her friend a half dozen times over the last few days. But she supposed it wasn't easy to be thousands of miles away from home when disaster struck.

"There was a small leak in the bookstore," she told her again. "A *tiny* puddle in the back, by the kids' play area."

"Damn it. Should have had the roof fixed last year. I *knew* that and put it off anyway."

"It's a *very* tiny leak, Donna. Honestly. The store did not float away."

"Okay, okay, I know I'm being a little obsessive…"

"Just a tad," Terry agreed, smiling as she closed the refrigerator door and picked up the glass of tea off the table. Taking a sip, she said, "Just enjoy the rest of your time with your folks."

"To tell you the truth, they're jumping up and down on my last nerve."

Terry laughed, pulled out a chair and sat down. God it felt good to think about something else besides her own situation. Her brain had been running in circles over Aidan Reilly for days—and she *still* had no idea how to handle what was getting to be a more and more complicated relationship.

Of course, to Aidan, it probably wasn't complicated at all, she thought wryly. It was her own fault she'd made the mistake of feeling more than she should have. Now she just had to figure out what to do about it.

"Don't get me wrong," Donna said, "my parents are great. But they spend all their time giving the kids chocolate, which hypes the little tormentors into outer space and then they drive me insane."

A sigh of regret whispered through Terry as she wondered what her life would be now, if Eric had only lived. He'd be twelve now. Almost a teenager. She closed her eyes and tried to imagine that sweet baby face as it would be now, and couldn't quite pull it off.

She'd always wanted children. At one time, she'd assumed she'd have a houseful of them. Now, it looked as though those dreams had been buried with Eric. She was alone. And despite what she felt for Aidan, she was going to stay alone.

Shaking her head a little, she said, "Sounds like things're just the way they're supposed to be then."

"I guess. I'm just ready to be home."

"Yeah," Terry said softly. "So am I."

"Tired of small-town life?" Donna asked. "Ready to go back to Manhattan and start whipping those fund-raisers into shape again?"

Truthfully, Terry thought, but didn't say, *no*. She liked Baywater. She liked having neighbors, even though they were only on loan from Donna. She liked the small-town feel, the slower pace, the sense of community she'd experienced when the hurricane swept through.

And mostly, she liked Aidan.

Instantly that quick grin of his filled her mind. His dimple. The deep, stormy blue of his eyes. The gravelly voice in the middle of the night. The callused fingertips sliding over her skin. His laugh. His humor and strength.

She liked it all.

Oh dear God.

She'd really done it.

She'd fallen in love.

Sitting up straight in the ladder-back chair, she stared blankly at the wall opposite her. Why hadn't she noticed this when there was still time to prevent it?

But then, maybe she'd never had a chance against it. She'd felt something new, something incredibly strong and powerful from the first moment they'd met.

She'd known then that he was different. That he could be dangerous.

She just hadn't realized *how* dangerous.

"Hello? Earth to Terry, come in, Terry."

"Huh? Oh." Shaking her head, she grabbed up her tea, took a long drink and swallowed the icy liquid and felt the chill of it swamp her right down to the bone.

But it wasn't the tea giving her the shivers.

It was the knowledge that she'd given her heart to a man who wouldn't want it.

"Oh, no."

"What? What's wrong?" Donna demanded.

"Oh, I've made a big mistake."

"Sounds bad."

"Couldn't be worse."

"And is the name of this mistake Aidan?"

"How'd you guess?"

"Not really a big jump," Donna admitted, and she couldn't hide the delight in her voice.

"You don't have to sound so pleased about this," Terry muttered, grimacing at the phone she was clutching tightly enough to snap in two.

"Why wouldn't I be pleased? Two of my closest friends find true love and happiness? This is good news."

"Hah!" Terry leaned back in her chair. "As far as Aidan's concerned, we've found sweaty sex and completion."

"And you?"

She sighed. "Donna...I'm an idiot."

"No, you're not, sweetie," her friend crooned. "You fell in love. That makes you lucky."

"No. It just makes it harder to leave."

"You're not going to *stay* and see what happens?"

"Nope." Terry stood up, walked to the window and stared out at the sun splashed backyard. The sky was blue, white clouds drifted lazily across the sky and a puff of wind teased the brass chimes into a soft tune. It was as if the hurricane had never come.

And she knew, that once she was home, buried in work, in the familiar, this feeling for Aidan would go away, too, and it would be like these few weeks had never been.

If a part of her was saddened at the thought, it was just a small part. The hard reality was, she didn't want to love someone again. Didn't want to risk loss again.

After Eric's death, Terry had been lost. Devastated. She'd spiraled into an overwhelming need for risk. She'd put her life on the line time and again, chasing down thrills, adventure.

She hadn't really taken the time then to realize that

she had been, in a way, chasing death. Her own life had felt inconsolably lonely. She'd missed her son desperately and hadn't reconciled with her family enough to find comfort there.

Instead she'd jumped into a whirlwind of activity that was dangerous enough that it kept her mind too busy to grieve. Her heart too full to break.

Until that one morning five years ago. Waking up in that hospital bed, she'd finally faced the sad truth. That she'd become as empty as her world had felt. That she'd chased danger so she wouldn't have to face life without her baby. And that was a slap in the face to the love she'd found with Eric.

Since that morning, she'd changed. Built a life that was based on giving. On helping. On reaching out a hand to those who felt as alone as she once had.

But if she were to chance loving Aidan, wouldn't she be going back into the danger zone? Wouldn't she be handing the universe another opportunity to kick her in the teeth?

"Terry?"

"Sorry," she murmured, still half lost in thought.

"You're really shook, aren't you?"

"Yeah, I guess I am," she admitted, grateful at least to have this one old friend to talk to. To confess her fears and worries to.

"You know what? I'm coming home early."

"You don't have to do that," Terry said.

"I know. But I miss my own place anyway."

"Donna…"

"I'll be there tomorrow or the next day."

"Okay," she said, already planning her return to Manhattan. She wasn't running, she told herself firmly. She was retreating. Quickly. "And, Donna?"

"Yeah?"

"Thanks."

Two hours later, Liam opened the door to the rectory himself.

The housekeeper was out doing the weekly grocery shopping and the monsignor was in the church hearing confessions. Which left Liam to wait for the roofer to arrive and give them an estimate.

But when he opened the door, he didn't find Mr. Angelini. Instead a tall, curvy blonde with summer-green eyes and a quiet smile greeted him. Instantly he knew who she must be.

"You're Terry Evans."

"Father Liam Reilly?" she asked with a smile. "Aidan didn't tell me his brother was psychic."

"Oh, I'm not," Liam said, opening the door wider and waving one hand in invitation. "But Aidan's described you too well to be mistaken on this."

She stepped into the foyer, her cream colored heels making quiet clicks on the gleaming wooden floor. Liam closed the door, then faced her, a beautiful woman in an expensive, beige suit and yellow silk blouse. She looked…uneasy and Liam's instincts took over.

"Can I get you something cold to drink? We have soda, which I would recommend over my housekeeper's hideous iced tea."

"No. Nothing, thanks," she said and walked with him into the living room off the hall.

"Please. Sit down."

She took a seat on the sofa and Liam perched on the coffee table in front of her. There was unhappiness in her eyes and a wistful quality about her that tugged on his heart. Now he understood why Aidan had fallen so fast and so hard. The wonder of it to him was that the man was still struggling so against it.

"What brings you here, Terry?"

She inhaled sharply and looked around the room before shifting her gaze back to his. "Direct. I like that."

He nodded, waiting.

"Aidan told me," she said, "that you were going to use the ten thousand dollars from the bet to replace the church's roof."

He smiled. "Did he?"

She opened her purse, dug inside for an envelope, then pulled it out and studied it. "I don't know if you know this already, but he had planned to give you the money anyway, even if he had won that stupid bet."

His eyebrows lifted. "No, I didn't know. But it sounds like something Aidan would do. He's a good man."

"Yes," she said, running her fingertips idly across the back of the envelope. "He is."

"And you love him."

Her gaze snapped up to his and Liam smiled. Even if he hadn't been expecting it, he would have spotted the sharp jolt of emotion in her eyes. And it made him glad for Aidan. It was high time his brother found something that meant as much to him as the Corps did.

"You sure you're not psychic?" she asked, giving him a wary smile.

"Oh, I'm sure. But if you don't mind my saying so, it's easy enough to read your eyes."

"Great. I'm an open book." Terry shrugged slightly. "I hope Aidan's not in a *reading* mood."

"You don't want him to know?"

"No," she said it softly, firmly. "Neither one of us was looking for this, Father—"

"Liam," he corrected.

"—Liam. What happened between us...well. It doesn't matter."

"You're a lot like him," Liam said.

She laughed shortly. "No reason to be insulting."

He grinned, liking this woman more and more and wanting to kick Aidan's ass for even taking the chance of losing her.

"Anyway," she said, "that's not why I'm here."

"Okay, then why?" he asked, bracing his forearms on his thighs and leaning in toward her.

"For this," she said and handed him the envelope.

Confused now, Liam opened it, looked inside and stared in stunned shock. Her personal check for twenty-five thousand dollars, made out to St. Sebastian's, was nestled inside.

Lifting his gaze to hers, he said, "Not that we don't appreciate the donation, we do. But that's a big check. Can I ask what motivated it?"

She snapped her small purse closed again and folded her hands on top of it. "Ten thousand wouldn't have been enough to get you a new roof, Liam."

"True, but that doesn't explain your generosity."

She inhaled sharply. "Let's just say that I've come to like Baywater." She jumped to her feet and walked briskly across the room to stare out the front windows at the trees that lined the driveway. "It's a nice place. Nice people. I'm going to miss it. And I wanted to help in some way, before I left town."

"You're leaving?"

She turned to look at him nodded, and looked down, but not before Liam saw the gleam of regret in her eyes.

"When?"

"A day or two."

"Does Aidan know?"

"No—and I'd like your promise that you won't tell him."

"Are you going to?"

"I don't know yet."

Sighing, Liam set the envelope down on the table beside him, walked toward her and took both of her hands in his. "Is there some way I can help you?"

She smiled briefly and shook her head. "No, but thanks for offering."

"Are you sure you want to leave?" Liam asked, wondering how in heaven two such stubborn souls had managed to find each other.

She drew away from him and shook her head. "I didn't say I *want* to leave. Just that I am."

He smiled sadly. "That makes no sense at all, you know."

A short, harsh laugh shot from her throat. "Maybe not. But its something I have to do."

"Maybe you should tell Aidan how you feel."

Now she did laugh. "Oh, no." Shaking her head she said, "Even if I was willing to take a chance on love again—you know as well as I do that Aidan's not interested."

"He cares for you."

"Yes. I think he really does." She started past him, headed for the front door. "But it's not love, Father. He doesn't want that any more than I do."

"Are you sure about that?"

"Sure enough."

Liam followed her to the front door. She opened it before he could and then stepped out onto the small porch, shaded by a climbing wisteria vine.

"Thank you again," he said, "for your donation."

"You're welcome, Liam. It was nice meeting you," she said and took the two steps to the sidewalk, leading around to the parking lot behind the church.

"Terry?"

She stopped and looked back at him, bright green eyes shadowed with pain.

His jaw tightened and though his every instinct was to help, comfort, he held himself back—knowing somehow, that she wouldn't welcome it. "My brother's an idiot if he lets you get away."

She shook her head. "Sometimes, Father, getting away is kindest all around."

She left then and Liam stood in a splash of sunlight wondering how in the hell he could wake his brother up to reality before it was too late.

Twelve

Twelve

Aidan smiled as he pulled into the driveway at Donna Fletcher's house. Dusk was just settling over Baywater and the sky was still streaked with dark reds and orange. A slight wind pushed at the trees and from down the street, came the shrieks of children playing. Next door, Mr. Franklin was mowing the lawn and the older man nodded and waved as Aidan stepped out of his car.

He grabbed the still hot pizza box from the passenger seat, then snatched up a bottle of merlot he'd brought to go with it. Grinning, he headed for the house.

He'd been thinking about this moment all day. Through the work, through the joking around with the other guys, in the back of his mind, Aidan had been planning a nice, quiet night, with Terry cuddled up close beside him.

Funny. A couple of weeks ago, he never would have imagined that a cozy night at home would sound so damn good. But then, a couple of weeks ago, he hadn't yet met Terry Evans.

And ever since he had, his world had taken a subtle shift.

He shook his head and sprinted the last few steps to the front porch. Didn't want to think about what he was feeling. Didn't want to examine anything too closely. Better to just shut up and enjoy it.

He used the bottom end of the wine bottle to tap on the door and when it swung open, his smile dropped like a stone.

Terry stood there, wearing a pale beige suit and high heels. Her makeup was perfect, her hair styled and surprise flickered in her green eyes. "Aidan? You said you couldn't make it tonight."

Frowning, he said, "I got Monk to cover for me."

"Oh. Well."

His brain tried to work. He could almost hear the gears grinding slowly inside his head. She wasn't expecting him, but she was dressed to the teeth and ready for...*what,* exactly?

He glanced past her then and noticed the suitcases stacked in the foyer. Ice settled in the pit of his stomach as he lifted his gaze up to hers again. "Going somewhere?"

Clearly nervous, she licked her lips, pulled in a long breath and said, "Yes. Actually, when you knocked, I thought it was my cab."

"Your *cab*."

"To take me to the airport."

"You're leaving."

"Yes. I'm going home."

"Tonight."

"Yes."

The ice in his stomach melted with a sizzle under a sudden onslaught of fury. She was looking at him as if he were a stranger. She was *leaving*. And didn't look sorry about it.

"Without even telling me?" he asked. "Without saying a damn word?"

She blew out a breath that ruffled the wisp of bangs drifting across her forehead. "Aidan, don't make this harder than it has to be."

He laughed shortly, harshly and felt it scrape his throat. "Not really sure if I could do that."

He felt like an idiot. Standing there in jeans and a T-shirt, clutching a swiftly going cold pizza and a bottle of wine—while she stood there and told him she was leaving.

Shouldn't he have known this?

Shouldn't he have *felt* something? A warning of some kind?

"So what was the plan?" he snarled. "Were you going to call from the airport? Or just let me show up here to find you gone?"

She stiffened and her lips flattened into a grim line. "Donna will be here tomorrow. She could have—"

Another laugh, tighter, harsher than the first. "That's great. You were gonna let *Donna* tell me that you were too chicken to face me."

"That's about enough."

"See? I don't think so."

He dropped the pizza and thought seriously about smashing the stupid bottle of wine against the side of the house. But instead, he tightened his fingers on the neck of the bottle and clung to it like a safety rope. "I thought we had something."

"Really?" she asked, temper clearly spiking inside her now, too. She folded her arms over her chest, hitched one hip higher than the other as she tapped the toe of her shoe against the floor. "And what did you think we had?"

That left him speechless. Hell, how did he know the answer to that? He shoved one hand across the top of his head. "I'm not sure exactly. But whatever the hell it is, it was worth more than *this*."

Disappointment flashed in her eyes briefly and was gone again in an instant. In fact, he couldn't really be sure he'd seen it at all.

"Aidan, go home. This little…interlude is over. Let's just get back to our lives, okay?"

"Just like that?"

Behind him, he heard a car pull up and the short blast of a horn.

"That's my cab."

He turned around to glare at it, and when he looked back, Terry already had her suitcase on the porch and was closing and locking the door. He felt as though he was back in the hurricane. As though the world was suddenly moving too quickly for him to keep up.

He knew he should say something, *do* something, but instead he stood there like a moron as she walked past him, rolling her suitcase behind her, its small steel wheels grinding against the pavement.

He was still standing there when the driver opened the passenger door to usher her into the bright yellow cab. She stopped, hand on the door's edge, to look at him. Then she gave him a ghost of a smile and said, "Goodbye, Aidan."

Alone with his wine and his stone cold pizza, Aidan watched in silence as Terry drove out of his life.

Two weeks later, the Reilly brothers were considering voting Aidan out of the family.

"My point," he yelled as he grabbed the rebounded basketball and took off at a trot toward the end of the driveway.

"Your point because you fouled me," Brian snapped.

"It wasn't a foul."

"It was a *shove,*" Connor told him.

Aidan sighed, wiped his arm across his forehead and sneered at his brothers. "Sorry, girls. Didn't know I was being too rough."

"You know," Brian said, starting for him, "I'm thinking it's about time for somebody's clock to get cleaned."

Aidan tossed the ball to one side, braced himself and waved one hand. "Bring it on, tough guy."

"What the hell's wrong with you, Aidan?" Connor demanded, grabbing Brian's arm as he started past him.

"*Nothing's* wrong with me. You two are the ones doing all the griping."

Liam picked up the basketball, bounced it a couple of times and nodded at Connor and Brian. "You two go get a beer. I need to talk to Aidan."

The other two stalked off, muttering darkly and Aidan turned, walking toward the water bottle he'd tossed down an hour ago. Grabbing it, he uncapped it, took a long gulp then fired a warning look at Liam. "I don't want to hear it."

"Tough."

Aidan snorted.

"You miss her."

Aidan stilled. His hand fisted on the water bottle and he stared at it as if it held the secrets of the universe.

"Shut up, Liam."

"Not a chance. You're making a jackass of your-self and driving your brothers to plan your murder. When are you going to admit you love her?"

He shot his oldest brother a hot glare. "This is none of your business, Liam. So back the hell off."

The sun was hot and the air didn't stir. It felt heavy, thick. And too damned crowded around there for Aidan's comfort.

"You're my business, you idiot." Liam moved in close, shoved Aidan and demanded, "Do you think we don't know what's going on? Do you think no-body's noticed that ever since Terry left you've been a complete beast to be around?"

Fury spiked inside him, then just as quickly drained away. Hell. Liam was right. They were *all* right. With Terry gone, nothing felt good. There was no reason to get up in the morning and going to sleep brought no comfort because his dreams were filled with her. Then he'd awaken in the dark with empty arms and a hollow heart.

"She's the one who left," he pointed out in a dark murmur.

"Did you give her a reason to stay?"

"No." He'd wanted to. Wanted to say something that day on the porch. Wanted to tell her...*hell.*

Still clutching the water bottle, he dropped to the shaded grass, drew his knees up and rested his fore-arms atop them. When Liam took a seat nearby, Aidan started talking. "Just before Uncle Patrick died," he said, peeling the label from the bottle of water, "and left us the money that started this whole mess…"

"Yeah?"

"I went to see him. About a week before he died. Just before I left, he took my hand and he said—" Aidan closed his eyes, to recapture that moment clearly "—the worst part of dying, Aidan, is to die with regrets. Don't make the mistake I did. Do all you can. See all you can. Don't die being sorry for what you *didn't* do."

"I'm sorry he felt that way. He lived a good life," Liam said.

"Yeah, but he lived a quiet life. He never went anywhere, never did anything. I don't want to be that way." He shook his head firmly. "Don't want to die with regrets, Liam."

"And this has what to do with Terry?" His brother asked.

"Don't you get it? If I let myself be in love, I'm tying myself down. Giving up the space to explore, to dare, to risk."

Liam stared at him for a long minute, then shook his head and laughed. "Every time I think maybe you're not a moron, you prove me wrong."

"Thanks," Aidan muttered. "That's helpful."

"Did it ever occur to you that Uncle Patrick might have meant something else?"

"Huh?"

"He never married, remember? Lived by himself most of his life, kept to himself. Mom says he was a shy man in his younger days, so maybe that explains some of it."

"Your point?"

"My point is, Aidan, maybe the regrets he spoke of were more about what he'd missed emotionally in his life. Maybe he regretted never being in love. Never finding a woman to cherish. Never having children."

He hadn't really considered that before.

"Yeah," Aidan said, "but…"

"Aidan," Liam continued, stretching his long legs out in front of him, "you've already done more in your life than most people ever will."

"True."

"Do you really believe, being the kind of man you are, that having someone to love and to love you, would change all that?"

"Well…" His brain was working now, circling around, backing up, going forward again. Trying to shift all of Liam's words into an order that didn't come off making him feel so damn stupid.

It wasn't working.

"Love doesn't *end* your life, Aidan," Liam said, snatching his brother's water bottle away and taking a drink. "It makes it *better*. If you're smart enough to grab it when you have the chance."

"Yeah," Aidan said, feeling the first trickle of hope seep into him like a slow stream in high summer. "But what if she doesn't want me? What if she tells me to get lost?"

Liam snorted now. "Since when do you turn your back on a challenge?" He smiled. "Besides, I don't think she'll turn you away. Before she left, she gave me a check for twenty-five thousand dollars. For the church's roof."

"She did?" Stunned, Aidan stared at him. "Why?"

"She said it was because she liked Baywater and wanted to help. I think it's because she loves *you* and wanted to feel somehow a part of things here, even if she was leaving."

Aidan thought about it for several humming seconds, then jumped to his feet. Glaring at Aidan, he shouted, "Well why the hell didn't you say so?"

Liam laughed as Aidan ran all the way to his car, jumped inside and roared off.

Terry set her teacup down on the polished mahogany table and the click of fine china on wood sounded like thunder in the quiet penthouse. If she listened hard enough, she could probably hear the pounding of her own heart. It was too damn quiet. Too lonely. Too…*empty.*

But at least it wouldn't be that way for long.

The last two weeks had been a small eternity. Back on her home turf, she'd tried to step right back into her normal everyday rhythm. But it was no use. It wasn't the same, because *she* wasn't the same.

She'd changed. And there was no going back— even if she'd wanted to.

When the doorbell rang, she ran for it. Her socks hit the polished marble floor and she slid all the way to the wide double doors. Laughing at herself, she opened the door and froze.

Aidan stepped inside, closed the door and grabbed her.

Held up close to his chest, she felt his heartbeat thundering against her and she knew she'd never felt anything more wonderful in her life. Being in his arms again set her world right. Everything felt in balance again. As it should be.

As it was meant to be.

"Aidan," She managed to say, "What're you—"

"Just shut up a minute, okay?" He blurted it out, then held her back so he could look at her, staring into her eyes with an intensity that burned right down to the heart of her. "God, you look good."

She smiled and would have spoken, but he rushed right on, not giving her a chance.

"I came all the way here to tell you something." He took a deep breath, blew it out and blurted, "I *love* you, Terry. And I want you to love me back."

"Aidan—"

"Look," he plowed on, outshouting her, "I know why you've protected your heart so long. I understand. About Eric. About all of it."

Her eyes filled with tears, but she blinked them back, unwilling to have this vision of him blurred.

"But you can't do it forever, Terry. I finally understand that. Look, I risk my life everyday in my job. And I never minded before, because I really didn't have all that much to lose. Well now, I *do*. I'll keep taking the risks, because that's the job and it's a risk worth taking. But so is loving you."

Her heart swelled to bursting and her chest felt too tight to contain it. "Oh, Aidan, I—"

"Terry, I'm not the same guy I was when I met you." His blue eyes went dark and stormy, filled with emotion that reached out for her and shook her to the soles of her feet. "You've affected my work, my life. You filled my heart. I don't want to wake up another morning without you. I need you, Terry. And I hope you need me."

"Oh, Aidan…"

"I know love and marriage and all the rest of it is a *big* risk. But I want us to take it together. Can you do it, Terry? Can you love me? Marry me?"

His fingers tightened on her upper arms and she was grateful for his firm grip. Otherwise, she might have melted into a puddle at his feet.

Smiling up at him, she said, "Yes, I love you. And yes, I'll marry you. Today. Tomorrow. Whenever you want. Because I'm not the same, either. You filled me, when I thought I would never be whole again. And the last two weeks without you were emptier than anything I've ever known."

"Thank God," he muttered and pulled her close again. Wrapping his arms around her, he bent his head to the curve of her neck and inhaled the soft, floral fragrance of her. And for the first time since the evening she'd left, Aidan felt his heart beating again.

"There's something else you should know though," she whispered and he pulled back to look at her, waiting.

"I'm pregnant."

Stunned, he blinked at her. "But. You said. The pill. We. You."

She grinned and shrugged. "Apparently, they're not a hundred percent effective."

"Yeah. But. I."

"I was coming to see you, Aidan, to tell you. When you rang the bell, I thought it was the realtor come to list the penthouse."

"You were coming back to me?" he asked with a smile.

"Yeah," she said softly. "I was going to find a way to *make* you love me."

"Babe," he said, inhaling sharply and grinning now to flash that dimple at her. "You already did that."

He pulled her in close again and whispered into her hair. "I'm happy about the baby, Terry. Terrified, but really happy. But are you okay with it? I mean, after Eric. Aren't you scared?"

She nestled in close and felt her fears dissolve in a well of love. She had been scared. When the pregnancy test turned up positive, fear reared up and nibbled on her. But then she realized that if loving Eric prevented her from ever loving another child, then she was cheating both herself and the memory of her son.

"Yeah," she admitted quietly. "I'm a little scared. But I'm also *alive,* Aidan. For the first time in a long time, I'm really *alive.*"

She pulled her head back and looked up at him. "I want to love you, Aidan. Laugh with you. Fight with you. Build a family with you."

He brought his hands up to cup her face and smiled down at her. "You'll never be sorry you took a chance on me, Terry. I swear it."

"We took a chance on each other," she whispered and leaned in to meet his kiss.

Epilogue

Two days later, the sun was sinking against the horizon. Most of the speeches were finished, the Marine band was tuning up and the grounds were packed. There were never enough bleacher seats, so most people just brought lawn chairs and blankets, spreading out across the area.

Battle Color Day, when every Marine dignitary available was on hand for the Corps celebration.

The speeches were mercifully brief, the Drum and Bugle Corps stirred the blood and the Silent Drill team brought the crowd to utter silence.

There was something magical about watching men snap out precision moves, each in time with the other, with no sound but that of a rifle butt smacking into a gloved palm.

There was a sense of pride that rippled through the awestruck, motionless crowd.

A kind of pride no civilian could ever truly understand.

And as the Silent Drill team moved off the field, Tina Coretti Reilly, Emma Jacobsen Reilly and Terry Evans soon-to-be-Reilly, chatted in lawn chairs alongside their mother-in-law, Maggie Reilly.

Tina leaned out from beneath the rainbow striped umbrella, attached to her chair and held up a thermal jug of ice tea. "Anyone?"

"No, thanks, I'm good," Emma said, leaning forward, trying to strain her eyes to watch for a certain red convertible.

"Terry?" Tina asked.

"Yes, thanks." She took the plastic cup of tea and swallowed a sip before saying, "This is all so…"

"Amazing, isn't it?" Maggie said and gave Terry's hand a pat. "I always get teary at the official functions. And I'm so glad you're here with us for this."

"So am I," Terry said meaningfully, "and *this* I wouldn't have missed for anything."

"I hear that," Tina said on a laugh. "The Reilly Triplets in coconut bras?" she laughed again, clearly delighted at the mental image.

"Their friends will never let them forget it," Emma said smiling.

"And neither will we, dear," Maggie said and pulled a video camera out of the straw basket at her feet.

Terry laughed and looked at the older woman with the sparkling blue eyes so much like her sons. "You're going to *tape* them?"

"Of course I am," Maggie said, turning the camera on and winking at Terry. "Never pass up a chance for a little blackmail material on family."

"Ah, the Reillys," Tina said, leaning back in her chair and sticking her feet out to cross them at the ankle. "You gotta love us."

"We *are* fun," Emma admitted.

"Oh," Terry said, as she leaned back to sip her tea and enjoy the moment of solidarity, "I think I'm going to be very happy in this family."

"Look, girls," Maggie called out, excitement squeaking in her voice. "Here they come!"

A shining red Cadillac convertible slowly rolled along the main drive. Liam sat at the wheel, waving to the crowds, an enormous grin on his face.

Aidan, Brian and Connor, all sat on the trunk, their legs in the back seat. Each of them wore a coconut bra, a grass hula skirt and the grim expression of men trapped with no way out.

But as the crowd cheered, the Reilly triplets each lifted a hand in a wave—and met their humiliation like Marines.

* * * * *

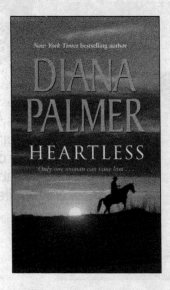

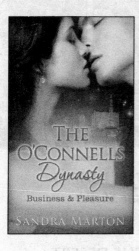
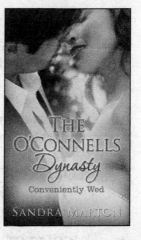

 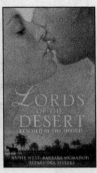 

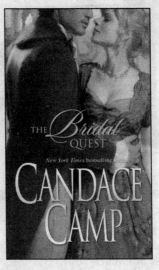

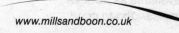

millsandboon.co.uk Community

Join Us!

The Community is the perfect place to meet and chat to kindred spirits who love books and reading as much as you do, but it's also the place to:

- Get the inside scoop from authors about their latest books
- Learn how to write a romance book with advice from our editors
- Help us to continue publishing the best in women's fiction
- Share your thoughts on the books we publish
- Befriend other users

Forums: Interact with each other as well as authors, editors and a whole host of other users worldwide.

Blogs: Every registered community member has their own blog to tell the world what they're up to and what's on their mind.

Book Challenge: We're aiming to read 5,000 books and have joined forces with The Reading Agency in our inaugural Book Challenge.

Profile Page: Showcase yourself and keep a record of your recent community activity.

Social Networking: We've added buttons at the end of every post to share via digg, Facebook, Google, Yahoo, Technorati and de.licio.us.

www.millsandboon.co.uk